Praise for *In War Times*

"*In War Times* is a novel of great historical reach—fr... the Kennedy assassination and beyond—and profoun... ambition, expressed with an unmistakable ease of execution and a master's sureness of touch. Kathleen Goonan has come through to the kind of control that makes every startling fresh development—and this novel bristles with astonishing moments of development—seem inevitable. Not only does Goonan know that Charlie Parker and Dizzy Gillespie changed the world, she understands that every vision of the future conceals a deep yearning for one's own specific past. That's real wisdom." —Peter Straub

"Paralleling the evolution of modern jazz with the creative ferment of science, Goonan delivers a bravura performance." —*Publishers Weekly* (starred review)

"Only Kathleen Goonan could have created this complex interweaving of jazz, physics, love, and war." —Joe Haldeman, award-winning author of *The Forever War*

"*In War Times* is an intense labor of love . . . a warm glass of fine, intoxicating whiskey that should be savored as thoroughly as possible." —*Starlog*

"Kathleen Ann Goonan goes against the grain of a lot of twenty-first-century SF by using sci-fi tools to create serious novels of ideas, and she's done it again: This is a truly humanist, and feminist, take on what's important for our future." —Gwyneth Jones, award-winning author of *Bold As Love*

"Sometimes a book makes me stop and think after I've finished it. Occasionally a book will make me stop and think during it. Rarely will a book do both. *In War Times* is one of those rare books whose ideas live in your mind long after you've finished and make you think about them for a time afterward." —*SFSignal.com*

"*In War Times* is a labor of love, a fact made evident on every page by the immediacy of its characters. I feel like I know these people. It's a darn good story, too, that will keep you up well past bedtime." —David Marusek, author of *Counting Heads*

"A provocative and at times intensely moving novel . . . at once deeply human and intellectually challenging." —*Locus*

Also by Kathleen Ann Goonan

THE NANOTECH QUARTET

Queen City Jazz
Mississippi Blues
Crescent City Rhapsody
Light Music

The Bones of Time

In War Times

KATHLEEN ANN GOONAN

TOR®

A TOM DOHERTY ASSOCIATES BOOK
NEW YORK

This is a work of fiction. All of the characters, organizations, and events
portrayed in this novel are either products of the author's imagination or are used fictitiously.

IN WAR TIMES

Copyright © 2007 by Kathleen Ann Goonan

Edited by David G. Hartwell

A Tor Book
Published by Tom Doherty Associates, LLC
175 Fifth Avenue
New York, NY 10010

www.tor-forge.com

Tor® is a registered trademark of Tom Doherty Associates, LLC.

The Library of Congress has cataloged the hardcover edition as follows:

Goonan, Kathleen Ann.
    In war times / Kathleen Ann Goonan.—1st ed.
        p. cm.
    "A Tom Doherty Associates Book."
    ISBN 978-0-7653-1355-3
    I. Title.
    PS3557.O62815 2007
    813'.54—dc22

                                    2007005165

    ISBN 978-0-7653-3243-1 (trade paperback)

First Edition: May 2007
First Trade Paperback Edition: August 2012

Printed in the United States of America

*This book is dedicated to Thomas Edwin Goonan
and to all of those who served in World War II.*

THANKS AND ACKNOWLEDGMENTS

FIRST AND FOREMOST I thank my father, Thomas E. Goonan, for his invaluable contributions and unflagging patience in helping me create *In War Times*. My mother, Irma K. Goonan, with her good cheer and wonderful sense of humor, helps me through each day. Thank you, Mom and Dad.

Thanks to Pam Noles for her ability to hear the unstated harmonies in the story through countless rereadings, helping to make them resonate, and passionately believing in the book. Thanks to Sage Walker and Steve Brown, my staunch past and present readers, whose clarity and responsiveness are invaluable.

Mimi and Jim Rothwell took time from their very busy lives to scan my father's wartime photos. Thank you!

David Hartwell, editor extraordinaire, worked unflaggingly on the manuscript, helped create a novel from a mountain of stories, and supported the book with great dedication. Denis Wong, his assistant, gave feedback and took care of details; he has my gratitude. I also thank Tom Doherty for his support.

Nat Hentoff kindly gave me permission to quote Charlie Parker's epiphany from his and Nat Shapiro's classic, *Hear Me Talkin' to Ya*, published in 1955. Mr. Hentoff's long career in jazz and support of jazz is well known; my father recalls reading his columns in *Downbeat*.

I also thank Sir Max Hastings for writing *Armageddon: The Battle for Germany, 1944–45*, which illuminates a part of WWII that is often glossed over, and for generously giving me permission to include a quote from it. Another important book was Gregor Dallas's *1945: The War That Never Ended*. Research on the VMA2 gene included in *The God Gene* by Dean Hamer influenced the "Midway" chapter.

Permission to quote Lewis Thomas's *Late Night Thoughts on Listening to Mahler's Ninth Symphony* was given by Penguin Press; the *San Francisco Chronicle* gave me permission to include a quote from Dizzy Gillespie.

The poem "On Hearing That His Friend Was Coming Back from the War," by Wang Chien, was translated by Arthur Waley and appears in *More Translations from the Chinese* (Knopf, 1919).

I am also grateful to the authors of the fifty or so books I read for background; they are listed at www.goonan.com. *A Woman in Berlin*, for instance, published anonymously, is a harrowing picture of Berlin during and after the Battle of Berlin in 1945; many other books corroborate the details included by the author. *Tuxedo Park*, by Jennet Conant, is an intimate and detailed account of how private enterprise, universities, and the government worked together to develop the top-secret SCR-584 and the M-9 antiaircraft director. *The Birth of Bebop*, by Scott DeVeaux, is an important work of scholarship upon which I depended.

Murray Juvelier flew in an observation plane that accompanied the *Enola Gay* on August 9, 1945; I would like to thank him for the time he took to talk to me in Fort Lauderdale. He gave me invaluable details about the planes, the flight, and the experience.

I strove for an accurate accounting of real events, but any mistakes are my own, not those of my sources.

My most heartfelt thanks, as always, to my husband, Joseph Mansy. He is the boy who went inside the Messerschmitt caves near Oberammergau, Germany, when his father taught at the NATO school there.

Everything is determined by forces over which we have no control. It is determined for the insect as well as for the star. Human beings, vegetables, or cosmic dust—we all dance to a mysterious tune, intoned in the distance by an invisible piper.

—Albert Einstein
The Saturday Evening Post
October 26, 1929

∞

[Bergander] and his family listened avidly, if perilously, to the BBC. He heard the famous "black propaganda" broadcasts of the British journalist Sefton Delmer, and—far more effectively from the Allied viewpoint—Glenn Miller and Benny Goodman. To young Bergander, American music possessed the status of holy writ. He thought: people who make music like this must win the war.

—Sir Max Hastings
*Armageddon: The Battle
for Germany, 1944–45*

In War Times

Stateside

1941: PHYSICS AND JAZZ

I remember one night before Monroe's I was jamming in a chili house on Seventh Avenue between 139th and 140th. It was December 1939. Now, I'd been getting bored with the stereotyped changes that were being used all the time at the time, and I kept thinking there's bound to be something else. I could hear it sometimes but I couldn't play it.

Well, that night, I was working over Cherokee, and, as I did, I found that by using the higher intervals of a chord as a melody line and backing them with appropriately related changes, I could play the thing I'd been hearing. I came alive.

—CHARLIE PARKER
Hear Me Talkin' to Ya

∞

I knew we were making something new. It was magic. Nobody on the planet was playing like that but us.

—DIZZY GILLESPIE
San Francisco Chronicle
May 25, 1991

1

Washington, D.C.
December 6, 1941

D R. ELIANI HADNTZ was only five foot three, though she had seemed taller in the classroom, and Sam had not suspected that her tightly pulled-back hair was a mass of wild black curls until the evening she sat on the edge of his narrow boardinghouse bed. A streetlamp threw a glow onto her pale breasts as she reached behind her head and yanked out the combs, made crooked by the intensity of their lovemaking.

Her loosened hair cascaded down her back and hid her face. She took a deep, shuddering breath, and sat with her elbows on her knees, staring out the window.

When Sam reached out and ran a finger up her spine, she flinched.

He had no idea why she was here.

Sam Dance was an uncoordinated soldier. To someone less good-natured, his last name, chosen by an immigration officer on Ellis Island a few generations back, might have seemed like a cruel joke. Because of his poor eyesight, the Army had not accepted him when he first volunteered in 1940, even with almost three years of chemical engineering classes at the University of Dayton under his belt. But while working as an inspector at a Milan, Tennessee, ordnance plant, he heard of an outfit in Indiana recruiting at a used car dealership trying to reach an enlistment quota. He hastened to their office, and was finally allowed to join the Army and serve his country.

Sam stood out because of his height. His intelligence was less visible, but must have been noticed by someone in the Army. Plucked from daily twenty-mile marches through inclement weather in North Carolina, he was sent to D.C. for an intensive course on a potpourri of esoteric subjects. The class met in a hastily assembled temporary structure on the roof of a War Department building.

The subjects, up to now, had been curiously disparate. Codebreaking, mechanical engineering, advanced calculus, and now theoretical physics rushed past, taught by an odd assortment of flamboyant Europeans with heavy accents and accompanied at the end of each week by a test.

Properly appreciative of the warmth into which he had been suddenly deposited, Sam was always in his seat each morning at seven A.M. when Dr. Hadntz opened the door, set her briefcase decisively on the bare metal desk at the front of the room, and draped her coat and scarf over the back of the desk chair. She always began her lecture immediately, chalking formulas on the board which he was sure represented some of the most rudimentary knowledge that she possessed. She was an exiled physicist from Budapest. The Army, of course, had not provided the students with an extensive background, but it was rumored that she had worked with Curie, Wigner, Teller, Fermi. Everyone who was anyone in theoretical physics.

Dr. Hadntz was the fourth instructor in a two-month course that rotated speakers weekly.

He and his classmates were being sorted out. The question was: By whom and for what?

Sam did not know whether Eliani Hadntz, as she sat splendorously naked on the side of his bed, her chin in her hand, was reverie-struck, paralyzed by guilt (was she married?), adrift in matters of speculative physics, or wondering what to have for dinner. The steam radiator clanked, and his Crosley, which he had switched on in a fit of awkward nervousness when they entered the room, played "Mood Indigo." Ellington's brilliant melancholia infused the moment.

He realized that he didn't know a thing about Dr. Hadntz except that she was intellectually renowned, part of a generation in which European women felt free to follow their own genius to the shrines of physics in Berlin, Copenhagen, Cambridge, Princeton. And that she was part of the mass exodus of physicists escaping the advancing tide of National Socialism. Dr. Compton, one of Sam's professors in Chicago, had brought Szilard and Fermi, both refugees, to lecture at the university while he was there. They brimmed with a strange mixture of dread and excitement— love of information for its own sake, insights that seemed to be unlocking the secrets of the physical world, and fear of the technologies such discoveries might lead to.

Dr. Hadntz rose from the rumpled bed, still deeply contemplative, her hair falling around her like a curtain. Crossing the room, she stood for a moment, still naked, directly in front of the window.

Deeply surprised at her immodesty, Sam jumped out of bed and pulled the blackout curtains shut, certain that she had been fully visible in the glow cast by the streetlight. A bit confused, he tentatively touched her hip, and she shook her head: no. She went into the bathroom, taking her bag. He heard her lock the door to the adjoining room, where a soldier by the name of Mickelmaster got roaring drunk every other night, then she closed Sam's door. Water ran for a few minutes.

She emerged wrapped in a towel and rummaged through the pocket of her overcoat, which hung over the wooden chair in front of the desk. "They have not given you many luxuries here," she said, as she pulled a cigarette from the coat pocket. Her lighter snapped open and flared briefly in the dark room.

Sam smiled. "You have no idea." Hot water, warm air, privacy, and electric lights to read by were prized commodities, and he did not know how long he could hold on to them. His inherent sense of tremendous awkwardness returned, a downward sensation like falling from a plane before you pulled the rip cord of your parachute.

Cigarette dangling from her mouth, Hadntz put her arms through the long sleeves of her white blouse, pulled on lacy underpants. She turned up the volume of the radio. Then she seated herself on the end of the bed, cross-legged, her back resting against the metal footboard. "You said something."

"I said—"

"I mean on Monday. During the first lecture. You asked some very interesting questions."

It was now Saturday evening. Their eyes had met and held on Tuesday, and on Friday they had dinner together.

"Your background is in physical chemistry. You were at the University of Chicago."

"For almost three years." On scholarship; his family was not wealthy, and he had also worked at night in a bakery the entire time he was in school.

She pointed her cigarette toward a dark shape in the corner. "Is that a musical instrument case?"

"Saxophone."

"You play with an orchestra?"

"Jazz." Sam loved jazz—as did most people his age. It was the popular music of the day. But his devotion was intense, encyclopedic; almost a calling.

"Good. Jazz requires a supple mind." She leaned toward him. He wanted to ask to share her cigarette, but it seemed too intimate a request and he flushed slightly in the dark. She was, of course, older than the hometown girls he knew, and European, but it had still happened so quickly, although certainly not against his will.

She said, "I have been working on quantum processes in the brain."

He did not like to look puzzled in front of her, but he was. "I don't understand."

"No one does. I was a medical doctor, like my mother, and then, quite briefly, a Freudian psychologist. Freud argued with me, but he could not convince me. I decided that it was not the answer. That was when I became interested in physics."

She knew Freud? He could not help computing. She must be at least twenty years older than him. She didn't look it.

She lowered her voice. He could barely hear her over the radio. "How does an atom *decide* when to emit an electron? I have been working on deciphering what we call consciousness. The quantum nature of our brains; the nature of will. Of course, I am positing that there exists more altruism than not." She frowned. "Or perhaps, just hoping."

She sucked in her cheeks, drawing from her cigarette. "I am attempting to . . . not to change human nature, but to try to understand it. So that we can use it to our advantage, as we have used mechanical processes to our advantage. I envision a vast computational network that is capable of helping us make changes according to what is truly best for each one of us. What do we all want? Food. Shelter. Love. Hope. Contentment. Challenge. Community. I have had all of these. Because of luck, I have been part of a tremendous intellectual community. But now, most of those people whom I so deeply respect—close colleagues of mine—are working on something that could destroy us all." She sighed. "As could this, perhaps. Nobel and Gatling thought that dynamite and machine guns would ensure perpetual peace, after all. But what is beauty? What is freedom? We all know what they are, even if they sometimes seem impossible to describe. We all want them. Perhaps we can choose, together, among the possibilities, if we combine the best of what we all want."

Abruptly, she got out of bed, crushed her spent cigarette in the heavy glass ashtray on Sam's desk, and finished dressing, her movements impatient; angry. "I have left their project. I regret to say that I contributed to it in many ways." She looked up at Sam. "We are in a race with the Nazis to create an atomic bomb." A grim, ironic smile quirked briefly. "Does this surprise you?"

Sam had heard rumors of this, had intimations that such a project was under way. Before he'd left the University of Chicago, one of his close friends in the Physics Department had become involved in some project with Fermi that he couldn't discuss.

Still, he was shocked. "Yes."

"I could probably be shot just for telling you this directly. I do this because there is so much at stake. We don't know what might happen if a nuclear explosion takes place. It might be never-ending. It could destroy everything. The world."

He stood and grabbed his trousers from the floor, glancing at her as she attached silk stockings to garters and slipped her feet into stylish two-toned high heels. Her black wool suit was cut differently than the ones American women were wearing now, but it was clearly well made, expensive. Sam found her sexy, scary, enchanting.

"I am always followed, although I think that tonight I have probably given them a good pretext for being here with you alone." As if she could feel the sudden final plummet of his heart, she turned and gave him a quick, unexpected hug, rested her head against his chest for an instant, and let go.

Opening her scarred leather valise, she took a manila folder from a huge accordion file that fell open from the lid. As she did so, he saw that in the bottom of the valise was a steel box, about the size of a hardcover book, locked with a heavy padlock. She touched it with her fingertips. "There is only one of these. I created it in Paris. I am not sure how it should be used."

"What is it?"

"I don't know what to call it. For me, it cannot be named." She set the folder on the desk, then closed and locked the valise. "These are the plans. I am leaving them for you to use. The product they will produce requires a catalyst—a chain reaction. *This* is the reason atomic fusion must take place, but I no longer have time to try to integrate this with the project they all have in mind, the atomic bomb."

She shrugged into her jacket and buttoned it over her simple white shirt. "My ideas do not matter to them. These scientists and your government are focused on only one goal. I think it is possible that some of my colleagues are simply curious, or drunk with the power of creating something that could destroy the world."

Handing him the two-inch-thick manila file, she said, "This is not the only copy. I have given this information to several of my friends. But they are all too busy with bombs to even consider it. While I do not blame them, given the gravity of their task, and the speed with which they think it must be accomplished, I am deeply sad that this avenue to peace might be disregarded."

"Which friends?"

"You would only be intimidated by their names. I believe that you have the ability to understand much of what I am positing, despite the fact that you have had only a few years of college. You asked good questions; you grasped my answers." She smiled—not at him, but to herself, as she bent to pick up her valise. Then she looked at him. "I should tell you. I gave you a test different from the other tests. It was much more difficult. Your answers were very good. The solutions worked, and you found them using unusual avenues of thought."

Her hand was on the doorknob.

"Wait." He put the file on his desk and grabbed his shirt.

She shook her head. "No. I have done all that I can here. My daughter is in Budapest with my parents, and they are in danger. I counted on others to help. They could not."

"You have a daughter?"

"My only child. She is twelve. My husband was a mathematics professor. He died several years ago. I'm not sure what is going to happen. They don't want to let me go. They tell me that they are doing the best they can to get my family out, but I don't believe them."

"Who is 'they'?"

She dropped her hand from the doorknob, gave him a look he could not read, kissed him on the lips briefly, then opened the door. Hastily buttoning his shirt, he bent and slipped into his shoes, then grabbed his coat.

"Do not follow, please. I must leave alone. It is important that you do not arouse the interest of those following me. They must think that this was just a sexual tryst."

He went to the door and watched her go.

In her foreign suit, she looked like a woman from another time and place. As she left the room, she did not look back. The authoritative sound of her heels on the wooden stairs at the end of the hall diminished and vanished.

He closed the door and leaned his back against it, disturbed, exhilarated, and puzzled. Her words had carried powerful admonitions. She knew things that few other people knew. And this amazing woman had entrusted him with this knowledge.

There was nothing much to do but turn on the light and the radio, sit down at the desk, pull out the papers, and try to understand what she had left him.

Dr. Eliani Hadntz was a Magyar Gypsy by blood.

And, she thought, adding to her leather bag a toothbrush, tooth powder, and extra stockings for eventual bribes, a Gypsy now by trade. She carefully lowered two hats into a shared hatbox, one flamboyantly red with a large feather, the other small, tailored and black, with a veil, the hat of a completely different woman than the one who would wear the red.

In the cosmopolitan climate of Europe in the twenties and early thirties, having exotic blood had been an asset. But being an intelligent woman was even more of an asset. After the war ended in 1918, learning, and steady progress toward that sleek, fabulous future in which machines would one day do away with physical labor, were prized. One stunning scientific discovery after the next was released to the world, though most people had not yet even absorbed the basic fact of evolution.

Throughout, though, there was terrible news from the Soviet Union. Her grandmother lived in St. Petersburg and refused to leave. The old lady's letters to Budapest boiled with anger toward Stalin and fear of the Germans. The Russians could see the German military buildup and were responding in kind. She hoped her grandmother's fiery letters were still arriving in Budapest, but the chances of that were slim.

The telephone in Hadntz's room rang. She did not answer it and, finally, it stopped.

The call made her nervous. No one who knew where she was staying, at the Hay-Adams on Lafayette Square in Washington, would call her. The War Department had a messenger who memorized any communiqués she was to receive and delivered them in person. The only person on the street when she left Sam's rooming house had been a blonde, probably a prostitute, smoking a cigarette as she leaned against a lamppost.

Dr. Hadntz had been issued tickets for the night train to Chicago; she was supposed to return to the Manhattan Project. Instead, she would go to New York. By tomorrow she would be on a boat carrying munitions to England.

A German, Otto Hahn, had done much of the chemistry work that in 1939 led to the knowledge that uranium atoms could be split. His exiled Jewish colleague in this work, Lise Meitner, confirmed the physics. Their conclusion, confirmed by Neils Bohr, was that it was theoretically possible to release previously unimaginable amounts of energy.

And thus it was possible to create an atomic bomb.

Surely the Germans, knowing this, were far ahead of the United States in this regard. It was a hopeless race.

But she had the stuff of human mind in her briefcase. Not actual, physical brain matter, but data. The roots of all bodily processes, including, therefore, the mechanics of consciousness.

This information had to be placed in the hands of those who wished to defeat National Socialism. Those who wanted to retrieve an enlightened, cultured Europe. Those who wished Vienna, London, Copenhagen, Berlin, and Budapest to continue to contribute to the arts and to learning. To freedom of mind. There was so little depth here in America. So little time. Everything was new, less than a few hundred years old.

The labor of millennia was being destroyed overseas, and she was wasting her time here. She could convince no one of the importance of her work. Perhaps they would listen in London. Perhaps not. She had an appointment with British Intelligence, but she couldn't stay there long, either.

Mr. Dance was the most intelligent of the students she had lectured in the past three months and a lovely, awkward young man. She hoped the material she had given him was convincing, for it was as important as the future of the world.

Her device did not fully work, not yet. The new design was better. It was still imperfect, requiring more research, more thought, more experiments and experience. She had had glimmerings of how the device would perform, and with it had seen vast suffering as well as joyous possibilities. If only she could stay—the United States was truly the center of all that she needed to make the device work. But she couldn't leave her family to fate.

Science had turned its attention, lately, to how life had begun. She felt, sometimes, as if she was using life to create something better than what had ensued— using it to create another level of life, one that would be better for everyone, each according to his own lights, not hers. The optimism felt after the Armistice, when it seemed that war might be ended forever, was long vanished. Complete disorder and its attendant suffering was abundant now. Poland was ruined; Russia was being overrun; London staunchly survived beneath a steady rain of bombs. The human world—its social order, its trade, its ability to function—was in chaos, and much worse threatened. It was a mad descent into the worst of what humans could be and do.

She hoped that Dance might understand her paper, the possibilities contained therein, and pursue them. Use them. To create his own device.

She felt a bit worried about seducing him. He seemed to take it all much too seriously. She hoped that someday he would understand why she had done it, apart from the fact that he was utterly attractive.

She finished packing; made sure that she had the papers she needed to get her where she was going.

Then she opened the briefcase and unlocked the steel box inside. Opening it, she took a deep breath, then lifted out her present product.

This time it was resinous, compact, filled with computing power which most of her colleagues simply would not believe possible. Far beyond the top-secret Norden Bombsight, beyond even the new computers nourished by the tycoon Loomis at Tuxedo Park and his friends at MIT, it was informed by a biological computer that communicated with what was called, in certain physics circles, the non-local universe.

In short, if human consciousness was the time-sensitive entity she believed it was, this device could be called a time machine—although that would be a clumsy, inexact way of describing it. It would meld the latest discoveries in physics with the latest discoveries about biology—a connection that very few scientists, with the exclusion of James Watson, ventured to consider.

It was a machine, but it was a machine that affected the physics of consciousness and of human behavior. It could, if distributed throughout the world, possibly affect the course of history. She had invented a device that enhanced a human sense— the sense of time, consciousness itself. It would enable humans to use the constant expansion of the universe, in much the same way that the previously invisible power of electricity had been harnessed and was now put to all kinds of positive uses, just as the microscope revealed worlds which before could only be surmised inaccurately, and as x-rays were used by Curie to see into matter deeply and precisely.

She knew, though, that her present device was incomplete, dangerous, a bit like direct current. She still was searching for refinement, for control.

Searching time, searching thought, searching possibilities in which others might call the future. To her they were all just possible avenues of time, which were always occurring without being sensed.

She activated it with a simple switch and felt it whirr gently in her hands. Her fingers rested in hollows she had fashioned for them of a new, permeable, conducting material, which completed the circuit. It would no longer require the starting boost the switch had given it.

Using her thumbs to turn the dials on the device's face, she watched her adjustments register as two dots of light that merged into one on the tiny screen. Then she moved her right thumb and took one dot of light into a quadrant that was geometrically described on the bottom of the screen.

She called what then happened to her "splintering." Perhaps it was simply her imagination, but time stretched around her, dividing and dividing again, so fast that any gaps in consciousness seemed smooth.

This had always been happening—not just to her, but to everyone, though it had been impossible to witness. There were a truly infinite amount of times, spilling like stars into the vacuum, never-ending, always expanding. But like microbes and far-away galaxies, before humans had invented the tools to see them, the inner workings of time were not available to humans.

But splintering was the wrong word, she suddenly realized. It was more like a bloom of matter on some surface, expanding until it linked with other blooms. What was it like? Being a part of it rather than an observer, she could not know. Perhaps it was as if she became infused in some medium, the medium in which time existed, like a drop of food coloring expanding in treelike tendrils through water, finally losing definition with agitation. Or maybe it was a sudden, softer expansion, but always there was this sense of infusion, and linking, and blending, this awakening of vision and the vast possibilities to which her present time, in all its boundless descriptives, was a doorway. It just depended on which way she turned once she had gone through it.

What would happen if all these blooms, all these possibilities united suddenly? If she crossed some edge? If the blooms infused one another? Who or what might she become? How many times could she do this without risking her connection with the present, with her daughter?

Was she simply imagining these other presents, the one in which Hitler died at birth, or another in which the Germans were not sent into poverty to pay for the Great War, another in which her mother set a vase of five roses instead of seven on the lace tablecloth one afternoon in July 1919? All blooms, all splinters, all soft and sharp at the same time, each of them a decision that could not be changed without knowing the possibilities, the outcome, of a single action. The only constant seemed to be her own consciousness, her own point of view.

The phone rang again, penetrating the brilliance, the intensity, of the splintering, where it seemed as if she were living many lives at once. Spent, shuddering, she managed to put down the device and to flick the switch that turned it off. Sweat ran down her forehead.

This world was her present world—the world where Poland had been brutally subjugated, and then, Holland, Norway, Denmark.

To find the possibility of change, she had to go through the steps. Find a catalyst, a place where the very bonds of atoms were broken, loosing particles which until now had been held in place by—by what? Gravity? Time? Were they one and the same? After getting her daughter out of Budapest, she planned to go to Berlin, where surely the Nazis were at work on the atomic bomb. Given their head start, which thus far had given them a great military advantage, they had to have been working on it for several years, and they had to be farther along than the Americans. But if she needed to, she would return to the United States, by any means possible.

She locked up the device and wiped her forehead with a towel she grabbed from the bathroom rack. She looked in the mirror over the sink.

Now, *there* was a wild woman. She smiled, imagining the dear voice of her mother telling her that she was too thin, that she should not have those hollows beneath her cheekbones, that she should take time from her studies to eat! Her hair, mostly black, but beginning to be streaked with white, fell in spiraling curls down both sides of her face, the lines of which deepened every day. She flattened her hair back and held it with combs, twisted it into a bun, powdered her face, applied bright red lipstick, and looked into brown eyes that seemed to be envisioning vast distances. She did not look like . . . herself. She closed her eyes, pressed her fingers against her eyelids, and looked again.

Better.

Donning her scarf and coat, she picked up her bag, her hatbox, and her valise, took the elevator downstairs, and walked through the plush lobby straight into a cab that was waiting for someone else. "Union Station, please," she said.

Sam Dance was a thoughtful person. His mother was deeply religious, from Quaker roots, but he was not remotely so. Still, she had imbued in him a richer sense of the dimensions of humans than most men his age had.

In his robe, he seated himself at his desk and tuned his radio to WLW, which carried clear-channel dance music from Cincinnati. He slowly turned the pages Hadntz had left, trying to absorb it all. Trying to make sense of what had just happened.

Trying to understand this gift.

For a gift it was; apparently the life's work of the strangest woman he had ever met. The strangest person of either sex. His mind was pulled along the straight rails of her reasoning as a wrench to a giant cyclotron. He did not know how she had learned what she knew about the genetic basis of life, the quantum nature of the mind. He went over where she had probably been, whom she must have studied with. Freud, she had said. A medical education. Work with x-rays. This much was clear in her computations of the probable structure of something she was calling a parallel spiral. A history of the advances in biochemistry during the first three decades of the twentieth century was included. These ideas amazed him; they had not been taught in school. He learned that some people believed that a molecule called DNA contained the mechanism for passing on hereditary information. Many of the papers in the file had been published. The more recent ones remained unpublished.

He paged through the mechanical drawings and saw a strange object that excited him.

The drawing was not titled—in fact, the edges were ragged, as if all identifying matter had been torn off.

The central part of the object was round, with eight circles projecting from its core. Two vacuum tubes were inserted into the holes on opposite sides—no, three, he saw, studying the side view, where the circle was a rectangle and its innards contained a cathode tube, described by neat lettering. There was no scale in the picture, but judging from the other tubes, this cathode was unimaginably small.

Some kind of generator—one not yet made, as far as he knew. An incredibly small electronic miracle. He turned the pages slowly as the night wore on, reading neurology, biology, physics. He read about how in 1928 Frederick Griffith did an experiment with pneumonia bacteria and mice that proved that the molecule of inheritance was DNA, not the protein surrounding it, as others had thought. But what exactly *was* DNA? What did it look like, how did it actually work? An unpublished paper by Dr. Eliana Hadntz asserted that, based on x-ray chrystalography photographs she had made of the DNA molecule, it had to have a structure like a curving ladder, which separated and integrated itself into other such structures in order to pass on its information. She had apparently just completed this paper when Hitler invaded Poland in 1939.

Gradually, he realized that she was trying to figure out what organic life was, and how it differed from inorganic matter. She was a medical doctor and also a physicist; she was trying to unite the two disciplines and devise a technology that would harness the power of human memory, human thought, of whatever consciousness was, on a very fine physical level, in the realm of quantum mechanics.

His room grew cold, and he neglected to bang on the radiator.

He forgot to eat until it was far too late to do so.

He fell asleep at the desk, and woke at five thirty in the morning.

He went to the window where she had stood, raised the window to a shock of cold, and leaned into darkness.

Everything—his understanding of the nature of life and of time—had changed for him. Overnight.

Several hundred miles north of the Hawaiian island of Oahu, six Japanese aircraft carriers rolled on mountainous swells, awaiting orders.

2

December 7, 1941

S AM WOKE AROUND NOON on Sunday after little sleep. Weak sunlight glowed at the edges of the drawn shade. His desk was empty once again save for his Crosley. The papers he had pored over until dawn, now hidden under the mattress, had given him strange dreams that he could not now recall, though their luminous essence lingered. The four walls of his dull green room seemed alien now, like the room of a stranger.

He got out of bed and gave the ring at the bottom of the shade a sharp tug. Outside, afternoon shadows were already creeping across the street, and a lone black car passed below. One man wearing an open overcoat with his scarf hanging untied strode west, and tossed a cigarette butt on the sidewalk. The dark limbs of bare trees stood out against the row of town houses, many of which, like this one, were now rented by the military. On 14th Street, a block away, a trolley car passed, and three young, well-dressed women strolled uptown.

After shaving and dressing, Sam walked over to 14th. Turning left, he passed the Piggly Wiggly and Steelman's Liquor, both closed on Sunday. Scholl's Cafeteria would be packed with late-service churchgoers. Peoples Drug had a phalanx of smiling, white-uniformed women behind the counter, all expecting large tips. He passed both places and continued another block to Frank's, a drugstore with a newsstand and a soda fountain. Frank had the best prices he'd found in this neighborhood.

A bell jingled when he opened the door. Several men slouched at the lunch counter, drinking coffee and reading the newspaper. Cigarette smoke curled above them, mingling with the smell of newsprint, magazines, stale coffee, and the grilled cheese sandwich Frank flipped on the grill. An account of a football game issued from a radio—*nice block!* Sam heard—nestled between haphazardly stacked pots on a shelf above the grill.

Sam gathered a dismembered *Washington Post* from between salt and pepper shakers and napkins, and took a stool, going first to the funnies. Krazy Kat. The Katzenjammer Kids.

Frank, a cigarette hanging from his mouth, said, "Can I get ya, Sam?"

"Pancakes and two eggs over easy. Got any of that sausage from the market?"

With a nod, Frank started a fresh pot of coffee. "Not much news today. Somethin' about the Germans at a place called Tobruk. Somethin' about Libya."

"Who's playing?"

"Dodgers and Giants. Station WOL."

The Brooklyn Dodgers, a New York football team, were in the National League. They had been around since 1930. "Who you rootin' for?"

"Got a little money on the Giants."

Sam's breakfast restored his feeling of normality. Time returned to its obvious linearity. *Fumbled the pass* . . . the radio said. He grabbed a pack of Chesterfields and an *Evening Star*, which had a morning edition on Sundays, and headed out the door. A brisk walk might clear his head, but otherwise did not seem palatable. He had a vague impulse to talk to someone, but didn't know who. No one, he supposed, except Hadntz; he couldn't discuss this with anyone. He had been charged, for some reason, with this great, weirdly ephemeral responsibility.

Back in his room, he tuned his radio to WOL. What could be more normal than listening to a football game on a chilly December afternoon? Against this backdrop, while the sun made a perfectly normal two-o'clock transit across the sky, he lifted up his mattress and retrieved Dr. Hadntz's papers.

It was not remotely possible for him to figure out where her notes would lead, what the device she had proposed might actually do, much less look like. He'd passed over the sparse sketches quickly, trying to suck out the theory, thinking that if this really was a machine, he might be able to design a better one than she had if his mind was not pre-set. He turned a page. "On the Relationship Between Quanta and Consciousness." Could either be truly fathomed, as forces, as objects, or either? Mathematically described? Used for the purposes of world peace—used for anything at all? He began to try to follow her reasoning, wishing for another cup of coffee, and in its place, he lighted a cigarette. *Three yard line . . . nice block! . . . twenty-seven-yard line . . .*

A new, urgent voice cut in. *We interrupt this broadcast to bring you this important bulletin from the United Press. Flash. Washington: The White House announces a Japanese attack on Pearl Harbor.* Immediately after this terse announcement, which might have come from one of Hadntz's other versions of the present—which she claimed flocked around the one he was experiencing, geometrically expanding with each instant, filled with other selves birthed from this one—the broadcast of the game continued. *He's down on the ten-yard line . . . it's a long pass—he dropped it!*

The crowd roared.

Had he just imagined it?

He looked out the window. Everything was the same. No one rushing onto the streets, no sirens. *They're going for a field goal . . .*

Keenan, his oldest brother, twenty-six and married, was stationed at Pearl Harbor.

He opened the window and stuck his head outside, into the cold air, elbows locked as he leaned on the window sill.

You would love Honolulu, Sam. It's a little old seaport, great bars, the most magnificent weather in the world. Maybe someday I'll be able to bring Sarah and the boys here. Last week Heck and I drove out to a place called Kaena Point. You've never seen a road like this. Just a narrow track sketched on the side of a cliff. Life on a battleship isn't half bad . . .

There had to be something on the radio. He turned the dial. There. Passed it. Go back. *By shortwave radio, brought to you by Golden Eagle Gasoline. Go ahead, New York.*

An ominous silence. Had New York been attacked as well? Were German bombers on the way to Washington, having taken off from some hidden base in the Caribbean, or an undetected carrier in the mid-Atlantic? As he reached to turn the dial, the CBS broadcast resumed.

The details are not available. They will be in a few minutes. The attack apparently was made upon naval and military activities on the principal island of Oahu . . .

The broadcast, in which "Oahu" was badly mispronounced by announcer John Daly—Sam had heard Keenan say it—lasted twenty-three minutes. Reporting moved from the Pearl Harbor attack to the certainty of war with the Japanese, to Manila, and to Thailand. He hoped to hear more about the attack but searched through static in vain. Symphonies, a radio drama, Sammy Kaye's program *Sunday Serenade*, football.

Throwing on his overcoat, he raced down the stairway and out the door to the nearest phone booth, on the corner of 14th Street, and put through a collect call to home. "You're lucky to get this connection," said the operator. "For some reason we're starting to get jammed. Ma'am? Will you accept a collect call from Sam Dance?"

"Of course."

"Ma?"

"Sam! Oh, it's wonderful to hear your voice. Are you all right?" She sounded puzzled; he had never called home before. It was too expensive.

His mother's voice was familiar, comforting. He didn't want to tell her anything at all that might disturb her, that might jar that comfort from her world.

But he had to. "I'm fine, fine." Somewhat disoriented by Hadntz's assertions, but this was nothing compared to his sudden fear for Keenan.

"Where are you?"

"Still in Washington."

"We've had a little excitement around here—Peg and Jonathan announced their engagement last night."

"She's so young!"

"Yes, Pa and I told her, but she *is* eighteen, and they do seem to love each other. You know that she was accepted at State, though."

"I didn't know. I'll have to congratulate her. Listen, Ma"—he took a deep breath—"Pearl Harbor has been attacked."

"No! Oh, no! When?"

"Apparently the attack is going on right now. I just heard it on the radio. But that's all. They didn't say anything else except that the Japanese have attacked."

"Keenan said that Pearl Harbor was too far for them. We're not even at war, Sam! How could they just . . . attack? I didn't raise my boys to go to war! I don't . . . Here. Talk to your father."

"Sam? Is that you? What's your ma all stirred up about?"

"Pearl Harbor's been attacked by the Japanese."

"You're sure?"

"I think it's true."

His father was quiet for a moment. "Let's hope we hear from Keenan . . . soon."

"Let's hope." Sam didn't know what else to say. "Listen, I should go; this is costing you a fortune."

"That's all right, son." His voice was heavy, his words slow and deliberate. "Thanks for calling. We love you."

"Turn on the radio and see what you can find."

Shadows were long now; the temperature was dropping. People were coming out onto the street. An elderly woman wearing a housedress and flowered apron rushed down from her stoop, wiping her hands on the apron as he approached, and grabbed his shoulders. "Young man! You're a soldier. I've seen you in uniform. What's going on?"

"I don't know anything more than you," Sam told her gently. "Go inside and turn on the radio."

"We can't find a thing!" She was as frantic as he had been a few moments ago. Somehow, sharing the news with his parents had distributed the worry, transferred his terrible knowledge to a network of concern and support. She took his arm. "You come in and find us a report."

Sam and the woman's husband, Jack Medson, pulled easy chairs next to a beautiful shoulder-high radio in the comfortable living room and bent their heads toward it. Mrs. Medson brought in a plate of the hot doughnuts she'd been making, and coffee in delicate china cups on saucers. Sam thought the couple was probably in their mid-sixties.

"Thank you, ma'am. If I remember right, there's a BBC news show on this shortwave band about now." From the speakers issued a symphony of frequencies as he tuned it. "Here we go."

I'm broadcasting from the roof of the Honolulu Advertiser, *which just narrowly missed a direct hit. Thirteen miles away, Pearl Harbor is taking a beating. Heavy clouds of smoke are billowing from the munitions dump. There are fifty casualties—*

"Only fifty!" said Mrs. Medson, standing between them, her clasped hands together. "Thank God."

Sam was silent. He didn't believe it.

"Hitler's involved in this, you can bet your bottom dollar," said Jack. "We'll be at war with the Germans too by tomorrow. Damned good thing. It's about time."

"I'd better get back," Sam told them. "The Army will be issuing orders." He felt distanced from everything. It couldn't be happening.

"Thank you so much, child. Here, let me get you a bag of doughnuts." Mrs. Medson patted his shoulder as she handed them to him. "Careful—I put a jar of cold milk in with them. You stop in anytime, you hear?" Jack stood, and they shook hands.

"Nice to meet you, Mr. Dance," he said quietly. "I wish you luck, son."

Back in his room, Sam put the grease-darkened bag on his desk next to the radio, which had finally succumbed to broadcasting news of the attack. It was getting dark, but he didn't turn on the light.

He opened the bag, took out the jar of milk. The cleaned jelly jar reminded him of home. His mother sterilized every jar she got to reuse for canning, and they resided in a bin in the basement, a shining, fragile heap that caught the afternoon sun.

Mrs. Medson's doughnuts were much like his mother's, although his mother used more nutmeg. He consumed them as if they were holy, as if he were in a state of prayer, or in the only communion in which he believed, that of family and friends. A community of shared memories, warm tableaus he could see and almost touch, almost live again.

He finished them off. The room was completely dark, and the streetlights had not come on. They were apparently in blackout.

The situation was grim. A second wave of Japanese bombers targeted Barber's point, Schofield Barracks, Hickam Air Field. As he listened helplessly, the Pacific Fleet was brutally destroyed, without warning. It was the work of renegades who did not respect international law. One did not attack without declaring war. Even Hitler, presently bombing civilians in London without mercy, had formally declared war on Poland, England, France, and Russia.

Sam twisted the empty bag between his hands, set it on the desk, and did not turn on the light.

Keenan had always been the person closest to him in the world. Older, so always more accomplished. But his buddy, his protector, his friend, the one he shared everything with. Keenan had taught him to fish, to play baseball, to climb trees. To take chances that he was not by personality inclined to take.

Of course, that had changed somewhat over the years. Keenan was married now, with children; it had been more than a year since they had seen one another. But they wrote frequently.

Sam's own hometown girlfriend had up and married someone more available, just a year ago, but she had never responded to his voluminous letters with anything more than a postcard—something he could now view as having been a large clue to their incompatability. Keenan had helped him through that, as he had always helped him with everything, reading Sam's long letters patiently, responding in kind, throwing in and eliciting all those daily details that made life one's own—funny, tragic, but something to be shared.

Sam opened his desk drawer and took out the sheaf of Keenan's letters, and set the pile in the center of the desk. But he did not, could not, read them.

The window shade was still up, reminding him that Hadntz had been in this very room only twenty-four hours ago. Such a short time, but so much had changed. He held to the plain, physical facts for a moment: the flat hardness of his desk, the soft circle of light shed by the desk lamp, the bare winter street outside, where a woman sat on a stoop across the street, dressed warmly, smoking a cigarette.

What was Hadntz's game? Was she a German spy? Had she given him these improbable plans as an act of sabotage? And if they were workable, why had she chosen him? If her story was true, he had to consider the fact that he had probably simply been chosen in haste.

Suddenly he realized why she had stood in front of the window. She had even said why. She wanted this hand-off of information to look like something else.

And though he never thought about it, he was considered to be intelligent. He loafed through school, and his history teacher in particular was outraged when he was taken out of class to be tested and his scores were exceedingly high. He was here, in Washington, absorbing the latest in scientific advances, theoretical and applied.

Hillbilly music, which Sam loathed, blared from behind the wall. He stood and pounded on the wall, something he'd never done before. "Hey! Turn that crap down! Don't you know we've been attacked?" The answer was an increase in the volume. Sam turned up his own radio so that he could hear the ongoing reports.

The announcer's crisp voice, ranging through international news of battles in China and Russia as well as the Pearl Harbor attack was strangely soothing, affording him a space to think.

If Hadntz's theories turned out to be true and usable, if he could possibly build a device such as the one he had glimpsed in her briefcase, like the one in the plans she'd left him, what might the device do? How could it facilitate the peace of which she had so fervently spoken, now that Pearl Harbor had been attacked? There was no going back. A quick Japanese defeat, perhaps? Since the Japanese had been laying waste to China, Burma, and wherever else they could wage their self-proclaimed war against white colonialism with great success, that didn't seem very possible. They were a formidable enemy.

He began to study her papers once again, trying to make sense of the equations, as well as her stilted English. Some of the papers were in German; he would have to have them translated. But by whom?

As the night continued, time disassembled, became sharp, discrete scenes. Keenan, a freckle-faced kid, running ahead of him on the path to the Puzzle River, turned and grinned, his face a heartbreaking pale flash, a mere glimpse. Keenan hollering, *Just swing out and let go of the rope! The water will catch you! Jump!*

If he could build and use this mythical device proposed by a mysterious, mystical genius, could he change what was happening to his brother right now? He continued reading Hadntz's papers:

> If, as I believe, everything is physical, then time must have a shape. Proposed: to discover the shape of time, and use that information, conjoined with information about how life changes matter—*we* are matter talking and thinking—and use those discoveries in a technological fashion, to improve humanity. To end human suffering. Something organic—live—presupposes a seed, a germ that contains the genetic program of the entire organism. Life unfolds according to time, in a rhythm.

He put the paper down. If he could he insert the seed that might change this present, where would he do it? *Here . . .* or *here*? How would he know? What havoc might he reap, what lives might he shatter? Where, in these papers, did she consider this?

Yet—he *would* do it. He would swing out now, on the end of the rope, unafraid, and arc through the hot summer day, or through suddenly fractured history, where death reached in without notice, snatching loved ones—if he only knew how.

His head dropped onto the desk, but he battled sleep, fearing nightmares, while listening to the radio for any scrap of news about what might be happening to Keenan Dance.

But as the radio poured news of fire and explosions into his ears, he dreamed of bright childhood, the glinting river, the cornfields of Ohio, where Keenan ran, parting the great, tall rows, toward the Puzzle River.

The next morning, he was pulled out of class, this week with a plump, bald German refugee, and taken to a small room in the basement. He was seated on a chair while two men in suits sat on a desk like mirrors of each other, both with one leg on the floor, and asked him questions about Hadntz's visit and demanded to know about their affair and where she had gone. A blond woman, a Major Elegante, was also there, taking notes, sitting on a chair in one corner, but she didn't speak and barely glanced at Sam.

"Well," he said, "it just happened very quickly. I can't explain it." He held up his palms in question. "Who knows what love is, how it happens?"

"Love!" One of the men actually snorted.

"You don't think she could love me?" he asked. "Why not?"

"I think we're getting sidetracked," said Suit Number Two.

"She is a very beautiful woman," said Sam. "It wouldn't be proper for me to say much more about it. You say she's gone?" He slumped back into his chair, shook his head. "After all that. How could she just leave?" He looked at them sharply. "Maybe something's happened to her. She must have had some kind of accident. Maybe she's in trouble. Are you looking into it? I didn't do anything to her. I mean—"

"Look," said Number One. "Just let us know if she gets in touch, okay?"

He was relieved when they did not question him further.

He had already determined that, whatever the cost, however complicated, and no matter what the roadblocks, he would figure out Hadntz's plans.

And use them.

The Washington, D.C., course in which Sam had been enrolled was abandoned: Every serviceman had to be a soldier now, first and foremost. And, Sam thought, perhaps the professors suddenly had a more urgent task. Or his contact with Dr. Hadntz was suspect, and he was to be trusted with no more secrets. In the fashion of the Army, they had of course not been told what the course was intended to do, but he was certain that he and his classmates now had more information about certain aspects of theoretical physics, codebreaking, and other classified information than most people in the Army.

Whatever the reason, within a week he was on the train back to Camp Sutton, in North Carolina.

On the way, he was given leave to go back to Middleburg, Ohio, for Keenan's funeral. It was a disorienting slice of time from the past, with all the old neighbors, except that Keenan was absent.

Even Keenan's body was absent from Katzan's Funeral Home on 5th Street, where his large family gathered.

Keenan was permanently entombed in the USS *Arizona*.

Camp Sutton, North Carolina
January 1942

B ACK AT CAMP SUTTON, Sam began to write his stories of the war down for Keenan. Or anyone, really, just someone, some target for his profound loneliness, as if Keenan had been his twin. He tried not to hope that the strange papers he'd been given might open a history in which he could see his brother again. But some future Keenan was the one he kept in mind as his audience.

Writing his narratives was a way of keeping Keenan alive in his own mind. *You are still there—somewhere.* And there was also the feeling that Sam had to live more fully, absorb every detail with enough appreciation for two, because he was fortunate enough to still live, because his eyes were still filled with color, his ears with sound, his mind with thoughts.

This was my war, he would tell his brother. This is what I did to defeat our enemies, to take the world through the war, past the war, and then to continue the fight. This is what I saw and what I learned.

We were somewhat surprised to get Christmas Day off after turkey and dressing, cranberry sauce, pumpkin pie, and nuts. (I believe there is an Act of Congress designating Thanksgiving and Christmas Day menus for the armed forces; I hear they even have holiday K-rations for foxholes.) After dinner we had a home-talent "entertainment"; some singing with mimeographed song sheets, and our company magician, Joe Kocab. We were released in the early afternoon.

I wound up with Jimmy "The Mess" Messner, Kocab, Stan Slates, Bill Porter, and others; we got cabs to a local roadhouse jammed with mostly rookie soldiers and local denizens. Kocab, Slates, and I were sitting in a booth with a slight buzz on when a drunken soldier staggered by.

Kocab said, "Hey, buddy, get me a beer!"

Instead of telling Joe to go f—— himself, the drunk said, "You'll have to give me a dime."

Kocab said, "Sure," and took his hand, laid a dime on his palm, and folded his fingers over it.

The drunk staggered a few steps, looked in his palm, and came stomping back, irritated, shouting, "I said you have to give me a dime!"

Kocab said, "I'll give you *another* dime, but you have to take care of it." Again he took the drunk's hand, put the same dime in it, and folded his hand shut. The drunk immediately opened his hand, looked in it, and shouted, "Give me my money!"

All of this was entertaining Kocab immensely, but the soldier was too drunk and too irritated to realize how the money was "disappearing," and by this time his drunken buddies were showing up to defend their buddy against the world, and our buddies were showing up to defend us, and the rest of the customers moving in to find somebody who looked like he had a target painted on his jaw.

Slates and I were trying to move our contingent toward the door; by the time we moved two or three outside, the others were edging back into the hot zone. This went on for some time before we got all our crowd loaded and moving to another roadhouse.

But something else is happening too, something just as momentous. I'm still trying to understand. I wish I could explain it to you.

Just before I left for the Army, Jack Armstrong—you remember him, Fred's brother—and I were discussing an idea he had about bouncing radio waves off airplanes to see where they were. My argument was you were bouncing waves off a cylindrical body, so there was damned little echo. And that they would be so scattered in space that you wouldn't get an echo to give you a blip.

Nothing wrong with the concept—we need amp; that is, power. Concentrated power that is just not available. What I'm working on has something to do with that idea, but it's infinitely more complicated.

Anyway, a better life is nearer than I thought. I've only been here two weeks, and now I'm off to Aberdeen Proving Grounds for a course in generator maintenance.

Or so they tell me.

Aberdeen Proving Grounds
February 1942

THE ABERDEEN PROVING GROUNDS were a warren of barracks and classrooms. The Aberdeen Back-and-Forth, an ancient train of wooden cars with time-smoothed wooden seats, met the passenger trains and buses and ran back into the living areas. On the day I arrived . . .

It was a wildly sunny day, false spring, his mother would call it, with white clouds scudding across a brilliant blue sky and bare tree branches waving as if their reawakening was already a fact, though snow was predicted in a few days.

Sam took a seat and surveyed his new waypoint as the train made slow progress inward—barracks, offices, test facilities, labs, and big guns. Lots of them.

After a short walk from where the AB&F dropped him off, Sam stepped into a barracks room about a hundred and fifty feet long and forty feet wide, with a worn wooden floor and many tall, narrow windows. He checked his orders: This was the right place, and a loud one. Soldiers shouted back and forth to one another, meeting and greeting and arranging their belongings, as they banged open their footlockers, cursed and bantered with cigarettes hanging from their lips, bluing the air with smoke.

He saw two rows of very public cots, and at one end of the barracks a private room for the senior NCO, which had a very luxurious appointment: a door, presently closed. Sam stood next to the shower room and toilets. The whole place smelled of a thorough, recent cleaning with bleach.

It was more promising than Camp Sutton, where there had not been a minute of time nor an appropriate place to examine Hadntz's papers or even properly mourn his brother's death. His entire hometown had turned out for Keenan's memorial service, but he'd been accorded only two days to travel there and back. Keenan still seemed strangely alive, still present, somehow. Perhaps that was the importance of seeing the body of the deceased—to fully know that life, whatever it was, had departed. By now, a black-marbled school composition book that held his missives to Keenan was almost full. He'd have to pick up a few more at the PX.

But right now he had a non-canvas roof over his head, and heat that would not rage out of control and kill them, as had happened to some unfortunate soldiers in Camp Sutton when a jammed stovepipe set a tent on fire. After he'd threaded through his fellow soldiers, chosen a cot beneath a window, made the bed, and arranged his belongings in the footlocker, he got out his book of the moment, *The Thin Man*. Lying on his cot, he became absorbed in the novel, able to ignore the surrounding curses, the dull, constant boom of munitions, and any tone of voice that might presage his being asked to perform some task. When lost in a book, he could sometimes even stop thinking about Keenan.

When a duffel bag thumped onto the cot next to him, he didn't look up.

"This *sure* as hell beats a tent in the pouring rain."

Sam had never actually seen the man who possessed this particular voice—a nasal New York accent, used heartily, full of good cheer and humor, though often tinged with dark irony. But he had heard it every morning for weeks at Camp Sutton, often in the same scenario: Freezing rain creeps down Sam's neck. It is still dark at Camp Sutton; the appellation "morning" seems misapplied. The first sergeant barks out names down the line while the company clerk holds an umbrella over him.

"Wellman."

"Here, sir!"

"Winklemeyer."

Silence.

"WINKLEMEYER!"

The spring-stretching sound of a screen door opening. "Yo!" *Slam.*

It had been like that every morning, rain or shine. The man with the New York accent never did get out of bed for roll call.

Winklemeyer, in the flesh, had put in an appearance.

Of medium height, slightly stocky. Sandy hair, reddish complexion. A short, faint scar above his left eye. Sam later learned it was the result of an imprudent mixing of certain chemicals in his father's lab when he was fifteen. Mischievous blue eyes, which he turned on Sam.

"Al Winklemeyer. Wink for short."

"Sam Dance."

"Good book?"

Sam held it up so he could see the title.

"Hammett is a helluva writer. Let me borrow it when you're through."

Sam hadn't run across many people in the service who liked to read. "Sure."

"Like jazz?"

You had moved out by that time. You know I like jazz, but this was my epiphany:

Casting about on the radio dial for something to listen to about 7:30 P.M. on a summer evening I was electrified by a swing band playing breakneck music in perfect pitch, harmony, and tempo, apparently without effort. At that time, I was in 9th grade, and not a popular music fan. That evening changed my life.

I happened upon Jimmie Lunceford playing from the Larchmont Casino. The name of the piece was, appropriately, "White Heat." I had another shock when I heard his theme song, "Jazznocracy." Just as fast, intricate, flawless, and awesome. I was smitten, never to look back.

I rushed downtown to Jimmy the Greek's to bring my friends up to date, and to make sure that we were together, comfortably ensconced the next Sunday at 7:30 to listen and exchange thoughts on what we heard.

There was at that time no affordable equipment to record radio broadcasts or live music. I had a Wilcox-Gay Recordio player which had no speakers, but it did have an AM transmitter which I could tune to a dead spot on the radio spectrum so I could tune it in on any radio in a city-block radius for clear reception. I tuned in to the Larchmont Casino and had the same electrifying experience. We all did.

About this time Wilcox-Gay brought forth a wire recorder to the retail market; the wire was soft iron, easily recorded with an electromagnet; also easily broken by a crimp in the wire. The break was also easily repaired: just knot the broken ends together. I couldn't afford one, however. We had to get our music on shellac records, 75 cents and 45 cents, 78 RPM; Lunceford, fortunately, was 45 cents, not a deal breaker. A dud on the second side, however, was a deal breaker for a prospective freshman.

Within our group, however, I think that we managed to buy all of Jimmy's output for that critical year or two. As our affinity grew, along with our nascent record collections, we met frequently for the purpose of entertaining each other with our latest finds, from the likes of Goodman, Shaw, Ellington, Billie Holiday, Claude Thornhill, Raymond Scott Quintet, Wingy Manone, Tommy and Jimmy Dorsey, Jimmy McPartland, and the like, culminating in an early-winter meeting on a Saturday night in our basement for the purpose of formally organizing the Squounch Club, dedicated to drinking beer and listening to jazz.

"Yo!" repeated Wink. "I said, do you like jazz?"

"Who doesn't?" It was the music of the day. The only people who didn't like jazz, as far as Sam could tell, were the Nazis. "Once I heard Lunceford's 'White Heat,' I never looked back."

"You speak truth. Listen, Dance, what say we find out what kind of trouble we can get into? We've got all night. I hear Ellington's in Baltimore this week. If we play it right we might be able to get to the Block and back before roll call."

They did, just barely. Hanging on the stage at a theater in the entertainment district of Baltimore, listening to Ellington and owl-faced Strayhorn exchange ideas, they missed the three o'clock train and had to hitchhike. During the evening, they discovered that they both played several instruments—Sam, the piano and sax; Wink, the violin and trumpet. Wink, an ex-premed student, had switched to chemistry, which angered his father—that, and the fact that he had blown up a portion of his dad's glass factory while performing an experiment.

Their lift dropped them off several miles from the front gate. As they walked briskly through the cold, many-starred night, thin, brilliant lines of fire streaked out over Chesapeake Bay.

"What now?" asked Wink.

"Tracers for the shells. I think they're developing firing tables."

"Round the clock."

"The Army never sleeps. Besides, you can't photograph the flight path in the daytime."

"Well, I certainly intend to sleep." Wink found that their room was perfectly situated to answer roll call from the window behind his cot, and claimed it was proof he was blessed.

On Saturday morning they were marched to the pistol range for sidearm practice, where they shot at paper targets, but they were really at Aberdeen to study a range of technical information, beginning with basic electricity and moving on to not-quite-explained heights of ordnance and advanced weaponry, according to their first quick lecture, delivered with no frills by their commanding officer.

Saturday noon, they were set free until Monday reveille. "This is how the better half lives," exalted Wink, as he rummaged in his footlocker, from which organization had ebbed within minutes after inspection.

Sam pulled a worn black case from beneath his bed and opened it. "Plenty of reeds." Music was the one constant in his life, the place where it seemed that, at least for fleeting moments, things could be set right, where a perfect world truly existed. "D.C.?"

"New York. I know the territory. I grew up on Long Island. A baby sax? That's pretty cute."

"Easier to carry than my alto."

"You any good?"

Sam shrugged. "I've had a few paying gigs. You know any places in New York where we can sit in?"

"A couple. After hours." Wink removed a violin case from his footlocker and set it on the floor.

"Machine gun?"

Wink grinned. "The world is not yet ready for my jazz violin. I have proof of that."

"That first time Artie Shaw used strings—"

"Agh, we all puked when we heard that. My violin is not shy background stuff. But I play this too." He pulled a cornet from a cloth bag, eyed it critically, spit on the bell and polished it with the bag, and slid the horn back into the bag. "I saw Beiderbecke when I was thirteen."

"No kidding!"

"I used all my earnings that summer to buy this cornet. My old man was fit to be tied. I was working in his factory and after that he wouldn't give me my own goddamned money. Put it in a bank account. He said."

"You got it yet?"

"Hell, no. Still lazy and undeserving, apt to waste it on the same kind of nonsense. But, as you see, I'm no longer working for him."

They got the last available room at the YMCA, grabbed a beer and a bite to eat, then headed to 52nd Street. The marquees were blacked out, but there was still enough light from cars and windows to read sandwich boards arrayed down the street, heralding one jazz luminary after another. Sam felt the rush of liberation and excitement that a city always gave him, a sense of intense, profligate possibilities.

Wink whistled. "Let us pray; this must be heaven. Teagarden, Hawkins, Eckstine."

Over the next few hours they kept up a frantic pace, moving from one tiny club to the next, buying as few of the exorbitantly-priced drinks as possible. When Red Norvo took a break they dashed across 52nd Street to catch Lester Young and Coleman Hawkins in a cutting contest, Hawkins deep and moody with perfect unexpected pauses; Young with a lighter, more facile approach, a virtuoso of freeing a melody exactly when it needed to be liberated into a present of wild notes strung together with the barest of connections.

The audiences were exclusively white, as was usual in upscale venues. Sam was no stranger to racism—no one in America was. His parents were strangely free of it, but all towns and cities had their black and white side of the tracks. In North Carolina, at Camp Sutton, he had seen it head-on in their forays to town. Black and white drinking fountains were labeled, and when he'd tried to talk to the band members at one of the jazz tours that came through town, he was confronted afterward in the parking lot by a band of local vigilantes with sticks, who warned him not to "fratenize" with niggers again, and to tell his soldier friends the same. He didn't have to; most of the other soldiers in Company C shared this attitude.

By that time he'd already spent the past six years on the other side of the tracks, listening, and was more used to the obverse—the foray into black territory to the after-hours joint on the other side of the tracks. He'd never been physically threatened in those instances, though, as he had been in North Carolina.

But even here, in New York City, it seemed that blacks were discouraged from mixing with white audiences—although he thrilled to spot Coleman Hawkins, whom they had seen onstage earlier, at a club across the street an hour later, sipping a beer and listening with deep concentration to a subtle, witty saxophone duel, couched within a big-band setting.

At the early hour of one A.M. they found themselves out on the street, pleasantly buzzed. "So where's your sit-in place?" asked Sam.

"Minton's. It's in a hotel in Harlem. West a Hundred-and-eighteenth around Seventh. You don't need a union card there."

"Why not?"

"Minton's got some kind of pull, I guess. All the musicians jam there. I was there a few months ago and saw Cab Calloway and a pretty damned good singer. Young girl. Sarah Vaughan. Didn't dare try to play, but we might get up there for a minute or two before we get kicked off."

"Which train?" asked Sam, with a grin.

"The quickest way, of course," replied Wink, deadpan. "Take the 'A' Train," written by Billy Strayhorn, had recently been a big hit for Ella Fitzgerald and Duke Ellington. The words were ostensibly based on Ellington's directions to Strayhorn on how to get to Harlem.

Although they were the only whites on the street in Harlem, they drew no looks, which gave Sam a strange feeling of liberation after spending years as the lone, barely tolerated white guy on dark streets and in juke joints. The revolutionary music he'd heard in the poorer parts of towns and cities had been commandeered by white promoters and white musicians, and smoothed to Glenn Miller dance-band precision, where the surprises so important to Sam were few and far between.

Sleet slicked the sidewalk. Music issued temptingly from the briefly opened door of the Black Cat as someone ducked inside. Sam wanted to go in, and a minute later wanted to try the next club they passed, but Wink was resolute. "We're going to the headwaters. You'll thank me. There it is—Minton's Playhouse. On the next corner." Ahead was a marquee that read MINTON'S PLAYHOUSE, which they entered through the Cecil Hotel.

Minton's was tiny, and many of the handkerchief-sized tables were taken. Everyone in the audience seemed, like them, to be lugging instrument cases around with them. Battered cases of various shapes and sizes sat on the floor next to men leaning forward avidly, accompanied by beautifully dressed women. Sam and Wink found seats right next to the stage and ordered a beer apiece. The place smelled of long-vanished fried chicken and cigarette smoke.

The piano player assayed halting, entire chords, violently augmented or flatted, linked by the trumpet's fleeting expressionistic runs. The drummer intrigued Sam. He used all four limbs independently to produce near-melodic lines with his various percussives. The bass player wore an expression of deep concentration, plucking notes from within what seemed an entirely different timeline from the other musicians. The fractured music formed a fascinating entirety.

"Who's playing?" Wink asked the waiter in a loud whisper, breaking the strange, complete quiet of the listeners. Several people turned and frowned at him. The waiter leaned close.

"Guy named Thelonious Monk. Oh, sorry—Thelonious *Sphere* Monk. Pettiford on bass, Kenny Clarke on drums, Dizzy Gillespie on trumpet." Another musician pushed his way past their table, holding his music case overhead.

"Sax," said Sam approvingly, as the man stepped onstage, opened his case, and slipped the strap over his head.

"That's Bird."

The Bird guy wore a soiled T-shirt, a fancy black overcoat with a fur collar, and sunglasses. The wrinkles in his pants were accentuated by the single brilliant spotlight illuminating the small, dingy stage, where the grand piano and drums took up so much room that the rest of the players barely had room to stand. The band swung into a number so fast it was indeed dizzying, accompanied by shouts from the audience: "Play it, man!" "That's it! Blow!" Apparently silence did not reign during fast numbers.

"Strange," remarked Sam.

Wink's eyes were closed. After a moment he said, "Flatted fifths."

"Start and stop just anywhere."

"Playing with rhythm."

The spoken phrase "Salt *pea*-nuts, salt *pea*-nuts," was repeated several times, separated by a beat that kept Sam strangely unbalanced along with the octave jump between "salt" and "pea."

When the "Salt Peanuts" piece was over, another trumpeter climbed onto the stage. Dizzy looked at him and smiled in a predatory way. "All right, then. 'Sweet Georgia Brown.' A-flat," he said, and counted out the beat.

Sam and Wink looked at each other, sharing the knowledge that A-flat was not an easy key.

The new trumpeter frowned for a few bars, not even blowing. Finally he kicked in with a few notes, but they were in the wrong key. Shamefaced, he climbed down. Dizzy stopped blowing for a moment to smile once again—this time, Sam saw satisfaction in that smile. The strange key, the challenge, was a way of testing aspiring players.

But, as the numbers passed through his being, each unique—"I Got Rhythm" in B-natural played at breakneck speed; something called "Epistrophy" which Sam had never heard of before—Sam realized that this music was more than just a challenge.

It was a new way of thinking about music, about notes, about keys, about rhythm. When they played "Anything Goes," anything did. Quick triplets. Forays that skipped across the face of a melody like a stone across water, veering in and out of keys. Octave bounces as in "Salt Peanuts."

Pettiford and Monk left around three, but Bird and Diz seemed oblivious to their absence. Bird, eyes closed, face glistening with sweat, leaned back and let loose with something entirely new in the world, a long wild phrase that Diz promptly echoed without a mistake. In what seemed the middle of a lightning-fast unison run, they stopped abruptly.

Parker squinted against the glare of the spotlight. "Are those instruments I see there, boys?"

"You bet," Wink said.

"Come on up and play." *If you can,* was the unspoken dare—almost a jeer—familiar to Sam and apparently to Wink as well.

Though completely out of their league in this new land of utterly unique music, they hurriedly unpacked their instruments. Sam counted it a point in Wink's favor that he was quite as eager as Sam to make a fool of himself. Bird swung into something he said was "Body and Soul, D," but which, after the first introductory bar, bore only a passing resemblance to the original, which Hawkins had already revolutionized.

Sam followed Bird's lead, almost holding his own. Wink blatted out a few notes. Bird looked oblivious to the world but was actually exquisitely attuned to his backup men of the moment for about three minutes, while Diz, still playing, cast him annoyed sidelong looks.

Parker suddenly put down his horn, ambled into a dark corner, shrugged off his coat, whipped off his tie, and tied it around his arm.

"Hell," Diz grumbled. He stopped playing as well, dropped onto the piano bench, and wiped his forehead with a white handkerchief.

Sam and Wink began a dialogue. It was the first time they had ever played together.

Sam lost himself in the naked lineaments of pure, timeless tone. Wink played himself into what seemed like dead ends and then drew Sam with him over a chasm of skipped chords which, though unplayed, somehow resonated. Dizzy suddenly regained interest, and then Bird, his equilibrium restored, returned and joined Diz in a rapid, luminescent flight, leaving the two soldiers in the dust.

Afterward, Sam decided he had stepped into one of Hadntz's perfect worlds and lived a couple of lifetimes there. He and Wink soon brought their conversation to a good stopping point and climbed down from the stage, conceding defeat concurrently. While the audience, now swelled by a new party that had just wandered in, offered ragged applause—probably because he and Wink had given up—Dizzy and Parker swung into something that sounded like "Cherokee," except that it was about ten times faster and was like a roller coaster, the most impressive display of instrumental virtuosity Sam had ever heard. " 'Koko'," said Parker, just for them, when they had finished—evidently the title.

A light glared abruptly and descended stageward on a rope, illuminating the dapper man turning the crank. "Closing time."

"That's Minton," said Wink.

Parker picked up the tip jar and stuffed the entire take into his coat pocket. Dizzy blew out his mouthpiece and looked the other way.

"Want more?" Diz asked Wink and Sam as he packed up. "We're heading over to Monroe's. The party is young."

On the street, walking through cold drizzle, Wink peppered Dizzy with questions. "What do you call this stuff you play?"

"Modern jazz. You didn't do too bad. How's that?"

Wink said, "Don't know. I play the violin, though."

"Classical background. Music theory. That helps."

"It sounds like you're doing a lot of augmented thirteens."

Parker, who so far had walked ahead of them, constantly looking up and down the street, turned his head. "That's right. Ever heard of Stravinsky?"

"Yeah. In fact—"

"This way." Bird herded them toward a dark alley. Sam balked, and Bird said, "You know that the military put Harlem off-limits to servicemen?" He gestured toward a shadowy figure at the end of the block. "There's a cop down the street."

Sam and Wink followed the jazzmen into the shadows, while Dizzy said, "You owe that guy money, Bird?"

"Aw, shut up."

They entered Monroe's Uptown House as the band—same guys that had left Minton's earlier, Sam noted, plus a guitar and another trumpet—broke. "Might as well come on back," said Parker. They followed Gillespie and Bird backstage through a warren of narrow hallways to a cramped dressing room where they stopped in the doorway. Bird and Diz found seats in the general disarray and got out their horns.

"This is what I'm talking about." Diz played a few bars.

"Okay, yeah," said Bird. They jammed a few minutes, trying out the idea.

"That's like it. But faster," said Dizzy. Parker tried his own changes.

The next set was tight, stellar, astonishing, their music what jazz, in Sam's opinion, ought to be—pure improvisation within a framework heeded by only the slightest quote issued with a feathery touch or witty flourish. It was an entirely new music, in which each person made his own contribution, where individuality and freedom were the most important aspects, where each affected the other in a constantly changing fabric of sound—profoundly different than a canned solo in the middle of a big-band tune.

By seven A.M., the audience was three, including themselves. Parker packed up and left while the others were still playing. From what he'd seen so far, Sam figured he was looking for a fix. At the end of the set, Dizzy said, "Come on over to my place." Sam did not feel included in the invitation, and later learned that Diz often took musicians over to his house after playing all night to continue the jam.

Snow swept down the street in dense sheets as they watched the band of musicians vanish into whiteness, and a horse-drawn milk wagon passed, bottles jingling. Sam was pretty sure that this moment would always remain a high-water mark in his life.

Without a word they headed for the neon blur of a coffee shop. After hanging up their snow-encrusted coats and stomping off their boots, they slid into a booth. The place smelled of burnt coffee.

"What the hell would you call that?" asked Sam, after they'd sat silently for a few moments at the marred linoleum-topped table.

"Parker told us. Music. Just music."

"Gillespie called it modern music, didn't he?"

Wink grinned. "It's modern, all right. Modern, right out of this world. Bird said something about 'making it new.'"

"Making it new. Yeah. Needs to be done. Jazz was stultifying. So they're doing it. But how?"

"That's what I've been trying to figure out." Wink leaned forward on his elbows and stared at the tabletop.

The waitress slid a napkin, spoon, and coffee cup beneath his nose. "You want the coffee on your head or in the cup?"

Wink leaned back and allowed her to pour steaming coffee into his cup as he rubbed bloodshot eyes. "They're using two different scales."

Two different scales. *Two coinciding events, which come from their own pasts, share a few beats of unison, and then diverge into their own futures.* It sounded a lot like Hadntz's model of time, if Sam's interpretation was correct.

"Decided?" The waitress tapped her pencil against her pad.

"Well, look—honey, can I borrow that pencil?" Wink took it from her hand. "Thanks."

"Anything else?" she asked drily.

"The forty-nine-cent special," said Sam.

Wink nodded. "Me too."

The waitress left.

"Okay." Wink wrote the notes of the scale of C major on a napkin—C, D, E, F, G, A, B. "You got these notes and everybody thinks of them in terms of a scale. They're uniform notes, the same frequencies—"

"The same chromatic event—"

"Yeah. But in a different scale, in a different setting, so to speak, a chromatic event can take on a different meaning. A different color. I mean, like in the scale of C, G is your fifth—the fifth note from C."

"Yeah."

"So if you flatten the G, it's the same distance from both C's. It's called a tri-chord." He drew a line between the F and the G and labeled it G-flat.

Sam visualized the black and white keys of the piano, heard them in his head. "Okay."

"So think of the scale of G-flat." He wrote on the napkin, G^b, B^b, C, D, E, F . . .

"Well . . ."

"Here." Wink shucked his cornet from the cloth bag and played the scale of C major. "Now, G-flat. Now, the entire thirteen tones." He gave them a quick run-through. The notes reverberated in the small room, hanging in the air for a second before fading.

"It sounds . . . Asian."

"It's the chromatic scale. Bird mentioned Stravinsky. His compositions use chromatic scales." Wink put his trumpet to his lips and took a deep breath.

"Put that away, mister," said the waitress, sliding their plates in front of them. "You're disturbing the customers."

"That bum?" asked Wink, nodding at a scruffy man bent over a cup of coffee at the lunch counter.

"It bothers the cook."

"Genius at work," said Wink, but he bagged the cornet. "Do you hear it now?"

Sam nodded. "A scale frames a note—frames a chord. Gives it a certain sound. A certain feel. A certain *resolution.*"

"Right. And?"

"You frame the same note with a different scale, it's like . . . seeing the same thing from a different perspective."

Wink nodded. "It's like you're setting the notes free. It still makes musical sense, but in a whole new way. You're hearing every note in a whole new light. Other composers besides Stravinsky have done it. Not often, though. I've never heard it in jazz. These eggs are cold. Waitress!"

"They were hot when I brought them," she said from a stool at the lunch counter, and continued to page through the newspaper.

"So you're really combining two different scales to get new intervals. A new resolution. New chords."

"Not necessarily *played* but, yeah, *there.* You *hear* them. They *resonate.*"

The way events that happened halfway around the world resonated here. Forming a fabric of meaning and being.

The way Pearl Harbor had set Sam on his strange course, which might yield a music as yet unhearable.

Sam sat through the first class of basic electricity, which lasted three weeks, and got perfect scores on every test. His notes were perplexing even to him, when he examined them later—a running record of how electrical theory, which he already knew backward and forward from his college years—fed into and supported Hadntz's theories. Afterward, he had been advanced to the next class. Three weeks later, he was called to the CO's office.

"I've just had a look at your records, Dance," the CO said. "You've had three years of chemical engineering, and we've had you in Introductory Electricity, Part Two, for three weeks. You trying to waste the Army's time?"

"No, sir." Just trying to extend this warm, dry, passable-chow interlude as long as possible, and ferret out a place in mind and in a physical location to do his own work: to build the Hadntz Device, the HD.

The CO shuffled papers and found the one he wanted. "Part of your time in Washington is available only on a need-to-know basis."

"I wasn't aware of that."

"I need to know. What were you doing?"

"I suggest that you ask the Army. I'm not sure myself."

He glowered. "Well, look, we're putting you right on the M-9 lectures. Got people coming down from Bell Labs to lay it all out."

"What's the M-9?"

"Replaces the M-7. Classified."

Sam had had training on the M-7 Director, a fire-laying assembly which required several men to work as a team in order to send a missile to hit a moving target. Each time it was fired, the team had to calculate the trajectory, and custom-cut the fuse. It was time-consuming and not very accurate. "I assumed that everything here was top secret."

"Good. Dismissed. And Dance?"

Sam turned in the doorway.

"I suggest you get with the program."

Sam refrained from laughing until he was outside.

The M-9, it turned out, was the result of research at MIT, Princeton, and Bell Labs—the work of the most brilliant minds available to the war effort. Their goal had been to develop an electronic calculating artillery director capable of much higher precision (plus or minus two yards at 40,000 feet) than the mechanical calculation produced by the M-7 Director.

The first lecture started after lunch.

"When an electrical current flows through wire in a coil it develops a magnetic field that changes direction at sixty cycles a second. The changing voltage pushes the rotor around." The Bell Labs lecturer, Dr. Bitts, held up an object.

"This is a selsyn regulator. Of course, you guys all know what a selsyn is. Who's going to tell me? You, Hellman?"

Silence.

"It's a device that transmits the angular position in the generator to a motor."

They filed out around six; the men headed toward the mess hall and Bitts headed in the other direction. As of one accord, Wink and Sam caught up with him.

"Buy you a beer?" asked Wink.

"I've got an hour to kill before my car gets here. Can you get into the officer's canteen?"

"With you we can."

They found an empty booth and ordered beer. "That was interesting," said Sam.

"I'm just getting started."

"I've been thinking about something for quite some time," said Sam. "If you send out radio waves and bounce them off a target, you could get back information about direction and speed. But you'd need something with a lot of power to focus the signal. I don't know how you'd overcome that problem. Could this M-9 have something to do with it? I mean, what's powering it?"

Bitts looked at Sam, then at his watch. He slid from the booth with briefcase in hand and grabbed his hat with the other one. "Got to go. Thanks for the beer." They watched him walk with what seemed special haste through the evening crowd and out the door.

"What was that all about?" asked Wink.

"Just an idea I've been mulling over."

The next day Sam and Wink were called into the CO's office. "Bitts seems to think that you two have knowledge of a top-secret project and were trying to pump him for information last night."

Sam and Wink looked at each other.

"You were talking about some kind of reflective radio device," Wink said helpfully.

"That's right," said the CO.

Sam wanted to strangle Wink. It was not to be the last time. "It's something I've been thinking about, but there's a power problem."

The CO made some notes. "This is all your own idea."

"Yes. But it's pretty obvious. I'm sure that a lot of other people have been thinking along the same lines."

‡

"Not *that* many people," said Wink, as they headed back to their interrupted class.

"What?"

"Apparently not that many people have been thinking about radio reflections."

"I guess they have," said Sam. "Only we aren't supposed to know it."

Two men in suits came to talk to them, and once again, the blonde, Major Elegante. Again, she asked no questions. Just took notes. When she left, Sam still didn't know what her voice sounded like.

After a week, they were again in the now-familiar office of the CO. "Okay," he told them, after they'd saluted and sat down. "You've been turned inside out and deemed not to be involved in industrial sabotage or spying."

Sam started from his chair. "My brother—" His voice shook.

"I apologize. I know about your brother. Please sit down. You'll soon see why this evaluation was necessary."

Sam sat on the edge of his chair and wasn't sure what to do with his hands, which wanted to punch the CO in the face. He gripped his knees.

"Okay, look. You and Winklemeyer, having been duly evaluated, have been cleared to receive classified information. Bitts will brief you at "oh-five hundred" tomorrow. Classroom C."

"But—" Wink began to say in what was clearly a protest.

The CO silenced him with a look. "I don't want you guys to get swelled heads, but somebody has decided that you've got the smarts and you're to receive special attention. I disagree with that evaluation; your behavior doesn't show it. But I've been overruled."

"He actually apologized," said Wink after they left, this time with an order not to discuss their technological thoughts with anyone.

"He damned well better."

"They expect me to be up at that hour on a *Sunday?*"

Sam was thrilled.

A guard was posted outside the classroom; he waved them in, looking irritated—no doubt for the same reason Wink, bleary-eyed, was irritated. "Please close the door," said Bitts. Heat hadn't made its way into the room yet, and he still wore his overcoat. The heavy oak school table at which he sat held an insulated coffee pot, and Sam noted with satisfaction that they'd been thought of: three cups and saucers were there, along with notepads and pencils, and a plate of Danishes.

"Morning," said Bitts. "Help yourselves."

"Absence of 'good' noted," said Wink, pouring his coffee.

Bitts looked at Sam. "You're the fellow who wondered about the energy source."

"Right."

"It's called a cavity magnetron. It was invented by two Brits, Boot and Randall, and was offered to us as a down payment for the exchange of war information. It was brought here under the highest conditions of secrecy." He smiled. "In a suitcase, which they kept under a bed at their hotel."

"Which is why you thought that we were spies trying to pump you for information," said Sam.

"Now we know that you're just thoughtful guys trying to solve the same problem we've been chasing for years," said Bitts. "I've been authorized to fill you in on the details."

"Why?" asked Wink.

"We're going to need people in the field who know how the M-9 operates right down to the ground."

"We're the repair guys," said Sam.

"You could say that."

"Who's working on it?" Sam asked.

Bitts pushed notepads and pencils toward them.

"It's a collaboration between the military and private enterprise. I'm from Bell Labs. We developed the computer. MIT has what they call a Rad Lab and they've been developing the radio imaging—we're calling it radar, for radio detection and ranging—and integrating the magnetron into it. A guy named Loomis—a good friend of mine, quite wealthy—is an amateur scientist. Brilliant. He's been working, on his own and in conjunction with MIT, on the same problem you identified—how to generate the power we need to make radar more effective. Boot and Randall showed the magnetron to Loomis, and he grasped its importance immediately. He's brought everything together, including getting it into quick production. G.E., Westinghouse, Sylvania—different companies have the contracts to manufacture the components. It generates extremely short microwaves, and we have about a thousand times more power available than before."

"How?" asked Sam.

Bitts swung his briefcase onto the table, unlocked it, and took out a set of blueprints. Then he began to talk electronics and physics, and explained a major top-secret weapon of the war. Sam began his notes.

U.S. bombers are equipped with the top-secret "Norden Bombsight." I guessed, correctly, it turns out, that the M-7 was a derivation of the bombsight.

They are mechanical cousins, both manufactured by Sperry Gyroscope Company in Long Island, N.Y. Most of our "New York" contingent worked for Sperry, manufacturing M-5 and M-7 directors, hence, the interest of the 610th in having them aboard. As far as I know, none of the other 610th personnel are aware of the existence of the top-secret M-9 Director, or that the M-5 and M-7 will soon be obsolete.

The computer (M-9 Director) calculates the future position of the target and drives three selsyns to provide the guns (four 90mm AA guns) with instantaneous azimuth, elevation, and distance readings. The guns are ready to fire anytime after ten to fifteen seconds of tracking, with near-perfect performances.

The power to operate radar comes from a cavity magnetron, a hollow block of metal with a spherical interior that concentrates the signal to a point in the center of the magnetron and emits the signal from the antenna.

At this time radar is a war secret—and, in particular, the short (10mm) radar enabled by the cavity magnetron is a heavily guarded secret. The Germans are way behind us. They're using a longer-wave form of radar for London bombing runs. England has the Home Chain radar towers to give early alerts of the approach of German bombers, but again, these are still longer-wave. The short-wave precision of radar enabled by the cavity magnetron is a powerful new development. It will open all kinds of doors.

Obviously, radar won't be secret for long. Anybody with any sense that's paying attention is going to recognize that the enemy is doing something that gives them the opportunity to see where you are even when no lights are shining. You're still getting artillery in your proximity. Even without searchlights they're looking at you. In spy work when you find out something about your enemy you're not supposed to know, the first decision is about what use you make of the information. If you don't use it they keep using the technology against you. The inclination not to use it keeps it from being an advantage. That's the first rule of successful spy work.

Bitts reached under the table and pulled out a cardboard box. Opening it, he took out one of the main technological advances that would later be credited with winning the war. Outside, the dim winter dawn brightened, causing the piece of metal to gleam.

"This is a resonant cavity magnetron." Made of copper, the disk was about the size of a grandfather-clock pendulum. "It generates ten kilowatts of power and ten-centimeter radio waves."

"So far we've been using—what?—about two meters?" asked Wink.

"Correct. Two meters works for vague, general imaging, but this has made much more accurate targeting possible. With this, even a U-boat periscope can be spotted."

"Amazing," said Wink. "And am I right in assuming that this opens us up to much shorter antennas?"

"That can be installed on bombers, yes."

Sam did not say anything. He was stunned by how similar this magnetron was to the one described by Hadntz as a power source for her device, at least in output. It had been one reason he had begun to think it was just a fairy tale. He believed there was no such device.

Now there was. Sam picked it up and examined it.

Bitts gave them detailed information about how it worked; about how electrons were funneled around its circular core by a magnet. He told them, briefly, about another component of the M-9 system: the proximity fuze. Merle Tuve, a Carnegie-based physicist who bought his own black powder at a Georgetown shop and made his own vacuum tubes, had developed it. The prototype had recently been tested at the firing range in Dahlgren, Virginia. The fuze, which had a radio-controlled detonator, sent a spark when it was *near* a target, rather than when it hit a target. It was a technological development that might help turn the tide of the war against Germany and in the Pacific. Bitts said that the new computer-and-radar system was called the Signal Corps Radar 584, SCR-584 for short.

And, reflected Sam, it had all been foreshadowed by what he had learned from Hadntz's papers after that night in December. But this stuff was way, way back in the beginning of the paper. If *this* was possible, then—

A thought struck him. "If they'd had this radio detection system at Pearl Harbor—"

"They did," said Bitts.

"*What?*"

"Not this, but they had a long-wave radio imaging station that had just been set up and had not yet been tested for acceptance. It was only on at night. The operator had a trainee with him, and stayed over about ten minutes that morning. They saw blips on the screen and called it in. The plotters had just gone off-shift; the guy who answered the phone said that it must be regularly scheduled B-17's coming in from the mainland. Nobody expected the Japanese to attack."

Sam pushed back his chair. "Excuse me." He brushed past the guard and found a bathroom down the hall.

Inside, he locked the door, leaned against the cold tile wall, and vomited.

As he splashed water on his face, the cold light of winter dawn washed through a high window. He put both hands on the sink, leaned forward, and bowed his head. Thousands of men had died. Hundreds were entombed in the ocean, like Keenan, or had been burned beyond recognition in the tremendous fires set off by the Japanese attack.

Just having technology wasn't enough. It had to be used.

How many Keenans might be saved, if Hadntz's ideas, whatever they might lead to, actually worked?

Did time have a shape, as Hadntz suggested? Was it as malleable as music, demanding certain basics but open to improvisation?

The idea opened new doors, turning him mercifully away from his previous obsessive thoughts.

Sam sat on the wooden chair beneath the window and watched the tiny octagonal tiles on the floor form various patterns, depending on—what? Something his brain was doing, suggesting different ways of seeing. Maybe time was a pattern which one chose to see, out of several possible patterns. Perhaps one's genetic material—the DNA, which Hadntz claimed was malleable—determined the pattern one saw. Perhaps time was a series of tones—frequencies that humans interpreted and might eventually regulate with as much ease as electricity.

He sat there, thinking, ranging through possibilities as if they each had an azimuth and elevation, and he had a mechanism that could focus on them and enable or disable them according to . . . again, what? How could one measure the ripples from a stone tossed in a pond, interacting with an infinite number of other tossed-stone ripples?

He sat there till Wink came and fetched him.

⫶ 5 ⫶

The M-9

O KAY. NOW LET'S MAKE 'Twinkle, Twinkle, Little Star' modern. A-flat." Wink counted out the time, and it was fast.

It was midnight. Sam and Wink were in a deserted lounge building at Aberdeen.

After as many visits to Minton's and Monroe's as possible, including Sunday afternoon jam sessions, they had discerned that the harmonic rules within modern music were dictated by tones themselves rather than an artificial framework—scales—most commonly used in Western music. Rhythm, the other main component, also followed no previous form, and the music swung of its own accord, off balance and falling toward resolutions adroitly avoided. They had chosen the most innocuous song they could think of, and it was now so modern, so abstract, that its roots could barely be discerned.

Sam played a sixteen-bar solo, passed it to Wink, and they finished in a stretch meant to be in unison but that fell to pieces. They finished, breathless and laughing.

"That was your fault," said Sam, collapsing onto a worn couch.

Wink wiped sweat from his forehead. "Not so. You've been slacking off."

Wink had had Sam practicing scales in different keys until it seemed as though his fingers would fall off. Some scales, given the arrangement of holes on the saxophone, seemed almost impossible to play quickly, but Sam rapidly improved.

Wink filled at least part of the void left by Keenan's death. He was immediate, and radiated something akin to Keenan's relish for living to the full.

Studying his notes for the frequent tests on the revolutionary new information they were absorbing required all of Sam's mental energy, but he occasionally took out Hadntz's paper and tried to understand it in the light of what he was learning. Security was tight in the shops in which they worked with the components of the M-9, but Sam used the experience to think about what might be usable, in his immediate environment, if the Army allowed him to continue on his present track, in creating a prototype.

It seemed impossible, here at Aberdeen. There was no privacy. The shops were locked when not in use, and placed under armed guard. The M-9 and radar were top-secret.

He would need his own shop, specialized tubes, and other materials which he would have to synthesize out of disparate components. Parts of the process were simply not included in the Hadntz paper. He would have to deduce those on his own.

But . . . what if he was successful? What was Hadntz's real purpose in recruiting him? What if something unimaginably new *was* born, as she hoped? It would change . . . everything.

It's just a form of technology, he told himself. An application of science, like the M-9. Science was neutral—merely information. Technologies were focused. Human intent determined their development and use.

But human intent was what she proposed to manipulate. If an atomic bomb was possible, and it was in the works in Germany, wasn't it his responsibility to do something?

If the Hadntz Device worked, though . . . who had the moral authority even to use it?

She talked about averaging, about the device being available to everyone, even children. The genetic triggers of their time-sense would be different. The plasticity of mind that enabled learning would be replicated at will, rather than disappearing at an early age. She cited work in child development by an Italian doctor that proved these learning abilities occurred in discrete stages, and that if one stage was missed, the child would not have the same chance to learn as easily as, say, they learned their own language at an early age. Hadntz's paper ranged over a huge number of subjects, searching for a uniting theory that could then be used . . . but how?

Playing bebop was so demanding that it diverted him from this obsessive conundrum, freed the part of his mind that needed that freedom in order to even begin to understand.

"Hard work," commented Sam.

"Thinking is always hard work."

"Kind of like inventing radar."

"Yeah, but thinking about music is free. You need a lot of money to think about radar. Laboratories to test theories. Shops to create hardware."

"Big companies to produce the stuff."

"But it's all just electronic pulses."

"Like music."

Wink nodded. "I seriously think that there is a connection. At least in the fact that human minds are involved in the production of highly disciplined pulses. What moves me in modern jazz is the same thing that moves me when I think about the M-9. Both are an astounding confluence of thought, attempts to make it new that suddenly come together and bear fruit. Sometimes it seems as if art and science are very closely related. Both make me feel like humans have been stumbling toward the light for centuries, and now the sun has risen. Like you have to keep finding out all kinds of things that don't seem connected, and then someone will see how to unite them. There's the art of it." Wink tended to fall into such verbal reflection, and Sam found himself encouraging it; what Wink thought often reflected what he was thinking.

Sam wondered, not for the first time, whether he should share Hadntz's paper with Wink. He was cleared, security-wise, so the Army had solved that question for Sam. But Sam was still unsure.

They got to New York almost every weekend. If they left directly after their class wrapped up, they could be in New York in time for a nice dinner and a fair amount of music.

Hadntz's ideas about the quantum nature of consciousness sometimes came to the fore as Sam sat in Minton's listening to the concrete, seemingly isolated packets of information that made up modern jazz, strung together in a whole that made more sense the more he listened to it. And the more he heard, the more he craved, because it led his mind in one direction, a timeless one, bright, in direct counterpoint to the darkness that was now Europe and the Pacific. No one knew how the war would end. All of Europe might fall to Hitler, all of Asia to the Japanese. One, the other, or both, seemed equally likely. The reported brutality of these regimes made such futures, so very possible, seem unlivable. It was a tense time, charged with the immediacy of history in the making, the sense that everyone had to work very quickly, as hard as they could.

Bebop released the place to which Sam directed his missives to Keenan, a "somewhen" in which he still lived in the loops of time and space that Hadntz's paper seemed to reveal, a place where he and Keenan might be different than they had been here, where they might not even have the same common memories they'd once had, and yet would somehow be, ineluctably, Keenan and Sam, like a tune that could be played an infinite number of ways and still retain its identity. Modern music was jazz, yes, but jazz assuredly made quite new, something so new and different that, when contrasted to previous musical forms, a new understanding of the nature of time would be.

And modern music seemed to have some kind of relationship with the cutting-edge information about physics he'd received in Washington and in Aberdeen, and a relationship with the technological children of that information, the SCR-584 radar and the M-9 Director. With radar, the M-9 *heard* something that was previously ephemeral, just as these creators of modern jazz *heard* something that had always been there, but which could only be surmised with the mind and targeted with blindingly fast fingering, so swiftly that a new universe was called into being for the barest instant before vanishing.

Sure, the SCR-584 was new, and powerful. But Sam had to wonder what kind of weapons their enemies might be developing. Japan had used poison gas in China in the late thirties; Germany was using their own form of radar to send their bombers to London. When would their enemies be in possession of new and even more powerful technologies and weapons?

That was the other side of "making it new."

New was not always good. It was a risk. In modern music, it was release, the learning of a radical new language that pushed the known to unexpected territory, changing, it seemed to Sam, his very brain in the process.

But sometimes the new could be a deadly surprise.

In the world of physicists, ordnance testers, and musicians, there was no division between day and night. So the expedition to the M-9 testing was scheduled for four in the morning, much to Wink's disgust. The hour was perfect for music, in his opinion, but not much else.

They and six others who had attended Bitts's lectures boarded a bus and dozed for half an hour while being transported to the test site.

Sam stumbled from the bus into the frigid Aberdeen night and followed the others to a detached truck trailer on a hill, braced on all sides, its large doors flung open so that everyone could see inside.

They were instructed to fold back the hinged roof; after it was open to the sky one of them cranked up a parabolic dish, which was the radio set, so that it extended above the roof.

In turn, they moved the M-9 Director, the power generator, (which contained the cavity magnetron), and the tracking unit out of the truck, connected them with wires, and set up a folding chair next to each. Bitts turned the dial that powered the thing; the two banks of technology at the forward part of the truck lit, blinking wildly, then settled to a steady hum. And it was ready to go.

Ready to find, track, aim, and fire at a rapidly moving target. It was connected to a bank of four 90mm antiaircraft guns arranged as a battery, but not loaded with shells. That would have been done by one of the teams, were they in a battle.

After twenty minutes and a cigarette for everyone, it was still ready to go. The major accompanying them looked at his watch, at Bitts, and back at his watch.

The dials jumped to life. Bitts said, "Late start this morning. Gentlemen, you are seeing the tracking, on that screen, of your morning Air Force defense run."

One of them was manning the M-9, but the rest simply watched as, just as Bitts had told them would happen, the four guns rotated in unison toward the drone of propellers.

"It followed those goddamned planes," remarked one of Sam's colleagues on the way back, "like clockwork."

"And no fuse to calculate and worry about cutting right," said another. "Completely fucking automatic."

Sam leaned his head against the cold glass of the bus window and began to think about trajectories and then was dreaming about a trajectory of time in which Keenan was downtown in Honolulu the morning of the attack, on shore leave, and thus still lived.

They were in Minton's, and it was around midnight. Immersed in a sea of fast-moving thought meshed to notes streaming from the stage, notes that propelled his own thoughts about time and space and electricity in vast, dissonant leaps, Sam saw how Hadntz's device meshed with consciousness, linked inner and outer, large and small, how the totality changed with only a slight dissonance, how new thought, new paths, could suddenly appear, how time flowed and linked and grew, folded back into itself, and grew again. The multidimensional vision appeared quite suddenly, seemingly thrown up by the power of the music, the sheer concentrated force of thought made physical, transmuted to pulses of sound, of focused energy. The notes, time itself, were the bare lineaments of thought, forever falling into new configurations . . .

"Hey."

"Hey yourself," said Sam, considering whether to return the rude shove on his shoulder or employ a more friendly method of dealing with whoever kept nudging him.

"Soldier."

"Uh—sir?" Two MP's hovered over them.

One of them seized Sam by the collar, pulled him out of his chair, and spun him around. "You're off-limits."

Wink was out of his chair now, addressing the shorter one. "You're making a mistake. We are on a special—"

"Can it," said the other MP. "You're coming with us."

Minton approached. "Take it outside."

"You guys have had it," said one MP, when they emerged on One hundred-eighteenth Street.

"We'll see," said Wink, and Sam wished that he'd shut up.

It took them two days to arrive in the CO's office, and they passed those days in various jails, brigs, and holding tanks.

In the meantime, Sam gave much thought to making things new. "The notes are there; they exist. It's just a matter of using them in a new way. A new arrangement of vibrations. But you have to think about it in a different way first. You have to throw away the old framework."

Bribes from their dwindling cash supply allowed them to keep their instruments, and they worked out several new arrangements while in various cells, winning applause from some and comments related to serious hangovers from others. With each attempt, Sam felt the effort, the stretch, resonate back into him, felt it changing what he thought, and what he thought he knew, bouncing off some imagined future and adjusting, as he did when he did something as simple as deciding whether or not to open a window. Throw that all away too, he thought. Abandon the old framework.

"My mother used to take me to the art museums in New York because the old man was too busy to go with her," said Wink. They'd entertained a group of drunk soldiers to great effect in their last holding tank, but presently they were locked up right on the Proving Grounds, with its comfortingly familiar din of ordnance testing punctuating their musical forays with bebop-like randomness. "I saw a lot of astonishing things. They all seemed to have something to do with how machines were affecting humanity, or how we were moving into new ways of thinking about ourselves. I remember one of those fellows, Kandinsky. He's Russian.

"I was just a kid, and his stuff seemed to be all about speed, about velocity. I mean, these guys say that their music is modern music, and this art was modern art, and this concept that we're working on with in the M-9, this technical advancement, is a modern concept. Things have changed so much. A hundred years, no, *sixty* years ago, we didn't have telephones, electricity, automobiles. We're beginning to be able to use things that are invisible to our eye, but which can be proved to exist. What we're doing is taking the elements of physics, finding out new properties, using them in new ways like Kandinsky did with color and like Diz and Bird do with sound. The next time we go to the city—"

"If we ever go anywhere again—"

"We can find some Kandinsky. There's a connection. All this stuff is coming from the same place. Funny . . . I never really thought about it before . . ."

Sam suddenly resolved to tell Wink about Hadntz. "Listen—"

"All right, you wretches." An MP appeared at the door. They were ushered from their cell, and Sam realized that he still didn't know exactly how to tell Wink about Hadntz.

The CO did not greet them, and did not ask them to sit, as he usually did. He continued writing and said, "You two are in a hell of a lot of trouble."

Wink said, "Sir, we are just doing our part for the war effort."

"So I heard." He continued writing. "Men have been court-martialed for less."

Sam thought of Keenan, of how disappointed he would be.

"Sir, I hardly think—" began Wink.

"Don't bother." He finally stopped writing and handed each of them some papers.

"What?" asked Sam after glancing at his. "These are orders to ship out."

"We're in charge of hundreds of thousands of tons of ordnance?" asked Wink. "Just we two?"

"Had you going there for a minute, didn't I?" asked the CO. "The best way to keep you out of trouble is to give you plenty to do. And a strong word of advice—'special' is not a word you should throw around lightly in the future, particularly regarding yourselves." He looked down at his papers. "Also, thanks to that friend of yours, you are now officially warrant officers."

"What friend?" asked Sam, completely puzzled.

"A Major Elegante."

"Major—" Sam frowned, trying to recall who Elegante might be.

"You know this guy?" asked Wink.

"The name sounds familiar, but . . ." suddenly he remembered the silent blond officer, and kept quiet.

She was a direct link to Hadntz. What if Elegante really knew what Hadntz was doing?

Elegante, and others in the Army?

The thought chilled him.

The CO continued. "This will give you a lot of leeway in terms of how you spend your time. God knows why, but once you start to try and understand the Army you're lost, so don't even try. No one but you and a few commissioned officers will know about this status. Keep it that way. To everyone else you shall be and you shall act like staff sergeants, subject to all kinds of shit to which you will not object. Savvy? Now get out of here."

Nobody ever escaped the 610th to better themselves; if you were able to strike a deal with anyone the 610th would declare you "essential" and that would be the end of that. Being on "TD" (temporary duty) at Aberdeen, I was, however temporarily, under the command of my "provisional company" captain who couldn't care less where I went when I left APG.

Hearing that the Air Force was desperate for engineering officers, and thinking that two and one-half years of college would fill the bill, I met with an Air Force rep and he confirmed that I had the necessary education, and if I could pass their physical (with glasses!) they would be glad to have me. So I rushed to the clinic to get fitted for hi-power glasses, crossed my fingers, and held my breath.

All for nothing. My new liberating glasses were handed to me at the ceremony where they handed out our graduation certificates and our travel orders. I was no longer in alien hands; I was, as of this instant, back in the tender hands of my very own 610th. And not even a delay enroute!

⊣ 6 ⊢

Passage to War

THE *QUEEN ELIZABETH WAS* 1,100 feet long, the sister ship of the *Queen Mary* but not identical, about sixty feet longer. Normal trade for a ship of the *QE*'s size was 1,500 passengers. When I crossed there were 17,500 aboard.

The ship had permanent gunners for one shift, then would draft sub-gunners from the passenger list, which was mostly military. We got a certain amount of dry training, loading and unloading, so if we came under attack by airplane or submarine whoever was on the guns could return fire. The regular gunners would show up as soon as they could make it; we'd stand by as fill-ins if a gunner got hit.

Our gunner's pass got us on deck any time of day or night. The regular passengers were not allowed on deck at night, nor in daytime if we were under attack.

Being January, it was a cold, rough trip. The *QE* veered over the north Atlantic. We ran about thirty-six knots, top speed, all the time and changed course every thirty seconds at random, and so covered a lot of ocean. The direct travel time would have been on the order of three and a half days but we spent five.

Our stateroom was the cinema, which had a high ceiling. The bunks, stacked twelve high, were maybe eighteen or twenty-four inches apart; the guy above you was right in your face. Bunks were made of pipes with a grommeted canvas fly tied between them. Each soldier's space was two and a half feet wide and six and a half feet long. There was no padding, sheets, or blankets. You could wiggle around and get the canvas to approximate your shape fairly comfortably.

I took a look, decided I was going to sleep in the top bunk, and hoisted up my duffel bag. Up above was a wooden rack where everyone's duffel bag went.

The main dining room was not open to us as part of the crew. Ours was a crew dining room we occupied for fifteen to twenty minutes. It was a hidey-hole with a seven-foot ceiling and long board tables with tip-down stools.

As we had a crew pass to get where we needed to go we decided that the main dining room was the place to eat. We'd go up there about the time the last people popped into line so we wouldn't have to wait.

One day we arrived there just after they shut the door. We hammered on it and the main purser opened it. He was a Brit, and, next to the captain, a top dog.

He looked us up and down very coolly and described to us exactly where we were allowed to eat. Without raising his voice he tore us into little pieces and turned us out with an invitation not to try it again.

After that if we missed the open door we went back down to the crew mess.

It was two in the morning and on deck, in the middle of the north Atlantic, the temperature was well below freezing. Sam pulled his collar up and stomped his feet to keep them warm. He was on watch next to the fantail six-inch gun, watching whitecaps glint in the moonlight like faint chimeras, buffeted by gusts of wind fresh off the icebergs they'd recently passed. Removing his gloves, he clamped them beneath one arm and with numbed fingers tied his earflaps beneath his chin before putting the gloves on again.

In this desolate windswept place, Sam felt Keenan's presence, as he did more and more often as anger and anguish continued to occupy him. Keenan had been in the Navy for years. Perhaps he had sailed this route. Certainly he had stood watch on many frigid nights such as this.

Keenan was like Wink. Irrepressible. Keenan was the first to walk the railroad trestle over the Puzzle River. Once, he'd dangled from supports below the track as a train roared inches above his head. All the kids, including Sam, watched in horror, certain he'd drop to his death at any second. He came back laughing.

Sam wished for another cup of the electrifyingly strong hot chocolate that was brought to those on this shift, and composed, in his mind, his latest update, which he would write when he went off-shift. His missives were rough; he planned to go over them when they were finished, put them in context, smooth out the rough edges. He had ceased to anticipate that Keenan would remember everything he had known, if another world was leading him in a direction this one had taken; he went back and added details, sometimes, details about the flavor of the times, the tiny things.

The lounge is spacious, the grand piano grand; a suitable instrument for a concert or for Art Tatum. The lounge would accommodate a dance band, but there's no hope that one will take the stage on this particular cruise. It lacks a dance floor, but no doubt one will surely appear once the last dogface steps off the gangplank.

Instead, the room is nicely furnished with easy chairs and couches and is well populated with readers. In my visits two memorable piano players held forth—a black fellow with long supple fingers who was content to emulate Tatum, and a white boy with short stubby fingers who was more a Fats Waller type. They didn't seem to compete; just seemed to enjoy the opportunity to make use of a great instrument before an appreciative audience.

After the pianists left, the mundane silence demanded music. Sam unpacked his sax. Wink arrived with his violin case.

Everyone groaned when Wink opened it up. "Not that classical crap!" someone shouted.

But when Wink cut loose with a surprising unpredictable solo on "Take the 'A' Train," then backed up Sam on some Beiderbecke standards like "In a Mist," he raised appreciative whistles and commanded relative silence.

As Sam played, visions assailed him, as they always did when he got to playing this way. Keenan running toward the guns on the *Arizona*, his passage blocked by fire. Newsreel images of London Docklands bombings, smoke rising from fires breaking out everywhere. A green field rushing toward him as he fell. A split-second mathematical realization he would never recapture. The stamping feet and whistles in the interval before their next piece seemed distant, as behind glass.

Sam wished that at least one of the pianists had remained. Maybe tomorrow night.

But he never saw either of them again.

They reached Scotland. As the ship entered the Firth of Clyde's calm waters, low, bare yellow hills came gradually into view, as well as bits of land that proved to be islands as the ship passed them. The *QE* was not perturbed by the light chop whipped up by the brisk, cold wind. Eventually the fog burned off to reveal an estuary narrowing to the mouth of the River Clyde.

The uncertainty of the future was strangely exhilarating. They were safe from German subs now; underwater nets protected the firth, and Glasgow was out of range of German bombers. This would be their first staging area and his first taste of another continent. So far the war had been only newsreels, newspapers.

And Keenan.

Now it was without a doubt his war. Operation Overlord was the name of the invasion plan, and Company C was there to facilitate it.

But Scotland at dawn was peaceful. Large gray herons flew overhead and gulls in the thousands hovered over the QE, its welcoming party, and the only interruption of the hush. The smell of land was surprisingly distinctive after five days at sea. Civilians were up on deck now, leaning on the railings, and a deep mechanical thrum sent vibrations through the ship. Far off, a ruined stone tower caught the light of the sun.

Relinquishing his gun to the British gunner at the end of his watch, Sam grabbed a mess hall breakfast and hurried back on deck to watch the process of anchoring at the mouth of the River Clyde, still thirty-two miles from Glasgow. Standing at the wooden railing, he absently ran one hand over it, feeling the indented initials American soldiers had carved in the wood when they got tired of looking at the empty ocean.

Then Wink was there. "Glasgow's a helluva good drinking town. By all reports."

"We'll have to conduct some research."

Their first night on leave they found Teacher's Pub, where the bartender put out an hourly supply of Teacher's and sold no more until the next hour.

The pub's low roar consisted of the unintelligible English of Glaswegians. Sam caught the bartender's eye. "Another wee heavy and pale ale." Sam had no head for whisky, and avoided it, but he had discovered this local specialty. It was indeed heavy, subtly spicy, without any flavor of hops. The bartender poured the contents of the three-ounce wee heavy bottle into a pint glass and filled it to the top with India Pale Ale.

The guy next to him at the bar said, "You're a Yank too, eh?"

"Sam Dance. Company C. Ordnance."

Beneath a crumpled corduroy fishing hat, his barmate's face was lined with resignation; his eyes were far-focused, for an instant. He had apparently been allowed to grow a beard, black streaked with gray, though he wore some sort of U.S. uniform.

Sam asked, "You one of the Dirty Dozen?"

He returned from wherever he had been and turned to look at Sam. "Nah. Met 'em, though. There's actually thirteen of them, paratroopers. Thirteen is how many jump, in a stick. They are foul. Got free range on account of most of them are going to die, I guess. They're in your barracks—Hotspur Transit Camp—right now. I'm Angelo Rafferty, 4-F. Tried to join up a couple times but as far as they're concerned I'm not Army material. Bad back, they say." He polished off the second shot of Teacher's lined up in front of him, leaving one to last till the clock struck. "So I'm USO. Accordion. Been opening for Ella Logan."

"Doesn't she do that jazzy 'Loch Lomond'?" Sam had a hard time wrapping his mind around the notion of an accordion, which was inextricably linked to polkas, opening for her.

"Big hit. Million-seller. She's in town. We just got in from North Africa."

"What's it like there?"

"Hot as hell. Italians strafed us while we played. I buddied up with some paratroopers and they let me jump. Back's still the same as far as I can tell, works fine. Goddamned doctors. Don't know their ass from a hole in the ground."

The clock struck eleven, the bartender put out amber fifths of Teacher's, and filled the three shot glasses sitting empty in front of Angelo. Behind them pressed a crowd, thrusting empty glasses toward the bartender on either side of Sam, getting theirs before the supply ran out. Angelo tossed one back, chased it with an ale, and started nursing the second. Sam looked around for Wink. He was over in a corner, romancing a Glasgow girl, who was laughing in the dim light.

"Where's Logan playing?"

Angelo shrugged. "Dunno. I'm hoping we'll move on to London soon. I'm itchin' to be in France when it happens."

"Want to be up front, eh?"

"And kill those Nazzy bastards, you bet."

In Sam's opinion, the accordion would make an excellent weapon in the right hands. He envisioned Angelo squeezing out vast accordion riffs, fingers flying over the keys, knocking the SS dead in swooning rows.

Wink touched his shoulder. "How about a party? She's got a friend."

Outside, as they walked, fine drizzle gathered density until it dripped from their hats. Sam's girl linked arms with him. "What's it like to be a soldier?" she asked; or at least that's what he thought she asked, given her accent.

"Interesting."

"Ha! I'd wager you're the only one to think so."

The streets were not empty. People were leaving pubs, singing in the streets. Shouts and whoops echoed from the next block. They walked uphill for quite a ways and turned onto a side street. Reaching a tall, narrow town house, they were greeted by faintly musical bellows which grew louder as they climbed stairs. He and Wink were introduced to the father of Wink's girl and three of his roaring-drunk friends. Sam accepted a whisky and played the piano to enthusiastic applause. They even applauded his singing. Wink's girl sang along with him and had quite a nice voice, though her timing was off. Cold, damp air came in through an open window. The father, who had a better voice, pushed another whisky on him. "Play, man, play!" Oh, he was sheer genius, he was. He felt it; they heard it; Wink and his girl danced energetically, shaking the floor. They all sang, loudly, with unsurpassed gusto, and went *dah dah dah* when they didn't recall the words, which became increasingly often.

When Sam's horrendous headache woke him, he found that he had been maneuvered sideways onto a single bed; his legs hung over one side and his head hung back over the other. Rain beat at the small window.

He decided, once again, that whisky was not his drink.

Sam haunted pubs and read playbills for a week before he found out that Glasgow was Logan's hometown. It was probably the last place she'd play. She had friends and family to visit.

Sam and Wink's battalion had about nine hundred personnel but only twelve or so of them went to Glasgow to guard the shipment—four-million-dollars' worth of equipment and tools.

The two men spent their days ticking off invoices and organizing the cargo for transport. An officer noticed them riding the crane hook down into the lighter's hold; thereafter, they walked when he was around.

It took a week to transfer their several tons of machine tools in stages from the lighters which ferried the cargo upriver to "goods wagons"—small British boxcars—for the journey to Tidworth.

What kind of town could be named "Tidworth?"

A very small town, indeed.

Wartime England

JANUARY 1944–JANUARY 1945

Surely music (along with ordinary language) is as profound a problem for human biology as can be thought of and I would like to see something done about it. A few years ago the German government set a large advisory committee to work on the question of what the Max Planck Institute should be taking on as its next scientific mission. The committee worked for a very long time and emerged with the recommendation that the new M.P.I. should be dedicated to the problem of music— what music is, why it is indispensable for human existence, what music really means—hard questions like that.

—Lewis Thomas
*Late Night Thoughts on Listening to Mahler's
Ninth Symphony*

Tidworth, England
January 1944

A BOUT HALF THE TIME I spent in England was during cold weather. Coal was rationed. Pub owners were terribly embarrassed that they didn't have the means to keep beer warm in winter. They never really believed that Yanks preferred cold beer. "It's the war. Can't do anything about it; can't heat the basement."

We were living just outside of Tidworth, a village of a couple hundred. Lugershall was two miles away; county of Wiltshire. We could go to Andover, ten miles away or to Winchester, twenty-three miles to the south toward the coast. These were the nearest big towns with movies and dance halls. We'd take the Wilts and Dorset bus to Andover, go to the railroad station, and buy a ticket to London for a modest fare. It was about ninety miles—or may have been sixty. Anyway, it was a three-hour trip.

Our first barracks in Tidworth was a big corrugated iron gymnasium with a seventy-five-foot ceiling. There were a few windows up high. It was pretty dark; if you wanted to read in a bunk you had to use a flashlight.

We rented bunks from the Brits, double-deckers with a two-by-four frame and chicken wire on the bottom of the bunk. You got a cotton sack you filled with straw. The second time you got straw you were careful—you didn't move the first night so that it formed around your body and was then reasonably comfortable.

The gymnasium was turned into a field hospital for the invasion. They treated the lightly wounded there until they got better; then they were put in the repple depple, the replacement depot. Those men didn't return to their original company. Instead, they were slotted in wherever needed. This was an unpopular system.

We got evicted to a bunch of Quonset huts. They were attached by corridors so you could go between them. We stayed under cover for days. The fighter planes were looking for soldiers to strafe. The Army was a big proponent of the adage that "idle hands make idle people and idle people get into trouble." In the States, we'd spent hours in close order drill or doing calisthenics. All that stuff was off the books in England. At Tidworth, early in the war, a company performing calisthenics got severely strafed and suffered high casualties.

As soon as our equipment rolled in our work schedule jumped to twelve hours a day, six days a week. Sunday was a day of rest: we worked only eight hours. W. and I set up a battery shop, a fuel handling shop, shops to work on spark plugs, air cleaners, all kinds of welding equipment, gas and electric, for chassis repairs. The idea was to get equipment ready and to turn it around fast if it was out of duty.

We received all antiaircraft equipment that was used at that time. My main job was to take delivery of M-9 Directors. A crew uncrated and assembled the components of the M-9, as well as the four-wheeled trailer. They bolted the computer to the trailer, put the housing on top, and sent it up to us. We would plug it into an electric source, fire it up, and check out.

Test settings were built in. You turned it on and everything would go wild inside, revolve, settle down to humming radio tubes and lights. In eight to ten seconds it would be waiting for you to do something.

One turn of the dial put it in a factory-built situation with the answer printed in the manual. You check out dial one and it might show 130 MPH south, 27 MPH west, 2 MPH down. If it was within specs you went on to the next test. If it never settled down you looked for what was loose or missing—open circuits, unheated tubes that needed reseating. Tubes were shipped separately, 130 of them. You kept a log about what you were doing, what the outcome of the tests were. Let it sit a while to see if it changed. Troubleshooting was specialized search and rescue. They'd been through a sea voyage and rough handling.

We did this for three or four months and finally got to the point where the pressure was lessening. We had the troops well supplied and were doing maintenance of ordnance coming back from the field that needed repair. Work loosened up and we were allowed to take two days off every twenty days.

Wintertime England was everything that Sam expected—cold and rainy, a land of plentiful pubs. Knocked-down trees and cars up on blocks were scattered throughout the fields, intended as obstacles to the inevitable German invasion.

The train station had recently been bombed. The vicar's garden had a ragged crater in its center, and he had an ill-kept secret plan to landscape his "vicar's crater" for reference in postwar Memorial Day sermons. A pilot of local legend named Bellingham, who died in an encounter with a Messerschmitt the week before the 610th arrived, had a month earlier shot down a German reconnaissance flight over the town. Two Germans had survived, and were in the local hospital under heavy guard, protected from injury at the hands of the Poles and Czechs in the RAF unit. By all accounts, they were treated like weekend guests at a house party, were insufferably arrogant, and predicted a quick end to the war, in their favor.

When American soldiers walked down the street they were followed by children asking "Got some gum, chum?" When a woman in the Hart and Hind said to Jimmy "The Mess," in parting, "Keep your pecker up," she was puzzled by the resulting hilarity. Even after they found that this meant, "Keep a stiff upper lip," the soldiers never failed to be amused. "Knock me up," was another phrase frequently used by young women; it meant "Give me a call," not what it meant stateside.

Nearby, an old country estate was home to children evacuated from London. It was run by a breezy and incredibly good-natured young woman named Elsinore, whom Sam met at the pub. She put off all manner of soldiers and fliers as regularly as they identified her as good matrimonial material. This was, according to her, the minute they saw her easy facility with children.

"It's all this death." Her bobbed hair was dark and her eyes were dark too, in the dim light of the Hart and Hind. "They imagine themselves as happily married and me as the loving mother of their children and of course they will each have bloody four, no less." She laughed over her Down and Putny's Red Ale, her second since Sam had introduced himself and joined her at a small round table. "It will be a cold day in Bermuda before they catch me and I don't think I'll be having those children at all, thank you."

Sam did not propose, but regularly walked, in his few spare hours, through the winter garden and up the imposing stone steps of the estate with chocolates and tins of his mother's cookies for the children. "You needn't try to butter me up," Elsinore would say. But Sam liked sitting among the children, helping them tie their shoelaces or do their schoolwork, though he was less than helpful when it came to British spelling. It reminded him of home. Mrs. Applewhist, a thin, sixtyish woman from the village, also helped in the manor, but was somewhat suspicious of Sam for a good long while.

Wink thought he was nuts. "They're unbearably loud, rude brats. They kick and bite. Hard. Like wild ponies. And their noses run."

Sam's feelings were hurt by this assessment, as if the children were his own. "They're homesick and want their mothers."

"No reason why they can't learn to wipe their own noses. No kids for me."

Though he didn't want word to get around, for fear of being asked to do something tiring, Wink was by far the most athletic of the company. He'd been on the varsity football squad during his first year of college. Sometimes he disappeared to return drenched in sweat. When someone asked, he'd wiggle his eyebrows and say, "Wouldn't you like to know?" The truth was that he'd been out running along the deep, narrow English lanes. Considering the extent to which

Sam went in order to avoid being assigned any physical work, he found this completely voluntary and unnecessary activity a sign of insanity. Wink said it cleared his mind.

The only truly unpleasant character in the outfit was Belcher, a burly guy from Cleveland who complained day in and day out that he had joined to be a paratrooper and was being unfairly kept from combat, and who became more and more sullen the more money Wink took off of him at poker. The pathological liar of the company, Homset, was of course utterly charming and harmless once you knew you couldn't trust a word he said. He had two wives back home and was having a hard time sending both of them money, especially with girlfriends in London to entertain. Sam noticed that an odd trait of pathological liars seemed to be that they believed every word that the other fellow uttered. Jimmy "The Mess" Messner, Earl T., and Kocab, the company magician, were still with them as well, good drinking buddies and always ready to help out in a pinch.

As he and Wink set up the compound, Sam realized that they were creating the perfect place to try to build the device. He was living in a mechanic's dream, with machine and woodworking and automotive shops all around. The Yanks, like the British flyboys from the nearby airstrip, were self-starting and disdainful of authority, so Sam was well able to have anything built that he felt like having built. If he had brought in plans for a Rube Goldberg–type perpetual motion machine they would have built it; they would have built him a goddamned rocket ship.

Sam and Wink cordoned off one corner of a Quonset hut as an administrative office. Their desks, which doubled as drawing boards, were supported by packing crates; their workbench was a twelve-foot-long assembly of planks supported by two-by-fours, which quickly grew littered with greasy bolts, vacuum tubes, and M-9 components they were troubleshooting.

Wink headed off for a few hours of relaxation at the Hart and Hind after each twelve-hour shift. "What say we hoist a few," he'd say, flinging his jacket over his shoulder, standing expectantly at the end of Sam's footlocker.

At first, Sam agreed. But after a few such evenings, he saw his chance.

"I'm going to rest. Maybe I'm coming down with something."

"Elsinore will be there."

"Give her my regards. Maybe you can volunteer to take care of the kids."

After Wink left, Sam opened his footlocker and extracted a page from Hadntz's paper. He kept her folder with his composition books filled with letters to Keenan. With paper in hand, he walked through the tunnel to the Quonset hut.

Joe Kocab was there, wiping his hands on a greasy rag. He waved to Sam from across the shop and yelled, "Got those bolts machined today."

"Great," said Sam. "About time to knock off, isn't it?"

"Long past. I'm off to the H and H."

Sam set his page next to his drawing board. Sliding his T-square up and down the piece of paper he'd taped to the board, he used his triangles and pencil to render a precise mechanical drawing of one view of the device. As was the process in rendering many mechanical drawings, he had to deduce some of the measurements. Once he was finished with the drawing he'd have to go over it carefully to make sure that he'd created no discrepancies.

Absorbed in his work, Sam was startled to hear Wink say, from over his shoulder, "Got a burst of energy, eh?" Then he looked down at Sam's drawing. "What the hell is that?" He punched Sam on the arm. "Damn. That looks complicated. You some kind of spy after all?"

Sam picked up his brush and swept eraser crumbs from the drawing. He compared it to Hadntz's specifications. "Look the same to you?"

Wink studied it for a moment. "Yeah. But—"

"Think we can make it?"

"No sweat. Kocab's a genius. What is it, though?"

"I've got a lot more drawings to do before it will be ready." He carefully untaped his drawing. "I'll give this to Kocab tomorrow."

"Look, Dance. What is this part of?"

"I've been meaning to show you."

It took Wink three nights to make it through the paper. They sat together in their office, Sam on his stool drawing, and Wink reading.

Finally, on the third night, at around two in the morning, Wink slid the papers back into the folder. "You think this will work?"

Sam straightened on his stool to ease his aching back. "If it works, what do you think it will do?"

"She thinks it will change history. Cause us to mutate into better folks somehow."

"Anything more specific?"

Wink lighted a cigarette and began to pace. "Not much that I could put into words of my own, words that aren't hers. Who is Dr. Eliani Hadntz? I gather she's a member of the scientific establishment in Europe."

"The Army put me in a course, back in Washington, just before the war started, with different lecturers. She was one. Russian, by way of Hungary."

"What were the lectures for?"

"Never told us. But the science was cutting-edge." He filled Wink in on what he knew about the course, and about Hadntz. He didn't mention the sex.

When he finished, Wink was deep in thought. "Maybe she stole the plans."

"Possibly. But I don't think so."

"She some kind of spy?"

"I've been interviewed by security people a couple of times and I get the impression she's on our side. Or maybe her own side. A new side. I don't know where she is now, though."

"When did she give this to you?"

"December sixth."

"The quantum nature of consciousness, eh?"

"Well, our brains, which appear to generate consciousness, are composed of physical matter."

"Right."

"So the laws of physics inherent in matter are inherent in our brains and every cell of our bodies as well."

"Yeah, sure." Wink shuffled through the papers. "I found this stuff absolutely fascinating."

"So maybe your year of premed will help?"

Wink shrugged. "I hated medicine. I wasn't the best student. But I know enough to recognize that these are some strange . . . speculations, here. I mean, who in hell would dream that genes take this particular shape? Anyway, we're going to need some chemicals. I think I can rustle them up. Got a few contacts already. I love experiments." He tapped the tiny scar above his right eye. "Got this when I blew up one of Dad's labs."

"You told me. You've got the credentials."

"Damn right. I'm impetuous, foolhardy, play a mean jazz violin, and I'm an all-around great guy."

"So you're in."

"Well, sure. Otherwise you'd have to kill me."

Or somebody would. Sam wasn't supposed to know anything about Hadntz's paper, either.

As Sam had the metal components machined, he kept the parts of the device well separated, as if they might join together in the night like magnets and win the war for the Germans. He was superstitious of it in this regard. Everyone knew that the Nazis were very much ahead of the game when it came to science. If Hadntz *was* working for the Germans . . . but no. She was teaching real physics in the United States. Why give this information to a soldier in the U.S. Army if that was the case?

But why him, anyway? He could not answer that, except that Hadntz had been in a hurry to rescue her daughter, and she had liked him, and had no other choice. That night of sex and physics might prove to be his luck, his damnation, or just a great puzzle with which to while away the war. He might have been able to think that this was simply a wild theory she wanted to test, except that during that week of instruction she'd seemed the epitome of sharp intelligence.

Magnification was needed to solder the wiring, which was of a new and ingenious design. As Sam worked, late at night in a corner of the blacked-out engine-testing hut, he realized that the thing he was making would be capable of serving as a platform for an infinite number of computations.

Wink continued to be full of surprises. He spoke fluent German, thanks to his grandmother, who never learned English, and was sometimes called down to the POW camp to translate. Given the times, however, he used his smattering of French to much greater effect, in his romantic endeavors. He had a classy girlfriend in no time, a woman named Claire who managed lorry logistics and spent her spare time driving the little green Austin her father gave her fast enough to scare even Wink. Meanwhile, his frequent classical bouts with his violin might have made him unpopular had he not practiced out in the field, where his faint melodies seemed, softened by distance, like a shell-punctuated dream.

And he completely embraced Hadntz's vision. Sam thought that, for Wink, it was an intellectual lark, a puzzle, a technological challenge, a fairy tale of science. Fun.

For Sam, though, it was deadly serious. He was now deeply sensitized to death; couldn't bear to think about it. He saw death once, and not by design. As a result, he eschewed one popular form of entertainment, which was going up on Artillery Hill to watch the 101st Airborne practice jumps. Men spilled from the open bay like apples from a barrel, to become scattered black dolls in the sky. White chutes puffed open, flowering the sky with what might have been notes against the wavy staff of cloud strata, but two of the jumpers were made into quarter notes by the straight line sketched when they plummeted straight to the ground.

The meat wagon revved its siren, beyond the complex of barracks and Quonset huts and the dance hall. He heard that in combat they dropped the parachutists from only three hundred feet.

Belcher's complaints about being kept out of paratroop duty subsided.

⁞❙ 8 ❙⁞

The Perham Downs

TOGETHER, SAM AND WINK pulled several all-nighters working on the device, but work was temporarily held up while Wink went through various official and unofficial channels in search of necessary chemicals.

When a crate of musical instruments arrived one day, they were immediately requisitioned by Sam, Wink, Earl T., and The Mess.

Earl T. was a cadaverous young man, tall and pale with a sudden, bewitching grin. His hands spanned an octave or more; his playing was relaxed, natural, fully realized.

The Mess was inclined to bobbing his head and making peculiar *ch-ch* sounds, which, after he got his set of drums, Sam realized was his own internal drumbeat, in which he dwelt. He also had a knockout crooning voice, which Sam wished was more punchy, more along the lines of "Salt Peanuts."

With this promising group as its core, the Perham Downs, a swing band, was organized. The villages around Tidworth contained a number of small dance venues—church recreation rooms, town halls, and the like. The name Perham Downs had the strong ring of destiny; after all, the Perham Downs had been a military training ground for centuries. But the destiny they hoped for was a bit of extra cash and the strong possibility of attracting women.

"We do need a cover for our work," said Sam, as they posted the call for tryouts.

"Cover!" said Wink. "Hell, we need to have a smashing time and knock their socks off. We need to think in music for a change. Jog us loose."

Kocab, whom Sam had cajoled into performing a well-received magic show for Elsinore's kids, answered the call by walking over from his work at the garage one day, wiping his hands on a rag, and offering himself as first clarinet.

When Sam lifted an alto sax from the crate, he felt blessed. Pawing through the straw remains, he searched in vain for reeds, but found some in a village shop the following week.

The first out-of-town gig of the Perham Downs was in a square stone building in Shrewsbury. Sam insisted that The Mess drive their truck, and was rewarded by having a chance to gaze long at Stonehenge, silhouetted in the twilight, as they passed.

The hall had a professional complement of dressing rooms for men and women, a real stage with a real, moth-eaten velvet curtain, and not a drop of alcohol. This was discovered when the Perham Downs took the stage to warm up.

"It's impossible. An American swing band can't play without beer," Wink told the promoter.

Earl T. had begun a long-fingered strut along the piano keyboard, and a few girls stood expectantly at the edge of the stage, resting their heads on crossed arms and staring up at the band. In the center of the room an old man teetered on a ladder, trying to affix a mirrored ball to a light fixture.

"No booze?" Earl closed the piano with an air of finality and soul-deep regret.

Sam got out his polishing cloth and proceeded to remove corrosive fingerprints from his nickel-plated army-issue saxophone. Wink pulled the mouthpiece from his cornet and shook spit on the floor.

The promoter pulled nervously on his hat. "You see, it's against the pub regulations. They do not want us competing against them."

"So buy it from them."

He shook his head helplessly. "It is more complicated than that, I fear. We cannot offer it to the dancers because of the nature of the hall. I mean, it is not a pub."

By now, about thirty people were standing around in the large room. The promoter's partner came over. "What's the problem?"

"They won't play without alcohol."

The partner gave them a finely calculated look of utter contempt. "Yanks are famous boozers."

"Nothing but selfish louts. It's wartime. Our young men and women are in dire need of entertainment."

Sam clicked shut his saxophone case and picked it up.

"It is blackmail," said the first. "You are asking us to break the law."

"Who ever heard of a band playing without drinks?" asked Wink in a reasonable tone of voice. "Our manager didn't even conceive of such a possibility when he set this up."

"Our manager's an idiot," growled Earl T. "Maybe we need a new one."

"You're elected," said Wink, pretending to grow heated.

"I'm out of here," said The Mess.

The first promoter said to the second, "Well, do something. Or we'll have to give back the money."

The second promoter quickly exited the hall as the first took the microphone and said, "Not to worry, folks, the Perham Downs will commence playing in just a few minutes when a certain lack is made up." He glared at the band members. They waited without unpacking, feeling well within their rights.

Within ten minutes a keg was rolled onstage by two men and the pump set up. The musicians fortified themselves and once again unpacked their instruments. In a few minutes, the place was jammed with dancers, the mirrored ball glittered, and the band was making up for lost time.

Lunceford's "Jazznocracy" was their most-rehearsed number, and they began with that.

The Mess and Earl T. set up the railroad beat, the train barreling down the track. Wink and Sam came in with the train's horn as they approached a crossing. And then all hell broke loose.

They each took a solo, in the driving, frantic-sounding, yet well-controlled number. Their audience shouted, applauded, spun out across the dance floor, a swirling visual accompaniment to their wild swing.

After that, the ice was definitely broken.

After an hour, relatively drunk, they retired to a dressing room for a break.

It was very large, and filled with shadowy objects covered with a thick coat of dust. A broken rocking chair, a massive, scarred dresser, and a low table rested just beyond the pool of light that came from the distant ceiling.

Wink spied something off in a corner. "What's that?" He pushed his way through mounds of debris and raised the neck of a bass fiddle from a nest of broken furniture. "This is exactly what we need."

The Mess climbed over and examined it. "Looks sound. Needs strings. It would certainly fill that large hole in our arrangements."

"This falls into the category of moonlight requisition," said Earl T. "It's been sadly neglected."

"It's yearning to be cleaned up and played," said Sam.

"*Meant* to be," said The Mess. He shook his head. "It's a crime to treat a musical instrument in this fashion."

The promoter stuck his head through the curtain. "Are you too soused to get on with it?"

After they got back on the stage, it became apparent to Sam that without keeping up with them drink for drink, the listeners lacked the ability to gloss over their mistakes in timing and harmony. He realized this when complaints were voiced, loudly.

A young woman climbed onstage and began singing. This rather drew things together for a time as she was not bad; she claimed a pint of ale as her right. The crowd danced to sentimental favorites and called out their picks, becoming hot and disheveled and happy. Sam and Wink embarked on a modern jazz rendition of "Moonlight Serenade," but were dissuaded by angry shouts when it became clear that it was undanceable. "Stop that hobbyhorse music," yelled one woman, and Earl T. hurriedly swung into a slow, soothing number as the lights dimmed.

They called an end to it around two in the morning and the crowd dissipated. The singer had become rather attracted to Earl T. and sat next to him on the piano bench, kissing him passionately.

"He won't be much help," said Kocab. "Where's our promoter pals with our pay?"

"Early to bed," said Wink, "makes them wealthy. They seem to have slipped away."

"I vote the keg is ours," said Sam. "Fair pay."

They spent a few minutes wrestling it out the door and onto the truck.

"We do need that bass too," observed Wink. "We could get a lot more work with a proper band."

"Some practice wouldn't hurt either," suggested Kocab.

The bass was placed gently in the back of the truck on some moth-eaten blankets, also requisitioned from the depository of broken and discarded objects.

"What to do with that bass till things cool off?" asked Sam, as he backed the truck out of the courtyard.

"They won't come looking for it. Nobody will even miss it."

"But if they do."

"Wake up Kocab. That's his job—making things disappear."

Kocab directed them to the garage. "Nothin' up my sleeve," grunted Kocab, as he helped lower the blanket-wrapped bass into the center of a tower of gigantic truck tires.

No one ever asked about it. After six weeks, they pulled it out, polished it lovingly, procured strings, and auditioned those who claimed to play bass until Wink was satisfied with Grease, a slight, pale kid from St. Louis. The Perham Downs continued their ascent to local fame, assisted by "Moonlight," their new bass.

❙ 9 ❙

Elsinore and the Princess

S AM KEPT NAGGING Wink to go to Elsinore's beautiful, decaying mansion to entertain the children. He finally acquiesced.

They walked into the kitchen with their instrument cases early one evening and gathered an admiring crowd. "Keep back!" commanded Wink, holding his cornet over his head as if they might attack him. The children, who already stood well away in a quiet circle watching them, looked puzzled, except for one older boy with red hair, who laughed at Wink.

"What have we here?" Elsinore walked into the kitchen.

"You didn't tell her?" asked Wink.

"Tell me what?"

"It's a surprise," Sam said. "Sit down."

The red-haired boy pulled a chair from the kitchen table for Elsinore.

Without preamble they jumped into their modern jazz version of "Twinkle, Twinkle, Little Star," which they had renamed "Pleiades," beginning with two short, recognizable bars and then flying into what Sam thought of as a swift, stunning tour of modern jazz ideas—unison octave jumps, sudden key changes, and abrupt pauses. After one such pause, they did not resume playing. That was the end.

It was then that Sam realized that not only was the red-haired boy laughing but that Elsinore had joined him. Her whoops filled the large kitchen. Tears ran down her face. She gasped for breath, her arms clasped across her chest as she rocked back and forth. Finally she slid onto the floor, still laughing, and then all the children roared.

"I told you that they were rude," said Wink. "Despite the fact that Elsinore's performance is much better than ours."

"They're just not ready for modern jazz." Sam helped Elsinore up off the floor.

"You'll—wake—the—*babies*," she gasped, and then was off again, hysterical with glee.

The evening was not a total loss, though, for Wink. He met Elsinore's sister, who worked a radar tower in the Home Chain over on the coast, and they went off to the pub for a pint.

After the children were put to bed, Elsinore sat with Sam in the now quiet kitchen and chatted. To Sam's surprise and disappointment, most of her talk was of a flyboy she'd become smitten with.

He turned the conversation to the coming spring, and suggested that they renovate the flower gardens of the estate. Sam's mother was a founding member of her local garden club, and he'd grown up pruning, dividing, digging, and fertilizing, enjoying it as much as his mother did.

Elsinore's charming smile revealed her dimple. She grew excited. "Can't you just see this place with vases full of flowers? The children will love collecting them. Mrs. Applewist told me that the estate was once known for its gardens. Glorious, she said. A crew of four gardeners. There's something left of it. A perfect project for the children."

When Sam decided it was time to leave, Elsinore accompanied him through the great hall. He pushed open the front door. It creaked on its hinges, revealing a misty, moonlit landscape. Frosty night air rushed into the barely heated house, carrying the scent of woodsmoke. She clapped him on the back like a buddy. "What smashing fun for the children, Sam! See you soon, then?"

He walked back to the barracks alone in the dark, realizing that he too had wanted to woo the elusive Elsinore, and that he did not much like the role of "just friend" he had worked so hard to assume.

The stuff we were building roads with on Artillery Hill was gravel, but what the Brits supplied was "hoggin." Fortunately for the Yanks, Louis, the first Earl of Mountbatten, Supreme Commander of the Allied Forces in the Southeast Asia Theatre (cousin of King George V) owned a six-thousand-acre estate named Broadlands, just outside of Romney, Kent, which contained a large working gravel pit. I had to drive through the estate for half an hour to get to there.

I brought three or four loads back every day, as did each of the others of our small fleet. The routine was to drive into the estate a mile or so and pull under the hoggin bin. The operator would drop a load into the truck, record the weight, and hand me a slip.

To shield them from the dangers of the endless bombing of London, the two royal princesses were in residence, and on parade, as it were. I saw them three or four times a week, horseback riding on the mostly unpaved roads on the estate.

We would be driving at low speed and the girls would be riding at a canter or a walk, paying no apparent attention to us. They were, without fail, unaccompanied, and I never saw any sign of anyone lurking under cover providing any kind of protection. All of us visiting American soldiers, of course, were armed. It was never far from my mind how much firepower and visitor control would have been provided had the situation been reversed.

One day was an exception. I was driving a six-by-six dump truck and, as I came up out of the gravel pit, the truck seemed to drag on the right side.

I was in a large clearing with forest all around. I got out and discovered that the inside tire on my right-side bogey was flat, so I got out my jack and tire iron and jacked up the bogey.

At that moment, Princess Elizabeth rode up, out of the gravel pit, and for the first time ever, she was alone; Princess Margaret was missing! Well!! My book on protocol in addressing royalty in the performance of changing tires (pardon me, *tyres*), was missing, had never been issued, did not exist. What do I say?

As it turned out, she had been briefed on this very eventuality. She approached to twenty-five yards, made a right-hand turn, made a twenty-five-yard arc around me and my truck, regained the road, and continued on, out of sight. So there! Finesse. The next time we met on the road (with her sister, of course), she pretended that she had never seen me before.

Sam and Wink practiced what they thought of as modern jazz any chance they got. Sam convinced Wink that he should use his cornet rather than his violin in this endeavor, reasoning that they would thereby duplicate the instruments they'd heard used to create this unique sound, this new music. They sought out places where they could practice. This Sunday night, it was a storage room for jeep parts.

Wink's playing was full of fire and daring. After about twenty minutes he stopped in mid-phrase and said, "Okay. What's wrong?"

Sam let his sax hang from the strap around his neck. "You know what we need, don't we? A cavity magnetron. It's in the plans. I don't know how the hell we're going to get one. I mean, even when they ship us the SCR-584's, we can hardly pry the magnetron out of one of them."

"I don't see why not."

"Well, then the 584 wouldn't work, and since we're the ones who are supposed to get things working, it could reflect badly on us."

"How long are we going to need the magnetron? Maybe we could just shift them between the 584 and the device. Rotate them."

"Since we don't know what this is going to do or how long it's going to take, I'm not sure that's feasible. We might interrupt some process that would have to start over every time we removed the magnetron."

"Hmmm. I met some guys who might help. Bunch of paratroopers. The ones who don't wash. They're eating trout with drawn butter tonight, pheasant tomorrow night, and traded a few leftover boar roasts with Company B last week, all from Mountbatten's estate. Apparently they hunt and fish and help themselves to the earl's property as they please."

"So how would they get a magnetron?"

"Sort of the same way they're getting the chemicals. It would be complicated. So complicated that we wouldn't be blamed, and they don't care if they are. Although for them just getting one would probably be child's play. Fun."

"Just so long as no one gets shot."

"They don't have to shoot these guys. That's accomplished by the Germans, almost guaranteed. We just push them out of planes behind enemy lines."

⊰ 10 ⊱

London

WE NEVER DID go to the Rainbow Corner to see Glenn Miller. Miller played nightly for a couple of years. It was a walk-in with no charge for military personnel, a place to go and dance. But the Rainbow Corner was a sea of uniforms. Being surrounded by uniforms day and night, we suffered from Dreaded Soldier Fatigue. When we went to London, the first order of business was to find a place where there weren't any soldiers. Emil Keller found us one such place.

Emil Keller's dad was an official, with Karl Leitz, in the Leica Camera Company. When Hitler came to power in the mid-thirties Leitz helped Emil and his sister escape to England, where they had relatives. The thing Keller was most knowledgeable of was cameras. He found himself a job at a Leica camera store in Soho, a theatrical area of London and also an international area where different nationalities mingled.

When the war began, being a German national, Keller had to leave England. He became an American citizen, helped organize a Leica manufacturing plant in Canada, enlisted, and, with his technical background, wound up in Company C. When in London, we often went to a German restaurant in Soho, Schmidt's, that Keller steered us to. After British food, it was a godsend.

The hotels would be loaded up. The best place to stay would be a double-decker bed in a hostel with a shower down the hall that might cost one shilling. I stayed at what was formerly the Half Moon Hotel, which was five or six multi-story buildings in a campus arrangement, filled up with double bunks and operated by the Red Cross. Wink had a girlfriend, as usual; she'd bring a friend and we'd go pub crawling along the Thames.

Sam braced himself as the train to London halted. Outside, somber ochre fields were fringed with the upward strokes of ancient trees, black along fencelines, and scattered with yellowed sheep.

"Shall we help?"

Wink dropped the window open and thrust his head and shoulders outside, then fell back into his seat and closed the window, muffling the clank of machinery and shouts of men as they removed the section of bombed track.

"They're covered."

Rails twisted by bombs were removed and replaced, to be melted and recast. The trains were delayed, but it was a commonplace inconvenience, taken care of by the efficient Brits.

Wink relaxed into his seat, able to make it look as comfortable as a leather club lounger. The train jerked forward and chuffed Londonward once again.

They were the only soldiers to get off at their station. While crossing a tiny park, they heard a man hold forth on the evils of Churchill and of Parliament, preaching from a bench to no one in particular. Sam doubted that anyone was ever converted, even though Uncle Joe Stalin was now an ally and sucking down American war supplies with terrific appetite. England tolerated a much wider array of political views than America, though. Mrs. Dibdon, who recorded Sam's hoggin chits at her Mountbatten cottage and whose father was a lifelong Mountbatten butler, kept a large, glass-covered portrait of Stalin above her altar, and a keg of tragically cold beer for herself and the soldiers.

They walked to Schmidt's. The homely smell of sauerkraut hit them as they opened the door; the murmur of the civilian crowd rose and fell, and there was not another uniform in sight.

After dinner, they met Cindy, Wink's current London girlfriend, and some of her companions, for a night on the town. Transportation was Cindy's Mini.

As he had regarded it from the sidewalk, the Mini was smallest car Sam had ever seen, yet here he was in the backseat, a girl on either side and one on his lap. After an awkward moment she leaned back against him and managed to get an arm around his neck. "Might as well be comfortable. I'm June."

June's blond hair was cut in a bob below her ears. Her tiny red hat, anchored by a pearl-ended hatpin, matched her lipstick. The seams of her nylons, Sam had noticed as they stood outside the car negotiating seats, were the tiniest bit crooked, probably drawn on with an eyebrow pencil.

Wink's girl was driving too fast, given that she had little light to see by. All the women in England seemed to drive too fast. She glanced at Wink every thirty seconds until one of the girls said, "Watch the road, Cindy."

June said, "We're going to a place like the Crystal Palace, Yank. That's gone now. Burned down. Not by the war. Same thing, though. Like one's childhood has big gaps. I remember going there as a little girl, palm trees above my head and light streaming through. Good clothes, forbidden to run. I did anyway. Fell into a pot of something or other."

"Built just for the Queen's jubilee, right?" said Wink.

"Blood-sucking royals," said Sam, reminded of Mrs. Dibdon's unvarying description of her employer, Lord Mountbatton.

"No, I think they were bird-of-paradise," said June. All the girls laughed. Their various scents filled the car. Sam was reminded of his sisters. And then of his brother.

"Why so quiet, Yank?"

"Oh, he's just that way," Wink said.

"*He* makes up for it," said Sam.

The windows of their dance venue, a huge hall of glass reminiscent, as June had said, of the Crystal Palace, were painted black. Inside, a moderately good swing band played, and the thousand-strong crowd of British and American soldiers, WAVES, WACS, and WRENS, danced and drank with great energy, roaring with conversation and emitting clouds of cigarette smoke. June's little hat stayed tilted on her head as they danced, both slow and fast.

Around nine, the air-raid signal sounded. Sam, Wink, and Cindy wanted to stay. "This is a good band," protested Cindy, her arm around Wink's waist. But the other girls insisted that they find a shelter. As they hurried down the dark street with scuffling crowds, hearing bursts of laughter from time to time or someone calling out a name, a building not a block ahead of them collapsed in a wave of dust and rubble. Sam heard a child scream.

They ran across the street with the rest of the crowd. A fire blazed in the shattered building. Sam followed the screams, choking on dust and smoke, pulling on his leather gloves. A shrieking boy was trapped beneath a pile of bricks.

The heat was unbearable. Sam tossed bricks with ferocious speed. The boy's pants were on fire. Sam freed him at last, and carried him past the growing fire, over piles of rubble, and out of the building. He set him down on the sidewalk and a man with a water bucket doused the flame on his pants. Looking at the black mess that had been the boy's leg, Sam felt sick. A woman rushed up and knelt beside him, crying, "Bobby! Oh, Bobby!"

Sam went back to his group. June made much of him.

"Bloody goddamned Germans," said Wink, his face bathed in firelight.

"Sappers coming through," hollered someone behind them, and then the professionals were there.

Without discussing it, they went into the first pub they saw and found a table. "Sorry about the cold beer," said the waitress as she set pints on the table. "It's the war."

One of my rather strange friends in Company C was Howie Brost. His dad, under nom de plume, was a tin pan alley songwriter, a million seller, and one of the songs he was still collecting on was "Bye, Bye Blackbird." He was in the very center of America's songwriting business through the teens, twenties, and thirties, being, among other things, the Ray Henderson of the big-time songwriting team of DeSylva, Brown, and Henderson. They wrote songs for many musicals for stage and screen, including the Ziegfeld Follies and George White's Scandals, and for vaudeville stars—Al Jolson, Sophie Tucker, and many others. Some of their hit songs were "That Old Gang of Mine," "Five Foot Two, Eyes of Blue," "I'm Sitting on Top of the World," "Button Up Your Overcoat," and "Animal Crackers in My Soup."

Howie was a book collector and came to London equipped with a letter of introduction to a guy who managed a theatrical supply house. It was a huge warehouse in central London filled with stage props, costumes, all manner of equipment for stage productions. For whatever reason it also had a well-equipped library. When Howie came back from London, he came back with a very good selection of books to read. As soon as we read them he sent them home. I remember reading *Tristram Shandy*, *Jurgen*, and a number of others I don't recall at the present time.

The next morning, they were up fairly early, considering, and visited Schmidt's once again, for lunch.

"I'll take Howie's lead," said Sam, as they stood on a chilly corner after being fortified with steaks. One bone of contention between the Brits and the Yanks was that the Yanks were paid so much more than the British soldiers that they could afford such luxuries, and could therefore attract more women.

Wink threw down his cigarette butt and scuffed it out with his boot. "You would."

Sam knew that he didn't really care. Wink would be happy trying to find the chemicals they needed. "Well, I've got the letter."

Howie had wrangled a letter that authorized Sam to take what he needed for the war effort, with a warning not to abuse it. "This does not mean that you are entitled to rare folios or jewelry."

"I wouldn't know a rare folio if it bit me."

❧

Sam stood on the threshold of a great, dim warehouse, an ancient and vast store-house of time. This place had, according to Howie, housed theater paraphernalia for longer than the United States had been in existence.

He closed the heavy door, which was framed by massive hand-hewed timbers. Wide flooring planks had settled into a mildly rolling floor for unbridled, profligate objects of all descriptions that loomed in semi-darkness.

A ten-foot-high fireplace surround and mantel, fashioned of some dark wood, leaned against other tall, flat objects shuffled like cards into a mixture of grand wrought-iron gates and finely carved headboards. A long row of tables, as different from one another as a pack of mongrel dogs, stretched away to his right. A wash of yellow light splashed down the corridor that led to the heart of the place.

He headed toward the light. He needed a guide, someone who spoke the language in this country of ancient, well-used objects. To his relief, when he rounded the corner, he saw a man hunched over a high desk with several open ledger books spread out atop a mound of papers.

"May I help you, sir?"

"I'm from the U.S. Army."

"That's news." He did not look up.

"I have this letter." He pulled it from the interior breast pocket of his jacket and handed it to the man. It was improbably crisp, and rustled as he unfolded it. The man took it, squinted.

"I see. I'm Edwards. I'll see what I can do."

Sam followed him out into the dimness. As they trudged up six flights of open stairs, Sam could see down into cubicles filled with time embodied in matter and measured off in square feet; stacked, horizontal planes of time. Perhaps time was really like this: ever-opening rooms, like a vast apartment building, but extending into dimensions that they presently could not see . . .

"We might find something you could use here," said Edwards.

Sam hoped so; they were on the top floor, with their chances of finding something accordingly diminished. The smell of time—spicy, dusty, oily, and just plain dirty—was giving him a headache.

Edwards pushed his way through some fairly new art deco side chairs toward a row of huge, rococo radios. "I'm not sure but that they've already been looted; after all, we don't need working models. But it comes in by the truckload and something could definitely be overlooked."

Sam and Edwards examined the radios, shoving and pulling them about, before finding one with actual innards.

"This looks promising." Sam took a screwdriver from a pocket and removed the back. He relieved the mahogany cabinet of tubes, wires, dials, crystal, brackets—anything remotely useful. These he could use to create a dedicated environment in which to produce Hadntz's Device, or modify and recast to fulfill an entirely different function from that for which it had been created. He put them all into his duffel and carefully replaced the back of the radio, kneeling on dusty floorboards, as Edwards watched.

He descended the stairs behind Edwards, feeling as if he had not found anything he really needed. Pausing at the third floor, he asked, "Mind if I look around here a bit?"

"Suit yourself. Don't have a spare torch."

"I've got one."

After passing what seemed like a mile of hanging clothing, he came across a tall shelf stocked with someone's ancient mineral collection, and then things more recent. He collected three watches with glowing radium dials; his inventor's brain insisted on them. He found a rock labeled U-235 on a little stand beneath a bell jar, and three retorts of various sizes, each with a mysterious residue on the bottom, and rocks of clay sediment. He picked up one of the rocks and trained his torch on it, just able to discern that it was veined with the channels used by primitive life to form itself, according to Hadntz's paper, which seemed to contain all manner of speculation. Perhaps this might be a template for the circuits he was trying to invent.

Nearby, in a box of jumbled books he rummaged through to perhaps find something rare for Howie—not that he had any idea what that might be—he found a large art book of Kandinsky prints. Remembering Wink's mention of Kandinsky in relation to modern music, he picked that up as well. He also took a book of translated Chinese poetry, filled with references to rain, rivers, mountains, and longing, because the lines he scanned resonated with his seeming distance from Keenan.

He returned to the main level, and walked across the ends of aisles until he again saw the man at his post, part of his bowed head and his desk lit by a small, contained disk of light. Again, the man did not look up as he approached.

"Excuse me. Do you want to see what I have?"

His head jerked up. "What? Oh, yes." Edwards fussed around and pulled out another ledger book and carefully logged Sam's finds. Sam had a dizzying vision of Edwards's mind, no more and no less full than this warehouse, knowing exactly which object was where, a precise map of pure things, removed from their context, awaiting some kind of transformation.

"That will do. Good night." Edwards waved his hand and then used it to turn a ledger page. Sam was dismissed.

When Sam stepped out onto the street, blackout reigned. The damp air smelled of smoke.

Sam headed toward their regular meeting place, a favorite pub, hoping Wink would be finished with his gathering expedition. Despite the scent of fires, the buildings he passed were intact; the Germans were still targeting the Docklands, although a lucky bomb had fallen on Buckingham Palace. Lucky for the royals, actually. It made them seem less isolated, more like all the other suffering Brits.

But after several long blocks, he decided that he must be lost, and turned to retrace his steps.

And then, someone was walking next to him. Right next to him, closer than a stranger would. "Hello," she said, and he recognized Hadntz's voice.

She wore a dark, heavy coat, a black hat, and boots, and thus was almost invisible. "Come with me," she said and linked her arm through his. Then he realized that someone was next to Hadntz; he saw a pale oval face floating at Hadntz's shoulder.

"Is this him?" The voice was that of a girl. An impatient, disdainful girl.

"Yes," replied Hadntz. "Let's go now."

"How did you find me?" asked Sam.

Hadntz was silent for a while. On the corner they passed a blacked-out pub—not the one he'd been headed for—from which music and conversation emanated. Finally, she said, "It was not easy. Think of a method analogous to your radar."

"Radar?"

"Of a sort." They walked quickly, and he automatically kept note of the streets they turned onto, and how many blocks they went before turning. A few cars crept past, headlights dim through tiny holes cut in material covering them.

He said, "We've been trying—"

"I know."

"Where are we going?"

"You'll see."

Finally they came to a neighborhood of tall, separate homes—mansions, in his vernacular—made over into small hotels and guest houses. She turned onto a sidewalk punctuated by the dark shapes of a formal yard gone ragged and they climbed broad steps to a veranda. Paint flaked off on his hand when he grasped the banister.

Dusting off his hands as Hadntz pushed open the green door, he walked into what may have been originally a ballroom. Floor-to-ceiling windows, draped with blankets, were set in a vast expanse of faded, peeling floral wallpaper. Children darted about, squealing and laughing. Small groups of adults on odd sofas and chairs pushed into scattered groups engaged in lively conversation, but he heard no English words. Most of their clothing was foreign; worn yet elegant, the clothing of war, of refugees, of travelers who moved with no settling place in sight. A small coal fire in an ornate stove contributed an acrid undertone, but not much heat where he stood.

Hadntz flung her scarf over a hatrack festooned with winter gear; rubber boots waited in empty pairs on the floor. He kept his own coat, but helped Hadntz out of hers and hung it up.

The girl's curly black hair fell, gloriously long, down her back as she divested herself of a black coat and a sheared-wool hat that looked Russian. She glared at Sam. Hadntz spoke sharply to her in a language that flowed like music. She replied just as sharply, flung her coat on the floor, and walked away, her back straight as a plumb line. Then she stopped, returned, hung up her coat, and left again without a look at either of them.

"My lovely niece, Katya." Hadntz managed to convey irritation and pride in the same tone.

"Not your daughter?"

"No." Hadntz's reply was weary. "I have not yet found her." She greeted the crowd in the main room. "I'd like to introduce a colleague of mine. Sam Dance." Nods and polite murmurs lasted a few seconds.

Then an old woman jerked out of reverie and beckoned Sam close. She smelled of talcum powder and spoke a few words in Romany. Hadntz smiled gently and stroked the old woman's hair, a pensive look on her face.

"What did she say?"

Hadntz hesitated, then said, "She wants to know if you're the one who's going to save us."

"What?"

The woman closed her eyes. Her head nodded forward.

"She's lost everyone. Follow me."

Hadntz led him down a flight of stairs at the back of the house. "The kitchen is in the basement, which works well for us. We are able to stuff ourselves while we are bombed." Down a short corridor with irregular stone walls that might have been built centuries earlier, she pushed through a swinging door.

They entered a cavernous room. The electric bulbs hanging from the ceiling had a makeshift look; the gas sconces on the wall had probably been there for a century. A vast slab of pink marble in the center of the room held several candelabras with unmatched candles and two clean, gigantic pots. Odd tables and chairs were scattered about. The drainboard overflowed with an assortment of clean dishes, knives, pots, and pans. Onions and potatoes filled huge baskets. A deep niche held wrapped cheeses and jugs of cream. The stew bubbling on the hob was fragrant with smells he could not place. Hadntz asked, "Will you have supper with me?"

"I'd love to."

She took two flowered bowls from the open shelves. "Goulash. Which means everything we could get with our ration cards in one big pot." She ladled goulash into the bowls and set them with bread on one of the tables, then lit a candle.

The goulash was delicious—worlds better than Army slop.

Hadntz's face was deeply shadowed in the flickering candlelight. Within their co-coon of silence, Sam had the sensation of being completely removed from his own time, neatly cut out and re-inserted in hers, which radiated quiet but intense depths. It was like a very strong memory of someplace he had never been, or had forgotten, until now, as if he might be reliving this room and the words they spoke.

She said, "You are working on it?"

"Yes. I've told my friend, Allen Winklemeyer, about all this. He's read your paper, and he's helping to create the . . . device?"

She nodded. "I see now."

"See what?"

"Winklemeyer is the new factor that I've been trying to account for."

"I needed some other input."

"Of course," she said. "I should have realized that. Don't worry. But after this—no one else must know." She put down her spoon, reached into her dress, and extracted a small tube from her bosom. "Microfilm. You may keep it."

Sam suddenly had a sense that this might be his only chance to ask questions, and that he had no time to waste. "Look. How do you know that DNA carries genetic information? And that bit about life in clay. How did you come up with that?"

She tapped the microfilm canister on the table with some impatience. "Right now, we have no time to discuss it fully. I've tried to answer some questions you may have in this. I have made some important modifications. For instance, I included a paper titled "Studies on the Chemical Nature of the Substance-Inducing Transfor-mation of Pneumococcal Types." It was published last year by Oswald, Colin, and Maclyn—a very important paper which shows that DNA carries genetic informa-tion. And I recently visited my friend Schopenhauer. He's preparing some lectures on the connection between physics and biology, to be given in Glasgow. He is calling the series 'What is Life?' "

"But the shape—"

"I admit that there is information in here that is not presently proven, not widely known. I include more of my own papers. With the war, it has been impos-sible to publish. It is all considered secret information. You won't find any papers about the atomic bomb. Yet you seemed to believe that it was possible when I told you about it."

"All right." Sam took the canister. "Do you have a way to look at it now?"

"I have the original papers." She got a notebook from her large bag and returned to the table, shoving her bowl aside. They bent their heads over it as she paged through it. He glimpsed equations that looked fascinating.

"What is this X?"

"It's what I'm working on. A model of time as it relates to our consciousness and our consciousness as relates to our genes."

He raised his eyebrows in question.

She said, "We were just talking about them. Genes are the nucleic acids through which everything about us is expressed. I theorize that these tiny segments are turned off and on at particular times by inner and outer forces. They control our physical bodies, including our mind, our brain. I believe that the physical shape of these genes are mirrored by the structure of time. In other words, the force we call time, which extends from this point equally in all directions, can also be expressed as this double-helix model, and events are turned off or on according to the way sub-atomic particles interact with that which we call consciousness." She wiped her mouth with her napkin, leaving a smear of red lipstick on the smooth, well-worn white cloth. "I do not know what we are, really. Some kind of monster, it seems, right now. I have seen things that beggar the imagination. Things too terrible to speak of.

"But—well, here it is. Subatomic particles communicate with one another. They seem to be able to influence one another from great distances because they are actually the same particle. Time is an illusion that we all share, because we are actually a single microorganism. But within that which we call time are forces which we may be able to manipulate by manipulating our DNA. It determines how whatever time is ordered.

"Let us say that pain and suffering can be minimized. What is the order that we can put into ourselves so that we might avert, or minimize, that pain and suffering? What is this disease of humanity called war? What is the sulfa drug that can kill whatever infects our minds and causes war, at the atomic level? For us, time is biology; biology, time. What if we can inoculate *this* time with a bit of the time that is causing the disease, and thus resist it? What if the part of us, the time of us, that survives this cure, is the part that is the least evil? Can we thereby create an era in which we prosper? A time in which we do not suffer? A time in which we continue to explore and to learn? A time in which we travel the universe, a time in which we *understand* time, and ourselves, and all of nature, and yet continue to move toward an ever-changing model of perfection, of happiness?"

She tapped the paper with a long red fingernail. "That is why I have written this. Think about the beams we are using now. The Germans follow a radio beam to London. They have to stay on that beam. Our own radio beams—microwave beams—emit energy that bounces off of the German planes, and we interpret that information through the motions of photons on a screen. If we are the tower—if our consciousness is an interaction with matter and our DNA is the receiving dish—can we send out a 'ping' to another point in time, which is not 'the future' but contiguous with now, and receive communication in return? Correct our course by inserting the antibody of a particular mode of behavior? Evolve a new sense so we can 'see' where we are going, see where a particular path might take us and avoid it?" She sighed. "We tried to do that after the Great War, which seemed for a time to have inoculated us against another. Hitler used that abhorrence to his advantage, though. Why couldn't the German people have ignored him? Why couldn't he have died in that war? Would another Hitler have arisen instead? Are these forces inevitable, or are they manipulable? I have put this theory into a language that those of many nationalities share, the language of mathematics. I—"

The air raid siren sounded, like the cry of a great beast rising from vast depths.

She grabbed his hand and pulled him toward the door. "Hurry! We must help the old people and children downstairs. I have to find Katya. She has taken to trying to watch the city burn from the roof. She laughs as the bombs fall. She doesn't seem to understand that one could fall here. Or maybe, since she has lost her mother and father and brothers, she is hoping for that."

Sam shouldered his duffel bag and they ascended the stairs through a steady stream of people making their way down.

"No Katya. No Katya," she muttered. "Have you seen Katya?" she asked several people they passed, and continued upward.

When they reached the main room, she put an elderly gentleman into Sam's keeping. Sam shepherded him to the stairway, then realized he was too frail to descend without help. He supported him from the front, holding on to his thin waist with both hands, so as not to block the entire stairway. After the toothless old man was seated Sam rushed upstairs.

The house shook from a nearby impact.

A feeling like that of leaves rustling in the wind, touching one another repeatedly, settled upon him. He was in a reverie of summertime Puzzle River, the walk through the forest, still deep then, still mysterious with all that was unknown, in childhood, and then the final run toward the bluffs behind Keenan. Keenan was always ahead.

"Wake up, Yank." The rude light in his face pulled him from brilliant joy, this knowledge of Keenan's presence. He opened his eyes and shut them against the glare of a torch.

The man holding the torch helped him up with his free arm. "You're all right. Good." He squinted at Sam. "What day is it?"

"March first, 1944."

"All right, then."

"Wait!" he called as the man turned to leave. "The basement."

"Nobody here but you. We've checked."

Sam got to his feet, heaved his bag onto his shoulder, and walked through the shell of the dark house. His head ached; he brushed his hair with one hand, dislodging plaster that rained to the floor. A fire flared briefly in the ballroom, and he saw, then, that there were no dead bodies, no evidence of habitation, not a stick of furniture, even burnt. He appeared to be in an abandoned house. He touched his head. It was sticky with blood.

He pulled out his own torch and checked his watch: 11:43 P.M.

His chest constricted in panic. What had happened? Where had they all gone? How did they get here in the first place? Hadntz had said that it was not easy to find him. Were they all in . . . some different place? Or was this some kind of new vengeance weapon devised by Hitler's scientists, one that removed people and left usable property behind?

He recalled his sensation of being cut out of his own time and inserted into Hadntz's. It had not seemed radically different, but maybe it was. Perhaps that scene simply coincided with a scene from his time, the way that two different scales might frame the same note in modern jazz, giving it a different nuance in each instance, a whole different past, presaging a different tonal future.

Had he dreamt the whole episode? Had he drunk too many ales, stumbled into this empty house to sleep it off?

But no. No. Here in his pocket. The microfilm.

Something . . . had worked.

⫶ 11 ⫶

Birth

IN THE END, it wasn't necessary to pilfer a cavity magnetron using the complicated system of trades and payoffs set up by Wink.

They were unpacking and organizing ordnance when Sam, having pried the lid off a crate that purportedly contained engine blocks, whistled. "Take a look at this."

Wink set his clipboard on the crate he was tallying and looked over Sam's shoulder. "Magnetrons?" His shoulders slumped. He was the picture of disappointment. "This takes all the fun out of it."

Sam cleared a space on top of a crate and began lifting them out, one by one. "Heavy." Their copper interior and permanent magnets gave them a bit of heft.

"Come on. They can't weigh more than a few pounds."

"You could help."

Eleven cavity magnetrons soon stood on the crate. Each eight-holed copper disk was sandwiched between metal squares. Wires spiraled around the core, then twisted outward, leaving their tight circle for a more relaxed arc, like tendrils searching for something to latch on to.

Sam searched in vain for paperwork. "Who do you suppose these belong to?"

Wink took another delicate, savoring sip of the Mountbatten whisky, pilfered from a stone building on the edge of the estate by Wink's friends, the paratroopers, swirling it in his moonlight-acquired snifter, which he kept with the bottle on a shelf, hidden by heavy, greasy machine parts that no one would have any use for. "I guarantee you that somebody is going to want this whole shipment. However, considering that it's top-secret, I really don't understand how they're to be distributed. So we're going to borrow one and see how it works on our . . . device, and then use it in one of the M-9's when the rest of the parts get here."

"Sounds reasonable to me," said Sam. And it did. He could not help wondering whether Hadntz, knowing of their dilemma, and possibly disappointed in his progress so far, had somehow managed to steer this shipment his way by using her government contacts. He would not have been surprised.

It was about 2 A.M. The wireless gave news of a victory at Saipan, after a horrific naval battle with the Japanese.

Sam paused in his work, trying to shake the images of obliterated battleships, the blood and thunder of battle, the perfect, unique individual lives that were suddenly gone forever. His heart took a few skipping beats. He could not help thinking of Keenan, trapped in the sunken *Arizona*. Had he found an air pocket, which ran out? Had he been killed instantly, on impact?

He forced himself to resume his painstaking task beneath a large magnifying glass he had wired over his workbench. He hunched forward on his stool. Nearby, at the airstrip, planes took off; landed. The space around him smelled of diesel fuel, stale coffee, and Wink's careful daily allotment of what he now referred to as His Lordship's Drink. Wink slapped down cards on a crate, playing his perpetual game of solitaire, having completed his work on a chemical bath through which electricity would flow.

No one bothered them here; they'd built a private little shed in one corner of the vast garage and also used it for music practice, the noise of which discouraged visitors and encouraged imprecations and good-natured derision; comments about stampeding wild animals and the elephants which must be hidden within. "A goddamned circus," Wink told Jake. "It's a whole different world in there. God's truth."

Sam wasn't sure that the bomb impacts he thought he heard outside were real or imagined; the concussion he'd suffered in London had various side effects, including sleeplessness.

They had spent many hours comparing the two papers—Hadntz's original, and the microfilm version—but it seemed as if the original had been stretched and changed in so many ways that they just gave up and started all over again, figuring that whatever she had done, Sam's strange experience proved that something, at least, had happened, and probably due to her changes.

Sam soldered what he hoped was the final wiring connection and stifled a yawn. "Ready?"

Wink shrugged and moved a stack of cards to another stack. Later, recalling the scar on Wink's forehead and how it got there, he decided that Wink might have the flaw of always erring on the impetuous side.

Sam flipped the toggle switch that gave it power.

The apparatus hummed. Current flowed through a large rectangular pan, which was about four inches deep. Across the top was soldered an arc of new material, Plexiglas, which came from the gun turret of a B-17 that had exploded while on the runway with a full load of ordnance. A pump with a pressure regulator was attached by a thin pipe. Inside the pan was the liquid Wink had painstakingly distilled in a series of chemical processes described in the paper. As it turned out, the radium from the watch dials, the residue in the retorts, and the silicon Sam had picked up in the warehouse had all been necessary; Sam supposed that his repeated readings of the paper had helped him in his seemingly serendipitous choices.

He and Wink leaned over the metal table. The visible wires glowed, emitting a small, rainbowed spectrum that Sam saw reflected from his hand and from Wink's face when he looked up and they stared at each other.

"What's happening?" asked Wink.

"I can't tell. Give it a little more oxygen."

"I foresee the strong possibility of bugs."

Nothing much happened for about an hour. Wink went back to his solitaire game, but Sam continued to watch the liquid through the dome. "Look!"

"Are these . . . lines? Crystals forming? Is it turning into a solid?"

"I don't think so. They're certainly delicate-looking."

"Like wires. Different elements precipitating into these forms, I guess . . . they're all different colors."

"Changing colors."

"Like a kaleidoscope."

"And changing shapes too."

"Three-dimensional."

"Maybe more. She describes dimensions that we can't see. Not yet."

"Hell," said Wink. "Must be the whisky."

"What?"

"Pictures. I see pictures."

"I don't. But I hear music."

"Yeah. But pretty faint." Wink bent down, pressed his ear to the Plexiglas.

Sam laughed. "Gotcha! Music from the hall. It's Saturday night."

"What in God's name are we doing here, then?"

"Not much, as far as I can tell," Sam said, walking around one side to check a connection. "But I don't think this is from the dance hall."

"There seems to be this . . . jelly forming here." Wink bent down to look inside the shining contraption.

Sam said, "Do you hear music now?"

Wink said, "Yeah. Definitely not from the dance hall. 'Koko.'" What they'd heard Parker and Gillespie play in Harlem. "But there's something different . . . different pianist, I think. Plus a bass."

"Maybe we've created a radio."

"But what would we be picking up?" They'd heard no recordings resembling modern jazz so far, and did not really expect to, because of the continuing musician's strike—and it could be that Parker and Gillespie would not be popular even if they were recorded. No one else in the Perham Downs had any idea of what they were trying to do, and local revelers didn't appreciate undanceable music, even if it was played well, which it wasn't.

The music, faint already, faded. After a moment, Wink said, "What the hell. We were hallucinating."

"Both of us? Hey!" He saw a spark and reached for the switch.

In the moment before the explosion, he thought he heard "Koko," as loud and clear as if he were standing next to a musician he could never hope to emulate, the tones an exquisitely controlled transportation system to ecstasy. During the explosion, he thought of Kandinsky's flying-outward lines, heading from a nucleus of utter darkness—the magnetron itself, but more than that: time, emanating with such speed that this present caught him, created him, informed him intimately in every cell and in every thought and action. After the explosion, it seemed, once again, that he was in paradise—summer at Puzzle River, infinite fields of tall green corn, a sweaty baseball glove on his hand, the sting of catching a hardball—until he realized that Wink was dragging him across the concrete floor.

They managed to contain the resulting fire, just barely. They stood, breathing heavily, in a warehouse that now stank of smoke as well as oil.

"Can we put this down to just another strafing run?" asked Wink.

The device was black, melted, ruined—except for the cavity magnetron, which they were able to retrieve and burnish after the mess had cooled.

"Back to square one," said Wink.

Feeling deeply weary, Sam examined the blackened object.

It had the irregular shape of a small cow pie. It seemed opaque at first, but now that it had cooled, it had a hard, ceramic-like finish, like dulled obsidian.

Sam lifted it from the floor and put it on the workbench. It seemed heavier than it ought to be. All in all, it resembled some kind of artifact found after a bombing raid, objects of twisted and melted metal which, shorn of their original purpose, demanded a new way of thinking about them, a fresh method of observation, if one were to use them again.

Its reflective surface was suggestive, all potential, as if it could burst into life, might once again come alive with music. Holding it between his hands, Sam had the fleeting sense that some kind of circuit had been completed, a movement of as yet unnamed subatomic particles, and decided that it was just a sensation brought on by having studied Hadntz's detailed speculations for so long.

He shoved it to the back of the workbench, with all the bolts and wrenches. No one would notice it.

∥ 12 ∥

Intelligence

THE HOSPITAL DAY ROOM was a good place to get lost. I'd read in their library and once in a while looked at the register. One day I saw that a guy from home was there. Ray Johanson. I think you knew him. I didn't, but I knew his brother, Pete.

We found Ray and fixed him up. He didn't have any clothes to get out of there so we found him a uniform and a visitor's ticket to the Tidworth Ordnance Club. The Ordnance Club was British and had beer and a small menu. We had a few complimentary tickets and counterfeited them so we wouldn't run out.

Ray's girlfriend showed up; he'd been going with her for four years between battles in Africa, Italy, and France. He was a dispatch rider for Patton, loved Patton like a father, and wouldn't fight for anyone else. He swore he was going to head out for Patton's outfit. All he had to do was get there without getting picked up by MP's and thrown into the repple depple. By the time he was better they changed the policy—if you put in for an outfit in combat they would send you to them, and when the time came he was off to Patton's outfit.

A week later, he and Wink went to the Ordnance Club to eat.

Wink said, "What's on the menu today? Specialty of the house—bacon sandwich. Just like yesterday and the day before." The "bacon" was a thick slice of raw pig fat. The bread was genuine enough, though thin.

"Do I have Dance and Winklemeyer here?" The British voice behind them sounded official, as all Brits did, save Cockneys. It was their accent.

They looked at each other. There was no way out. They turned and saw a British major.

"Gentlemen, come with me."

Major Bedwick seated himself behind an imposing desk, folded his hands, and hunched forward. "I have been hearing things about you."

"Good things, sir, I hope," said Wink. He was ignored.

"It seems that a particular American soldier, Ray Johanson, has been seen leaving the hospital in his robe and going to your quarters."

"Which we do share with a good many people."

"After which he emerges clothed in a uniform with a pass to the club, where he meets his girlfriend."

"Sounds like just what the doctor ordered," said Wink.

"Yes, well, the rumor is, like the rumor about the whisky that vanished from the Mountbatten private stock, is that you may have had something to do with this arrangement."

They were both silent.

"The point is that you are schemers." He pushed back his chair and began to pace the room with hands clasped behind his back. "You are capable of manipulating the system to your advantage."

Wink said, "Sir, we are simply bringing our Yankee ingenuity to bear on the many different crosses that one must bear in wartime, to boost morale and keep everything running smoothly."

The major stopped pacing, raised one eyebrow as he looked at them, and said, "Well, men, perhaps that is the reason you are going on this little trip."

"How little?" asked Wink.

"Frankly, I have no idea. You are just to get in that automobile waiting out there for you and do as you're told."

"That Rolls-Royce?" asked Sam. "I'm not dressed for the occasion. Have you spoken to our CO?"

"I might," said the Major, "if you make it necessary. As I have mentioned, there really are things I ought to tell him."

"Well, throw me in the briar patch," said Wink. "I'll bet that Rolls has a bar."

Sam tried to memorize the distances and the turns, as usual. The driver, dressed in a suit, chatted affably about the weather, the raids, and the bloody awful Germans and how Stalin was going to crush them once and for all. However, when asked questions, he said, "I am just the driver, sir."

After an hour, during which Wink and Sam were silent—Wink searched the refrigerator and found it contained only an empty gin bottle—the driver turned right onto the winding driveway of a large, red manor house.

"Rather astounding place," remarked Wink.

"Amazingly . . . ugly."

It had sprouted many wings which were stylistically unconnected to one another, and had a vaguely German air because of the half-timbers. Bicycles littered the front steps, and at least one was propped next to each of the multitudinous doors.

"This is it?"

"Not quite yet, sir."

Behind the manor were long, low buildings, obviously war-built. The driver parked the Rolls. They followed him to a back door. The guard said, "G'day, sir," and nodded them in. The driver then led them up two flights of stairs and down a wide hallway. Opening the door, he motioned them in, hung his hat and jacket on the coat stand, and took a seat behind the desk.

"Just the driver?" asked Wink.

"Don't worry. You didn't give anything away. Can't blame me for trying." He offered them cigarettes, which each accepted. Leaning back in his chair, he propped up his feet on the desk, lit his own, put out his match with a flourish, and tossed it in the ashtray he'd settled on his lap.

"So who are you?" asked Sam.

"You don't need to know."

"Your child's bedroom?" asked Wink, glancing around.

"Someone else's child, I'm afraid, although I find the Peter Rabbit wallpaper comforting." He tilted his head as smoke drifted upward. "You know, of course, that we have radar. It's a war secret, but you are in a position to know about it, so I presume I'm giving nothing away in telling you that."

"Correct." Sam smoked his cigarette in a leisurely fashion, leaned forward to flick the ashes into the ashtray on the desk.

"It helped us survive the Blitz. The Germans knew we had something, of course, but couldn't figure out its exact nature. However, something happened to the radar the night of last Saturday. All of our stations picked up an object at the same time, and that object was triangulated as being in your shop. Your very shop, gentlemen. It was a radio object, some sort of transmission that canceled our beam. What was it?"

Wink, uncharacteristically, said nothing.

The man took his feet off the desk and resumed an upright position with an accompanying screech and thump of his chair. He took out some papers from the top drawer, tapped them to straighten them, and handed them to Sam. "Might it have been something like this?"

Wink leaned over Sam's shoulder.

The contents of the paper resembled Dr. Hadntz's plans to a startling degree. There were differences, though, and omissions. Sam paged through the papers, studying each one, trying to decide what to do, what to say. He was pretty much on his own here—at least, he hoped he was. Wink was a bit of a wild card, but so far that had always been for the best.

He returned the papers to the desk. "Where did you get this?"

"Answer my question."

"Might I have some tea?"

No Englishman could refuse such a request, and while it was fetched, Sam considered.

Something about the device, quite startlingly, had worked. But what?

This was not an American officer they were speaking to. He had no jurisdiction over them.

He returned with the cups of steaming tea, set them on the desk, and resumed his seat. "We know about Dr. Hadntz," said the man, whose identity, in Sam's eyes, had morphed from the driver into The Driver. "We know that she took a device like this out of the United States. And," said The Driver, looking at Sam, "we know that she took a particular liking to you. Now we detect this . . . effect. Exactly where you were. In addition, she vanished into Hungary several months ago."

But Sam had seen her in London.

Or some version of London. He suddenly had a vision of tableaus, like cards, shuffled by a careless hand. Each card, each tableau, was somehow contiguous with the others, but held its own universe, which fled outward from the flat plane of the card into many-dimensional realities, each with its own history, its own emotional justifications.

The Brit continued. "If her . . . invention . . . falls into the hands of the Germans, they can obviously wreak havoc on our radar. And probably deduce how it works, as well. We will lose one of our few advantages. This could easily—very easily—turn the tide of the war against us."

Sam's relaxation was total. He didn't know what Hadntz's invention did—but neither did they. He had a very strong feeling, though, that it was something much more radical than interfering with radar.

He didn't know whether the British knew this or not. He guessed not. There had been nothing, in the plans he had just looked over, of theory. Nothing about the twin helix. They were only a set of mechanical drawings that included a close facsimile of the top-secret cavity magnetron.

"Did you build one yourself?" asked Sam.

"Answer the question, please."

"What did it do?"

The Driver sighed. "Very well. We did make this device. It did nothing of note other than blow some fuses. It did not block our radar."

It did not contain the modifications Hadntz had given Sam in the house in London.

The telephone rang. "Excuse me." A pause. "Who wants to know? Oh. Major Elegante. I see." He replaced the phone in its cradle. "Come, then. It seems that you're wanted at home. An utterly integral cog in the assembly of jeeps for Overlord. You see," he said gently, "we wanted to ask you to work with us. I'm sure we could have made some arrangements. The United States is supposed to be sharing scientific information with us unilaterally. But apparently that has its limits, according to a certain Major Elegante. I'll see that you're driven back—you'll excuse me, but there is something else I need to do now. Good to meet you both. Perhaps we'll meet again."

They didn't speak until after the drive back, the route of which Sam once again memorized, although there were no signs. They made their way to the flight line, where no one could hear them.

"A shame he didn't offer us lunch," said Wink.

"He got us off quickly so as not to share their beef Wellington and fresh vegetables and trifles."

"Not to mention full-strength coffee. I'll bet they drink a lot of it at that place." Nearby, teams of maintenance workers swarmed over several battered Spitfires that had limped home after an engagement with a phalanx of German bombers the night before. Engines roared to life and then stopped. Propellers, windshields, and tails were replaced as they watched. "How did that guy ever get back?" Wink wondered, pointing at a plane that had a two-foot-wide hole in the side.

"Do you want to go on with this?" Sam asked.

"You've got to be kidding."

"I'm suspicious of the whole thing now."

"You weren't before?"

"Apparently they've kept an eye on us."

"Of course they have. We're working on something the Brits don't have. I'm not at all sure that our own CO doesn't know we're up to something and has orders to protect it. War secrets, and all. There are agents all over the place, I'll bet. Didn't you say they questioned you about Hadntz in D.C. right after she gave you the plans? Who is this Major Elegante, anyway?"

"Elegante was there."

"Did you tell me this before?"

"No."

Wink whistled. "Damn. We're valuable, Dance. Look, last week we figured out how to make those Bell Lab computers work. Rescued the whole M-9 program. They didn't have a clue. It would have set things back for months—who knows if another shipment would have even made it over here. The ship could have been sunk. They ought to give us some bloody medals."

"That's *damned* medals to you, Yank, and don't you forget it."

The Bell Lab computers, which calculated where a moving target would be, were actually sine- and cosine-shaped fiberboard wrapped in wire. None of the M-9's they were testing from the huge shipment had worked. After a lot of elimination, Sam had finally figured out that it had to be the boards. After more elimination, he realized that the boards had been slightly warped in shipment. So slightly warped, in fact, that it was not perceptible by ordinary perusal. He'd deduced it after studying the entire setup, and he and Wink quickly made the lot of the M-9's functional. Then they submitted a report with suggestions about how to prevent this problem in the future.

Sam said, "I think that whatever Hadntz incorporated into her most recent plans—"

"Which she gave you in London, under the noses of the Brits—"

"Well," Sam smiled, "it *seemed* to be London. Anyway, it was a vital change."

"Right. Actually, it was a lot of little things."

"Fine-tuning, like figuring out that the slightly warped fiberboard was causing the whole beautiful M-9 Director not to function at all."

"And that's how she made the whole London thing happen."

"I wonder if she knew that's what would happen. She said something about it having been difficult to find me. I don't think it would be too hard to find me here."

"Depends on where she started from."

"The Brits can't find her."

"No doubt if we went looking, we couldn't either."

Sam sat on a rock and lit a cigarette. Wink leaned against it and lit his own. They smoked in silence for a moment.

Then Sam said, "Let's call it off."

Wink looked at Sam, a startled expression on his face. "What?"

"I mean, we have no idea what we're doing, who we're working for, really. Even if Hadntz really has the best intentions in mind, I'm not sure that she really knows where this is going. Maybe we're part of a big chain of labs manufacturing this thing everywhere, and when they're ready, they'll all link up and—"

"I kind of thought that was where this was all leading to," said Wink. "Some kind of huge, overwhelming change. Like—yes, nuclear fission is possible. But what if they make a bomb that creates an explosion that never stops, that changes everything into one huge chain reaction?" He tossed his cigarette away. "Damn, where's the whisky when you need it? Look, Dance, we trust each other, right?"

Sam smiled. "Can't play jazz without trust."

"*Especially* not modern jazz. I know why you're doing this. Because of your brother."

"Because people are being killed. Not just him. He keeps me going, though. Why are you doing it?"

Wink perched on the rock and stared across the field of damaged aircraft. "This war is like a huge dark cloud of hate. I'm not sure that we really know what's going on over there, across the channel. But I know that all the scientists and artists fled before it. They're bellwethers, I would think. Maybe more sensitive than most people. Needing more refined conditions in which to work."

"All the European lecturers and professors had a story about why they left Europe," said Sam.

"My father kept all kinds of scientific journals and papers in his office. I guess his dream was to be some kind of professor, and instead he wound up with a factory. But it's no secret that the Germans know about the possibility of nuclear fission. It's no secret to anyone in the world who was up on those kinds of things—mathematics, physics. Who knows what kind of secret weapon the Germans are working on right now? Like the guy said, any little thing could turn the tide of this war. Maybe this is it."

"But if this works, will it stop the war? Or will it ruin everything?"

"Hadntz apparently believes that it will stop the war," said Wink.

"And I have another question. Do our guys know we're working on this, or just the Brits?"

"Obviously, Elegante does. Beyond that, who knows? She may be some kind of wild card herself. Or maybe they're just giving us enough rope to hang ourselves."

After the war, Sam figured out they'd been taken to Bletchley Park.

A few days later, The Mess knocked on the door of what they euphemistically referred to as their "office."

"Yo," said Wink, cracking open the door, the better to disguise his stash of whisky, which he was not inclined to share.

"We got company."

Sam joined Wink and looked out the door.

About ten British soldiers were methodically searching the garage. They'd clearly started at the front and were working their way back. Sam thought that maybe they had about fifteen minutes.

"Get Kocab," he said to The Mess.

He watched The Mess stroll across the garage, picking up a wrench on the way, and incline his head toward Kocab's. Kocab picked up the large rag he used to wipe his hands and casually walked toward their office.

As the soldiers worked their way closer, opening and slamming locker doors and rummaging through toolboxes, Sam said to Kocab, "It's heavy," and slipped him the device. Kocab accepted it, and then Sam saw it no more. Kocab walked back toward the jeep he was assembling, stopping to chat with The Mess on the way.

A moment later one of the searchers opened their door and squeezed into the cubicle. "Where did you get that?" he demanded.

"What?" asked Wink.

"All this bloody whisky, that's what."

Wink had to sacrifice half of their stash to the guy.

"Nice decoy," said Sam after he was gone.

"Shut up."

When Kocab brought it back the next day, he said, "What is this stuff?"

"War secret," said Wink.

"Right. Well, it definitely had some kind of effect on me."

"You'd better lay off the strong drink," said Wink.

⊩ 13 ⊩

Calibration

SAM HAD WORKED a fifteen-hour shift, but was awakened by a rough shaking an hour after he fell into bed. Something heavy was tossed atop him. "Suit up."

"For what?" He was sure that Wink, on the next cot, was awake, but feigning sleep with all of his considerable skill.

"Mission over Berlin. Be at the flight line in ten minutes. Here's your pill."

"Why didn't you say there must be some mistake?" Wink said, after they left.

"You're provoking the gods," said Sam, zipping himself into the flight suit and shoving his feet into his boots. He stood and swallowed the Dexedrine they'd left.

Another torch glare provoked moans. Wink's silence did not protect him. "Suit up. Ten minutes."

Wink was on his feet in a flash. "Yes, sir!" Crisp salute.

"We're calibrating," he told Sam as they walked through the chilly night.

"I figured that out."

Sam's B-17 was called Sally Rand; he had a brief glimpse of her well-endowed red-clad figure while climbing the ladder. The interior was close and dark. He was to sit next to the bombardier, a man called Henk, he'd been told during the pre-flight briefing where he met Glenning, Mason, and the other crewmembers.

In front of Henk was a small, glowing screen—one that Sam had undoubtedly assembled and tested a few days ago. Henk was intense and quiet, and so was everyone else when they heard that their mission was to bomb Berlin. The assumption, both by the Allies and by the Germans, was that Berlin was safe from daytime bombing raids, and the more precise targeting such raids would allow.

Sam's perception of himself as an irreplaceable cog in the war effort evaporated as he zipped and buckled himself into his gear. The survival rate for these missions was low. Their hospital was filled with men who'd been wounded by shrapnel ripping through the thin aluminum skin of their plane, or by bullets fired from the German planes as they came right up to the B-17, or by the huge 88mm antiaircraft guns protecting German targets. They might even be trying to get rid of him because of what he knew.

The plane bounced down the short runway. He had by now seen thousands of takeoffs, and many botched attempts. It was a breath-holding proposition as to whether the plane would actually take off before it reached the end of the strip or crash into Bedder's field, long since cleared of valuable sheep and cows. His radio crackled. "We're off, boys."

Sam nervously adjusted his oxygen mask. The plane was not pressurized; the first bullet hole would have depressurized it. England vanished beneath him, a beautiful blur of deep green, and then there was the Channel, patterned with white-edged scallops which were waves. Suddenly everything vanished into mist. He calculated their speed, their trajectory, and when they emerged into a world of gold and ruby–drenched cloud his breath was taken away by its beauty. He was suspended above this beauty, on his very first airplane flight, inside the latest weaponry of death.

"Come on back, Dance. You're to check out the ball turret setup." Glenning helped him settle into the gyroscopic Plexiglas sphere suspended beneath the belly of the plane after Mason climbed out. "You're not the man for this kind of mission. Too tall."

He began to check out the computerized gyroscopic sight. The information was transmitted to him through blips of light on a tiny screen; he had only to rotate and superimpose his own dots for the sophisticated device to calculate his own plane's speed and the speed and curve of the target, which the simple sight of humans could not do with any great accuracy. Calculus at work. Had Newton dreamed of weapons? Of course; catapults and such. But mostly he dreamed of pure information. Rather like Hadntz's dreams, except that she had tried to use her information positively, knowing the negative ends to which it could be turned.

But there was no way to control how a technology might be used.

The clouds cleared and he assumed that they were still over France. Miller's "Moonlight Sonata" played over his headphones from a radio station near Tidworth. Despite his heated clothing he was cold. The pilot of one of the Mustangs escorting them caught Sam's eye and gave him a quick smile: he was that close. East was the blinding sun and then out of it German fighters that seemed to have come from above. His Mustang friend peeled off and engaged the Messerschmitt in gunfire.

There was no time to trade places with Mason. Sam did not think; his training thought for him. He pointed the guns at the Messerschmitt 109 and was rotated into firing position. Firing in short bursts, as he'd been taught, he thought that perhaps it was one of his bullets that pierced the fuselage of the other plane; assuredly, it was the Mustang that sent it down in a spiral of smoke and flame.

Alert and cool now, he stopped thinking about anything other than being suspended above occupied France, defending tons of munitions and the nine other lives on his plane. His headphones were filled with technical messages from the navigator or engineer to the pilot, mixed with excited chatter when they began cutting through the harrying German planes.

They were one organism, bent on survival. He'd never had such an intense feeling before; the instantaneous communication, the bond as each engaged in a specialized task. And a deeper pride: his fix had worked. Although he had been tested and re-tested, knowing, intellectually, that lives depended on him, being here brought home the seriousness of his own small part in the war effort, and after that it never left him. One must execute all things to the best of one's ability, unslowed or deflected by bullshit—bureaucratic pettiness, human jealousies, or greed.

Rotate the cramped sphere hanging in all this beauty. Fire and fire right there into the face of the German hidden behind his mask. Hope the frost would clear from his goggles; there, it had. Dizziness and panic; has his oxygen tube crimped or come loose? Someone finds the crimp; unkinks it. Breathing again, pure oxygen, and then the attack seems over and he is pulled from the turret.

"It works," he tells Mason through his radio microphone.

"You did great," Mason says as he takes over and Sam is deeply gratified at the compliment. At least they're still alive. Back at his post next to the bombardier, he finds that his own screen is not working.

By the time he fixes it, they are suddenly over Berlin, surrounded by flak meant to confound the sensitive tracking devices embedded in this machine of death. Mustangs and Messerschmitts everywhere. Parachutes fill the sky—more American POW's, if they survive. The 88's below boom ceaselessly. The surviving B-17's are westward blips, their range exhausted. Sally Rand's target, a refinery, is below and amid a hail of ground-launched missiles. The bombardier lets go and a cheer rises through their shared mind: *Target hit!* Jubilance!

Turning from the now-high sun, Germans in pursuit. A shock rips through the plane; a shudder, a stall. A cry of agony: "God! Damn, damn! My fucking *hand*—" A sickening drop, the plane recovers, but low, missing one engine.

Across Germany they fly, trying to climb, then just trying to make it back. Talk of diverting to Switzerland then—no, the Channel and a dash. "Sweet, sweet!"

Mason dead, right where Sam had been, the ball turret. The entire crew crying, even himself.

Three B-17's lost and five Mustangs. And, as if peripheral, twenty-seven men. Target hit. Slosh of whisky downed after peeling off sweat-drenched suit.

Quiet, pulled-aside congratulations from the pilot—apparently the gyroscopic setup greatly enhanced their defense, his kill of a plane, their very survival and ability to go up again and kill the civilians as well as the soldiers of Germany. Much improved, a great breakthrough.

He'd heard rumors of firestorms deliberately started by the Allies. He hadn't believed it; even the Japanese targeted only Pearl Harbor.

Now he did. The Germans had indeed targeted civilians everywhere, and the Allies were not above it, either. The entire world was involved in such atrocities.

As was he.

During his plummet into sleep he wondered how anyone could get up and do this again in just a few hours.

But all fliers did, many and many times over until they too fell from the sky.

There were no soldiers in the barracks when he woke. It was four in the afternoon. He couldn't believe that they'd let him sleep in just because of a little run over Berlin.

But he now had a much better idea of what was happening across the Channel.

Was that why he had been sent? By Hadntz?

If so, he had a feeling that it was just the beginning.

⊰ 14 ⊱

Behind the Lines

S PRING BROUGHT SLIGHTLY warmer mists, the classic English beauty of deep gardens, but not hoped-for days with Elsinore.

After the bombing he sought her out more frequently. He realized that he wasn't going to the mansion just to be around the children. Maybe that had never been the case. If he had fooled himself, though, he probably hadn't fooled anyone else—not Wink, who teased him about Elsinore, nor Mrs. Applewhist, or even Elsinore herself.

But more often than not, when he went to the mansion, she was not around. Still, he did enjoy being with the children; they begged him to play the piano for them so that they could have sing-alongs after dinner. They still groaned if he brought his saxophone, except for the red-haired boy, Charles, to whom he had given a few elementary lessons. Even Mrs. Applewhist, always in her flowered cotton dress and well-worn green apron, welcomed him now that Elsinore was scarce.

Sam and Wink let the Hadntz Device well enough alone. Apparently, it required some kind of activation, which required what they both had decided might be nuclear fission. Obviously, that was not possible. So it stayed on the shelf, seemingly inert. "Though God knows what it's really up to," Wink remarked more than once.

Sam was desperately disappointed. He had placed his hopes on the device more than he realized. Some kind of easy out, some kind of no-cost solution. Magical restorer of life. But if it worked, why hadn't Hadntz built one and used it by now?

Perhaps she had, and had thereby left them behind.

There was news of terrible slaughter in the Pacific, in Russia. In Tidworth, the 610th continued the invasion buildup. The Perham Downs, gaining a local reputation and more players, were invited to many gigs, where they invented semimodern interpretations of old standards.

On his trips to London, Sam often now found himself at the front door of the theatrical warehouse, and tried to retrace his route to the house to which Hadntz had taken him. Perhaps he had to go inside, wander through the rooms of time first, and come out another door. He finally gave it up; if she wanted to find him, she would. If she still lived.

One day, as Sam stepped off the train at Paddington Station, a man in a black suit approached him.

"You are Samuel Dance?"

"Who are you?"

"I'm with British Intelligence. Follow me, if you please."

"I don't—"

"Here is my identification. We are working in conjunction with your OSS concerning a certain physicist whom you know."

Sam was silent.

"She has made a deal with us, but she requests your help. Only you." The man looked around. "Now, if you'll come this way, we need to talk in private."

With a good number of negative scenarios bouncing around in his mind, Sam weighed his alternatives.

"I would like to talk with someone from OSS about this."

"That can be arranged."

But he never actually met anyone from the OSS. They simply gave "permission" for him to participate in the operation. The upshot was that he was to be dropped behind enemy lines, in France. He could not talk about this with anyone when he returned.

At two in the morning, Sam and Wink walked somewhat unsteadily down a cobblestone street in Tidworth. In the distance, a few flyboys started up another chorus of "There Will Always Be an England," the words replaced by ribald substitutes at which they roared in laughter.

"All right. Spill." Wink gave Sam's arm a sharp shake, as if that might dislodge a recounting of what he had done while absent.

"Can't talk," Sam replied.

"Talk anyway. You're useless. You don't say anything, you don't do anything except what's required, and, what's worse, you've completely stopped practicing."

Sam kicked a stone out of the way and continued walking, hands in pockets. His head spun with unbearable images.

"You're telling me that some stupid command is keeping you from telling me what happened last week? Are we in this together or not?"

They were on the outskirts of town now. "Nice night," commented Wink. "Lots of stars."

"Lots of stars."

"Let's sit on that rock and watch them."

Sam shrugged and accepted a cigarette from Wink. They smoked in silence for a few minutes. Then Sam said, "I was with Hadntz."

"What?" Wink's voice was filled with amazement. "In London?"

"No. In Germany. And—I don't know. We went to a few places. Maybe Poland."

"I'm amazed, astonished, astounded. You were across the Channel. You went to 'a few places.' What kind of places?"

"I was dropped in France. Hadntz and I went to labor camps. I was her driver."

"Labor camps?"

"They're killing people," said Sam. "Deliberately and methodically. Working them to death making weapons. Look. I really don't *want* to talk about it. But I will tell you that Hadntz found her daughter. Alive. And the Germans are building incredibly huge rockets."

"How huge?"

"About fifty feet long. The ones I saw. I doubt we know how many they have— maybe thousands. Hadntz said that they're going to attach warheads to them. They have a pretty complex gyroscopic guidance system. But that isn't the worst thing I saw."

"My guess—the people," said Wink.

"They are starved, beaten, and worked to death. They are publicly killed for the smallest infraction, the least suspicion of sabotage, or even for not working quickly enough. But I guess it's the same philosophy our own slaveholders had. The Slavs and Poles and Gypsies—the 'non-Aryans,' whatever they are—are considered subhuman, just like the Negroes were to the slaveholders. It's a pretty convenient way to look at other people, if you can get away with it, and if you don't give a shit about them. It's a deep human trait. We all must have it. I guess it's one of the things that Hadntz wants to deal with, to change, but for the life of me I can't figure out how."

"She says—"

"If DNA does exist, and if it can be changed, and if it can be changed by her device, and if we can figure out exactly what needs to be changed—just the implications of DNA are staggering, never mind all the other stuff—I guess that's all just great. Unfortunately, our interpretation is a mess—"

"But it did *something*," said Wink, in his best come-on-let's-go voice. "The British looked for it, remember? It does emit some kind of signal. Or did, for a while. That's a start, isn't it?"

"I suppose."

"We've just got to keep trying. We have to make another one."

Sam laughed softly. "She's got you hooked, doesn't she?"

"You need to understand a problem before you can solve it. So—why take you over there?"

"It was a deal. She wanted British Intelligence to provide her with the necessary forged papers and transportation, and was willing to take the risk that she might be caught. I was too; it was voluntary. They gave me a choice. She was searching for her daughter in these camps. And she found her. The deal was that they would help her if she would take a witness they could debrief."

"Which was you."

"Which was me. I didn't find out anything specific from her about the device, anything we can use. She said she had nothing new, that the microfilm was still the latest version." Sam fell silent.

"You're tired." Wink clapped him on the back. "I'm sorry."

"Thanks."

⫴ 15 ⫴

Doodlebugs

IT WAS JUNE 6, 1944. The sky over England was dark with planes and had been for twenty-four hours. Artillery Hill, where Sam and Wink stood during a brief break, itself rumbled, the very deep ground of it, with the steady, droning roar.

"Where are they all coming from?" marveled Wink.

Sam had been an integral part of Overlord. All these planes, DUKS—ungainly-looking boats-on-wheels—mortars, and guns had passed through ordnance, assembled by them and those beneath them. Nevertheless, it was a wonder to see such concentrated power as the entire American force was mobilized and moved toward the coast.

They worked round the clock once the invasion began. Red Cross ships brought back horribly injured men, landing craft came back full of bullet holes, and planes ripped by big guns limped home.

The German defense of Normandy was more vigorous than expected. German Tigers were superior to Shermans; German equipment in general was better.

The war continued. But the Allies were, at last, on the continent.

The V-1 attacks started soon thereafter.

We were in England during the height of the buzz bomb attacks. The Krauts lacked gasoline and their big bombers ate up a lot of gas with little strategic success. They wanted to put the British population into a state of fear, but the bombings just made them mad as hell and determined to stick things out. The Germans filled the gaps between bomber attacks with V-1's. There'd be a big air raid once in a while, then the V-1's—buzz bombs, a bomb with wings and a pulse engine—would come. The Brits called them doodlebugs.

A pulse engine works like a stovepipe with a Venetian blind bisecting a cross section. The blind opens and wind blows out the exhaust gasses. The blind closes, a spray of gasoline explodes, giving a push, the blind opens, and the cycle starts again. Such a simple motor, and it went six hundred miles per hour, faster than planes.

When a buzz bomb approached, you could hear it. Sounded like a lawn mower. If it shut off, the whole pub would get completely quiet. Then you'd hear an explosion a block away or so. Instantly the room would roar back to life.

After ten weeks of bitter and costly fighting, Paris was taken. The Germans pulled back and sent forces east. The flow of new ordnance being sent over the Channel ceased; instead, it was sent directly to the continent. While troops celebrated in Paris, and despite Allied defeats, the generals decided that the war would end in December.

But there was no dancing in London.

The doodlebugs, essentially drone airplanes, could be intercepted by a plane flying close and creating turbulence, which caused the drones to crash. But that was risky. Still, the RAF were sent in great numbers to do just that.

"Where are we going?" Sam had to shout to make himself heard over the roar of the jeep he had borrowed, after repeated requests from Elsinore that he find one, as well as petrol. While that was a small enough task for him, he was beginning to regret letting her drive it. But he loved just being with her. She was always so strongly present, and he missed her terribly when he was not able to see her for a few days.

She barreled down tiny dark lanes as if by touch. Even though the three-quarters moon was out, they were in pure darkness once they were enclosed beneath a canopy of trees.

"Slow down! We might hit a cow."

She wrenched the steering wheel left, and he braced for the smash into the hedgerow. But miraculously branches just slapped the windshield and they bounced down a way which could not have been more than a cowpath through the forest.

Then they were in a field. Dark buildings loomed ahead. He heard the roar of an airplane engine. She pulled round to the side of a hangar and stopped with a jerk. "I hope I'm not too late."

Elsinore swung herself out of the jeep, combed her long, snarled hair in vain with one hand, and patted the pocket of her slacks. "Damn, forgot my lipstick."

Sam sensed someone behind them and turned, braced for a fight.

But the man's face bore a glad smile. "You came!"

A flyboy grabbed her round the shoulders, and Elsinore was enveloped in a crushing hug and what looked like an equally crushing kiss. "I told you I would."

"Who's this?"

"My friend. Sam Dance. Sam, meet Will Mitland."

"Pleased to meet you. Yank, are you?"

"Oversexed, overpaid, and over here. And after that ride, glad to still be here."

"She drives like a maniac."

"Like a man, you mean," Elsinore said.

"Oh, nothing at all like a man," said Mitland. They kissed again, this time more passionately, and Sam was thrown into a dark funk.

He was sure they did not hear him as he said, "I'll be at the hangar."

Walking toward the huge metal building, he hoped he wouldn't be taken for a German spy. But other than a terse nod or a "Yank," he was ignored.

Inside, crews crawled over the Spitfires, fueling up, testing engines, replacing spark plugs. The men were covered with oil and their faces were utterly serious.

The signal to scramble sounded.

Within minutes, the planes were in the air and engaged.

Suddenly Elsinore was beside him, gripping his arm with both hands, as they stood in a field in England and watched the warriors play out their roles. The night sky was illuminated by sudden fires that plummeted like falling meteors, explosions, and the far-away, almost imagined *aack-aack* of machine guns. It was a low, close fight as the RAF tried to wipe out the Messerschmitts guarding the heavy German bomber on its way to London so they could take it down.

As soon as the battle commenced, four meat wagons sped off down dark lanes to search out the fallen.

Will Mitland was brought back, less than an hour after he had left, retrieved from his burning plane, dead.

Elsinore, fighting her way through medical personnel at the ambulance, would not stop screaming. She was pulled away and handed to Sam.

Sam settled her in the jeep as best he could, after she scrambled out twice. He took the wheel. Bereft, now, of even the light of the moon, he turned on his slit headlights and retraced their route through ancient fields and battlegrounds.

They traversed the Salisbury Plain, where soldiers had massed for centuries, for confrontations and for training. He imagined that he could feel their combined being; all their hopes and wishes and love of family and home set against the vast and unknown darkness through which they crawled; Sam's speed, unlike Elsinore's, was limited by what he could actually see with his slitted headlights.

Elsinore beat on the dash of the jeep, sobbing, beyond touch or comfort, her curses rich and strange to him, drawn from deep times and handed down to her, curses of god and of men and of governments and of Germans. All he could think of was getting her home to the manor, home to her children, home to an absence as desolating as that which had informed him since December 7, when his world changed as well.

Sam pulled up in front of the mansion; he jerked the jeep to a stop with the hand brake and jumped out. When he tried to help Elsinore up from the jeep seat, she threw off his arms and got out by herself, very slowly. Then she just stood there, looking around at the moonlit night as if she would never move.

Finally he gently took her arm and led her up the broad stairs and through the wide front door, then toward the exceedingly wide staircase, which had accommodated two horses side by side during a long-ago war, according to Mrs. Applewhist. A crowd of silent children accompanied them.

Elsinore collapsed at the foot of the stairs, moaning "bloody Germans, bloody Germans." Sam gathered her awkwardly, glad that she was small and light, and this time she did not resist. He trudged upstairs. Charlie watched from the upstairs railing.

"Is she drunk?" he asked.

"No," said Sam. "A friend of hers just died. Which room is hers?"

More children gathered. They helped pull off her shoes and get her into bed. Mrs. Applewhist stood in the doorway. "What is it?"

"It's Will," said Sam.

Some of the children began to cry. Apparently they knew Will.

"Hush now," said Mrs. Applewhist. "Let's get the dishes finished. Sarah, you will read a story to the littles. Go on now. Out with you. Elsinore needs to rest."

At the sound of Mrs. Applewhist's voice, Elsinore opened her eyes, turned face-down on the bed, and sobbed. The older woman sat next to her, embraced her wordlessly, and smoothed her hair. Elsinore curled up tightly.

"We'll make do now, Mr. Dance," said Mrs. Applewhist, with a sigh. "I suppose we must."

Sam took the jeep and drove back to the base, himself seized with Elsinore's shivering, wanting, like her, to scream.

But not for Will. For Keenan.

He went to the workshop and threw himself into soldering a damaged M-9 component that had come back today, wishing that there was something, anything, that he could do to work on Hadntz's Device. The hiss of the blue flame soothed him, but the world around him seemed suddenly darker than ever.

In the following weeks, he gave all his free time to Elsinore, because she seemed to depend on his presence. Mrs. Applewhist reported sleepwalking and fits of hysterical laughing and crying, which his visits seemed to temper somewhat. He read Chinese poetry to her from the book he'd taken from the warehouse, the one that Howie had not claimed, saying that it really had no value, while she sat pensive in a chair next to the fire, and she said that the sound of his voice soothed her. They developed small rituals of tea and weeding the newly sprouted garden, and she did not talk much.

For the time being, he was simply thankful that he could help. Helping her helped him as well, he discovered. His darkness and his feelings of helplessness in the face of evil lifted so gradually he did not realize that it was happening.

Then her mood changed, suddenly. She wanted to get out; had to go to the Hart and Hind every evening. "Good to be among people," she said, taking his hand as they walked down the road at dusk. "I like a crowd." Sam learned to brace himself for the downward drunken spiral into which she was more and more prone to fling herself. Laughing all the way. Mrs. Applewhist disapproved, and Sam was worried, but Mrs. Applewhist, after a few long talks with Elsinore, said, "There's nothing we can do about it. I'm sure that she'll get better eventually."

"Maybe she should go to a doctor?" he asked.

"Oh, then maybe we all should," said Mrs. Applewhist, fine British sarcasm ringing in her voice. "This war is making everyone half-mad."

On this particular evening, after two ales, Elsinore became quite animated.

"I have a hard time persuading the children to carry their masks with them everywhere." Elsinore picked her own off the table and examined it. "It does make one look so like an insect." She donned hers quickly and turned herself into one, goggle-eyed and insect-snouted, eyes glassed-in ciphers, and rotated her head like a praying mantis, a slow, grave swivel. "What's in this thing, anyhow?"

"A charcoal filter. Takes the chlorine and various other poisons out of the air you breathe."

"But I hear they have worse. Wonder why they don't use it. Mow down an entire choking, gagging city. Pump it into the underground."

"Poison gas was outlawed after the Great War."

Her laugh a hearty, ironic, "O-HO!" which filled the bar, then trickled away as if it were brilliant sunlit water vanishing over a precipice in a waterfall. "Indeed. Why then, let's just outlaw the lot of this, say? Bombs and buzz bombs and rockets. Anything the sole purpose of which is to murder." She raised a glass. "I'll drink to that!"

They clinked.

He said, "Gasses disperse quickly. They're subject to things difficult to control, like wind."

"But, then, poison our water. And we can poison theirs," she added gaily, that dark bleak sparkle in her eye. "It all makes such sense," she persisted. "Poison the food! Poison the air! Mass destruction everywhere! A Democracy of Death! O children wear these!" Twirling the mask above her head again, as high as her arm would reach. "They will defend you with an ultimate and magical power. These masks will return your parents to you unharmed! You will walk into a new land to which war has never come!" She leaned forward. "Tell me. I know that you must know. What is the superweapon Germany is working on? The one that will subjugate the world? As if *U*-boats and *V*-rockets and *B*-for Blitzkrieg were not enough? And what will that start with? What letter of the *A*-for Alphabet are they reserving for the worst of the weapons, the A-pex of their ever-flowering creativity?"

She pounded the table with her fist, making her Red Hook Ale jump, and he wanted to unfurl her fist, clasp her hand, and comfort her with all that he was and all that he might ever be, although he knew that that was not possible. L-for Love, his mind said and the sudden truth of it both warmed him and cast him into despair. He didn't dare tell her. She was in a place past comfort, on the other side of love.

But she paused in her rant and took in his look with complete recognition.

"*D*-for Dance," she said soberly and pulled him from his chair. It was a fast tune and then a slow one and she clung to him for a second in silent entreaty, then lifted her head and said, *please, let's go home now.* And, *I'm sorry,* a whisper, afterward, as she lay naked and beautiful and spent in her bed.

Sorry?

To be so savage, she replied, and burst into tears in his arms.

He had fallen in love with Elsinore. He was not at all sure that she had fallen in love with him, but was not bothered by that. She was complicated. If he could comfort her somehow by being there, he would be there.

But the closer he got to Elsinore's physical self, the farther he seemed from her heart and mind. She still went from listless to manic at the drop of a hat. At dances, she sometimes cried hysterically on his shoulder as the band played. He soon realized that it was always the same song, and asked the band not to play it. Otherwise, he was tense the entire time they were there, thinking about how the next few notes after the lull between songs might be the ones to set her off. She was chain-smoking, and her face was pale, thin, and focused on something far off, usually over his shoulder, if they sat opposite one another with their tea.

But whenever he had to leave, she hugged him tightly and begged him not to go. "Oh, they won't miss you over there. Use your head. You know, make one of those dummies to sleep in your bed at night and . . . and pay a bunch of guys to answer roll call. You're clever. Think of something. I need you here with me, Dance."

"And they shall be named," she cast a wicked look at him, "Edwin, Branwyn, and—"

"Tin-tin."

"No, they must all end with *win*. I am in a winning mood. And this is a new thing beneath the eye of heaven. The Germans are but a mote in my eye." She was manic on this sea-cliff. He could see the radar tower thin and wavering to the east, so far away that it sometimes disappeared as if in a mist.

Another month had passed, during which time she had become increasingly possessive of him. He preferred this aspect to her stone-darkness, a blackness so profound that within it nothing stirred and no light penetrated. She would reach bottom and then begin her upward trajectory as if a launched rocket, bursting from negative to positive and then beyond. He knew there was something terribly wrong, and that he was doing nothing to help. Neither could the chaplain nor any of her multitudinous friends. One sign of her decreasing grip on reality was that it pleased her to talk about their imaginary children, their names all ending in "win" or "wyn"; to plot their characters and lives. He thought he was quite braced for her sudden turn away from him in some future, but hoped that they could move through that to something more like normal, like the normal she had been when they first met. He wanted to be that which saved her, or perhaps father the child who could. The best he could do, though, was be here as she weathered it. Only she could save herself.

He divided his free time between thinking about the device and spending time with Elsinore, or at least with the kids, feeling her essence around him in the huge old kitchen even when she was not there. He worked in the garden with the children, often in the evening and sometimes in the early morning. Red-haired Charlie took a particular liking to the enterprise. He carefully and sparsely sowed the tiny lettuce seeds, covering them tenderly, and weeded alongside Sam and Elsinore.

It was a season of growth and hope after a terrible winter. Sam was becoming very used to the place and did not think about what was ahead, when he would no doubt be transferred to the arena of war.

Around the time the lettuce was making its first fragile appearance, Sam became afraid. She was on one of her upswings, breathtaking as the arc of a Mustang as it rose to meet the enemy. Ever more bright, breathless, and smiling while lighting one cigarette from the last, she kept a bottle of gin next to her bed. She thrashed around in nightmare, and always cried out the same thing: "Give it to 'im Will! That's it!"

And then she took a Spitfire and went up.

He told himself afterward that he should have known. He should have figured out that she'd do something deeply heroic and mad. She had planned it, apparently, for weeks.

The uniform was the easiest part, he surmised. Getting to know the roster was a bit more complicated. Targeting the flyboy she replaced took guts. He apparently quite willingly drank more than he should have, considering he'd had but a few hours of sleep in the past five days. He passed out on the couch in her room. Littering the washroom floor with dark sheaves of her hair was the last thing she did before running down the stairs clutching his mask and hat, attired smartly in the RAF uniform, and riding her bike to the airstrip.

She simply jumped into the flyboy's hastily patched plane and took her place in the formation.

If Sam had been outside at the time he might have seen the battle. She fought valiantly, toughly, courageously. Apparently Jimmy had not only let her sit in his plane and learn how to operate the simple controls, but had given her detailed instructions. She downed a Junker, for which she would have gotten a medal had she been a legitimate flyboy.

That was not how she died, though. She ditched her smoking plane expertly on the water and was picked up. There was quite an uproar at the hospital when they cut off her seared uniform, and quite a puzzle until the groggy flyboy woke about ten hours later. He enlightened them, which was rather embarrassing for him, not to mention the entire outfit.

She was a sensation, a hero. For the next week or two, she was calm, her old rational self, the burn on her face bandaged and one arm in a sling, her short hair astonishingly fetching. They didn't quite know what to do with her. So they let her just go back to work.

She was in the garden shed when a buzz bomb fell. It was quite early one morning, but several children were gardening with her, as was Sam.

He was pulling weeds, thinking about what he could get done in the fifteen minutes before he had to leave. Charlie and three of the girls were staking tomatoes. Charlie wielded the scissors, cutting off lengths of string from a large ball of saved-up mongrel pieces knotted together.

Sam heard the ominous lawn-mower sound, leaped up, and tried to get to the children, to shelter them somehow, but the sound had stopped and then there was a geyser of black, finely turned earth spewing into the dawn-fresh sky, scattering and showering in great clumps. Sam was thrown into the trees by the blast.

Aching, but still conscious, he pushed branches and debris from him, realizing that his arm might be broken. The shed, crushed by the impact, was on fire. He finally struggled free of the tree and hurtled across the crater that had been their garden.

"Elsinore!"

She screamed hideously from the shed.

Sam ducked beneath the sagging lintel; saw her legs beneath a tangle of fiery garden tools, their wooden handles ablaze. Elsinore was engulfed by flames.

He grabbed her legs and pulled her out with strength he had not known he possessed, tossed dirt on her to smother the flames.

Her face was horribly burned, but her eyes were open. "Where are they?" Then she screamed, "Find them!"

Mrs. Applewhist and the milkman helped Sam search the bomb site. He saw an arm, and a bit of bloodied red hair, and pulled Charlie from the dirt. He was lifeless, his head shattered from a rock. Sam found the little girls a few yards away, sprawled beneath a wheelbarrow, which had almost torn them in half. They were holding hands. They must have been running away.

Then he heard another buzz; another silence. This bomb hit the manor house, taking many more of the orphans with it. Elsinore died later that day of her burns, in the gymnasium hospital.

It was random; senseless. It all came down to luck, good or bad. Elsinore was only one of hundreds of millions of non-combatant civilians who died in the war, killed by the insanity that surged through the world and, he feared, would surge again.

As if his life had become some kind of grim game he scratched out a mark for her in his being. Two of mine, he thought. Two of mine, and several millions of all the others, all of them dear to at least one other beyond belief.

All this dearness, gone from the world. It must set off a firestorm of aching loss, a dark wind which rose from somewhere within all of them, they who birthed this wind. There was no stopping it.

The image of her that lodged in his mind forever afterward was one he hadn't actually seen. It was the way she must have looked when she flew out over the Channel. Determined, cool.

Taking things into her own hands. Fighting all the way.

It was eventually discovered that the most effective weapon against the V-1 buzz bombs was the top-secret M-9 Director, which located, tracked, and shot down the terrible weapons.

Sam and Wink, being experts on the M-9, traveled around England during the next six weeks, helping to set up the fire directors, working out glitches, instructing crews, supervised by an American civilian. On noticing that some of the gun crews had penciled corrections onto the wall next to their chairs, Sam included the field corrections, which resulted in increased accuracy, in a report. His notes from his Aberdeen course, which stated that the M-9 would work perfectly using the firing tables developed there, were obviously untrue.

Soon a visiting inspection by a member of the design team did some detective work. Apparently the Army had provided tables for three-inch guns; the M-9 used a 90mm gun, which was somewhat different in diameter, but was deemed "close enough for aircraft work." The difference was that a 3" gun was 76.2 mm—quite an important difference, it was later discovered.

In August 1944, M-9's shot down eighty-nine of ninety-one V-1's launched from Antwerp. Not quite 100 percent.

But with corrected firing tables, this changed. The last day that Nazis launched V-1's, a hundred swept through the sky, at six hundred miles an hour, toward London.

A hundred were shot down by the M-9's.

After that the Germans didn't bother any more.

They had something worse.

Once we were experienced in handling buzz bombs, the Germans had V-2 rockets ready. When they started sending the V-2's nobody knew what they were. All of a sudden there was a huge explosion. Everything would shake. The building would fall down and there'd be a hole in the ground and debris in the air. A news photographer was shocked to see a rocket in the center of his developed photograph. That's how they found out what they looked like. They were too fast to be seen by the naked eye. So now they were looking for rocket launchers on the mainland most of time.

Looking at the grainy newspaper picture of the huge-finned rocket as it plunged into the London building, Sam was cast into darkness. These were the rockets he had seen with Hadntz. His own lack of faith in Hadntz's project had, perhaps, allowed this to happen. He should have been pushing, trying to figure out how to take it to the next step, never letting up.

The V-2's rained down on London, retaliation for the bombing raids that killed hundreds of thousands of German civilians. England and Europe were turning into a wasteland of rubble, a howling firestorm of released rage, out of control, with no discernable end.

British Intelligence once again grilled him, trying to pinpoint the launch sites. They were like giant ski jumps, usually concealed with brush so they could not be seen from the air.

Suddenly, the Allies had a new problem. Although the Army newspaper, *Yank*, daily warned of the German army buildup in the Ardennes, Allied command assumed that the terrain was too forbidding for a major attack to take place, and was caught completely by surprise when without warning, without even the barest hint of radio chatter, German forces poured down the center of France. The Germans, having realized that their communications were compromised, had switched to delivering oral commands.

German strategy, materiel, and the skill of their soldiers were all that Europe had learned to fear over the last several years of darkness. Allied troops were slaughtered in the snowy fields of France and Germany. Air support during those cloud-covered days was limited; the ground troops were on their own. Combat troops were held back as reserves. Hastily drafted cooks, bakers, band members, and all manner of non-combat personnel were thrown in as shock troops and front-line warriors.

Company C received orders to ship out in late December. Their destination was the French port of Le Havre, and then Camp Lucky Strike.

Sam and Wink devoted special skill to packing the components they had used to create the device. Sam kept the microfilm in a zipped inner pocket of his shirt at all times. Wink confiscated a typewriter and madly retyped the paper, with two carbons, cursing over the footnotes and his frequent mistakes while Sam redid the drawings on tracing paper and had them blueprinted.

Sam packed the device itself into his duffel, wrapped in some underwear. It still showed no sign of any kind of function. They decided that they had done something wrong, and determined to try again as soon as they had an opportunity.

And then, they waited.

⫴ 16 ⫴

France

January 1945

A FTER THE CROSS-CHANNEL invasion occurred on June 6, 1944, our mission in England started being reduced as troops moved forward through France. Within six months we were out of a job in England. In early January of '45 we loaded all our goods and battle equipment onto heavy four-wheel trailers, originally for 240mm ammo, which we used for our tools, heavy milling machines, punch presses, and stamping machines—everything we'd need to set up shop to supply troops on the continent. We also loaded up tanks and high-speed cats.

We took 400 command cars out of the motor pool. These were normally for officer use and were occupied by a driver in front, and sometimes three or four officers, but they were usually used for one. We had about 900 people so we put everybody in trucks and jeeps and command cars and took off for Portsmouth, England.

Our first night was spent in the Channel on a Navy LST headed for Le Havre. It was an overnight trip. We got the best food we had in England on that LST, just normal Navy rations.

When we landed at Le Havre, we drove off across a floating dock onto land. There was an MP waving everyone to the right-hand side of road. All of us were used to driving on the left-hand side in England; we didn't have any idea which side they used in France.

We drove from Le Havre about twenty miles out in the country to a big tent city, Camp Lucky Strike, a transit camp. It was the middle of January, and cold. Our assigned town was Muchengladbach, in Germany, and they kept us in Camp Lucky Strike until near the time when our town was to be taken.

Although it was six months after D-Day, nearby St. Lo was still occupied by a small group of Nazis. It was in our neighborhood but our troops passed it by; it was decided that St. Lo was not important enough to root out. While waiting at Camp Lucky Strike we kept our distance but visited a couple of country inns in the area and were able to get pretty fair wine and found out that French beer was not only warm like the Brits' but watery with very little flavor—no taste; good for nothing but chaser.

"Just like the good old days," said Wink, as a cloud of soot settled over them in their pyramidal tent, where Earl T., The Mess, and a few others lay on their cots, reading, writing letters, and sleeping. Rain, sleet, and snow were unrelenting.

The ordnance needed for occupation once the Allies crossed the Rhine was ready to go. But there was, presently, no clear route to Germany. The men lived in increasing apprehension of being sent to the nearby Bulge front, where there was scant chance of living more than a week or so under the joint onslaught of the Germans and the harsh winter weather. If the Germans got to the coast, France would be split into two fronts, and access to the Rhine would be further delayed.

Then Boots and Zenzer and Wilson, men who had been with the company since Camp Sutton, were called. In a unit that had been together for several years, their absence was felt. They heard that Zenzer died in a few days, Boots got a million-dollar wound, which is to say his right arm was blown off, and was sent back to England. They never heard what happened to Wilson. It was being called the Battle of the Bulge.

The war that was going to be over next week might last forever. Casualties were horrific. And hanging over it all was the threat of ever-new weaponry—above all else, an atomic bomb. The V-2 was bad enough, and the Germans were using it to great advantage in Antwerp. If what Hadntz had said about the German's head start, Sam thought that an atomic warhead for the V-2 couldn't be far behind.

But most people knew nothing of atomic research. They knew only that captured German soldiers still boasted of the Wonder Weapon that would soon end the war in their favor. Whatever it was, Hitler would soon have it operational. After the V-2 rockets, which were technological marvels, almost anything seemed possible.

No, the war wasn't over yet.

A few weeks into January of '45 they got orders to head out, just hours behind the troops that were at that very moment finally breaking through German lines.

There was still some fighting going on when we moved up the road to Germany on the ancient invasion route through France, Belgium, and the corner of Holland to Muchengladbach. We passed masses of German prisoners being marched toward Le Havre.

We had hundreds of command cars, and soldiers were saluting like mad and wondering where the 900 officers came from. Nights, we stopped along the road. There was no comfortable place to sleep. We tried the canvas on top of the command cars. You'd droop over each side. That gets painful. We slept in the fields on frozen dirt; took turns sleeping on the car seats.

The elaborate caravan had been jouncing through destroyed villages in France for eighteen hours, making slow progress. It was well after dark. Snow, at first a subtle pixilation in their headlights, was suddenly all-enveloping. The car in front of them veered right and stopped. Wink followed him into the snowdrift.

"We live and breathe as one," observed Wink. "Forever and ever, amen."

"Just so long as I continue to live and breathe," said Sam. "Are we supposed to sit here all night? I'd rather drive."

After fifteen minutes they concluded that indeed they were to sit there the rest of the night. "I'm going to take a look around," said Wink, and soon returned. "We're in luck."

The inhabitants of a nearby farmhouse were gone. They'd left behind nothing of value, but on the stone floor was a heavy wooden table. No fuel in the stove, but Sam ventured out and pried some planks from a destroyed outbuilding.

"Hot C-rations, that's what I like. Living like a king." Wink, ensconced on a ragged hassock, drank brandy from his tin cup. "Whoo-hoo! Warms you right up."

Damage to the age-darkened beams overhead was revealed only occasionally as the fire flickered. Sam was brewing ersatz coffee—roasted acorns was his guess—when the door burst open. Wind and snow rushed in. Wink jumped for his never-used rifle.

"I'm an officer, bud." And indeed, the figure wore an Army jacket, Army fatigues, Army boots, and spoke with an accent somewhat reminiscent of Michigan's Upper Peninsula—and in a voice undeniably a woman's.

"Damn, it's cold," she said. She pulled off her gloves, flung them on the table, and stamped snow from her boots. "Give me some of that brandy. I'm glad you finally stopped. I've been chasing you all day. You pulled out of Lucky Strike ahead of schedule."

"We're making up for gained time," said Wink, handing her the requested brandy in a cracked teacup.

Sam said, "Chasing us? What are you talking about?"

Her blond hair fell in wet dark waves around her face as she yanked off her woolen hat. "Bette Elegante. OSS. I'm here to debrief Sam Dance. Hello, Dance." She held out her hand, and Sam shook it.

"I've seen you before," said Sam. She had been there when the men in suits questioned him in Washington, the morning after Hadntz had passed him the plans. She had made them warrant officers, like a distant queen knighting them.

She had agreed to send Sam to France.

"You're the one who called when we were at that place in England," said Wink. "How the hell did you find us?" A gust of wind rushed in through the pantry and their candle flickered.

"Radar. Of a sort."

Sam was shocked. Hadntz had claimed to use radar as well.

"And why are you in the OSS?" asked Wink.

She shrugged. Wink offered her his hassock. She unzipped her jacket and sat down. "Why are you in the war? Same batch of reasons I guess. Got a cigarette?"

Sam took one from his shirt pocket and leaned over to light it for her.

Her face, in the candlelight, was that of a child. Pale and delicate, with an upturned nose. Wide blue eyes with dark, sooty lashes. Her mother, he learned later, had been a Russian immigrant with a deep ancestral hatred of the Germans. Bette's real name was Akalina, but she had changed it when she was twelve and somehow made it stick. She spoke Russian, and she had a decided bent for technology. Her father was a chemist and she the sixth and last child in a sea of brothers. Like Sam, her college education had been interrupted by the war. Unlike him, she'd had a "bloody hard time" getting the courses she needed for her degree.

"Look," she said, "it's not that mysterious. It's in your dog tags, Dance. If all else fails. But right now, luckily for me, it's just in your orders, pure and simple. You're where you're supposed to be, more or less. I just used this to find the exact place."

She leaned over and took a steel case from the outside pocket of her pack. It was five by five inches, three inches deep, with a tracking screen on one side. She handed it to him. "Turn it on," she said. The knob clicked as he turned it clockwise. A single pale green dot lit the screen. "See? You have coincided with yourself."

"Makes me feel a little bit too important."

"I wouldn't throw your dog tags away if I were you. Really, it's for your own safety."

"Right."

"For instance, if you get stuck inside of Germany. For instance, in that slave labor camp you went to with Dr. Hadntz."

"I didn't wear my dog tags. I guess someone decided that they might take them as a sign that I was an American soldier."

"You were tagged, nevertheless. We could have gotten you out, if we had to. If we had wanted to."

"Before I revealed valuable war secrets under torture," said Sam wryly.

Wink looked back and forth between them. "Somebody tell me what's going on."

"We can give you one of these too, Winklemeyer, if you're jealous."

"I'm not jealous. I'm afraid. This is a free man's nightmare."

"None of us are free any more."

Wink snorted. "What the hell are we fighting for then?"

Bette leaned forward. Her face was no longer childlike. "You call this *fighting*? I'll tell you what fighting is. My aunt is fighting on the Russian front right now. She's a tank commander. She has to control a herd of wild men who're ready to rape all the German women ten times over and burn their cities to the ground. They don't rest at night in cozy chateaus."

"Though I've heard they do drink a fair amount of whatever is handy." Wink poured himself another cup. "I'd say we're holding up our end in that regard."

Bette ignored him. "They're out sniping at the enemy, cutting their throats, never letting them rest. This war *means* something to them, soldier. If our side had five Pattons for generals instead of Eisenhowers, Bradleys, and Montgomerys, we wouldn't have lost twenty thousand soldiers in the past two months."

"Twenty . . . *thousand*?" Sam's voice caught.

"Maybe they should make you a general," Wink said.

Bette's glare was brief, but murderous. "I don't see why not. I could do a better job than the lot of them thrown into the stewpot and cooked into one." Then her smile was brilliant, again with that childlike innocence. "And speaking of stew, what's that delicious smell?"

Wink laughed. "Canned mystery meat."

"I've got baked beans," she said. "And chocolate, and a tin of Bordeaux sardines, and more wine than I can guzzle on my own." She rummaged through her pack and pulled out a parcel. "And a real surprise," she said. White paper crackled as she laid the parcel open. She frowned. "Looks like some kind of cheese."

"Covered in ashes," observed Wink.

Sam sliced off the end, tasted it, and found it enchanting. He made a face. "Terrible stuff. Just awful. Don't worry, I'll take care of it myself."

Wink and Bette would have none of that.

Their feast concluded with hard biscuits from Sam's rations. Bette turned out to be a serious jazz buff—not unusual, but it gave them some common ground. She was amazed that they had seen Diz and Bird. "They're legends," she said. "But I still have no idea what bebop actually is. No records. I've been out of the country since 'forty."

"Since before the war started," observed Wink.

"It might seem that way to you," she said.

By the time they bunked down, wrapped in bedrolls on the floor by the stove, they had been singing for an hour, gloriously loud, and swapping stories about Fifty-second Street clubs.

They were awakened rudely the next morning when a soldier burst in the door. "Fun's over! Time to roll!"

Bette threw off her blankets and jumped to her feet. Grabbing her boots, she began to pull them on, leaning against the wall.

"No Frogs," he said, but looked at Sam and Wink with envy. "Some people have all the luck. Not only do I have to sleep under a truck, but—"

"You'll salute when you address me," Bette said, stuffing her hair beneath her hat and throwing belongings into her pack. "I outrank you."

She rejected their prized command car, pulling a private out of another and ordering him to take it and follow the bullet-riddled Duesenberg she'd been driving. It took them ten minutes to get the snow off of it.

"You'll have to drive," Bette told Wink.

They pulled into the slow-moving line of command cars. Blackened by fire and shattered by mortar shells, the buildings cast no shadows on this gray, overcast morning. The freezing air was tinged with the sour smell of old fires, burning diesel, and dampness. Out in the countryside, bare trees flailed, buffeted by wind.

Bette lit a Chesterfield and retrieved a small stenography machine from her pack. She settled into her corner of the car. "Okay, I need to ask you a lot of questions."

"I'm not supposed to tell anyone about this."

"Winklemeyer has been cleared."

"How do I know?"

She pulled her valise onto her lap, ruffled through papers, and took out an order, which she showed him.

"You will understand through my questions that I am entirely acquainted with this entire mission from the time it was conceived. I know Hadntz."

After a few halting sentences, Sam moved into reverie, and the ravaged French countryside receded. The low promptings of Bette's voice were like the crows in the trees, flying into the gray skies of memory and bidding him to follow with his own inner vision, pulling his mind as if it were a kite on a string.

He recalled the medieval village, stone and half-timbered walls, cobbled streets, and the countryside they passed into, still bare and winter-brown, with unmelted snow on the hilltops. Women and boys were in the fields, plowing. Some waved as their truck passed. Cresting a hill, he saw a compound of low buildings surrounded by fences. Hadntz handed the guard their papers and they were found sufficient. The guard directed them to a small, neat cottage on the side of an assembly field.

Hadntz's black hair was now blond, braided and wrapped round her head in a coronet. She held her head high as she stood next to him. Sam passed for German: he was. But he was merely the driver, she the imperious commander, and so his speech requirements were limited. She had furnished him with a driver's uniform and a Glock, which gave him little comfort, surrounded as he was by men with rifles and machine guns in addition to their sidearms.

He followed her up the stairs carrying a crate of French brandy which he set in front of the kommandant's desk. He had to return to the truck for the fur coat and the fine cigars. With a nod, the kommandant accepted them and ordered one of the guards to take them to Haus #4.

Relatively small, it was nonetheless furnished comfortably—even lavishly. An obligatory oil portrait of the Fuehrer, whose image Sam had now seen in the kommandant's office and in several hallways, surveyed the room sternly. A crystal chandelier hung over the intricately carved dining room table. The room smelled of beeswax. Sam assumed that the woman dusting a display of fine china was a prisoner. She did not even glance at them as they passed through the room. A short hallway led to a bedroom. Their escort unlocked what looked like a closet door, and they stepped into an elevator, where five underground floors were registered on the arrow's arc.

"Five?" asked Bette. "Are you sure?"

"Yes."

"Did you see what was on the other floors?"

"No."

"And when you got out of the elevator?"

The concrete corridor of the fifth level down was utterly different from the faux-homey one through which they had accessed the elevator. The air was fresh and cool, piped in through vents in the ceiling.

They passed two telephones set in the wall, a water cooler, an office in which three professionally dressed women and one man in a business suit tended typewriters and file cabinets. Sam glanced inside an open door. Inside, two men were on their knees, working on a diesel generator.

Then they were walking alongside a block-long glass window. On the other side of the glass an enormous room housed men and women standing at long tables. The women's hair was bound up in white scarves. Men and women alike wore identical gray jumpsuits. They worked quickly and under heavy guard, their faces blank, assembling some kind of electronic component, twisting wires with pliers.

The glass room had been built inside a huge tunnel. He could see through the room, which he assumed had been built to protect delicate electronics, to the bare rocks of the tunnel beyond, and had to force himself to keep his own face expressionless. The whole thing seemed like a dream.

On a long wooden skid, a gigantic rocket was being assembled by a group of skeletal men. Some were ascending ladders; others lit the cave with brief flares from blowtorches. And in that light he saw a terrible thing: three men and two women hanging by their necks from a crane, their faces, in death, black, their bodies a background to what looked like ceaseless labor in the service of a war others had perpetrated, sweeping the entire world before it, crushing them in the physical manifestation of beliefs that were, in themselves, invisible as any thought, any religion, any emotion.

Sam was sure that their escort did not notice, as he opened the door for them, the anguish suffusing Hadntz's face for just a second. Even she seemed stunned at the vastness of this enterprise. Her expression echoed the hopelessness of the skull-like faces bent over their work. It all washed through him as if he were one of the hapless, naked humans falling from the ark of the world into the mouth of a volcano. The air inside was cool, clean, and scentless. No one spoke; the only sounds were those of the setting down of one tool for another, the occasional clatter of a search for the right bolt or wire to be plucked from the trays next to each worker.

He was startled when Bette offered him a clean white handkerchief. He had not realized that he had tears on his face. Wink stared grimly forward, and they were stopped in another squalid, bombed village. Starving children crowded around the closed windows of the car.

"Are you able to continue?" she asked, and followed this with technical questions about what he recalled concerning the work of the prisoners.

He returned to the room.

He and Hadntz had walked up and down the lines until they came to one old man with a straight spine and a nearly fleshless face which nevertheless held the vestiges of laugh lines. He was bald and wore no scarf; on one arm was tattooed a number, and his eyes were such a dark brown that they looked midnight-black, like Hadntz's.

Hadntz pointed to him and the escort signaled to one of the guards. The man was taken to the side of the room.

She was allowed to choose five others. They were all relatively elderly, except for one teenaged girl who could not maintain an impassive face. She blinked rapidly when she met Hadntz's eyes, then quickly looked down at her hands, which had not stopped moving in their assembly of weapons.

"After we left she talked about herd animals."

"Herd animals?"

"Yes. The refugees were in the back. She seemed determined not to talk about them, as if I might be a spy too."

As Sam and Hadntz passed through the gate he gripped the steering wheel tightly to keep his hands from trembling. She had seemed quite composed; he could no longer tell what her emotions might be. "Keep going," she said. "Then turn right as soon as we pass through the village."

In the rearview mirror, he saw that the prisoners were standing, holding on to the wood slats surrounding the truck bed. The girl took off her scarf and sat on one of the bales of hay in the back of the truck. Her dark hair tendrilled in the wind; her face was turned toward the sky. The cab of the truck smelled like hay, which was scattered on the floor as if tracked in by someone who used the truck to feed cows, and old cigarette smoke. Hadntz took a few deep breaths and turned her head briefly to glance through the rear window.

Sam said, "Who—"

"Quiet."

After a few minutes, she said, in a strangely normal voice, "I have been thinking a lot about herd animals."

"Herd animals?" He was so stunned by his recent glimpse of hell that he just fell into her conversation, unable to formulate the questions he needed to ask.

She was looking out her window, her face turned away from him. Maybe she was just casting around for some way to deal with the enormity of what they'd just seen.

"There are so many of them. Flocks, herds, schools. Among groups of mammals, there is supremacy. The wolf pack. A herd of horses. The leader of a herd of elephants is always a female. The village elects a mayor. The Indians have a chief."

"The Germans have a Fuehrer."

"Yes." Her voice now sounded muffled as if by a cold. "And it seems to me that they are following him without thought. He is to them as the leader is to a wolf pack, the stallion to the herd. The Russians do not feel the same way about Stalin, but they have less choice. The Germans have accepted Hitler completely. Each new, slightly more outrageous direction is embraced. It comes from Him. It must be Good. He has replaced God in their minds—infallible, all-knowing. Very necessary. Vital to them. As if they were just waiting for him to come along. He has created in them a very strong sense of identity, one in which those who do not agree with it are afraid to challenge."

"Did you know what we would see there?"

She looked at him directly. Her eyes were red; she had been weeping. "Yes. I have seen other places like this as well. It is happening all over Poland, Germany, Czechoslovakia. And worse. Why? How can people treat one another this way? What I am thinking about is how to remove or change this human propensity. What if we could somehow change this urge to be like all the others and to follow a leader blindly?"

"The results might be chaotic."

"Oh, of course!" Suddenly, she was screaming, face twisted, eyes blazing. "That would be so much worse than what we have now! I could only rescue these six from death and it has taken me a year to do so! Six people from thousands, brutally murdered by the pack at the direction of the master! They are forced to make instruments of death until they die of exhaustion and starvation, forced to do so by those who are pleasing their master—and keeping themselves from the same fate."

"But—your device. Can't you—"

"It is not working," she said, flatly. "Or . . . it does not work as I thought it might. At times, everything closes. Rolls up."

"What do you mean?"

She sighed. "There are dimensions . . . it has to do with resonance, with the vibrational qualities of subatomic particles. The same numbers I have given you, the same ideas, expressed mathematically. I have made them as simple as possible, reduced them as much as I have been able to, at this point. It has to do with how life itself took shape, the physics and the chemistry of cells themselves, as pure matter." She smiled slightly. "That is, in theory. In practice, the experiences I've had using the technology based on my theories have . . . given me a perspective that frightens me."

"I still have no idea how it might work," he said. "Or even, really, what it might do. I only hoped that, by now—"

There was anguish in her voice; in her clenched fists. "You are right. Of course you are right. I should have been able to do more. I am still working on it. Have been working on it. It is just hard to know *what to do first.* There is too much to do; too many terrible things to deal with." Then she seemed to quite deliberately unclench her fists, splayed her fingers in and out as a pianist might, and finally rested her hands in her lap. "It is why I have been thinking about herd animals."

"How would you change this herd propensity?" He spoke in a very calm tone of voice, one he might use with an upset child.

"Genetically." Her voice shook, but soon became even. "All the secrets of being and of behavior are locked within us. We are not simply apes with bigger brains, and even apes are not simple. Nothing is simple. The actions we take are determined from within. You really need to read Darwin. We breed animals to isolate certain characteristics. I want to understand the roots of our own characteristics."

"Turn the world into your breeding pen? Isn't that what Hitler is trying to do?"

She said heatedly, "My way would not involve murder. Instead of unlocking the secrets of matter to cause world-ending weapons, why not try to figure out why we do certain things, and how we might change that? How can we cure our own stupidity? It would be more satisfying to me than holding the power of a million suns in my hand."

"Are you the one who wanted me to come here? Was this your idea?"

"Yes. I made a deal with the British to get you here. This is something that you needed to see. This is what is really happening. This is what we are fighting. This is what *you* are fighting."

"But I'm not sure—"

Unexpectedly, she reached over and patted his arm. "I know. My device seems outlandish, impossible."

"I mean, I'm not even sure what it's supposed to do."

"Read the papers again. It's all there."

"But there are all kinds of unproven assertions, such as the function and structure of DNA, to begin with."

"They are true, though. Remember? I included several papers that show the latest discoveries."

"I need to get some of them translated," he admitted. "I'm not even sure in what language some of them are written. But still, how do you use that information, even if it's true?"

"Someday I hope to be able to teach you. When there is more time. Or you can begin at the beginning yourself, as I did, and prove it for yourself."

They did not return the way they had come. She had several sets of papers and passes, and stiffened every time they encountered another vehicle. Once, on a remote part of the road, she had him stop and sent him back to the passengers with a loaf of bread, urging him to be quick, just toss it in. A cold wind bit at his face. The passengers were huddled together on the floor of the cab, covered by straw. The girl nodded as she reached out a thin hand and took the loaf. The sky had thickened with gray clouds; he smelled snow in the air and he jumped back into the cab.

At dusk, they drove through a small town where evening lights glowed, illuminating the inhabitants of houses. Then the remote road was lined by a dense pine forest.

"They must be getting cold," he said.

"I cannot risk seeming to treat them well if we are stopped. There must be no suspicion."

"We're out in the woods. Don't you think—"

"Turn . . . here."

"Where?"

"Stop. Back up. There."

He had not even noticed the narrow track through the pines.

It was pitch-black now. She reluctantly allowed him to turn on his slit-covered headlights. Snow began to fall, and around them the tall pines whipped back and forth in the wind. "Keep going," she urged, when he suggested setting up a camp for the night. "It's not much farther." After half an hour they came to a cottage in a clearing.

"Come, come," she said, helping them jump down from the truck. The girl fell and Hadntz helped her up; embraced her. The girl began to cry. They hugged while the others made their way to the front door, which was open, holding their rags around them tightly.

The cottage was unused and dusty, smelling of the pine wood of which it was built. Sam lit candles and started a fire as the rescued people talked and laughed and wept. He assumed they were speaking Romany; it was the musical language he'd heard in London. One of the crates in the truck held a feast: a ham, bread, and wine, although Hadntz would not let them eat much. They had been starved and must recover slowly. She instructed Sam to boil water over the fire in a pot hung from an iron arm, into which he shredded ham. After the cut-up potatoes were cooked in the same water, he smashed it all together into a gruel.

The crate also held a fiddle. The old man picked up the instrument and sat on a stool by the firelight.

He began to tune the violin, but rested it on his lap frequently. By now the others lay near the fire on pallets which Sam had assembled from quilts in the crate, and all seemed asleep. Hadntz tried gently to take the violin and urged him to a place on the floor, but he shook his head violently and continued to tune.

When he was finally satisfied, he drew poignant harmonies from the instrument with the sweep of his bow. His face was impassive, but his tears flowed freely and glimmered in the firelight. Sleet beat against the roof. Sam went to the place in his being where Keenan now lived.

By the time they were finished, Bette had recorded many details: the number of prisoners in that room, the presumed population of the barracks above, the thickness of the walls, the number and placement of guards, the location of the camp, the town that flanked it. He had already given much of this information to the British, so he assumed they had not shared it with the Americans. Also, they had not asked nearly as many questions about what Hadntz had said.

"How did she get the requisition to remove the workers?" asked Bette.

"I don't know. We spent several days going to various German offices in Paris. She's resourceful."

Wink's comment from the front seat was a hearty snort. Sam couldn't put into words what he felt: that Hadntz was the soul of Europe, an amalgam of nationalities, intellect, culture. She absorbed the tribalism, the darkness, the deep enmities and purified all of it, circulating it through some deep, clear, groundwater of being.

He told Major Elegante about their similar trip to the V-2 plant at a camp named Dora, near Nordhausen, where workers were dwarfed by the massive rockets, as he had told the British, but there were things he did not tell her.

He did not tell her that Hadntz was thinking of her device now as something more organic and less mechanical, more invasive and intimate and less of the exterior world. He did not tell her Hadntz's speculations about the quantum aspects of consciousness, which took her a good hour, during which the mountains became increasingly shadowed by gathering storm clouds and wind buffeted the truck and those in back dropped out of sight of his mirror to huddle on the floor, but that was mainly because he wasn't sure he understood enough about it to repeat it.

He did not hand over the new microfilm she'd given him, and denied that he had any such thing.

He did not tell her that Hadntz had exacted from him a promise to dedicate lifelong efforts toward her goal, and that he knew that she had shown him the factory simply to impress upon him the necessity, although Keenan's death had already provided that. He therefore did not tell Elegante that he had been warned that this would most likely entail uncertainty and sacrifice unforeseeable at this point in time, and that he had still committed himself. He couldn't tell her that Hadntz's vision of humanity's possible future made him ring with real, yet unhearable harmonies, because that seemed terribly fanciful, utterly private, and difficult to articulate.

He did not realize for two decades that Elegante already knew this, possibly more fully than he did, before they ever met. And she did not tell him, either, at this point.

In the end, perhaps, it did not matter about the microfilm. When he and Wink denied knowledge of the device, she went through their duffel bags until she found it, tossed Sam's underwear back in the bag, and put the device—what Wink had taken to calling "The Cow Pie at the Center of Time"—into her pack.

Sam and Wink looked at each other. There was nothing else they could do.

She found the written plans amid his composition books, and took them as well. There was no company magician here to intervene. She paged through the other composition books for a few moments, reading bits of his narratives, raising her eyebrows from time to time, then returned the books to Sam's bag.

It was dusk. They were still amid ruined farmland. Bette let them out, took the wheel, and drove away, passing the line of command cars with a spatter of mud.

The soldier behind them relinquished their command car. "What was that all about?" he asked.

"Top-secret," said Wink.

"Right," said the soldier over his shoulder, sarcastically, as he walked down the slick road toward his original jeep.

Sam and Wink shoved their duffels into the back. Wink said, "Your turn to drive."

There was no town or village in sight. They passed through snow-covered fields. Occasionally the legs of dead, bloated cows, or even dead soldiers, were visible by the side of the road. Low ridges became purple in the distance and then it was dark.

"So," said Wink. "The OSS is involved."

"I guess. She's been on to us all along. She was there when the suits asked me about it in D.C."

"Apparently the British have an interest in it as well. They sent you to Germany, right?"

"Yes. But with the OSS's cooperation. I think that the Brits were more interested in the V-2 information, and with possible radar disruption. Look, I'm sorry I didn't tell you more. I didn't even tell Elegante how . . . terrible it all was. There aren't any words."

Wink waved his hand. "That's all right. But if this is so important, maybe they could supply us with decent materials and a dedicated work space, to begin with."

"It could be that Elegante is the only one that takes this seriously."

"Maybe that's it. Maybe she doesn't want to call any more attention to it. To us. To it."

The caravan pulled off the road and halted. They got out and stretched.

Wink stood with his hands on his hips, surveying the freezing landscape. "Looks like another warm, cozy night in the snow."

Germany:
The Angels of Electricity

JANUARY 1945–AUGUST 1945

Yet, even here there were trees in blossom; a scent of lilac and hawthorn came in waves from the ownerless gardens. After all, it was spring.

—GREGOR DALLAS
1945: The War That Never Ended

Germany at War

WE WERE THREE DAYS on the road. The final day we drove into Maastricht, Holland, exactly in the corner of Holland, with one border Belgium and other being Germany. The mode of travel was to follow the guy in front. There was a jeep in front of every section, followed by a hundred trucks and a hundred command cars.

We spent all our time in Holland in Maastricht, stopped along the street; our caravan was out of sight in both directions. Drew a crowd of Dutch kids. All spoke English; they took several languages in school—French, German, Dutch, English, Flemish, and Walloon. All the kids had big rolls of bills; wads of Dutch guilders. They'd buy all the money we had, any kind of official money except scrip, for double the price or more. The Army'd gathered up all the dollars and pounds so we couldn't escape into the countryside, but everybody had a few bills held out in case something along the road looked worthwhile.

We sat there for three hours or so. I suppose somebody was trying to find out where to go.

The deep arbitrariness of life was brought home to Sam as they followed the retreating Germans up the Stuttgart Line, through villages strewn with corpses and rubble, the stench of fire and death, where troops had been fighting only hours earlier, finishing the Battle of the Bulge.

Had Sam been disposed to perfect vision instead of severe myopia, he would probably be one of those perished soldiers, like Keenan. He felt his brother's loss constantly, like a phantom limb. In his composition books he told Keenan small details which only he would find interesting, things he could not put into reassuring letters home. Keenan alone would understand why certain things were funny, or the profound loneliness of a crystalline winter night spent in a foreign, snowy field. His mother would not appreciate the details of life in the wake of years of war, where the price of a prostitute was a few cigarettes, where advancing American troops left behind glittering caches of empty wine bottles liberated from cellars.

After they crossed the German border, the caravan stopped once more. The men availed themselves of the break by relaxing in one of the hastily evacuated houses on the town's main street.

His mother might understand the sense of familiarity he felt in the bedroom of a member of the Hitler Youth, with its model airplanes, a poster of the Fuehrer on its wall instead of the one of Count Basie he'd taken from the Count's 1937 appearance at the Lakefront.

Downstairs, the office of Dr. Klein, the dentist who was the father of this boy, was filled with books in French, German, and English, including a copy of Sinclair Lewis's *Main Street*.

Earl T. found and displayed to all of them, with evident relish, a stash of letters from the Nazi Party congratulating Klein on his good standing, and photos of Klein and his family at swastika-bedecked rallies. "This could never happen in the U. S. of A.," said Earl T., sitting in Klein's office chair with the photos spread out on the floor around him. He sipped Klein's brandy thoughtfully, beneath Klein's undergraduate diploma from Oxford, where he had studied literature.

"Hmmm," said Sam.

One night in Tidworth barracks, Earl T. came stomping in, shortly after lights out, cursing and bitching and cursing more; dumped his overcoat by his bunk, grabbed toothpaste and toothbrush, and still cursing, grouching, and bitching attacked his teeth and tongue, brushing and cursing and brushing and stomping around, red as fire. Asked if something was bothering him, if there was something we could help him with, it took some time for him to get his mouth clean enough for approximate discourse. While taking good-byes with his Thursday date, Doris, she was imprudent enough to remark that Earl kissed just like Albert. Somewhat miffed at such a tender moment, Earl had asked, "Just who in the hell is Albert?"

"Why, he's the black boy I date on Saturdays."

Sam was about to try and needle Earl T. about the fact that the pilots in an all-black battalion had won some battles, to see what his reaction would be, but a soldier poked his head in the front door.

"Let's go!"

The long snake was on the move again. They were heading to the German town of München-Gladback. The British and American spelling of the name was Muchengladbach.

In Muchengladbach, our destination, we ran out of daylight. When we got there nobody knew where we were going, though we found our way downtown and to the headquarters of Third Army in the City Building.

Muchengladbach was on the west side of the Rhine, which would not be taken for more than a month, so there were German troops about six miles away holding both sides of the river. We used blackout lights. You'd get a tiny amount of light on the road ahead; you could drive about two MPH safely. We just followed the guy in front. Most of the streets were heaps of bricks. A 'dozer had come through, scraping an open lane in some streets.

There was an MP on the street corner yelling, "Turn off the lights! We're under artillery range here!" So we'd turn off the lights. Halfway around the block another guy would yell, "Turn on your lights!" We had to stop at intersections to wait for a break in our own convoy and we did that for an hour until the brain in the jeep that started all this realized he was following the end of his own convoy, and that the head of the convoy was lost.

If you've never been in the Army, this all sounds pretty fantastic. If you have been in the Army, you'll understand. The troops even have a name for it: SNAFU, meaning, "situation normal, all fucked up." If it had taken until daylight, it might rise to the next level: TARFU. Meaning, "things are *really* fucked up." If it led to an extraordinary event, say a full-blown German artillery attack on Army headquarters, even the Army might declare that an event of FUBAR proportions had been achieved, meaning, "fucked up beyond all recognition."

A soon as it was light, somebody decided they knew where we were going— to a block of four- and five-story apartment buildings on Neusser Strasse. The residents had been chased out to make room for us.

I'd been driving since six A.M. the morning before with a break in Maastricht. We were pretty well pooped out. A truck loaded with Army cots pulled up. We each carried one inside, chose a room, and I was out like a light.

After ten minutes or so of sound sleep, an artillery shell hit the house across the street. We ran to the window and saw dirt falling back into hole, looked at each other, and went back to sleep. That was our intro to Muchengladbach.

The ground shook with the nearby impact of heavy shells; tanks roared past their windows; machine guns chattered occasionally; and all was woven into Sam's dreams, which were of destruction, and fires, and seeing Berlin from the air, knowing that people below were being burned to death.

He woke in a sweat, and found that the other cots were empty.

Downstairs, Wink was amassing a collection of culinary riches—bread, tinned meat, various liquors, and a few potatoes. He and the others then combined them with their too-well-known rations to make a rather fine meal.

Filing into the kitchen for dinner, they saw one of the tenants of the building, who retained one small room on the third floor for herself and her two boys. She pushed past them but did not look at them.

Grease, the Perham Down's esteemed bass player said, "She doesn't seem very happy to be liberated."

"Terrible story," said Wink. "Her husband was stationed here. She convinced him to surrender to the Americans. He was standing on the front porch, in full uniform, waving a white flag, when the tanks came through. Machine gun fire cut him in half."

"Imagine someone stupid enough to surrender to a tank," The Mess commented as they ate.

Those were the only words spoken at dinner, and the only sounds were those of forks hitting metal mess kits, and a constant undertone of explosions from, perhaps, nearby Düsseldorf.

The 610th settled in quickly, an isolated island of American technicians amid British forces fighting their way east. Stationed in the swirling cauldron of advancing and retreating forces as the Third Reich finally and slowly collapsed, Sam, Wink, and the other ordnance technicians were pressed into KP duty in support of the troops passing through town. But Elegante's interrogation—the mere fact of it, and her confiscation of the device—strengthened Sam's resolve to begin building another as soon as possible.

The Allies presumed that Hitler was in Bavaria, commanding from a hidden mountain redoubt, and that new and fierce resistance was in the offing.

West of the Rhine, though, "liberation" commenced, in grand style. Liberating was not confined to the prisoners in the local slave labor camp. It also applied to the property of the Germans, who had melted away as the Allies approached. Using handcarts, baby carriages, and toy wagons they took all they could carry, abandoned their houses—many of them destroyed—and fled east. Most remaining Germans hid in basements and bomb shelters, uncertain of the disposition of the Amis, the Americans. Most of their factories, which they had kept running up to the very last minute, were also deserted, save for a few in which Germans remained, surrendered, and stayed on as operators in return for food.

Though Muchengladbach had been deserted by the German Army, the thunder of big guns and frequent overflights by British, German, and American planes kept the war very much present. The Germans fought with all they had left—by many accounts not much, but they still made a fearsome display of force, and killed thousands of men—to keep the eastern bank of the Rhine. Germans surrendered en masse, and were marched to a nearby slave labor camp and guarded indifferently. Any who wanted to head for home could easily do so. Most stayed, for food and the chance to stop fighting what was clearly a losing war.

Muchengladbach, as well as Düsseldorf and Dortmund, which all lay directly on the invasion path, had been targeted for greater than fifty percent destruction. The

Allies had done a fair job of accomplishing this degree of damage. Muchenglad-bach was left without telephones and gas. Most streets were impassable, piled with bricks and rubble. Getting the power plant up and running was the first order of business. Sam and Wink were put on that detail.

American soldiers augmented their billets with carpets, kitchenware, furniture, and candles from the ruins of the apartment buildings around them, and the tech-nicians on Neusser Strasse were no different. But when a new guy, Zieberhost, was added to their unit, they found that he didn't understand protocol when he ac-quired a clock by poking a gun in the stomach of an old German man and demand-ing the finely carved clock on his mantel. Grease had been with him, but had been too afraid of what Zieberhost might do to try and stop him.

They liberated. Zieberhost robbed.

They kept a close eye on him after that, and dubbed him "Wild Card Zee." He didn't have the least idea why.

Surrendering German soldiers did not dare be taken with a weapon, for fear its possession might be mistaken for intent to fire, so there were stacks of weapons everywhere. Sam, playing cards with Wink, Grease, and Howie one night during the first week in their new parlor, watched Wild Card Zee stagger past with three ma-chine guns and struggle up the stairs. He'd taken over an upper room in which to dismantle, clean, and ship them home in pieces, to be reassembled later and used for aggressive defense purposes.

"Zee's a nut," said Grease, surveying his cards.

Howie, the book collector who gave Sam his intro to the theatrical warehouse in London, had turned his interest toward fancy hunting rifles, antique pistols, and ceremonial swords. "True. He wants to kill people. I'm building a nest egg."

Wink said, "I'm sure my future wife, bless her heart whoever she may be, will wish I had been that forward-looking. Gin. You really need to pay more attention." He swept three silver forks and one cake knife into his growing pile. "Your silver set is not going to be very complete, guys."

At a knock on the door, Wink drew his gun, got up, and opened it a crack. The town still harbored many German soldiers, some of them regular army, the Wehrmacht, who were eager to surrender. Others were ferocious SS, with their fear-some fight-to-the-death oath and culture.

Earl T. grabbed his pistol from the table next to him.

"He's okay," said Wink. "He's Russian. What say we serve him dinner."

They admitted Leonid, a bald human skeleton wearing rags and tied-together pieces of leather, which were the remains of a pair of boots. He staggered into the room, then crumpled sideways and lay motionless on the floor.

Earl T. cradled the Russian in one arm while passing a shot glass of brandy be-neath his nose. His bruised eyelids fluttered open.

"He has an unholy smell," observed Grease.

They sat him down and fed him broth from their feast; a little bread. His eyes brimmed with tears and his hands shook. Wink questioned him as he ate. "He's not a Jew. He said that all of the Jews were shot last week when the Germans knew that we were coming. They were in the process of being starved to death, but I guess it was taking too long."

No one spoke for a moment. The fire, made of wood pried from the shed behind the house, snapped in the stove. Overhead, Zee dropped something heavy and cursed. Wink resumed his questioning. After a few moments they nodded to one another, smiling.

"Long-lost brothers?" asked Earl T. He handed Leonid a cigarette and lit it for him.

"Better. He's a music professor from Moscow. Was drafted, lucky enough to be captured—"

"Yeah, he looks lucky," said Grease.

"And has spent most of the war working for the Germans. First he worked on a dairy farm and lived with a family. They weren't bad, he says. But for the past six months he's been making concrete submarines in a nearby plant."

"You understand him right?"

"The Germans are out of steel," said Wink, after a few more questions.

Sam added, "Radar won't see a concrete sub."

Leonid offered to cook for them until he was able to be on the move again. He wanted to return to Moscow, but was not certain that was a good thing to do. Wink explained, "He's heard that the Russians are treating former prisoners quite badly. Stalin figures that they must have surrendered too quickly. It seems, though, his commanders neglected to issue weapons for the particular battle in which Leo was captured. He had to fight with a scythe."

"I vote we try him out," said Sam. "Even a music professor is probably a better cook than any of us."

"Speak for yourself," said Wink, pretending to be offended. But it was agreed, all except for Zee, whom they did not need for a majority.

The main order of business was getting their shops set up. The deserted submarine factory a hundred feet from their garden gate was the perfect candidate.

The next morning, before dawn, Sam made himself some good, strong American instant coffee from a Red Cross package and sleepwalked Wink over to the submarine factory. Their footsteps crunched in the grit and dust from shelling. A woman walking past on the street, both hands in the pockets of a black overcoat, called out, hopefully, "Zig zig?"

Sex, the GI's had discovered, had become incredibly cheap. Sam shook his head. When they reached the front door, Wink mumbled something, dropped to the pavement, and leaned against the wall to finish his slumber.

Sam walked through the first floor. The weak light showed only indeterminate shapes of mammoth plant equipment, and the air was permeated by the smell of heavy oil.

Wink dragged himself through the door. Sunlight topped the building across the street and came through the windows full force, illuminating a mountain of metal reinforcement bars—rebars—at the far end of the building. Mike "Sunny" Sunmeyer, their new CO, had given them a week to clear it out.

Sam said, "Come see what I found yesterday."

Wink followed him upstairs, to a relatively clear, cavernous space. To one side was a large office with a heavy door.

Sam said, "Our new lab."

Wink brightened. "Smashing! We'll be back in business in no time."

They were back downstairs when a rebar clanged against the concrete floor. They drew their pistols. "Out!" said Wink.

About fifty feet away, a man rose slowly from behind a pile of rebar, his hands in the air. He said, "Pole."

"Take off your coat," commanded Wink. "No, don't pretend not to understand. Now!"

The prisoner jumped at Wink's sharp tone. Slowly, he eased off one sleeve, then the other, and let the coat drop to the floor. He was clad in a button-down shirt, fine wool slacks, and an unmarred leather belt.

"Too damned fat," said Wink. "I know him. He's a German."

"*Nein!* Pole!"

To Sam's astonishment, Wink shot over the man's head. The report reverberated in the plant. "Get over here, you frigging Nazi." As he began to shuffle toward them, Wink added, "And bring that coat. Turn it right side out."

"Stolen! I am Pole—"

"Cut the crap."

Sam had never seen Wink this way before. Wink herded the man out the door and down the stairs. Indeed, the coat, when right side out, was covered with German medals, and indeed, the man was somewhat corpulent, an impossibility for a Polish slave laborer.

Wink directed him to sit in back of the jeep. He kept his gun on the man, who now had a contemptuous look on his face.

Sam avoided piles of pushed-aside bricks as he passed shops emptied of every object—he knew they were empty because he had been in many of them and had seen the bare shelves. He pulled up in front of Company C's new office, which, handily, had been the office of an insurance company and came complete with desks and file cabinets.

"Get out," ordered Wink. He marched the German into the CO's office, where a clerk looked up, startled.

"Who's this?"

"Prisoner of war."

"Sunmeyer isn't in yet."

"Call him."

"No phones. We're working on getting field phones laid out. I'll take the information. I'm not sure what we'll do with him. Maybe the Brits should take him." He rummaged through a drawer, pulled out a form, and slapped it on a clipboard. In something that even Sam could recognize as terrible German, he began to ask questions.

"I do not speak to filthy Jews," said the man, and spat on the clerk, square in his face.

Wink hit the German on the head with his pistol butt. The prisoner collapsed on the floor. Blood flowed down his forehead.

The clerk wiped his face with his handkerchief. "Fucking Nazi."

They all stared down at the man, from whose head wound blood flowed steadily. He groaned.

Sunny opened the door and peered inside. "What's going on?"

They climbed back into their jeep. Sam put it in gear, but didn't start it. "I've never seen you act that way before."

Wink rubbed his face with both hands. "Maybe it was just for lack of opportunity, but I don't think so."

"Why not?"

"Maybe I'm nuts. It's unsettling—but it was very clear. I saw the good officer's obnoxious, smirking face before, and we were not in the factory. We were instead in a prisoner of war camp. Leonid's former home. I was actually there the other day, of course, disinfecting it for the German prisoners, so maybe I'm just remembering the general physical surroundings.

"Anyway, we were prisoners there. I had a whole set of memories about how the Germans pushed the British back and captured us the other night.

"So I'm in the exercise yard and on the other side of the fence, this guy, this exact same guy, I swear, is beating a Russian prisoner with his rifle butt. The Russian falls to the ground and the German just beats the hell out of him, then swings his rifle, smashes the Russian's head, and leaves him there. It was like . . . a new place in my mind."

"In other words, you're going crazy."

Wink nodded slowly. "Yeah, it certainly seems that way. Or maybe I just wasn't completely awake. What's the criteria for reality, anyway? It's damned hard to realize you're dreaming when you are dreaming. I mean, it is for me. Has this happened to you?"

Sam nodded. "Just . . . quick visions. I think that actually I've always had them—you know how you remember this or that, or imagine what might happen—but there's more . . . palpability to this. More . . . authority."

"Kind of frightening."

Sam nodded. "Indeed."

Upon arrival in Muchengladbach, we immediately began an endless round of chores: KP; dragging heavy, unwieldy rebar from the Weller submarine factory, loading them on trucks, and hauling them out to the country to be abandoned in some convenient field; guard duty (watching anything that someone would like to carry away or a place that someone would want to get into or get out of); and ash and trash (picking up garbage from the mess hall, trash from the various companies and work sites, and trucking it to the designated dump and unloading it).

Up to the previous week, the Weller submarine factory and the sub air-handling equipment factory next door depended on a retinue of slave labor. They occupied a stockade across Rheydt Strasse and traveled back and forth under guard. When Patton's troops came through the week before, the troops closed the two factories and released the slave laborers. Some of the laborers left town, and others moved to the city dump to live on the pickings.

So here I come with W. and a few other soldiers on our ash and trash mission having no notion of the new dump occupants.

As we back up to make our deposit the occupants move in on us, intent on first dibs on our succulent pickings. I am becoming very dubious about the developments, but without anything programmed to do about it.

We dump our cans and the occupants lunge at the garbage; an ancient crone comes up triumphant with a large piece of fresh-looking bread. A large lout a little slow on the approach but with overwhelming firepower knocks the crone ass-over-teakettle, in the process separating her from her booty; he retreats from the fray, stuffing his spoils in his mouth.

I am left with a decision. Do I point my gun at him? Arrest him? Turn him over to the authorities? What authorities? Shoot him? There is nothing in the guidebook telling me what to do.

In the end I do nothing—the same as everybody else. I am sure nobody had any intention of doing anything. Just look the other way and come back tomorrow and watch a similar performance.

At least I was spared the need to form a decision, or even a series of decisions.

This time I had little opportunity to review my options; next time I wouldn't have that excuse.

It's a dog-eat-dog world, but most of us don't get that close-up view.

Next: back to picking up and dumping rebars. Our route was east on Neusser Strasse out of town and toward the Rhine River. We were acutely aware that the Rhine was still in Nazi hands, our troops had not yet made the crossing, and the Rhine was only six miles from Muchengladbach; maybe three miles from where we dumped our bars. We dumped our load and someone said while we were this close we should drive up to the last hill and see what the battle site looked like. Yeah! See the war before it moves on!

We drove over the next hill, down the other side, and an American soldier jumped out of the bushes waving at us.

"Get the hell out of here!" he yelled. "You're drawing fire."

Sam was bone-weary when they dragged back to Neusser Strasse to an unexpected but wholly welcome scene.

Leonid was boiling a large kettle of water in the backyard for their baths. Rabbit stew, with carrots, potatoes, and onions, exuded a heavenly smelling steam from the kitchen. The table was set.

"This is *real butter*!" said Sam, after one taste of what he presumed was oleo.

"Impossible!" said The Mess. "How the hell did you get it?"

The butter vanished quickly.

Leonid was profusely admired. He smiled his first smile—tired, but genuine, and later that evening accepted a shirt from Grease. In the parlor, standing next to the stove, he removed layers of rags and threw them on the floor.

"Nothing but skin and bones," said Grease.

"What are those numbers on your arm?" asked Earl T., looking up from a solitaire hand he was dealing.

Wink translated. "He says the Germans liked to keep track. And I say, maybe they'll hang the bastards who did this." He got out his violin for Leonid to play after they'd cleaned up, but the Russian was dead asleep on the sofa.

Sam, though, did not get much sleep that night. In an empty bedroom upstairs, he got out his Hadntz notes and studied them. Her thoughts rang in his head, almost as if she were sitting next to him, speaking aloud in that wonderful, rich voice with the distinctive accent. She'd been seeing Leonid's world for years. This was her solution.

They needed parts, though. It was daunting to think of re-creating the whole setup, even if they had brought much of it with them from England. They were in an entirely new foraging situation, in a country completely destroyed.

But it had been a technological country. Surely they could find what they needed somewhere. They set up a lab on the second floor of the plant in anticipation.

⁘ 18 ⁘

The D & W Telephone Company

WHEN WE TOOK over the Weller Submarine Fabrique, my CO discovered that it was equipped with what turned out to be a twenty-four-line in-house telephone switchboard, with no feed from the MG system (*alles kaput*), and asked me if I could fix it. It provided in-factory phone service without going out to the city with each extension.

We were operating with an amalgam of field telephones, a twisted pair of wires in weatherproofing. When the Army moves, one of the techs gets a wheel of this wire and reels it off. You drag these wires over fences and rooftops and set up something like an old-fashioned switchboard, crank the magneto to generate power, plug in a manual connector, and get the operator, a soldier at a manual switchboard. The farther you get from the battery, the fainter the signal becomes. Our wire came all the way to Muchengladbach from Liège in Belgium so it took a lot of hollering to get anyone to understand you.

I took on W. as a partner. The system we were rehabbing in Muchenglad-bach had a central battery that provided power to each of the phones connected into it. So when we started putting it together the first thing we had to do was recharge glass telephone batteries. I assume they were kept charged off the city grid but we didn't have a city grid; there was no power at that time. This was very sensitive equipment, built to last forty years. Our battery shop was used to charging truck batteries; that was their main business. We lugged these batteries to the shop and explained that these were sensitive *telephone* batteries and that we had no backup. We instructed that they be put on a light charge and we'd pick them up in a couple of days.

He said he understood, so we went back to work on other phases of the phone business and an hour or so later had a message to pick up our batteries. What? We went to the shop and the guy says the batteries are ready, nothin' to it, just put them on a hot shot, they're ready to go. And they were, though we didn't have much hope for them. He didn't know what he was doing; we just lucked out.

We reinstalled the telephone batteries and threw the main switch. The switchboard sprang into action, giving me a small thrill, both because the batteries were not irreparably ruined and because the phone switchboard had life in it and responded to electric current. But was it damaged?

Step relays jumped into action. There, I already learned what a step relay was, by watching the initial action of the switchboard and applying a word that I had heard before in classes but had never seen demonstrated. I had a great advantage, which was that I knew nothing—had no preconceived ideas—about American telephones, much less German phones.

Other relays clicked, quite a bit of action for a few seconds, which slowed, and finally came to a complete stop. It just sat there, waiting. What next? It was all up to me. So—poke it and see what happens!

I picked up a telephone from the pile and plugged it into what looked like a matching outlet. Aha, it fit! The switchboard made a few encouraging clicks. I put the receiver to my ear (nothing mysterious here, it looked just like an American handset). After getting a dial tone (whatever a German dial tone might sound like, never in my life having heard one), I thought I might like to know how many numbers it would take to ring a number.

I dialed a number at random and got what I took to be a ring signal—only one dial to get a number? That couldn't be right! I kept trying more numbers, and with every try I got a ring signal. Then, at twenty-three—

"Hello."

"Who the hell is this?" I ask.

"Colonel Erbahr," he says. "Who the hell is this?"

Well, wasn't that an interesting answer. I spent the next minute extracting foot from mouth.

Early in the process we discovered an eighteen-phone setup next door in the submarine AC factory. Having no knowledge of how the Germans did it, I devised a system to connect the two systems together by using a cannibalized phone from the Weller system to hack into the AC factory panel, and a phone from the AC factory system to hack into the Weller panel.

Thus, we started the D & W Telephone Company.

The 610th had set up an office to hire qualified locals to further their mission. So it came to pass that one afternoon a German, Perler, was ushered into the presence of Sam and Wink, chief engineers of the Dance & Winklemyer Telephone Company.

Perler was of medium height, with a fine, pale complexion and faded blond hair. His small blue eyes were narrowed in disdain; his long fingers were well suited to fine electrical work. He appeared to be in his fifties.

The clerk said, "Maybe you can find a job for him. Supposedly he knows something about phones."

Sam noted that Perler narrowed his eyes still further at this characterization. "What are your qualifications?" he asked.

Perler stood very straight. "Chief of maintenance for Gladbach for the past six years. I know everything there is to know about this telephone system."

"Party?"

No Germans had been members of the Nazi Party, apparently. It was really not a fair question, but Sam felt like making him lie for some perverse reason.

"Of course not," said Perler indignantly.

"I think that we can use you. We've got the phones working but we're limited as to the amount of numbers we have available."

"I will take a look," said Perler.

Sam gave him a tour of the setup, which he inspected thoroughly. Sam thought he was somewhat admiring of their work, but perhaps he was just imagining it. They returned to their "office," a few folding chairs at the main switchboard.

Perler spoke one word: *"Querverbindungsatz."*

After Perler came on board and examined my handiwork he said that the phone system had special relays called *querverbindungsatz* which would do the job and at the same time recapture four customer numbers for our limited system. So we began our search through bombed-out Germany for *querverbindungsatz*. They were difficult to find.

We began visiting Düsseldorf, cadging telephone parts not available on our side of the Rhine. Düsseldorf is nearby, about eight or ten miles, had a lot of equipment we could use, and a working telephone system. Like Muchengladbach and all of Germany, the Düsseldorf office was part of the post office department, a government entity. From Muchengladbach it was about six miles to Krefeld, on the way, where we crossed the Rhine on a pontoon bridge (the highway bridge and the railroad bridge were destroyed by the German troops in an unsuccessful attempt to keep the Allied forces out of central Germany) and about two miles along the river to Düsseldorf.

Perler was very interesting to observe. He seemed to incorporate within his person the contradictions observed in many Germans in varied social contexts. In line with his status, he appeared to be about fifty-five years old. I was twenty-four, a member of the conquering army. He was deferential to me, not fawning, but maybe he was, and I just didn't notice it, having had my own expectations of his role.

However, I had ample opportunity to observe him in other contexts and settings.

W. and I provided cigarettes to Perler, although on a strange basis to out-siders. Cigarettes were a much more acceptable medium of exchange than any form of money; Germans just did not smoke if left on their own. When we took a break and offered a cigarette to Perler, it went into the pocket; if we wanted him to smoke with us, it took a second cigarette. In Düsseldorf, meanwhile, Perler was hauling out cigarette gifts and fawning over these guys who may have outranked him on the government (Nazi) chart, but worked in an entirely different district.

Our search for *querverbindungsatz* eventually led us to an obscure ware-house in the tiny village of Dahlhaus under the control of the U.S. Army Signal Corps.

When we got to the phone warehouse at Dahlhaus, the status situation was totally reversed. The warehouse manager, who was totally in charge (and his employees really snapped to) was reduced to jelly when Perler tore him apart as he explained that the U.S. Signal Corps had taken charge of the warehouse, and although they *did* have the *querverbindungsatz* we needed, a signed req-uisition form from the Signal Corps office in Köln was required for him to re-lease it.

Well! Perler, in cold Prussian that would have done General Rommel proud, explained to this hayseed Hitler that the U.S. Army *needed* this *querverbindungsatz*! it needed this *querverbindungsatz* now! And the very idea that the U.S. Army should retreat to Köln like a whipped dog to get a piece of paper that could be produced at this very counter in the next minute, and that you, mister manager or whoever you think you are, lack the authority to accept such a piece of paper, you can borrow my authority to accept it.

The manager, by this time actually shaking, ordered his awestruck staff to produce the *querverbindungsatz* and Perler whispered to me to write an order. The order was produced, dated, and signed by me, and we were on our way. Thus we had two faces—actually three, counting his toward W. and I—of Perler—fawning underdog, bullying commander, and deferential, defeated German. He was a perfect example of how deeply rank-conscious the Germans were.

The *querverbindungsatz* looked as though it had been designed by Western Electric for Bell Telephone Company in 1930; that is, it would attract no atten-tion in a telephone switchboard; totally anonymous. It was a black prewired circuit board ready to pop into a standard small-format interoffice automatic switchboard to increase its capacity by attaching another unit to it The basic difference in appearance between the *querverbindungsatz* and, for instance, a circuit board in the M-9 Director was the collection of electrical elements be-tween the input and output contacts.

On our way back, we stopped at a radio station and traded cigarettes for some speakers. This German radio announcer had been studying English secretly for three or four years, and this was the first day he had dared to try it on anyone who spoke English. He was oh-so-happy that we could understand him (his English was quite good; he actually had a British accent!).

A few days later we emerged from Düsseldorf telephone headquarters to observe a leaden sky promising a violent thunderstorm. We had the pontoon bridge to negotiate, and preferring to be in Krefeld, on the home side of the Rhine, before the storm struck, we sped to the bridge and were nearly across when the storm hit us, and hit us it did.

Between the end of the bridge and the top of the riverbank was a *volkspark* with huge gnarled trees that gave the appearance of an ancient orchard, with great limbs horizontal and vertical, headed every direction. I have to admit that this demonized forest really got my attention in that storm, for all of the limbs were in action, more or less independently, with some treetops revolving and some thrashing, with all of them threatening to blow away and some of them doing it. This small forest was probably only six or seven hundred feet to traverse, and with some artful dodging (terrified action, more like it) we were able to gain the top of the riverbank to gain the relative safety of the town.

Relativity showed its ugly head in the next minute. I was sailing along a clear street in Krefeld, no traffic at all, partly sheltered by a four-story brick building on my left (windward) side when my two German assistants in the rear of our weapons carrier screamed in unison, which I could barely hear over the roar of the wind.

At that same moment I observed several bricks bouncing on the street just in front of the truck. Looking back through the canvas cutout and through the open rear of the canvas cover, W. and I saw the street just beyond our tailgate was eight feet deep in bricks. Just ahead was a vacant lot which became our refuge until the storm moved on.

Krefeld, like Muchengladbach, had been heavily bombed during the war, some of it very late in the war, during the past several weeks. A bomb, exploding in a masonry building, which described many of the buildings in that area, might blow off the roof and the back of the structure and break the bonds between the vertical building front and floors, leaving it standing, an accidental booby trap ready to be toppled by a moderate wind.

"Damn," said Wink. "That was close."

When the storm subsided a bit, they got on the road to Muchengladbach. It was lined with stately trees, many of which now lay across the road. Sam gunned the truck through fields to get around them.

"Just a few seconds' difference and we'd have been done for," said Sam, as they entered Muchengladbach and its more familiar devastation. He glanced in the mirror. "What is Perler doing back there?"

Wink turned around. "Seems to be sorting through the equipment we got. Why?"

"I don't know. There's something strange about him. Yesterday afternoon he went up the stairs to the second floor, then came down and apologized. Said he was looking for me."

In the mirror, Sam saw Perler hold up one of the very specialized tubes they'd gotten, and then another.

"He knows those aren't for the phone system," said Sam.

"So what?"

"He's wondering what we're doing with them."

"We're just greedy Americans plundering his country. We're the new bosses. We're going to trade them for something, or sell them on the black market, or send them home as curiosities. What do *you* suppose he's thinking?"

"I don't know. But he's pretty smart."

"Given. So what?"

"I wouldn't be surprised if he had a key to our lab. I've seen him going up to the second floor a few times. But when I follow him, he's puttering around with some wires."

"Why would he want to get in there?"

"Curiosity."

"Weak."

"Not if he's a German spy. Or Russian."

"Hell, for that matter, British or American. We've had a fair number of people sticking their noses into this."

"I don't trust him."

The next two days, as he busied himself with integrating the *querverbindungsatz* into the phone system, Sam kept a close eye on Perler. He noticed that Perler seemed to be keeping a close eye on him.

"You have good schooling," Perler remarked, as he stripped some wires with a jerking motion.

"Thanks," said Sam.

"I am surprised at how quickly you got the telephones working."

Sam laughed. "Smarter than I look, eh?"

"I don't like Hitler."

"Neither do I."

"He is destroying what is left of our country."

"We're doing our best to prevent that."

"You're destroying it as well."

"Germany is still fighting. We don't have much choice."

"Yes," said Perler, finishing his connection and moving on to the next. After that he asked no more questions.

It was a week later, early in the morning.

The punch press was hard at work, stamping out aluminum mess trays using a die made by Al Hauk of Company C—without telling the officers—from rolls of heavy sheet aluminum they'd traded with the 611th in return for their share of trays. Munchengladbach was becoming a regular stop for U.S. military traversing the British sector. There were no public restaurants, no carryouts, gas was hard to get, repairs impossible, and they had many overnighters for meals and quarters. Word had spread about the punch press so Al and gang were making more die sets and planned to set up three other presses on a twenty-four-hour schedule to fill the demand.

Sam passed through the din and climbed the stairs to his new second-floor haven. Unlocking the door, he let himself in to their spacious lab—about twenty by twenty-five feet, but still in setup stage—and saw Perler, sitting on an office chair at a table. For once, he was smoking a precious cigarette instead of saving it for trade or currying favors. His forehead shone with sweat in the unheated room.

Sam put his hand on his pistol. "What are you doing here?"

"Look," said Perler, and nodded to an object that lay on the table in front of him. "Just—look."

"I can see it from here," said Sam. "Where did you get it?"

Although it looked as subtly foreign as all of the other electronic and mechanical parts in Germany, it was clearly a Hadntz Device.

Perler stubbed out his cigarette in the ashtray and put the butt in his metal cigarette case, snapped the case shut, and slipped it into his shirt pocket. "It was given to me."

"By whom?"

"A German woman. We are part of an organization that has been trying to assassinate Hitler. All of our attempts have failed. I give this to you as an act of good faith. To show you we are serious."

"Why?" asked Sam.

"Sit down," said Perler. "Have a cigarette." He got out his case again.

Sam pulled out a chair at the other end of the table. "I have my own. Here. I'll smoke if you smoke." He tossed one to Perler. Perler put it in his case. Sam tossed him another. He lit it and continued.

"In 1944, Rommel was forced to commit suicide for participating in one of our plots. We are presently trying to get some sarin gas to put down Hitler's ventilation shaft in Berlin."

"I thought that Hitler was in Bavaria."

Perler shook his head. "He is in Berlin, in his bunker. Speer, his minister of armaments, who is an architect, informed us of the presence of this ventilation shaft."

"Why?"

"Speer believes that Hitler is committing treason against the German people, as do I. Hitler's latest command is that the Gauleiters—men who have local control throughout the country, all of them quite loyal to Hitler—are to destroy anything that will be of use to the conquerors. Factories, dairies, anything and everything. You arrived in Muchengladbach before this order could be implemented, so the power plant was still available for your use. Germany has lost the war; it is just a matter of time before the surrender. But if it takes too long, all of Germany will be destroyed. Transportation, communication, manufacturing, waste-disposal plants—everything. We will starve. Hitler would like to kill us all, and he is taking steps to carry out his plan. He says that any Germans left are weak, non-Aryan, not fit to live."

"Shove that over here," said Sam. Perler slid it over to Sam, and he picked up the device.

It was encased in a network of circuits, tubes, and steel. Larger than the one they had made. Within the case, Sam could see that the substance had the same translucent qualities. When Wink and Sam had made theirs, they had made no such case. There was a dial on the case.

"Does this do anything?"

"There are glimmerings of . . . something. Several others of our group are trying to make a copy of this one. The woman told us that it was necessary to have a network of them to enable their use. But this one doesn't do anything. Still, when I saw the combination of tubes that you confiscated, I realized that you might be making one. That you might be one of us. That you might even have more of them, enough to facilitate its functioning. I gained entry to this laboratory, and my suspicions were confirmed."

"What was the woman's name?"

"She wouldn't say."

"What did she look like?"

"She had blond hair, blue eyes, a delicate face."

"Where was she from?"

"She had a Berlin accent."

"When was she here?"

"In December." Perler nodded toward the device. "After our close call last week, I realized that I should not keep this to myself. Mine was given me as you see it. Being an engineer, I have thought about how to make one, but without seeing the plans, I am only guessing. I believe, however, that you will benefit by incorporating a *querverbindungsatz* into the process, as well as other parts that you might not recognize, as they are German technology. I can help you. We are on the same side. I just need to see your plans."

"I want you to leave, for now," Sam said.

"But—"

"You are going to give me your key, we are going to leave, I will lock the door, and you will meet me back here in an hour."

He went to fetch Wink.

"Okay," said Wink, as the three of them, back in the office, drank Cokes. He had Perler's device in front of him. "For one thing, we can't get sarin gas. I've heard of it. The Japanese have used it. Unless there's some in Germany that we can liberate, there's nowhere else to get it."

"Maybe you could make some," suggested Perler. "Or get some anthrax. Anthrax would work. We have a network set up to put poisons into the bunker through the shaft. But we have to move quickly. Every day, Hitler destroys more of our infrastructure."

"How the hell do we know that you'd use it on Hitler and not us?"

"You would just have to trust me," said Perler.

They kept Perler's device, and put Kocab on immediately to make their lab secure, even against explosives. "Or magicians," said Sam.

"I'm not sure about explosives," Kocab said. "But we could weld some of that sheet aluminum around the inside. I can fix the door pretty well too."

They re-crated their equipment; nailed and chained and locked the crate shut. Then they let Kocab and Earl T. get to work. Wink remained to keep an eye on things; Sam was to spell him in two hours.

When Sam left the factory, Perler was sitting on a flight of concrete steps across the street, the only remains of a bombed building. His arms were linked around his knees. He rose when he saw them and hurried across the street.

"Can you get the sarin for me?" he asked anxiously.

"I doubt it very much," said Sam. He continued down the street.

Perler followed. "I need the device back."

They walked in silence for a moment, then Perler said, "I was foolish."

Sam said, "Maybe not. If, as you say, we're all on the same side, you've lost nothing. If we're not, you may have lost a great deal."

"Why would I even have shown it to you, then?"

"To get information from us."

"I have a daughter. She is fifteen. I am doing this for her. I don't want her and her children to grow up in a destroyed country, a country with no hope, like the Germany I grew up in, a country that can be easily swayed by someone else like Hitler."

They were passing a block of empty shops now. "She used to work in that drugstore. Now it is empty. Maybe it will always be empty."

"I'm not a magician. Winklemeyer and I have no connections with anyone who may be able to help you with your plans."

Perler said, "I suppose I can console myself with the thought that it didn't work, anyway."

"What did your contact tell you it would do?"

"Open new worlds," Perler said. "As if one really could." He stopped and looked around at the darkening ruins. "We could certainly use one. I was just holding on to straws."

"It's almost curfew. We'll see you tomorrow morning," said Sam. "You said we could get some telephone equipment in Köln."

"Yes," said Perler.

"Auf Wiedersehen," said Sam, and turned down Neusser Strasse.

When Sam returned to spell Wink, their helpers were at work downstairs on their machines. They sat on the floor and leaned against the wall of their lab. Wink wolfed down a sandwich that Leonid had made for him, and swigged a beer. A single light threw faint light on the heavy, grease-stained planks of the floor.

"So," said Wink around his mouthful of black bread and mystery sausage, "what do you think of Perler?"

Sam's dark, bitter beer was cold, satisfying despite the chill of the night air. "I suppose he must be right. There's a network of these things. Somebody's passing them out like candy. If he's on the level, we should tell someone."

Wink wiped his mouth on the napkin Leonid had wrapped the sandwich in, folded it carefully, and put it in his jacket pocket. "Like Sunny? Who's in charge here, anyway? My friend, we are living on the dangerous but fruitful edge of chaos, where no one is in control and anything could happen. We could bust into General Simpson's headquarters with a wild tale of vengeance weapons, but if we showed him one of these things, he'd laugh. Anybody would."

"I mean, we need to tell someone where Hitler is. If that's where he is."

Wink nodded. "Sure. And of course they'll believe us. I heard yesterday from a German that Hitler was ten miles away, on the verge of liberating them from our terrible yoke. You think that Perler is the one and only conduit to truth?"

"Somebody went to a lot of trouble to have that device made. Maybe they know more than us."

Wink snorted. "That's *definitely* possible. Wonder what Elegante did with ours?"

"She's on our side," said Sam.

"Maybe. Who's on anyone's side? I'm trying to figure it out." Wink got to his feet, put his hands on his hips, leaned backward. "I'm off to bed. Wake me up in four hours."

"Will do."

Wink headed toward the end of the factory, where someone's office held a couch.

Sam was left alone for a while. He fell into deep thought, imagining more than two melodies at once—three, possibly, or four, which merged from time to time, then diverged, strings spinning into space to loop back, perhaps, at some point, and converge. Startled out of his reverie by footsteps, he rose silently and drew his pistol.

Earl T. emerged from the stairway at first, followed by Kocab. They were panting, and carried a sheet of machined steel.

"Put that away and get the hell over here," said Earl T. "This thing is heavy."

The *querverbindungsatz* worked quite as advertised in the phones, and that was really the last major work we did on the phone system other than tidying up the telephone wire layout inside and out.

The dial system continued to work until the rainy day I was assigned to KP and the dial phones crashed forty-five minutes into my shift. It took me until a few minutes after my KP shift was over to find the trouble.

After that, it so happened that I was not assigned to any other duties like KP or ash and trash. I was just to stand by and keep the phone system running.

⊣ 19 ⊢

The Biergarten

IN THE BACK OF their apartment building, as with many German homes, was a courtyard with a summerhouse. Earlier in the morning than Wink rose unless death or something like it threatened, Sam sat at a desk overlooking the courtyard and closed up the papers he had been studying once again. Access to the German telephone system and warehouses full of detailed, advanced electronics was going to make this attempt a bit easier than their try in England. But he was still unsure how to proceed.

Lighting a cigarette, Sam watched sunlight glaze the roofs below and fill shattered buildings with deep shadows.

It was early April 1945. On March 7th, the Ramagen bridge across the Rhine had been taken miles south of Muchengladbach, but Germany had not yet surrendered, although many German soldiers and commanders had individually surrendered. The Werewolves, the fighting Hitler Youth, who had necessitated the complete destruction of several towns which were willing to surrender, had succumbed to whatever might cause twelve-year-old boys to stop fighting—perhaps seeing death firsthand. Generals Eisenhower, Patton, and Montgomery had together descended into the Merker salt mines to survey the discovery of hundreds of priceless paintings, tons of gold, and barrels of gold-filled teeth that the Nazis—Goering, in particular—had stored away for the time when they would resurface. Hitler had ordered troops and materiel east to defend Berlin against the Russians. When Sam pulled *volkspark* night patrol, he always took a potshot at "Bed-check Charlie," the Allies' name for the plane the Germans still sent out at twilight, in a futile gesture, to check Allied positions.

Seventy thousand refugees were on the move. Germans who had fled east to escape the Americans and British realized that the Russians were a far greater threat and were filtering back west. The neighborhood was filling up with German civilians reclaiming their homes or squatting in unoccupied buildings, surviving on potatoes, fruit, and the remnants of last year's home canning. Children played in the street, melting away before an MP jeep rounded the bend. The women sat on their stoops and talked with one another in the evening before curfew.

The summerhouse, pleasantly proportioned and open on two sides to what promised to be a lush, mature garden in another month, tugged at Sam's thoughts as he imagined happier seasons spent beneath its wide eaves. Its intact red tile roof was a moving filigree of tiny shadows as the overhanging, just-budding linden tree moved in the morning breeze. Red and yellow tulips blazed against the brick wall. A wide, dark-framed mirror hung on one of the walls. In the foreground was a statue of a figure carrying a basket overhead.

Sam had traded three packs of cigarettes for a Leica camera and film. He was now the company photographer, documenting the town, its people, and his buddies.

He opened the window. Grease, his roommate, said something rude about the influx of cold air and rolled over. Sam leaned out and took several pictures of the courtyard. The statue was in the foreground, and Sam hoped that he'd properly exposed the picture to get the effect he wanted: sunlight streaming down; a palpable sense of spring.

A girl and a boy edged around one corner of the summerhouse and looked both ways. As he watched, they ran up the walk to the back porch. Their footsteps on the stairs were quiet; carefully placed. Sam heard the door open and close, and they scurried down the walk, the boy holding a small bundle. Just as they went around the corner, the girl stopped, evidently feeling Sam's gaze. She turned and looked up at him. At that instant he snapped her picture. She melted away through the bushes.

He went downstairs. Leonid was in the kitchen, as usual, cracking some hard-won real eggs into a bowl for their breakfast. He was less cadaverous now, and had learned some English. His hair was a gray haze of fuzz on his formerly bald pate. There were always good smells here. This morning, it was bread baking in the oven.

"Who is the girl?" asked Sam.

"Lise. Karl. Ah . . . same grandfather?"

"Cousins."

Leonid nodded. "Cousins. Her mother . . . raped?"

"Raped."

"Yes, raped by Russians. They say. Then shot. Horse, eaten. Father, dead Luftwaffe pilot."

Sam was startled by the depth of sadness in his eyes.

"This was their house. Egg for them. Slice of bread."

"Good," said Sam. "We have plenty."

"Yes. Plenty. Much?"

"Plenty is the same as much, yes. But maybe even more than much. More than enough."

"I hope that someone takes care of my family this way." But he looked doubtful.

That afternoon, a group of GI's drove up in two six-by-six trucks. Sam was smoking a cigarette on the front stoop. A sergeant yelled from the window, "Want some booze? Rhine wine and cognac."

"How much?"

"Three hundred bucks, including the trucks."

"We've got plenty of trucks. One-fifty for the booze."

"Ah, hell. Two hundred for everything."

"Hold on."

In fifteen minutes he'd canvassed all the unwary GI's in the building, and came out with two-hundred dollars in cash.

We discovered that combat troops had liberated a winery nearby. A couple of guys went over. They had big horizontal storage tanks of wine. When the combat troops got in there they liberated it with tremendous energy. There weren't many corkscrews around, so they just broke the necks off the bottles and took their chances gulping it down. They all got drunk and kept filling their broken bottles at the tap. The last guy was too drunk to turn it off. When we got to it the wine was a foot deep in a huge cellar. We looked for kegs that hadn't been opened and hauled out what we could recover.

We sent a truck to Maastricht every week. De Kroon brewery there made wonderful beer. The deal was that we got to buy a liter per week for each guy in our organization as long as we had empty barrels to exchange for their full barrels. We went around Muchengladbach liberating glasses and mugs, beer coolers and piping, and those oh-so-precious barrels from bombed-out *biergartens*. I estimate that we're drawing close to 2,800 liters per week for C Company.

They began to set up a *biergarten* in their backyard, using the two sides of the summerhouse. The other two sides consisted of a fine bar, with brass railing, from the *volkspark*.

Sam envisioned an oasis in the middle of chaos.

And from that springboard, he and Wink prepared to begin their serious, real work.

⁘ 20 ⁙

Bergen-Belsen

O N A RAINY DAY in mid-April, Sunny's efficient clerk sought them out, carrying a paper. "This is kind of strange—I mean, the provenance—but we checked it all out and the orders are good."

Wink wiped his hands on a rag. "What are you talking about?"

"You and Dance are to take two bulldozers to a place called Bergen-Belsen."

Sam studied the orders.

They were written in a hand he recognized, from notes on her paper: Hadntz's. And it was stamped and signed by General Simpson.

They were to drive a hundred miles through enemy territory.

"I asked some questions while you were getting the 'dozers," said Wink, as they got ready to load them on the truck. "The German commander of Bergen-Belsen signed it over to the Brits to get rid of it. It's a hellhole. I don't know what they want with us. Except that they have a desperate need for earthmovers."

"Hadntz wants us there. She meant for us to see that she was somehow involved with those orders. We know that she's been working closely with the British."

"Fat lot of good our 'security clearance' has been to us," Wink complained as he checked the chains holding the 'dozers on the long truck bed. "I swear not to reveal the top-secret American method of peeling potatoes on pain of death."

They stopped in bombed-out Kaarst. Sam rolled down his window and handed the orders to the Brits. The chilly air was laced with cigarette smoke from nearby soldiers.

"I'm beginning to think that Hadntz's herd-animal ideas aren't far off the mark. Without Hitler in evidence, everything is falling apart," said Wink.

"Do you think the U.S. would be any different?"

"I think that our country has a pretty good framework for maintaining stability in the event of a president's death. My question is—if humans are changed, somehow, how will that affect the whole lot of us? How might it affect this situation?"

"If the brain is just a series of electrochemical events, and if DNA controls those events, maybe if they unfolded in a slightly different way, people would be . . . changed."

"Life could be just one big party."

"Well, at least we might be able to get on with things. It's going to take a lot of energy just to get this place back to where it was a few weeks ago."

"I keep thinking about Perler. Do you think he and his crowd have anything to do with things falling apart?"

A Tommie came up to Sam's window. "Two blocks west, then north."

"Thanks." Sam put the truck in first gear and it growled into motion.

On the outskirts of town, Wink said, "Look. Over there."

Next to the road, the muddy, trampled field was empty, but a few hundred yards away a wave of people trudged toward them, and they stretched to the horizon.

Their truck was slowly enveloped by the refugees. The mob split in half and trudged past the truck, a river of women and children, but some older men as well, many wearing bold-striped prison uniforms. Everyone, including the children, carried parcels. Some were just boxes tied with twine; others had suitcases. All of them moved slowly, their eyes dull, putting one foot in front of the other, simply heading east, away from a much greater threat than the Allies—the Russians, their mortal, ancestral enemy.

After they had passed, Sam saw that the field behind them was scattered with bodies—not of soldiers, but of civilians, dying as they walked.

"God," said Wink. "What can we do?"

They smelled the stink of the camp miles before they saw it, driving through a pine forest alongside a rapidly flowing river. Bodies became more numerous, at first randomly scattered and then stacked in piles. It was obvious that many of them had been shot. Smoke rose and flattened beneath a cloudy sky.

"They're burning the bodies," said Wink.

They stopped on what seemed the threshold of hell to wait for permission to enter.

On the other side of the gate, a range of humanity filled the trampled grounds. Some were moving; many were not. Starved men, women, and a surprising number of children slumped against any available prop. There was no way to tell if they were dead or alive, save that the open eyes of some observed incuriously. Many were naked. Some had been executed and left to lie where they fell. All were so emaciated that their joints protruded like knobs. Those involved in the liberation of the camp—soldiers, medical personnel—wore masks and cloths tied over their mouths, and moved purposefully through the living and the dead.

The Brit at the gate took one look at their 'dozers and waved them into the massive compound, bounded by barbed wire.

"We're here," said Wink. "Now what?"

"Let's try and find out who's in charge." Sam pulled off the main drag and parked off to one side, next to a sagging wooden barracks. They jumped down from the truck.

No one paid them any attention. Two British soldiers with guns accompanied an SS officer in leg irons, who observed all the activity with an ironic gaze as they moved him along.

A dozen hefty blond women, wearing uniforms—skirt and jacket, with tall leather boots—were marched past them under guard. One of them looked defiantly forward, chin high. The rest of them walked with slumped shoulders and bowed heads, looking at the ground. Weirdly, an orchestra played somewhere, its clear sweet strains infusing the scene with an incongruous harmony.

"SS women?" asked Wink.

"Guess so."

They made their way through a constant stream of guarded SS men dragging bodies toward a huge pit. Turning off to one side, they followed the stream of movement to the place where the bodies came from.

They stood before a mountain of naked, tangled bodies, their skin yellow, pale green, and black with bruises, stretched tight on a framework of bones. Crisscrossed with lines of darkened blood, their faces were hideously drawn and no longer seemed even human.

Wink said, "I'm going back to the truck."

"I understand," Sam said, but his voice sounded distant to him. He was hearing violin music in an isolated forest cottage, where the power of life rose up and triumphed over such scenes.

Hadntz hadn't been able to do much of anything.

"Move aside," said a Brit. "What are you Americans doing here anyway?"

"We brought those 'dozers over there."

"Behind the crematorium?"

"The what?" asked Wink.

"Where they burned the bodies. But that was too slow. They couldn't burn them fast enough. Only so many thousands a day." His words were clipped, unstoppable.

"So they dug some jolly big trenches next to one another and let the rendered fat seep out to help the burning. You're standing in front of a gas chamber. They were brought in trains and sorted as to whether or not they looked useful. All their clothing removed, the suitcases they'd packed put aside. Told they were to have a nice shower. Packed in tight with beatings. I mean as tightly as they possibly could be and the door barred. Gas took care of them in a minute or so, but they fought like hell, inside."

Sam realized that here the dead far outnumbered the living. The weight of their lost lives was palpable, unbearably heavy with hopes, dreams, yearning, fear, and love. Each remarkably complex person had been an entire universe. There was no way to encompass such loss, to understand it. One could not help trying, though, and that was what brought Sam to a complete halt at the edge of a dark abyss, beyond which meaning did not exist.

For the next hour, they wandered the camp, as aimless as the released prisoners. Sam passed out all of his remaining cigarettes, which were gratefully accepted. One soldier looked alarmed, and came over to talk to them.

"Don't give them any food. They just die, see? I gave one a biscuit and he took one bite and swallowed it and dropped dead. They can't eat anymore. Stomachs can't take it. Stay away from the barracks. They're full of shit. I mean it. Those people couldn't even move any more. There's been no water for a week. They just shat where they were. Everyone sleeping with dead bodies around them. Lice. Terrible . . . just terrible." He looked Sam square in the eyes and said, "I'm Jewish. Paul Franklin. From Lancashire. Now I know what I've been fighting for. This is hideous fucking evil and there is nothing else to be said about it."

He recruited them to help repair the water system, and found someone for them to turn the 'dozers over to, with some perfunctory paperwork.

"They had no water?" Wink asked Franklin, as they headed toward the waterworks past endless rows of low, flat barracks overflowing with the dead.

"And no food, either, for the past week. They're blaming that on Allied bombings, but the SS had plenty of food in that warehouse. They've mostly run off, disguising themselves. Innocent old farmers trying to get home to their families."

"There's a river right there," said Sam. It glinted on the other side of the barbed wire.

Paul made a sound as if he were being strangled, which ended up as a sort of laugh. Then he rubbed his face. "Sorry. They claimed the river was contaminated. They didn't want to make anyone sick."

Sam was grateful to be given the simple, straightforward job of soldering pipes. At least he didn't have to dig holes with the 'dozers they'd brought, nor push piles of bodies into the holes. There seemed to be a lot of dead children among the adults. His entire being ached, as if he were being squeezed inside a rubber strait-jacket. He sweated the pipe with the torch, hoped the joint was sound, and moved on to the next joint.

After three days of doing what they could, which included helping rig a system to pump water from the river, they prepared to leave. The 'dozers would stay behind. They allowed as many released prisoners as they could to crowd onto their truck. Sam gunned the engine and put the truck in gear.

Just then, a British soldier came round from behind the truck, waving some papers. "You're to take this," he said.

Sam was too tired to look at the papers. "What is it?"

"Don't know. A crate. Needs to go to the American army in Muchengladbach."

Sam leaned out the window. "Set it sideways, then. Somebody can sit on it."

The man took the papers back. "These stay with the crate."

In the second town they passed through they picked up two women who climbed into the cab. Both looked as ragged and destitute as the other refugees, except that one carried a new red alligator purse and the other wore shiny, new black boots. Both were trying to return to Holland. They'd been desperately hungry for three years.

Many of their passengers were prisoners from camps further east who had survived a forced march during midwinter to Belsen. Many more died along the way than had survived. Some were Russians who, like Leonid, were afraid to go home.

Refugees jumped off when they thought they saw a prospect of food or shelter along the way. Two died and were thrown off the truck. Others crowded aboard and Sam was forced to limit these. Some chose to enter a displaced person's camp they passed in Hagan.

Once they reached Wuppertal, they were on familiar ground, having ranged here with Perler to scrounge for telephone equipment. Perler had proudly pointed out the world's first elevated train system, fifty years old.

The Dutch women didn't speak much; mostly they dozed. Sam and Wink managed to get fifty loaves of bread from a food transport truck while the vehicles stopped next to each other in Mettman.

"What are we going to do with all these people?" asked Wink.

One of the Dutch women opened her eyes. "Can you take us to Maastricht?"

Sam and Wink looked at each other. "Sure," said Sam. "We know the way."

"I wonder if my mother is still alive." She began to cry.

When they got back to Muchengladbach, they got blind drunk in their own backyard. By common consent, without speaking, they stumbled into the house and returned to the garden with their instruments. Earl T. and Grease eyed them warily.

They had not spoken of what they had seen, even to one another. Jazz took them to that unspeakable abyss. Seemingly discordant, it still had a theme: darkness, despair, and *Weltschmerz*, a good old German literary term that Howie had taught Sam, meaning the sorrow of the world. He thought that he saw Hadntz there, sitting at the bar, her mind a portal that could take them through and beyond, a mind that knew all this, and more.

Their audience had fled long before they were finished. Leonid put them to bed at about five in the morning, saying, "I understand."

The next morning, some thoughtful person or persons saw to it that the crate they'd carried was taken to the warehouse and left inside. When Sam and Wink showed up, much the worse for wear, Sunny waved them over.

"They said this came off the truck you were driving."

Wink said, "I don't know anything about it."

"Well, this paper was stuck in the slats." The crate had been crowbarred open. Inside was a small, black barrel upon which was stenciled, with white paint, SARIN, beneath which was a skull and crossbones.

Sam stood on the periphery of the commotion, which soon included several officers. They took turns looking over the information. Finally, Sunny said, "I just can't read it. It looks like this bunch of papers fell into the river. We've got to get this out of here, though, and to a safe place."

At that point, Perler walked in. When he spotted the barrel, his footsteps faltered, then he continued to the storeroom to hang up his jacket.

Sam left the group to follow him. Inside the storeroom, he asked, "Do you know anything about this?"

"It doesn't matter," Perler said. "It is of no use to us now." When he turned, his face was grim in the low light. He looked beaten. "Evidently someone leaked the plot. The ventilation shaft was extended so that it is very high. It would require a ladder to get the gas in, and is now under constant guard." He looked Sam in the eye. "Remember this. Once someone takes power and controls the military, it is impossible to change things. I was hoping that we could, somehow. A fairy tale. But . . . perhaps some of our plans did work. I certainly never expected to actually see the sarin." Then he left, passing Wink, who stood in the doorway.

"Who put that on the truck?" Wink asked.

"Some Brit."

"So—something did work."

"If that's so," said Sam, "I don't like it very much."

"You and me both," said Wink.

"The only answer is to make our own device," said Sam, as they climbed the stairs to the lab.

"That's the only way we can be in charge. But in charge of what?"

"Tell me when you figure it out," said Sam.

⫴ 21 ⫼

The Children of War

I T WAS ALMOST MIDNIGHT, the first of May. Wink had long since collapsed, having been under various onerous orders all day; all orders grated and wore on him as they did on most of the self-starting men of Company C. The others, except for Sam, were inside with Leonid, enjoying some post-dinner schnapps. A bare bulb cast black shadows across the ragged garden. Work was progressing on their device, but just as slowly as it had in England. More slowly, perhaps, because they were comparing Perler's device to the one they were making, and it was a complicated, meticulous process.

Sam whirled at a rustling sound behind him, almost drawing his pistol.

"Ami?" It was Lise, wearing the same clean, pressed jumper with white blouse underneath. Her shoes were cracked and worn.

"Yes. I'm an American. Sam."

She looked at him for a moment, seeming confused, then patted her stomach. "Eat?"

"Wait." He climbed the stairs, got a packet of soda crackers and two slices of baloney, and wrapped them in a scrap of *Stars and Stripes*. When he went back outside, she was gone, so he set them on the bar and went back to work. He looked up at a sound, and the food was gone.

The next morning, as Sam enjoyed a smoke in the garden and gently reveled, once again, in his on-call status for phone maintenance, cheers erupted through the open windows of the townhouse.

Sam climbed the stairs and stood in the open doorway. A celebratory bottle of sparkling Moselle wine was making the rounds. "What's up?"

"Radio report—Hitler's committed suicide in Berlin. He was in a bunker there," said Kocab. "Shot himself in the head. The Soviets found him, a woman, and a dog, in a courtyard above the bunker. They'd been doused with gasoline, but didn't burn completely."

"And Eisenhower was so convinced that he'd left Berlin for Bavaria," said Earl T. "I've been saying we should have tried to take Berlin."

Wink said, "How many times have we heard the bastard was dead? I'll drink to it anyway. Pass me that bottle." He took a swig and handed it to Sam.

The Moselle, cold from the cellar, was beaded with condensation. Sam took his drink with a concurrent dose of realization.

"He was right," he said to Wink, quietly.

"Perler."

"So what does that mean?"

"Right. What does it mean, anyway?" asked Grease, picking up on what Sam said, but referring to Hitler's death rather than Perler's prescience, about which he did not know. "Aren't there plenty of Nazis to take his place?"

"I doubt it," said Kocab. "Remember when Roosevelt died?"

"Yeah," said Earl T. "They were kind of amazed here in town when the war kept going."

"I'd say that it's true for the Germans, though. Leader gone, war over."

The Perham Downs were reborn at that moment. Everyone got out their instruments, tuned up, and played all kinds of pieces, badly at first, but they rapidly improved. Sam caught Wink's eye, said, "Sweet Georgia Brown," and they were off. After playing the theme rapidly for two bars, they launched into a modern jazz rendition. For once, the guys just sat and listened.

Sam sailed through the changes, modulating the time, blending with Wink's key changes with initial dissonance and resolving briefly before heading to new heights.

The sheer act of playing filled him with joy. He played for Keenan, *to* Keenan, a Keenan alive, somewhere, celebrating in a bar, buying everyone a round.

Then Sam sobered. Even if the war here was over—still doubtful—the war was not over in the Pacific. Thousands of men might still die.

They ended in an unmodern minor key, and the last few bars were a question phrased with a few bare notes.

Later that afternoon, as Sam and Wink washed steins, Lise reappeared with her cousin Karl. They stood at the edge of the garden, poised as if ready to flee. Sam motioned them inside and they advanced hesitantly, holding hands.

"Here, have some peanuts," he said, and gave them some to shell. They picked up the shells and stuffed them in their pockets after gobbling down the peanuts.

Armed Forces Radio was having a musical interlude. Suddenly Karl, who looked about ten years old, smiled.

"Ben-ny Good-man!" He grabbed Lise by the waist and hand and danced her around awkwardly for a few steps.

"No!" She backed away from him and spoke to him low, and in German, for a minute, before Wink interrupted, nodding at the children.

"It is all right. Okay."

Lise stared at him with suspicion.

To Sam, Wink said, "Evidently her uncle—Karl's dad—listened to American jazz, which was a huge family secret and great embarrassment."

"Dangerous too."

"Definitely." Wink turned to the kids. "Hitler *kaput*."

Lise's blue eyes widened. She shook her head violently. Karl said, with great certainty in his reedy voice, something in German, which Wink translated: "Hitler can *not* die."

On May 8, 1945, the rumor came around that the Germans had surrendered, that we were getting a holiday, and we would have to turn in our ammunition, not necessarily in that order. The result was, of course, that we all immediately shot twenty rounds of carbine ammunition in the air to 1) celebrate winning the war and 2) avoid turning in any ammunition. In addition, the guys who had souvenir guns and ammunition mostly shot that in the air. We had our own war on Neusser Strasse that day.

The summerhouse, as if charged with regenerative powers, became a local haven. American forces were strictly prohibited from speaking to any Germans or giving them food or help of any kind. However, being in the British sector isolated Company C from the rest of the Army and kept enforcement of this draconian ruling quite lax.

The kids showed up every day. Sam gave them small jobs while Zee, Earl T., and Grease hauled picnic tables and benches from the *volkspark*. The kids, using buckets, brushes, and rags, quickly made them usable.

Konrad, a serious boy with short blond hair and wide blue eyes, fed Wink the wires of fairy lights which he strung from a linden tree and along the top of the brick wall. Karl and Konrad handed speakers to Wink who, on his ladder, attached them in a configuration which, after some rearrangement, he declared acoustically satisfying, and created metal connectors so they could be removed every night.

The first day, as they rested from their exertions, Sam offered the band of kids cold Coca-Colas, freshly pulled from a barrel of ice.

"Here, I'll open it for you," he said to Lise, getting a bottle-cap opener from his pocket.

She didn't speak English, but she knew what the opener was for. A tiny frown; she shook her head vigorously, grabbed the Coke, and sat down on the sun-warmed flagstones. The other children joined her.

They rolled the bottles between their hands for ten minutes while Sam washed and dried glasses and checked the ice, which came from the newly repaired ice plant. Finally, Lise offered the Coke to Sam to open. Still, she didn't drink it. With her thumb over the top, she shook it and then let out a geyser of Coke. After they had all warmed their sodas and taken the sting out of them, the German children sat in spring sunlight, drinking warm, flat Cokes.

Under the bar, open coolers held Coke, Rhine wine, pink Moselle champagne, Krefeld cognac, and schnapps, all on ice. The beer cooler on the bar was connected; the *biergarten* was ready for business.

Each day, after they gathered all the cigarette butts to take home to trade for food, the kids loaded the coolers, swept the courtyard, and straightened the tables and chairs. Their landlady, Emma Tillman, spoke passable English and stopped by for a beer and a chat every evening. According to her, life during wartime had not been all that difficult, despite rationing of food and clothing. For the most part, they had not felt the sting until the war neared its end.

One night while bartending, Sam heard a familiar voice: "Any wee heavies here, my man?"

"Rafferty!" They shook hands over the bar. "Your drink is Teacher's."

"Oh, I'm not so particular."

The USO accordion player Sam had met in Glasgow still wore a beard, now mostly gray. His creased face was tanned; his eyes clear and smiling as he took a seat. Some weight had been lifted. "Nice place."

"Thanks." Now that the *biergarten* had come together, it provided an oasis of peace each night, when the smashed desolation of Germany was blanketed in darkness, and the floods of desperate refugees collapsed for another night of hunger-shot sleep. "So where have you been?"

"Italy, mostly. Playing for soldiers in foxholes. Found a stick of paratroopers to hook up with and made seventeen jumps. I've been playing for the past month over on the front lines. Up near Xanec." He leaned back in satisfaction, both hands on the bar. He looked even more satisfied when Sam came up with a bottle of Johnnie Walker Black and set it on the bar next to a shot glass.

"Next best thing to Teacher's. On the house."

"Hey," said Wink, overhearing.

"We could use some entertainment, don't you think? Rafferty plays the accordion."

That night, Rafferty donated an astonishing 78 to the cause. "Koko" was the roller-coaster tune by Dizzy Gillespie and Charlie Parker that had enlightened them at Minton's. He said, "These guys are amazing. Never heard them before this. On account of the musician's strike, I guess. But if this is any proof, jazz is gonna be a whole lot different after the war."

:| 22 |:

The Major

THE FOLLOWING NIGHT, a blonde walked into the *biergarten*.
Fairy lights glimmered in the linden tree, and the scent of some sweet night-blooming flower was rich in the air, blending with the delightful undertone of good, fresh German *bier* as it flowed from the tap.

The soldiers at the *biergarten* relaxed on barstools, chairs, and picnic tables, talking, drinking, and listening to Sam's growing jazz record library. There was no dancing; fraternization with German women was forbidden, and the town's residents were subject to arrest after curfew, anyway.

In the midst of "Koko," which Sam figured he could slip in at least once an hour, Sam looked up to see Major Bette Elegante right in front of him, in uniform, leaning on the bar. "Can a girl get a drink here?"

"Right away, sir!"

She grinned.

As they drank and talked, Sam was struck by the feeling that Bette seemed immensely familiar to him, even dear. This seemed odd. He had spent only a few hours in her presence, and hadn't necessarily expected to see her again after the last time. It didn't seem sensible that his heart should leap. But it did.

Her face glowed in the light of the Chinese lanterns as she sipped beer. She was knocked out by "Koko," and made him replay it so many times in a row that they had a mutiny on their hands. Her vibrant laugh echoed in the night as the hours passed and she seemed to relax, shedding some unseen burden.

And she was beautiful, down to the tiny nick on her right earlobe, revealed when she brushed her hair back with one hand.

Maybe it was as simple as that.

At three in the afternoon of the following day, as Sam was setting up after another wearying day of trying to track down Perler, Bette walked in once again.

She looked waiflike in a tight red dress and massive fur coat—never mind that Sam thought she could probably toss grown men over her shoulder.

"Like them?" She wagged her right foot, ensconced in a two-toned heel with several straps, and pirouetted on the flagstone patio of the Dance & Winklemeyer Biergarten, loosening her coat so that it fell from her shoulders. Her hair swung out as she turned. Silk stockings gleamed on her long legs. She pulled the coat tight and rubbed her face in it. "Mmmm. There's something to this fur stuff. All I need are boots and trousers and I'd be warm in a Moscow winter."

"I think this is the first time I've seen you out of uniform. You look absolutely smashing." Sam polished glasses with a white cloth. Soldiers would soon start drifting in.

Bette leaned against the bar, sipping schnapps. "I've got two great dresses they made me in London. One is in the German style. One is made to French specifications, down to my underwear."

"French underwear, eh? How is that different?"

"None of your damned business."

"Is that the French dress?"

"This is my American dress. Story is that I'm a Russian woman forced into slave labor in Germany. You, Mr. Nice American Soldier, have given me this fine American dress from New York."

"Right. I carried it in my kit in the Ardennes? I wrote to my mother and asked her to send one of my sister's dresses? No, they'd howl. They work hard for their money. I know. I tell Ma that I have this German girlfriend, this tiny little thing, and could she please send me a fancy dress from New York so that I can impress her? Just run over there from Middleburg, Ma."

"I'm sure that they have nice dress shops where you come from. But I guess you're right."

"It would make much more sense for you to be wearing a real German dress, one that I've stolen from some departed fräulein's closet."

She frowned. "I thought so too, but then I really wanted to wear this." A sigh. "I'll get out a fräulein dress. I've got several."

"What's the point, anyway? I have a bad feeling about this."

"Oh yeah. I was going to mention that soon." She pulled his orders from the pocket of her coat and handed them to him.

"Berlin? I'm just getting settled in. The D and W Biergarten is looking forward to a very profitable spring. I'm going to drink beer, relax, play cards, listen to records, and practice." And do some important work in the lab. He was seized with anxiety at the thought of more postponement. "The world-famous Perham Downs have an engagement tonight in Krefeld."

"World famous?"

"Well, maybe just company-wide famous. Our dance band."

"And you play?"

"Alto sax."

"A dime a dozen, Dance. Tell them to get another saxophone."

"I'm the bandleader. This will to be a huge loss to the war effort. It's to help morale."

She finished her schnapps. "We leave in two hours. Class A uniform."

They made slow progress through the overflowing farm wagons, carts, and foot traffic—Germans fleeing the Russians, who had finally captured Berlin, as well as captured Poles, Czechs, and Hungarians released from labor camps. Their car, a striking black Mercedes recently driven by high-ranking Nazis, repelled the usual hordes of begging children who clustered around jeeps, certain of a handout from G.I.'s. Men and children startled Sam with a Nazi salute. "Are these the Germans who had nothing to do with anything?" asked Sam.

"I don't see many women saluting," said Bette. "They learn how to hide what they think."

Sam almost laughed. He was sitting next to one of the least repressed women he'd ever met, a spy who swore like a man. He caught himself. "My sisters complained that they couldn't do all the things I could do. It made them pretty angry at times. But the war has changed that."

"Not much. I mean, I can shoot, but I could before the war. I can fly—"

"You fly?"

"I was in the Civil Air Patrol before I was recruited. I own a plane with three other women from my hometown. A yellow Piper Cub. We have a flying club. That's why we joined the CAP. They'd pay for our fuel. We had patriotic reasons for it too—"

"Right."

She looked a little annoyed.

"Can't take a joke?"

"I don't—" she began heatedly, then said, "I really get quite serious about these things."

"What are we doing in Berlin?"

"Intelligence. I need to meet someone there. We need to find out how much the Russians know about Hadntz's Device. It seems to have some sort of . . . potential. We're going to be fighting the next war with the Soviet Union. We need to establish lines of communication."

Sam felt a pang of guilt about withholding information about Perler. "Aren't they our allies?"

"You don't trust Stalin any further than you can throw him, Sam. He's a murderer on a grander scale than Hitler. We just cut him off from Denmark last month. Hear about that?"

"I'm going to stick with you. You know everything."

"I'm briefed. I just know what I need to know. I sure as hell don't know much."

"More than me. I'm just a cog."

"You're—"

"I don't mind. I just want to do my part as best I can and then get back home. I want to finish my education. I was working nights before I joined up and going to school during the day. If I was doing nothing but going to school, I could knock it off pretty quick."

"You want to be an engineer?"

"It's not glamorous work. But it's essential. The country is going to need engineers like never before."

"What kind of engineer?"

"I want to be the kind of engineer that can do just about anything. Now, what the hell are we doing in Berlin, again?"

In their billet, a sparsely-furnished flat without gas, running water, or electricity, Sam spent a half hour practicing the use of a camera concealed in a matchbox. It was made by Leitz, the company where Keller's father had been an officer, and was rather amazing. When he opened it, there was a compartment of real matches. The operation of taking the picture was concealed by the act of striking the match and lighting the cigarette.

"No, no," she said. "Hold it in your hand like this. Bring it up to eye level, above the cigarette, as you strike the match." She guided his left hand, in which he held the camera. "You *are* right-handed?"

"Yeah. I'm just not particularly adept."

"Let's go over that again."

It took them another hour or so to prepare for their expedition. Then Bette locked the door behind them, to protect the bottles of water, tiny camp stove, food, and candles they'd hauled up. They descended narrow, scarred stairs and ventured out into ruined Berlin.

"How do you like your promotion?"

"Not much," Sam growled, imprisoned in a lieutenant's uniform. "I think I could be court-martialed for this." He carried two flashlights in his pockets. Bette had her own, as well as a small wireless, in her bag. Between them, they had three guns.

She linked her arm with his, and patted it with her free hand. "No, you're completely cleared for gigolo duty."

They walked between mounds of rubble, and passed countless blocks where only the ragged foundations of buildings remained. Berlin stank of bodies trapped under concrete, unfound and just beginning to thaw, and of feces and urine.

Sam was wildly uncomfortable holding the arm of a woman dressed to the nines. Beaten people shuffled past, picking through refuse wearing shoes held together by knotted rags. "I feel like I have a target on my back."

"Stop complaining, Dance. I'll protect you."

He had no doubt about that. In addition to her more obvious guns, Bette had a pen that was a gun as well as a stiletto, and shoes that extruded a knife from the heel. "Although I think they're misdesigned," she had grumbled as she sat on the single chair to squeeze her feet into them. "It would make more sense for the blade to come out of the toe. I'm sure it was designed by a man. I have to take the damned thing off to use it—not exactly subtle."

Bette prevented Sam from giving his two packs of cigarettes to anyone, even after he saw one woman bend over and pick up the pinched, soggy butt he had thrown away and drop it into a tin cup.

"She'll trade a bunch of them for a loaf of bread," Bette told him. "We're not here to save Berlin. It's beyond saving. See that gang of boys? Can't be any older than twelve. I guarantee that two weeks ago they were slaughtering everything that moved with machine guns. If they were honest, they'd tell you that they haven't lost—that the Fatherland has been betrayed. They've been taught since they were born that it's impossible to lose. Have you heard about Hans the Rocket Boy?"

"Who?"

"The SS was putting children in these rocket-fueled planes as test pilots. The kids were doomed. The planes couldn't be landed. The wheels dropped off to reduce drag once they took off. Hans managed to land it though, and when he got out he was wearing lederhosen and he looked like he was twelve years old. Actually, he's all of sixteen."

"I wouldn't have minded flying a rocket when I was sixteen."

Narrow lanes had been bulldozed through some of the streets. Roman aqueducts still supplied a trickle of water, but all of the waterworks, the pumps, and underground pipes were completely out of commission. Every few blocks, they saw long lines of grimy, exhausted-looking Germans, most of whom had passed the last few weeks of fierce battle in underground shelters, waiting to pump water. Two Russian soldiers sitting on a stoop called out to Bette.

"What did they say?"

"What do you think? They want to mate with me. They would pay me handsomely with cigarettes."

"They probably think I'm your pimp," he said grimly.

"That's enough out of you. There's the place . . . yes, there on the next block."

The setting sun shot an orange glow through a shattered building, and they walked through its jagged shadow.

A smiling Russian in a broad-shouldered gangster-type suit with a mended lapel greeted them at the threshold of what was now a club. Sam heard strains from a pretty fair dance band inside. Bette wore a red hat with a huge white ostrich feather sweeping down on one side of her head, and her face was behind a fine black veil studded with tiny rhinestone sequins.

"Five dollars each," the Russian said.

"Five—"

"Pay the man, dear," said Bette, jagging him with a sharp elbow. It was breathtaking. But once they sat down he had to buy two ten-dollar shots of vodka. The small fortune he'd been given was as nothing in this wasteland. Bette tossed back her drink and smiled. "There, now." She stuck a cigarette in an ebony cigarette holder. "Can't stand those ugly nicotine stains. They're *so* hard to get out of white gloves." She'd shrugged off her coat, revealing that her gloves extended to her elbows. "I really should have brought the mink wrap instead."

Sam bit his tongue. It was her show.

The room danced with candlelight. A few generator-powered airstrip lights hung from bare steel girders, blotting out the night sky, but they only served to give a bit of dim illumination to the goings-on. A woman in a long, tight-fitting, black dress took the microphone and crooned "Shine On, Harvest Moon" in Russian. The people at the next table clapped rowdily.

A man in a frayed business suit dropped into the empty chair between them. He said to Bette, "That is a marvelous hat. Where, may I ask, did you find it?"

"At a little shop on Avenue Montaigne in Paris."

"Will you excuse us, please?" he said to Sam, and they began conversing, very quietly, in Russian.

After a moment Bette threw back her head, laughed, and kicked Sam under the table with her toe. "Could I have a cigarette, dear?"

Sam thought the light was way too dim, but he commenced chain-smoking and taking pictures with his amazing matchbox camera.

At four A.M., they were back in the billet, and Bette had him photographing the papers she'd been passed. He'd taken pictures of one set, in which he recognized drawings of the Hadntz Device—though again, configured slightly differently. Now he was on the second set. "Supposedly these are from the Kaiser Wilhelm Institute for Physics. Heisenberg's work. They were doing atomic research."

"For atomic bombs?"

"Of course. Heisenberg discovered nuclear fission, and he was a Nazi. Word is, though, that Hitler wasn't pursuing a bomb. He put everything into his vengeance weapons. But apparently the Russians have hauled off the heavy water and the uranium. Which is very bad luck. I don't know why Eisenhower left all this to them." She was becoming angry.

"I suppose that we haven't succeeded in developing an atomic weapon. We would have used it by now."

She didn't look at him. "Did you get that page there?"

"You're tired," he suggested.

"I'm mad as hell. Our guys fought all that way and then those pissant generals left Berlin to Stalin. We could have had it."

"Scuttlebutt is that it would have made for a pretty big fight. With Stalin. We've had enough, we got what we wanted, we don't need more territory."

"Neither do they."

"I thought you were Russian."

"I'm an American. And I think we've been had. Finished?" She folded the papers, fed them into the false back of her belt, and buckled it.

"Wow," said Sam. "You're a real spy."

"Shut up before I belt you one. Pun intended. Let's go."

Her blond hair gleamed in the dim light of the Hindenburg lamp. Delicate features. Blue eyes.

A thought struck him. "Did you really give that device to Perler?"

"What are you talking about? Who's Perler?"

"Perler is—"

"You're right. I'm tired. Let's go. This place makes me sick."

As they gathered their things, he said, "It strikes me as very odd that you don't want to talk about Perler. He had one of these devices."

"Be struck all you want, Sam. Don't forget the tripod."

Soon they were out of Berlin, driving down small, winding roads through the German countryside as the sky changed from black to gray.

As he drove, she folded and unfolded a piece of paper. Each time she unfolded it, she studied it for a moment, looked out the window, then folded it again and put it away. Each time she seemed a little more agitated.

Finally he said, "What are you looking at?"

"Private business."

"Oh."

She was silent as the sun rose. They drove through the blasted remains of what had been a forest. Shell-ripped trees rose from mud through which refugees slogged past the dead—soldiers who had fallen in the last defense of the Reich, mostly old men and boys. Then she said, "I'm not sure it will do any good."

"What?"

"Looking for my cousin."

"What cousin?" He was ready for some food and a nap, in that order. They were behind a band of Germans, men and women and children, all of them carrying everything they still owned.

Finally the crowd parted to let him pass. Several obediently raised their right arm in a Nazi salute as the Mercedes nosed through them. Sam stopped the car.

"What are you doing?" asked Bette.

"I'm really tired of this." He rummaged in the backseat and found the American flag that Bette had removed when they neared Berlin, and tied it onto the antenna.

"I think we should go," said Bette quietly.

"I was just getting ready to go."

"No, I mean to Ravensbrück. It's on the way," she said, and then he saw she was crying.

He put his arm around her shoulder. For a moment she hesitated, then dropped her head against his chest.

She whispered, "I'm just very afraid of what I'll see there. I'm not sure I can do this again."

"Again?"

"I've been to Auschwitz and Treblinka already. It's unspeakable."

He put the car in gear and moved forward again.

"I wouldn't recognize this cousin, and he wouldn't recognize me. We've never met. My mother is very upset about him. I just asked questions, looked at the records—oh, they kept very careful records, Sam. The sheer magnitude is numbing. I finally found a comrade of his, a soldier from his unit. He said that he thought that Mikhail might have been taken to Ravensbrück. That's all I know." She wiped her face and blew her nose. "It's unimaginable. So many people. Just . . . gone."

Bette had no trouble getting them into Ravensbrück. She spoke Russian, flashed the appropriate cards. Sam saw looks of sympathy on the faces of the Russians who had taken over the camp.

Together they roamed hastily established hospital wards, which were for the most part places where former prisoners could die clean and in peace. One nurse told them that they'd been able to save only about twenty percent of those they liberated. He helped Bette comb records until his vision blurred. Though he never suggested that her quest was hopeless, he knew that it was. And he knew that she did too, but was driven by fury, doggedness, a thoroughness of being which he increasingly admired and respected.

"We can never be whole again," she said, after five days of heartbreaking search, on their way back to Muchengladbach. "Not after this. Not ever. Let's get out of here. Head west."

After several hours, he said, "This is beginning to look somewhat familiar."

"We're getting close to Nordhausen," said Bette. "Near where you went with Hadntz." Her face was drawn; her eyes and nose were red from bouts of weeping. The next time he glanced at her she was asleep. Curled against the door, arms crossed, she moaned and muttered. He shook her.

"What?"

"You were having a nightmare."

"We'll stop." She directed him down ever smaller roads until they came to a mansion on the bluff of a river. He was so tired that he was practically driving in his sleep. Several command cars were parked in the sweeping driveway.

"Come on, Dance." She led him up the steps and threw open the heavy, beautifully carved wooden door. Just inside, a private drew a pistol. "Halt."

Sam glimpsed a beautifully appointed room. A fire blazed in the fireplace. A crystal chandelier hung overhead; heavy damask curtains were open, admitting gray twilight.

Two men stood at a large table, studying a map. One of them looked up.

"Elegante!" he said. "I never know when you're going to turn up next. Come in!"

"Jervowski! So good to see you again."

After a brief dinner, they were given adjoining rooms. The door between them was open; Sam saw Bette reach into her ditty bag and pull out a small book.

"What are you reading?"

She looked up. "Oh. Didn't see you there. Chinese poetry. Full of mountains and rivers and loneliness and a hell of a lot of drunken poets. It soothes me." She shut the door.

Sam fell onto his bed fully clothed. The next thing he knew, he was wakened by Bette. Her hair was wet and she smelled of soap. She wore a long T-shirt.

"Move over, Dance." She lay down next to him. "Just hold me. I'm feeling very sub-par."

He gathered her close. Some time during the night, they made love quietly, as if they had done so a thousand times, and then went to sleep.

In the morning, he awoke alone.

He got up and looked through both of their suites, taking in for the first time just how sumptuous they were.

Her small bag was not there, and, when he looked out the window, the Mercedes was gone. Women, he reflected, were always leaving him.

He missed her.

While availing himself of the luxurious shower, he was struck by a thought. Grabbing a heavy white towel, he rushed into the bedroom and dumped the contents of his bag on the floor and did not see it.

It was gone. No. There it was.

The camera. Full of exposed film from Berlin: the Russian-found Hadntz plan.

Bette was not a careless person. Either she would be back, or she intended him to have it.

He dressed and went downstairs in search of coffee and followed tantalizing smells coming from the rear of the mansion. Through open French doors, he saw Captain Jervowski, who waved him in. "Sit down."

A middle-aged woman holding a silver coffee pot asked, "Kafe?"

Sam nodded, asked the captain, "Where is Major Elegante?"

The captain shook out his napkin with an abrupt gesture. He frowned. "She got a call. Said to tell you she had to go to Moscow. Though heaven knows why she would want *you* to know such a thing. She said to give you a jeep from our pool."

On hearing the captain's clear irritation with his importance to Bette Elegante, Sam decided that the wisest course would be to keep his smile, as well as his growing sense of joy, to himself.

Just before Sam left, the captain came out and handed him a large, sealed envelope, and without comment turned and went back into the mansion. Sam drove down the road a while before pulling over and opening the envelope.

Dance:

I didn't try to wake you. You were exhausted. This is the first place they've been able to catch up with me in a week. Damn.

I'm at a loss to explain what has happened, except to say that I don't know where the future will take me. I have a lot of work to do. Important work, I think. It looks as if the war will soon be over for you. Not so, for me. What I'm trying to say is, something seemed to happen, for both of us, I think, but it can't matter. What I'm trying to say is— and this is very hard for me to say—don't wait for me. It will be a very long time before I come home—if ever.

All my love,
Bette

Beneath the note was her book of Chinese poetry.

Loss, rain, and mountains. Her gift to him.

His sense of desolation was muted by the note—strangely, because it held little hope. Yet, for him, it held all the hope in the world.

The Halfway House

O N A JUNE EVENING, Sam and Wink walked at a good pace toward the outskirts of town, where tank-blasted Muchengladbach gave way to linden-
flanked streets filled with beautiful homes. Wink's new girlfriend, Elsa, had one
such home. Her parents had fled to Munich. They remained there, but she returned,
found the house livable, and opened it up to the trickle of refugees returning from
the east.

Sam half-expected Bette to show up at any moment, in spite of her note, but she
did not. There was no way to get in touch with her. Still, he felt her presence, and despite, or maybe because of, her sudden disappearance, he knew that her own feelings mirrored his. Since Berlin and Ravensbrück, the perspective of Sam's writings
had subtly changed. The imagined reader was no longer just Keenan, but someone
in the future, for whom he kept a record.

Perhaps Bette.

Chemicals were distilling in their lab, and they could only wait for the long process to finish, drop by drop, which was why Sam had agreed to an evening's absence
from the lab.

"It's a floating population." Wink was talking, as usual, not only enamored of
Elsa, but enthralled by the fluidity of the inhabitants, and the stories he heard as he
eavesdropped. "They might stay a night or two, get some sleep and a little bit of
food, and move on. Elsa's got a heart of gold. And a basement overflowing with potatoes."

"It's free?"

"Of course not—are you nuts? She charges. It's a lot of work. But it's lovely. Her
father was the *Bürgermeister*."

"Probably piled up a lot of loot."

The imposing house, constructed of gold-colored bricks, was damaged only on
the right front porch, where a bomb fragment had fallen. To the left of the large front
door, a vase of fresh-cut forsythia, the bright yellow flowers spraying out in a circle,
were centered on a small table. Two elderly German men sat on porch chairs, smoking cigarette butts, and looked warily at Sam and Wink as they climbed the steps.

When they walked into the front room, lavishly furnished with Beaux-Arts couches, chairs, and tables, conversation stopped. Sam counted nine women and three men in the parlor and glimpsed a few more sitting at a vast dining room table in the next room, all looking at them with curiosity and some suspicion.

After Elsa emerged from the dining room and welcomed them, the low murmur of German returned. The windows were open, the long drapes pinned back, and the cool night breeze dispelled the fusty smell of the refugees, with their ragged clothing and improvised shoes. Electricity had not been restored to this part of town, and candles cast their glow from the mantle. Striped silk wallpaper, blackened in the corner where the porch roof had been, caught the flickering light.

They took two empty chairs and lit cigarettes. The Germans turned their heads longingly and Wink said in a low voice, "I can't go passing out cigarettes here every night—they'll get the butts. There's Elsa."

She brought them glasses of Rhône wine. She was buxom, and although otherwise thin, she was not as emaciated as most of her guests. "I am busy right now." She kissed Wink on the cheek and returned to the dining room.

Sam took a sip. "Tastes familiar."

"Well, yes, it's part of last week's requisition. But we have some extra crates."

"That depends on your definition of extra."

"Got those records for the *biergarten* in return."

"The Billie Holiday?"

Wink nodded.

"Excellent! That source does need cultivating."

"I thought you'd approve. In fact—there he is. Our underground jazz buff himself." Wink waved one of the men over. "Hans!"

Hans was short, and the grip of his hand was strong and confident. "I speak English," he proclaimed. "I hope it is good. I worked on it in secret for many years."

"He ran a radio station in Koblenz."

"Yes," said Hans. "I have more records, if—"

"Don't worry," said Wink, patting his pocket. Sam had watched him stuff them with cigarettes before leaving. "We definitely want the records."

"I have something more. Come upstairs."

In his large front bedroom—secured, no doubt, with his cigarette supply—was a mahogany four-poster bed. Covered with what was surely a hand-crocheted spread, it was neatly made. Next to it, on a night stand, a light was provided by a Hindenburg lamp. On top of the bed were—

"See!"

"Where did you get these? It's amazing." A saxophone, a cornet, and a clarinet lay in a neat row on the bed. The saxophone was dented; the cornet likewise. The clarinet was marred with long scratches.

"Would you join me in some playing?"

"Gladly," said Wink.

From the bottom drawer of his dresser, Hans took out a rag-wrapped bottle of Bordeaux. He opened it while Sam and Wink played experimental blats on their instruments.

"Let's tune to middle A," Wink suggested. They pushed and pulled various sliding metal parts on their horns until their middle A's sounded the same. After he poured each of them a glass of wine, Hans joined in.

"Okay," said Wink. "How about—"

" 'Sweet Georgia Brown,' " said Hans. He tapped out the time with his foot and they lit into it, veering and swaying, hitting a few sour notes.

"One more time," said Sam. "Let's try the chorus this way—" He played a few notes. They began again.

An admiring crowd crept into the bedroom. At a look from Wink, he and Sam both took off into "Koko," by far their favorite; each time it was different. They could not, of course, approach the way Diz and Bird did it, not by miles. But it was always new. They stretched it out, taking long solos, devising new call-and-response lines, ending up with a race to the finish and the cliff-hanging ending.

By now the room was packed. The Germans applauded and cheered and slapped them on the back.

"This is living," said Wink. "This is really living."

New musical thoughts surged through Sam like wildfire. It was almost like the time of his epiphany, in the mid-1930s, when he'd heard Jimmie Lunceford play "White Heat" on the radio. As Sam played, he was deep in another time, and his choices synched to that time. He worked in quotes from "Jazznocracy," "Sing, Sing, Sing," "White Heat," infusing into them all the ecstasy of hearing them for the first time on the radio.

Then he saw Dr. Hadntz.

She was sitting on the floor in the doorway. She wore a long, patched skirt, the stripes of which must once have been brightly colored but were now faded, and a white cotton blouse. Her hair, now black again, was held back from her forehead by a kerchief. Standing next to her was the old man, the former slave laborer, holding his violin and bow.

Sam nodded to him. He raised his violin and joined in.

Wink faltered for only a second, then met the Gypsy-infused rhythms and notes halfway. Hans, completely stymied, stopped playing. Sam twined his own notes into the garden of sound, which grew from this new strange seed, this melding of musical histories.

The violinist played with fierce abandon, his jazz instinctive and pure. Wink picked up his theme and played it with him for eight bars, in unison. Sam took the final three bars and used them to sweep into a new flight, which nevertheless referred back to the theme. His deep excitement fused into a steady, brilliant glow of certainty. There were no wrong notes, not then, not that night. Together they wove a new harmonic, which reached down to the very foundation of matter, where particles flickered in and out of existence, mirroring themselves elsewhere in absolute perfection, and then created a resonance of unheard, perhaps unhearable notes, which they all nonetheless strove for, and their striving, their thought, called those notes into being like a new world, with new horizons so wondrous that they could only come to life through sound.

It was, truly, a jazznocracy.

When they finally put down their instruments, there was profound silence. It was the kind of silence one sometimes felt in a church or in the wilderness—a living silence, filled with something beyond them all.

The violinist nodded briefly toward Sam and Wink. Hadntz rose, dusted off her skirt, and nodded toward them. "Thank you," she said.

Then they slid behind a wall of refugees and slipped from the room.

Sam and Wink both put down their instruments and made their way to the door of the bedroom. Running downstairs to the street, they looked up and down.

"They're gone," said Wink.

"I've seen the man before. He's one of the people Hadntz rescued at the refugee camp."

"Damn, he's good. More than good. He did something to me. Like Biederbecke. Like Bird."

"Exactly," said Sam. "And that was Dr. Hadntz."

"What?"

"The woman with him."

"No kidding. So she appears, and then vanishes. Doesn't even speak. Kind of like what happened to you in London, I guess, except that she didn't leave any new information."

"Maybe she did." Sam's mind still rang with new resonances.

People in the house were again talking, and Hans put on a record in his bedroom, which they heard faintly.

"Is that—"

"Yeah," said Wink. "Bird."

Of one accord they went back into the house to see what other riches Hans might have to offer.

Sam's second visit to the transients' house, the following week, did not end up quite as positively.

Hans was not there, and Hadntz did not put in an appearance, in spite of his hopes. Wink was on a nearby couch with Elsa, presumably saying the things that young lovers say in such situations. Sam was on his own, seated in an overstuffed chair, sipping beer, and trying to listen in on conversations he only half understood.

A new crowd was there; apparently the population changed pretty rapidly. Several Germans, including one surprisingly young, strong-looking man, sat at a card table playing cards and talking. Sam thought he may have been SS; certainly he was someone who had passed the war in a more privileged situation than the other refugees. Sam heard the word "Adolf " a few times.

Wink stood up. Elsa did too, and put one hand on his shoulder. He shook it off and strode over to the card players and started speaking rapid German.

He was a master of languages, and had easily picked up Platdeutch, the border-town German spoken here, a polyglot of all the nearby countries, modified by the local accent. Now he fired it at them for a good long time. The man stood threateningly before the women next to him pulled him back down into his seat. When Wink was done, after about twenty minutes of harangue, sweat stood out on his forehead.

"What was that all about?"

Wink's hands shook as he lit a cigarette. "They were wishing that Hitler was back. Saying, in fact, that he'd be back soon, that he's not really dead. They were talking about how wonderful he was and how the rest of the world destroyed their beautiful civilization. I told them that Hitler is to blame for this whole goddamned mess. That he created a world war and all this misery, and that he was a thug and a criminal and anyone who followed him was an idiot. Europe is in ruins because of him and his fucked-up ideas. How many people are dead? Who knows?" He gulped the rest of his wine. "Come on, let's go."

"I want another glass."

"I said, let's go."

"We are the occupiers," said Sam, "and I think it's a good idea for us to sit here and occupy this room for as long as we damned well please."

"That's the last wine I cart over here. The whole world is wrong and they're right. It borders on insanity."

The room was much quieter now, and the Germans were clearly discussing Wink, though in low tones, while occasionally looking over their shoulders at him.

Sam sipped his wine slowly, and Wink did the same, underlining the fact that Hitler had indeed lost the war.

Now that work was dying down as the German surrender took hold, Sam and Wink had time to get to work on the device. They had a clearer idea of what they were doing. Their travels through the technical wasteland of northeast Germany had yielded a lot of electronic loot. In addition, the German chemical industry, highly advanced, provided them with the kind of equipment they needed to refine the chemicals called for when they combined the two microfilm records they had—the papers Hadntz had shown in London, a seeming age ago, and the ones he had photographed in Berlin. They called Keller in to consult on the optical aspects of its creation, but showed him only the tiny segment of plans that he needed to see.

They called it the HD2; the second incarnation of the Hadntz Device.

One evening, Wink looked up from his examination of the papers. "Time for the blood."

"Did I hear you correctly?" Sam turned down the radio.

"Didn't you see this? Requires DNA. Which we have, right?"

"So does that moth over there."

"This is *ours*, bud. We can spit into this solution if we like, but don't you think that blood is a little more refined?"

"Echoes of Tom Sawyer," said Sam. "But what's the lead-up?"

"Remember the theory sections, about her proposed structure of DNA? It seems that there's proof that it carries our genetic information. I remember a little bit from premed. There's a discipline called molecular biology." He frowned. "They've been working on this stuff since the turn of the century. But . . . I don't know. . . . Anyway," his voice brightened, "to make a long story short, some genetic material is required and I say it might as well be our blood."

So they each made a nick in their index finger and squeezed some blood into the clear solution. It swirled slowly and voluptuously through the heavy liquid. Wink picked up the beaker and shook it. "Okay. That's that." They'd laid in a supply of brewer's yeast as a growing medium for whatever was to occur. They'd procured their present cavity magnetron via the local—and exceedingly rich—black market for military goods.

Sam was beginning to think of it as a terribly long, involved cooking project. "It would be a lot easier to build a rocket."

Wink sighed. "Yeah. I think that's her point. I wonder how long we wait this time?"

Not long, it turned out. Power raced through the solution, and they both had to look away from the glare it generated, and step back from the heat.

Again, Sam heard the music—possible forays of notes, each suggesting the next, partnered by harmonics so beautiful, so unique, that he had an instant of wishing that he could write them down. Maybe this is what it's like for Bird, he thought. Rafferty had brought Bird-lore with his record, including the fact that Charlie Parker was too busy thinking to write anything down. The next idea was always building on the last one, or crowding it out, as lightning struck again and again.

The landscapes this present lightning illuminated, though, were once again horrific. As the music faded and vision kicked in, he saw images of death and destruction, mobs rioting, soldiers shooting at random into a crowd. He saw young soldiers of all nations sacrificing themselves for some imagined peace, some longed-for utopia.

And he saw, in the last moments, Hadntz's paper, her thoughts, suffusing his mind, and wrenching his future from him.

"What—was that?" asked Wink. He was still leaning on both arms over the table, as was Sam.

"What is this?" asked Sam.

It was a clear, oblong object, about the size of a paperback book.

Wink straightened and crossed his arms. He nodded his head for a long minute, biting his bottom lip. "Good thing we weren't planning on using the magnetron again. So, did you see the process of how the hell this thing went from some kind of broth to something that seems to have no moving parts?"

Sam shook his head. "Seemed like it only took a minute or so." He looked at his watch. "Except that we've missed lunch and dinner."

They could only agree that at some point they had become saturated with something—some medium that invaded them, rearranging them as if they were composed of notes. And as if they were modern jazz, their previously predictable notes were taken apart, renewed, and reassembled.

"At least that's how I felt," said Sam, as they sat next to the device later that evening. "And afterward, I felt astoundingly refreshed. Still do."

"It's rather frightening," said Wink.

They regarded the product, which had gone from transparent to a milky opalescent-green solid.

"I don't see anything, anymore," said Sam.

"Nor hear anything, either."

"Maybe it's finished. Done it's work. *Kaput.*"

Wink shrugged. "Or maybe it's storing up information. Looking for new targets. Maybe it will swing into action, like the M-9, once it finds something. Like other people. And do the same thing, whatever it was. It was kind of like what I'd imagine hiking to one of those really high mountains might be. Oxygen thin. View infinite." His voice became gentle; quiet. "Infinite," he repeated.

They settled on a hiding place for the device: in plain view.

They flipped a coin; Sam lost. Gathering his courage, Sam picked it up. Nothing happened, which was as he had hoped; he was not reassured by the unpredictable effect it had had on them already.

Although they thought of various assays and tests, they performed only those which seemed unlikely to cause it damage. It remained at 98.6 degrees no matter what the surrounding temperature was. It was hard, but not brittle, and smooth as polished aluminum. To Sam's relief, nothing about it seemed to leap out and into him. He slid it like a book onto one side of the shelf above their work table, a shelf heaped with magnets, wires, screws, oily rags, and the other detritus of mechanics.

The following week, he was loading metal trays on a truck bound for Düsseldorf when Wink punched him lightly in the shoulder.

"Where's Perler?"

Sam put down his load. "I don't know. Why?"

"We've been robbed."

Upstairs, Sam beheld a two-foot-square area where a wooden floor used to be. Wink had moved the desk that had covered it to one side.

"How'd he do that?" Sam knelt and looked down. Directly beneath the hole was a boiler. He could see its rusted top, cold with disuse. Sam stood up. "Why didn't we think of this?"

"It probably took him all night."

"Maybe all of several nights. These boards are three inches thick."

They split up and searched his haunts. He was nowhere to be found.

"I know where he lives," said Sam. "Above the drugstore."

He hadn't been down that street in a while. Now it was coming back to life. Where before, there had been nothing for sale, there were now a few things—used clothing, cooking implements, and the like—in dilapidated, but opened, storefronts.

When he came to the drugstore, though, he was surprised.

It was neat, intact. The sign had been repainted. Its windows sparkled—no small accomplishment on these dust-ridden streets. The door stood open, and he went inside.

On the shelves were modest stocks of various items. A small stack of bandages; two tins of tooth powder; a bottle of alcohol. It was thriving compared to most of the shops.

Behind the counter stood a young, blond woman. She was strongly built, was neatly dressed, and had Perler's eyes.

"Can I help you, sir?" she asked, in well-rehearsed English.

"You're Perler's daughter?"

She said nothing.

"He's been working with us on the telephone system."

She nodded, seemed to relax a bit.

"Have you seen him?"

She shook her head. "Gone," she said.

"Where?"

"My English—"

"Cut the crap!"

She lifted her eyebrows and raised both hands. "Would you like to buy an aspirin, sir?"

"Would you like to meet my commander?"

The bluff worked. A brief look of fright crossed her face.

"Tell me. Now!"

She gestured. "East. His . . . brother. Berlin."

Beyond their grasp. There was no way to find one person in the morass of Germany, where everything was shattered. The little store seemed airless, and Sam's feeling of loss was odd, profound. The colors of the things on the shelves became intense, and he was drawn into their brightness, the glittering bit of evening sunlight on the bottle of alchohol . . .

"Sir! *Ami!*" The sting of ammonia cut like a knife through his skull.

He coughed, pushed away her hand, and returned from wherever he had been. The small, dark store enclosed him, except that the low evening sun that came through the open doorway now illuminated the stolid face of Perler's daughter. On the wooden counter between them lay a broken ammonia capsule.

"Okay?" she asked, her voice anxious.

"I'm sorry," he said. "How much?"

She looked puzzled.

"For the smelling salts." He gestured.

She shook her head. *"Nien."*

He got out a pack of Pall Malls, set them on her counter, and left.

Near the end of July, their German idyll was drawing to a close.

The *biergarten* was by now a true garden, suffused with blossoms. Blue-flowering vines covered the back wall, illuminated by colored lights swaying in the night breeze.

Lise and Karl had grown especially attached to Sam. Lise haunted the *biergarten*, sitting in the shadows in the evenings. Occasionally, when Rafferty played a German song on his accordion, she broke out in a smile and forgot herself, danced, or sang along. But her world was gone, and so far there was little to take its place. There were thousands of children like her in Europe. Most were not lucky enough to know who their parents were, and most of the parents were dead, anyway. The children were settled in displaced persons' camps. Lise, at least, lived with her cousin, near the house in which she'd grown up. The GI's became her new family; they were her pals; she was their adopted child

When their orders came to leave, Sam was most concerned for Lise. He left her a huge stock of cigarettes—money was of little use—and his parents' address. He took her photo, standing straight in the street in front of the town house, and took pictures of all the children, of the *biergarten*, of the strange and golden time between when war was over and they need no longer fight and the time when the stark numbers prefiguring starvation became overwhelming and the work of rebuilding Europe began.

But the 610th was not out of the war. They were just moving to the Pacific. They were to load up all of their equipment, head back to Camp Lucky Strike, and wait for a boat at Le Havre. Once back in the United States, they were each entitled to two weeks' leave, after which they were to set up ordnance shops on LST's—Landing Ships, Tank—in San Francisco and sail west to supply the troops fighting Japan.

It was an emotional time. Most of the men had girlfriends, to whom they bade farewell. They had a huge party with all of the Germans.

On the morning of their departure, Sam stood in the vacant *biergarten*. It felt like a crossroad, a place where the past and future had come together, where something good had been created from ruins.

It was the place where Bette had appeared, in her red dress, and asked for a drink.

He heard a rustle behind him and turned. It was Lise. She stood at one corner of the bar.

"Goodbye, Lise," he said. He took a step toward her, but still shy, she turned and ran.

He went to a rose bush he had carefully rejuvenated, got his knife from his pocket, and cut a long stem for her. Glossy, dark green leaves framed the perfect rose. He wrapped the thorny stem in his handkerchief and set it on the bar. "This is for you, Lise," he said.

When their caravan was finally ready, the townsfolk turned out, crying and waving. As they drove off, he finally saw Lise, running alongside, holding her rose up. "*Auf Wiedersehen*, Mr. Sam," she shouted. "*Auf Wiedersehen!*"

"Goodbye, Lise," he yelled in return. "*Auf Wiedersehen.*"

We will meet again.

The caravan turned, and they were on the road to France.

The following day, it rained. The heavy trucks slid down slick hills, and the soldiers were drenched and chilled.

Around two in the afternoon, when they had stopped for a brief rest, a colonel drove up in a command car, driven by a private. "Winklemeyer and Dance?"

Dirty and tired, Sam asked with some apprehension, "What?"

"Orders. I'm to take you to the nearest base and get you on the first plane to the States."

"Guess this shoots our leave," said Sam, after he and Wink read their orders. "Look. What's that at the bottom. Isn't it Hadntz's writing?" They had seen enough of it.

TAKE IT WITH YOU, the familiar scribble read.

∷ 24 ∶

Circumnavigation

S EEMS LIKE THIS is building up to something," remarked Wink as they stood on the tarmac in Le Havre. It was around midnight, and supposedly a plane that would take them to the States was due to land any moment.

"No kidding," said Sam. "I wish I didn't have to carry everything I own on my back while it happens." His own duffel was perhaps overly full of books. They had shipped anything worth shipping home from Germany, keeping with them only what they needed. "Where do you think we're going?"

"To a nice warm interrogation booth in Washington."

Once on the plane, they zipped up their jackets, pushed their duffels against the skin of the plane, and slept on the floor all the way to Washington, D.C.

Upon arrival they were handed new orders by a bored sergeant and transferred almost immediately to an outgoing plane.

"The Pacific," said Wink, as they read their papers. "Out of the frying pan and into the fire."

"We're the advance guard for Company C, maybe. While they get to party for two weeks and see their girls, we've got to get the setup plans ready. Think that's it?"

"Maybe," said Wink. "But then, why the message from Hadntz on the first orders?"

None of the planes they boarded were designed for comfort. Sam and Wink slept on lumpy mail sacks, rope hammocks, and cold steel floors, and were gradually transported to Hickam Air Force Base on Oahu.

They had flown all night from San Francisco. Sam asked permission to crouch next to the pilot's seat so that he could watch dawn tinge the horizon and grow into day. His heart felt too large for his body as he looked down on a series of intensely green islands set in an intensely blue sea. "That's Oahu," said the copilot. "There's Pearl."

"Where's Kaena Point?"

The copilot pointed to a spit of land pointing northward. Keenan had driven out there, one day shortly before he had died.

Sam didn't have to be told where Pearl Harbor was. It was a blue bite taken from lush green land, filled with toy-sized ships, crowded with roads and buildings, the place where Keenan had died. Where Keenan still was, trapped on the *Arizona*. The water was so clear that he could see the sunken battleships—long, gray ghosts. For a moment before the plane turned and the rising sun seared his eyes, Sam thought he could see shattered parts of the ships scattered across the floor of the bay. He bowed his head, and held on tight as they landed smoothly and braked hard.

They were instructed to wait in a large, open hangar on wooden chairs near the desk of a bored private whose main function was to guard them. He read a comic book while tilted back in his chair with his feet on the desk.

"Is it possible for me to go over to Pearl Harbor for just a short time?" asked Sam.

"Hell, no," said the private, without looking up.

Rage and frustration boiled up in Sam.

"What kind of a deal is this?" Wink demanded. They were, somewhat oddly, rather tired, considering that their only responsibilities for the past two days in the air had been to sleep, read, and survive the drone of the propellers. Wink gestured toward the hangar's opening. "Isn't that the Aloha Tower?"

"It's out there somewhere."

"Well, it couldn't take more than a few minutes to run us down there. I hear they've got great bars in Honolulu."

"Look, you wanna beer, go down the hall to the canteen. They got beer."

"No, I want a bar, a genuine Pacific island bar, full of rowdy sailors throwing chairs around. I want a Polynesian beauty on my knee. I want to hear ukuleles playing in the moonlight as surf sighs softly on the sand and beer bottles crash into the garbage can."

The private finally looked up. "Hey, I can use that when I go downtown tonight. Those Polynesian babes just love poetry. I'm gonna have a whisky and chase it with . . . you know, one of those exotic South Pacific beers from all the *fine* breweries we got here in the Islands. I'm gonna get drunker than nine hundred dollars. I'll pick a fight and get my nose broke and get thrown out on the street and go to jail. I do that just about every night. It's fun here in Honolulu."

"Sadist," said Wink.

They sat down. "Guess that didn't work," said Wink.

Sam got up again. "I need to speak to your CO."

The private sighed, but got up and left the room. In about ten minutes he returned with a tall, heavy officer who had a stern, tanned face.

They stood and saluted.

"At ease. I'm Captain Harris. Hawkins says you're disturbing his cultural activities."

"Sir, my brother was on the *Arizona*, and I was wondering—"

"Ah. I see." He was silent for a moment. "You would have had the best view of the harbor from the plane. I'm afraid there's nothing to see at the site. There's no memorial. We're still at war here. Your orders are short and sweet and don't give me any leeway. You absolutely must be on the next plane out of here, without delay. I'd like to help you son, but—"

"If I could just—stand on the dock—" Stand there and look out, out, over the blue water, with the mechanical din of the military base at his back. Just to know what it felt like for Keenan, to stand where he might have stood . . .

"It is just not possible. I am sorry." He shook Sam's hand. "Damned sorry."

After the captain left, the private said, "I'll be right back." Soon he returned with a cold bottle of beer from the canteen for each of them. "Least I could do," he said, his eyes averted.

"Thank you," said Sam.

He drank his beer in the open doorway, breathing deeply of fresh Pacific air mingled with the smell of diesel fuel, watching the most beautiful clouds he'd ever seen blanket the peaks of steep green mountains, and promised that he would someday return.

It took them another two days of flying to reach what looked like a speck in the ocean. "What's this?" asked Sam, leaning over the pilot's chair.

"Tinian."

"Looks pretty small. Lots going on, though."

"Largest airfield in the world," said the pilot.

"Maybe we're getting off here?"

"How the hell would I know? I'm just the driver. You've got some kind of special clearance."

And indeed, their orders had elicited confusion at every juncture, but they were checked and rechecked and always found to be genuine.

They were given cots in a storeroom. "It's nice to be special," observed Wink. They were roused at midnight. "Dance and Winklemeyer?"

"Yeah, we're that well-known crack combat team." Wink turned over and pulled the blankets up over his head. "I want mine over easy; bacon crisp."

The bare bulb overhead glared in their faces. "You're to report to hangar D immediately."

"Hurry up and wait," said Sam. He paused to splash water on his face from a water fountain they passed.

Security was tight at the hangar. A sergeant came by and gave them each two white pills.

"What are these?" asked Wink.

"Cyanide pills. Don't allow yourselves to be captured."

They were silent for a few beats. Then Wink said, "In for a penny, in for a pound."

At two A.M. they took off into a Pacific night spangled with stars, having been told that they were "observers."

Their plane was a flying instrument bank. "Is there anything you guys haven't got?" Sam asked of one guy calibrating an oscilloscope.

He glanced at Sam. "They're trying to get it from every angle."

"What?"

"You don't know?"

"I'm trying to find out."

"That plane up ahead is carrying an atomic bomb. They're going to drop it on Hiroshima, a city in Japan. If the weather's right."

Of one accord, they moved to a place where they wouldn't be heard. "I just don't understand," Wink said. "How did we get here?"

"I have a theory."

"I do too." They were both silent for a few moments.

"How the hell does she do it?"

"A better question in my estimation is 'why.'"

"'Why' is all right. 'Why' has a nice ruminative texture. We could kick 'why' around for quite a while."

"Hey, you guys know anything about radar? This screen seems to be on the blink."

Wink said, "Sure! You know, competent repairmen are very hard to find. We've been imported from halfway around the world to fix this very thing, sonny."

As the three planes flew, they got the heads-up that targeted Hiroshima. Chatter and tension increased.

Jake, the radar man, seemed calm and serious, but Sam detected some nervousness. Jake said, "I guess this will work. They've done tests, I gather. I think that one of the main problems for us is that there's going to be a huge shock wave that we have to outrace." He looked around at the plethora of photographic and other recording material that filled the plane. Oh." He got up and came back a moment later with dark goggles. "You can't look at it without wearing these."

"So what's the military significance of Hiroshima?" asked Wink.

"As I understand it, none. It's filled with Japanese civilians."

"What?" asked Wink.

"I've heard that this bomb is so powerful that we just want the Japanese to see what it can do."

"Oh," said Wink.

"Excuse us," said Sam, feeling sick.

They went to their stashed gear. Wink cleared his throat. "Time to get it out, you think?"

"From what I understand about Hadntz, I think this is what we came to do. They have a plan, she has a plan."

"Do we even have to get it out?"

"Might as well." Sam looked around the plane. "Looks like an empty window over there. We can just . . . hold it up."

Sam opened his duffel bag and found the spare shaving kit where he'd stashed the newest manifestation of Hadntz's plan. "I don't think it's good for us to be here. There's going to be a lot of radiation."

"Maybe that's the point. Us aside, I mean. Maybe this is the kind of force it takes to activate this stuff. Subatomic particles flying everywhere, if I recall some of those lectures correctly."

The Hadntz Device was still a solid, smooth oblong piece of material. Sam held it in his lap as they fast approached, over a dawn-tinted azure sea, what looked like several large islands. He could see the *Enola Gay* out front, and then below saw the T-shaped bridge that Jake had said was the target.

He caught his breath as a huge bomb fell from the *Enola Gay*. As he watched it fall, it exploded in midair.

Even wearing his goggles, Sam was blinded for an instant. When he could see again, the world looked unbelievably sharp and intense in a light more powerful than humans had ever before seen. Illuminated below was destruction on a grander, more lethal scale than he could have imagined.

This was what she had been talking about. The light of a million suns.

His vision was now darkened by dancing flash-shaped shadows wherever he looked. As he held the device to the window with both hands, it warmed to considerably more than his body temperature, but was not too hot to touch. He imagined that it stirred within his hands, and he saw it become transparent, for an instant, shot through with twisted, glowing threads of light that looked as though they extended into infinity. Through the device, he saw a monstrous, towering cloud, taller than the planes, dwarfing them, as the plane shot forward and pitched wildly, caught in the shock wave of the atomic explosion.

For a moment, Sam saw time as a foam, clear curved surfaces that shared each side with a different reality, his own consciousness sliding across one of myriad bubbles, held by a surface tension more intense than gravity: many worlds, infinitely multiplied, forever existing, holding their stories to them with a force that was being shaken, below him, with newly released particles whose bonds had previously been impossible to shatter. He—whatever he could be said to be—was simply packets of information, loosely related, the bonds of which could break, be rearranged, and relink without apparent dissonance. It all happened as smoothly as getting off the plane with the now wildly celebratory crew, he and Wink handing back their cyanide pills, and getting on the plane that would ship them out.

"So that's what Hadntz was talking about," said Sam, when they were next alone.

They were in the fuselage of a Curtiss C-46, amid a shipment of crates, lying down with their heads propped against their duffel bags, flying east over empty ocean. "That's what her colleagues were doing; that's what she rejected."

"And she claims that her device, which I suppose we have baptized, in a way, will be a much better alternative," said Wink. "Everything's changed now. We used to live in Before. Now we're living in After. I'm not sure what happened down there, but it must have been horrific. Japan will surrender now." He sighed. "At least the war is finally over. The whole war."

Sam couldn't stop thinking about all of the death he had witnessed, not only while flying over Hiroshima, but over Berlin, in France, in Bergen-Belsen, in Ravensbrück. He thought of all the children of war, so many of them now without any living relatives, having to make their way through life alone. Lise and Karl were only two of hundreds of thousands in Europe alone. And the war had raged in Asia with just as much destruction.

If he'd ever wished for revenge against Japan for Keenan's death, he realized, he'd had it.

"Let's look at it again." Sam sat up and got the metal box containing the device out of his duffel. Unlocking the box, he took out the device and set it on a crate.

It glowed, almost as if it might ignite on the instant. Yet it retained its same neutral temperature, not cold, as it was in the unheated fuselage of the plane, but not hot, either.

Sam held it between his hands and stared into it, shook his head, handed it to Wink.

Wink turned it every which way. "Something's happened to it."

Sam said, "As I recall from my Chicago lectures, an atomic explosion releases all kinds of particles. The bonds of the atom are broken, and all of the energies that have held them in place—"

"Stunningly powerful energies—"

"Unimaginably powerful energies—are released. The existence of a lot of these particles have only been theorized, of course, but they must have reacted with the device to produce this change."

"But what does the change do?" asked Wink. "What does it mean?"

"According to Hadntz's paper, it means that . . . I'm not sure . . . the genetic material of those within range of this device—whatever that is, but it's a limited distance—changes. Hadntz posits a structure kind of like a twisted ladder. The rungs of the ladder split apart during transmission of genetic material and link to another open-ended ladder, which then resolves into a new ladder."

"Therefore, something in us has changed. I felt something pretty amazing back there, when the bomb went off."

"Yeah." Wink nodded. "I felt . . . I don't know. I didn't even feel like a single person for a few instants. It was as if I was witnessing it for countless other people, people who needed to know what was happening. I was overwhelmed."

Sam nodded. "Just being in the vicinity of an atomic explosion couldn't have been good for us. I wonder what happened to the device."

"Maybe we'll never know. Maybe it was all just a pipe dream of hers. To end war forever."

Sam recalled the promise he had made her: to follow this path wherever it might lead.

But what if the path had just . . . ended?

They went over "The Hump"—the Himalayas—saw the Ganges, surveyed the Middle East from twenty-six thousand feet, and landed in a world that had just crossed a cusp of change from which it could never return. After that, there were many short hops in airplanes, made in both daylight and darkness.

"Around the world," remarked Wink at one point. "At least I can say I've circumnavigated the globe."

❘ 25 ❘

Victory

THEY WERE RETURNED to Company C at Camp Lucky Strike in the midst of a great victory-in-the-Pacific celebration. The Japanese had agreed to an unconditional surrender. The soldiers were wild with relief.

The enterprising men of Company C had set up a makeshift canteen. The line extended down one of the streets of Camp Lucky Strike as far as the eye could see. All over the camp there were similar lines as beer was distributed to enhance the celebratory atmosphere.

They were all there—Earl T., Jake, Kocab, Keller, The Mess, Grease.

When Earl T. saw them approaching down the road carrying their duffel bags, he shouted, "Hey! The conquering heroes are back!"

"Where'd they send you?" asked Jake, as they dropped their packs, wiped their foreheads, and accepted bottles of beer.

"Just more scut work," said Wink.

"Naaah," said Earl T. "Bet you guys dropped those bombs, eh?"

"You're absolutely right," said Sam. "We won the war singlehandedly."

"Great job. Glad you're back. We've got to get rid of all this booze."

"Always ready to do my part," said Wink.

"What about that bomb, anyway?" said Earl T. "It's something, isn't it? Truman said it's harnessing—now, what did he call it? 'The basic power of the universe.'"

"Here's the *Stars and Stripes*," said Howie, taking a folded copy from under his arm. "I'm getting all the issues I can. I suggest you guys do the same. Truman says, 'The force from which the sun draws its power has been loosed against those who brought war to the east.'"

"They say the Germans were working on an atom bomb," said Jake.

"I guess it was a closer thing than we thought. Damn. If they'd had one of those—"

"But why didn't we use this earlier?"

"Probably wasn't ready," said Howie. "It says, 'The battle of the laboratories held fateful risks for us as well as the battles of the air, land, and sea, and we have now won the battle of the laboratories as we have won the other battles.'"

"Amen," said Sam. "Let's drink to the battles of the laboratories."

They drank to that, and then to a great many other things.

They partied for two entire days, around the clock, passing wine bottles back and forth, singing, and even urging Wink and Sam to play, much to their surprise. Once they began, the other members of the Perham Downs got out their instruments and performed some appropriate tunes, gathering a large audience of beer-swigging soldiers. "We'll Meet Again," "Coming In on a Wing and a Prayer," It's Been a Long, Long Time," and finally—their masterpiece—"Jazznocracy."

Played out and getting thirsty, the Perham Downs granted Sam and Wink a final chorus. "Go ahead," said Zee. "Play some of that Chinese music."

"'Epistrophe,'" said Wink.

The excitement and joy that the others felt did not fully touch Sam. He threw in minor notes, modulated into a mournful riff.

Wink pulled him relentlessly back. He jumped an octave and came down on the tritone.

Modern. New. Sam smiled inwardly, followed, and invented with renewed enthusiasm.

They finished up with "Salt Peanuts," just to even things out.

When they were lined up to get on the boat at Le Havre the following day waiting to board the *Robin Sherwood*, they waited in line for two hours, and were becoming restive.

"Just let us on this goddamned tub," shouted Zee. His sentiments were echoed by several other soldiers.

"Look," said Earl T. "Isn't that Sunny? Down there at the end of the boat. Who's he with?"

"That's the harbormaster," said Jake. "Wonder what they're up to."

Sunny pulled a wad of bills from his pocket, began to peel them off.

"What the hell is going on?" said The Mess.

"He's paying him off, that's what," said Kocab.

Finally, the two men shook hands. Sunny turned and shouted, "All aboooaaard," with a huge wave of his arm.

It was discovered that the harbormaster had had orders to keep them in Europe so that they could return to Germany for an undetermined amount of time as part of the occupation. Sunny, who was independently wealthy, had persuaded him to let the 610th be the last group of soldiers out of Europe, although he denied it in the strongest manner possible. He was their hero.

The return trip was a continuation of the party, nothing like the trip over. The summertime Atlantic was flat. There was no need to hide among icebergs. There were no speed rolls. The freighter, having been used as a munitions transport, was gutted already, and filled with hammocks, which they accepted without grumbling. There was nothing but music, smoking, card games, and a nice, rolling sea.

They were free. They had done their job. They were going home.

Sam was leaving Europe, where he'd met Bette. He had taken to reading her book of Chinese poems, which were often about mountains and rivers, but just as often about parted lovers. He wondered if he ever would see her again. It seemed that few of the lovers in the poems did, but the form their longing took was exquisite.

Wink and Sam said good-bye to one another as the boat docked. The Army was loading GI's onto several trains, depending on their final destination. Sam was on a train to Ohio; Wink was headed for upstate New York. They were still in the Army; no one knew when they would be discharged.

They had each other's contact information—the addresses of their parents' homes—and made an agreement to meet in New York the following spring, on Easter eve at Minton's, figuring that this would be a time when both would be guaranteed to be free for at least a few days.

Sam had the device in his duffel. "It's your baby," Wink had said. "And the war's over. Maybe it worked. After the bomb, do you think anyone would be insane enough to start another one?"

Sam's group was called. "Easter," he yelled to Wink, as he hoisted his duffel bag and headed away from the war.

He thought.

Back Home

1945–1957

Yet I never weary of watching for you on the road.

—WANG CHIEN
A.D. 830, "On Hearing That His Friend
Was Coming Back from the War"
Translated by Arthur Waley, 1919

⊰| 26 |⊱

The New World Order

WHEN WE LANDED, we were still under orders to go home for fifteen days and report to our Texas camp. While home I got a fifteen-day extension by mail, followed by a twenty-two-day extension, followed by an order to report to Fort Benjamin Harrison, Indiana, on November 15 for discharge. As you can see, the military was in near collapse.

Right after Sam returned from overseas in late August, while on leave at his parent's house, his father called him to the breezeway door. Two men wearing black suits greeted him.

Sam accompanied them past the baskets of apples, corn, and cucumbers his mother had placed out for sale and steered them to the orchard. In relative privacy there, he turned down their job offer without much thought and got rid of them, which was harder. He still had no notice of discharge, but they seemed to think it would come soon, which was a cheering thought. Even though the OSS seemed convinced that the device did not "function," whatever that might mean, they did not believe he had lost it. He knew that they coveted it and were irritated that they did not have it and that was the long and short of his job offer—unless they were also after the photos Bette had left him in Germany. After they were gone he sat in the breezeway with his dad the rest of the afternoon, chatting and drinking beer.

Something in him was exhausted. Maybe, like many other G.I.'s, he had gone through things so strange that he just needed to reassure himself that the world was normal, that his wartime experiences had been some kind of fluke. His childhood home seemed like a good place in which to try to recapture some sense of surety.

Keenan was everywhere, and nowhere. It was as if he might breeze in at any moment, toss his hat on the hook, give their mother a hug, and say to Sam, "How about tonight, kid? The Odd Fellows are going to be whooping it up again and I've got an engraved invitation to the mayhem." His old room was still the same, even though he'd moved out years ago—a bookshelf filled with boyhood books, Boy Scout Eagle pin in a small cardboard box, his knife collection in the center drawer of his desk.

The war was over, but Keenan was still dead. Sam realized it slowly, day by day, as he steeped himself in their old haunts—the Puzzle River, Jimmy the Greek's, the now overgrown ballfield that Square Man Belford had carved out of an unused field years ago for his son and friends.

Hadntz's device had actually done nothing much, despite some promising signs. Maybe the entire war had been an hallucinatory dream—their labs, meeting Hadntz, being alone with Princess Elizabeth when she rode carefully around him that early morning on Mountbatten's estate. If not for his composition books, and Keenan's absence, he might have been able to persuade himself this was so.

At a complete loss as to where to put the device with which he was left, he finally incorporated it into a chest-high radio at his folk's house. This radio of his childhood, outmoded by a new, smaller model, had been relegated to the attic. Sam impressed upon his parents his sentimental attachment to the radio, but somehow did not care if it was destroyed in a fire or taken to the junkyard.

Sam made a side trip to Chicago to cheer himself up.

Don Bunnel and I spent a Sunday afternoon in '45 with Red Rodney in a tiny bar on the west side of Chicago, fed him drinks at our table between sets. I told him I had been hearing his records on Dave Garraway's WMAQ show; he said no, that was Diz. Red had no records yet, but he had Dizzy down cold.

Wink was the only person he knew who would appreciate this. He sent him a postcard about it, but got no reply.

After I got the discharge order, I started to scout for a college and got the serendipitous news about Purdue's schedule; the special semester began that very day. I went over, applied, and was accepted almost instantaneously.

He was pleased to read in the *Stars and Stripes* that the remainder of his education would be paid by the G.I. Bill.

He found a tiny apartment in West Lafayette, Indiana, a roommate named Carl Wetherald, who ate exactly one hamburger a day and wore only bib overalls—Sam dubbed him Overalls—and applied himself to electrical engineering, as there was no room for more physics or chemical engineering students. The program was fast-paced, with few breaks, and he was always taking more than the normal class load. There was a push to get the vets out and into the workforce.

But after everything he'd done in the war, it seemed easy. His saxophone gathered dust, although he still listened to jazz avidly, and kept up by listening to the radio and reading *Down Beat* and *Metronome*.

The members of the 610th were scattered into the postwar landscape, trying to pick up their delayed lives or start new ones. Sam tried to get in touch with Wink, but all of his postcards were returned. Sam figured he must have moved. He was probably just as busy.

Nightmares pursued him, dreams of burning children, dead children piled in mountain-high, tangled heaps of bodies, of orphans shunted around Europe to displaced persons' camps, of red-haired Charlie, blown to pieces, like thousands of other children in the war.

When he woke at night, sweating, he got up, smoked cigarettes, listened to the radio, and turned all the lamps on, trying make it look like the light of day, when such things could not happen.

Except that they happened in daylight, on thousands of bright, sunny days.

Hadntz had surely shown him why her device was necessary. It was too bad that she had left out the next step.

Sam made a trip to his parent's house. He removed the device from the radio and took it to the physics lab at Purdue in the middle of the night. The lab was relatively unpopulated at this hour except for a few hardcore physics nuts, so he was able to test the device with a Geiger counter in privacy. He was relieved to see that it was not radioactive—at least, it emitted no particles that the Geiger could pick up. Able to think of no other place that was as safe, he returned it to the radio in his parent's attic and tried to forget about it.

On an overcast March morning in 1946, while drinking his morning coffee at an oilcloth-covered table in his apartment, he opened the Chicago *Tribune* to the full text of a speech Churchill had given at Westminster College in Missouri:

> From Stettin in the Baltic to Trieste in the Adriatic an iron curtain has descended across the Continent. Behind that line lie all the capitals of the ancient states of Central and Eastern Europe. Warsaw, Berlin, Prague, Vienna, Budapest, Belgrade, Bucharest and Sofia, all these famous cities and the population around them lie in what I must call the Soviet sphere, and all are subject in one form or another, not only to Soviet influence but to a very high and, in some cases, increasing measure of control from Moscow . . .

Was that where Bette was now? Moscow?

Sam could see Churchill, stubby and powerful, his cigar, his black hat, his growl-face, and his transformational, childlike smile. The ex–Prime Minister's words, spoken with his special dramatic flair and import, brought back the real world. Sam was not doing his part.

But no. It was not true. He *had* done his part in the war. It was not his fault that the world had taken this turn, that the threat of atomic war hung over them, that

Stalin was now their enemy again, that small wars all over the globe holding the line against "Communism" seemed inevitable. The great promise of victory was diluted, withheld, by this new threat—the threat against which Churchill had warned, but that Roosevelt and Truman chose to ignore.

Maybe, though, it *was* his fault. He'd buried the device, tried to forget about it.

By this time it was only a month until Easter. It would be good to see Wink again.

By being even more frugal than Overalls, although it was a tight race, Sam saved enough money for his Easter weekend in New York. He even had enough for a bus ticket. Hitchhiking would have been cheaper, but not as dependable timewise.

Their agreement was to meet up at Minton's at midnight, Saturday. It was only nine o'clock when Sam arrived. He had slept on the bus and was not planning to spend money on a room. He could sleep on the way back.

Fifty-second Street was life squared. One glimpse of The Street and Sam knew once again joy, verve, the pleasure of being alive.

The marquees ranged down the street, brilliantly lit, a celebration of postwar electrical freedom. The Famous Door. The Club. The Onyx. All these riches were spread out before him. The only thing limiting him was time and money. Which one to choose? He saw all the well-known names: Pettiford, Art Tatum, Red Norvo.

Then he spotted the Three Deuces marquee. The names leaped out at him. Charlie Parker and his quintet. Miles Davis, Max Roach, Tommy Potter, and Duke Jordan.

It was a thrill to see Parker's name up in lights—he was getting his due. Sam recognized the other names from *Down Beat*. Maybe Wink was right. The world had been made new, and all wars were at an end, despite Churchill's pessimistic Iron Curtain speech. This must be so. Otherwise, modern jazz would not be so appreciated.

At any rate, he thought it a good sign.

He paid and crowded in among men wearing ties and jackets, most of them holding a drink or a beer in one hand and a cigarette in the other. He habitually went hatless, but other than that, he fit right in after getting a cold beer.

Squeezing toward the bandstand, he was transported to that night five years earlier, when he and Wink had been privileged to see Bird at the latter stage of his unfledging. His brain became a device tuned and retuned by Bird's notes; he was tossed like a plane in a wild storm across the astonishing sky of the man's mind. Though he'd collected what records he could afford, being here was so much richer than listening to records that it was like comparing a flat drawing of a street to walking down that street alive with people, talking to them, going into shops. Here, he could interact, see as well as hear, watch the man bring the notes out from where they flocked within him, building pressure until they burst forth as complex fragments united by tone, by instrument, by his fast-moving fingers, a blur on the keys of his alto sax.

Sweat ran down Bird's face. Despite his seeming success, his suit was as rumpled as before. In *Down Beat* Sam had read that the guy had had a nervous breakdown out in California. Well, now he was back on his feet. The Miles Davis guy on the trumpet wasn't half bad, but he was no match for Dizzy Gillespie.

Almost expecting to feel Wink's tap on his shoulder, he remained well after he ought to have left, to absorb all that he possibly could. When the band finally broke, he realized that it was almost midnight.

Sprinting down the street, he flagged a cab, damn the cost. "Minton's, Harlem," he told the driver. "Step on it."

As the cab reeled him through the neon wonderland of New York City, so dense with possibilities, joy sped through him; leaped out and met the neon lights as an equal in brilliance: soon he'd see Wink again.

He paid the driver with some of his last few dollars, and sped inside.

The place was packed. Monk was there, pouncing out ineffable chords. Fats Navarro was on trumpet. The sound in the tiny place ranged from overwhelming to intimate as Sam waited. The audience here ranged from the suited, as on Fifty-second Street, to men dressed in more shabby clothes, many with beards and wearing berets—in imitation of Diz, he supposed—eyes closed, intent on the music.

Wink never showed.

After Minton's closed, Sam sat on the sidewalk out front. A kick from a cop woke him up at dawn. "Get moving."

But where?

Pulling out his address book, Sam squinted at Wink's entry. Parents in upstate New York; he couldn't possibly go there.

But—he could call.

He converted his emergency three dollars into coins and nursed a cup of coffee until around nine A.M. It was, after all, Easter, but he was hoping that Wink's parents would choose a late church service.

He went to the back of the coffee shop, closed the door of the phone booth, and got the operator to dial his call after depositing many coins.

A woman answered. "Hello?"

"Mrs. Winklemeyer?"

"Who's this?"

"Sam. Sam Dance. Allen's Army buddy."

"Oh." Her voice went flat. "What do you want?"

"Well, I'm trying to track him down. I wondered if maybe something—"

"What is wrong with you, young man?"

"What do you mean?"

"What are you trying to do?"

A man's voice came on the phone. "Hello? Who is this?" he demanded.

"Sam Dance. I don't know if you remember—"

"If you call back, whoever you are, I'll have you arrested. My wife is hysterical."

"But—"

"Allen was killed in occupied Berlin. Whoever you are, Sam Dance knows that. I'm warning you." He slammed down the phone.

Sam held the phone in his hand and stared out through the glass of the booth.

In front of him, the lively scene of waitresses shoving plates at people sitting at the counter blurred. He concentrated on his breathing. Tried to orient himself.

Wink had not died in Berlin. Of this he was sure. Wink had crossed the Atlantic with him on the *Robin Sherwood*. Wink had given him this very telephone number as their boat docked.

But . . . he had not written. None of Sam's letters had been returned.

Wink had disappeared into the folds of time.

Sam slammed the phone onto the receiver and wrenched open the door.

"Mister, are you all right?" called out the waitress as he made his way unsteadily to the door.

The street was cool, the air fresh on this spring morning. It did not suit his mood. He shook with anger.

Damn Hadntz, and her device.

What else, *who* else, might disappear next?

He stuck out his thumb to start the long ride home.

The OSS kept after him, sending two guys to his frugal apartment after his first year of study. They again wore black suits, and again grilled him about the device. He simply claimed ignorance. He burned to ask about Bette—could think of nothing else—but didn't know if she was supposed to know him. Maybe they were trying to find out about her as much as the device.

One of them sat on his desk, dangling one leg and smoking a Lucky Strike, while the other made himself comfortable in the only chair. Sam wished that Overalls would put in an appearance, but he was out eating his hamburger of the day.

The two men hammered at Sam for a while about responsibility and patriotism and finally added in the promise of a good salary and when even that failed, left. But apparently this visit was automatically scheduled on the same day every year. He endured it each time unmoved. He wanted nothing more to do with intrigue, with the device. He just wanted to be left alone. He accepted that things had changed, that the world that he and Wink had inhabited had split, and that he had lost Bette. Perhaps even she had parted from him in the profound way that Wink had. His feelings about the device were not pleasant. The device, as he saw it now, had nothing to do with Hadntz's dreams of peace. It had, instead, to do with loss. And he'd had enough loss.

He did not feel sorry for himself, particularly when he compared his situation with that of the refugees in Europe, especially the children. But it was time to accept the loss, the changes. He forced himself to go through the motions—study, eat, even listen to jazz on the radio and read *Down Beat*. Jazz was his only salvation—timeless, an ever-moving Present, an infinite Now.

Sometimes he dreamed of Hadntz. It was always the same dream, brief and simple and not even very dreamlike. She wore an elegant dress of midnight-blue satin, a string of pearls, and heavy, foreign-looking black shoes. She spoke only in mathematics and he never remembered exactly what she said. Sometimes he dreamed of Bette, and he welcomed those dreams. He didn't have any hope of ever seeing her again, though. She'd probably forgotten him long ago.

As for Keenan, his desperate longing for his brother had modulated into simply missing him, daily. Any thoughts of revenge had been burned out of him by his witnessing the act that ended the war in the Pacific. If that wouldn't satisfy him, nothing would.

He felt guilt, apprehension, and a vague sense of failure at having abandoned Hadntz's dreams. But it was time to accept reality.

The diary-keeping had become a habit, and he continued it. He went through his composition books and added a lot of details, refined his past entries, but did so only for himself, to make an accurate record.

When it came time to make a career choice, remembering the fires of Europe, he went with the field of fire protection.

Finally, he graduated. It was 1947. Everybody was making money after the war. He quickly got a job at a large engineering firm. He thought he had a good idea, a moneymaking idea, and took it to the brass. They weren't interested.

So he made a phone call, then another. He took a long weekend and went to Aberdeen and was met at the gate by a man he'd known in the Army. This time the guy had a few more decorations on his sleeve.

Sam gave a presentation to a committee later that afternoon, and a few days later he got a phone call offering him a temporary contract with the War Department.

He had created the job. They'd even accepted his budget proposal—adequate, but not unduly inflated. Carefully thought out.

He got a modest number of War Department buildings outfitted with sprinkler systems. It was a start.

27

Reunion Blues

I N APRIL 1948, Sam held a reunion for the 610th.

It came about by accident.

He was living in Cleveland, working for an insurance company while he developed more government proposals.

It was a Saturday night in February and he was at a jazz bar, the Carousel. He was with his latest in a string of girlfriends, Doris Figley. Jimmy McPartland was playing. He was Dixieland-oriented, but when his wife Marion took the lead during the bridge, she was airy, impressionistic, modern. A strange mix—though Doris couldn't understand why, since she knew little about jazz, and was getting tired of rushing down the street to see Sarah Vaughan during the breaks.

"Dance!"

Sam turned. "*Kocab?*"

The company magician was cleaned up, well-dressed, and sported a wife, whom he introduced. Sam quickly recovered from his surprise. "What are you doing here?"

It was Kocab's turn to look surprised. "Lived here all my life." He patted his wife's hand. "And here's my childhood sweetheart. We've got a little girl. You think our parents are going to let us move away? Besides, who would do the baby-sitting if we did."

After a few drinks, Kocab said, "We ought to have a reunion."

An instant of fear passed through Sam. He'd have to endure Wink's loss afresh. Eventually, Kocab talked him into it—he couldn't find any logical reason to object.

By the time the night was through, Sam had agreed to find a venue, and Kocab was going to take care of the invitations. This was deliberate. Sam couldn't face trying to contact the others. After his experience with Wink, he didn't know what would happen.

The room Sam scouted out was perfect: right size, right price, even right acoustics. He nervously checked and rechecked the bar arrangements, the food setup, the DJ's directions. By six, the reunion was off to a swinging start. The guys were trickling in, many with wives and some with girlfriends, poking fun at one another, swapping stories.

Wild Card Zee held forth to one group. "Hell, yeah, I'm up on a hill on the edge of town, got enough guns, some loudspeakers that play calliope music when I see somebody comin'. They all think I'm nuts in town. They keep away and that's what I like. Tell the little kids, keep away from the nasty vet!" His laugh, a hoarse crescendo, echoed and haw-hawed over the low roar of the rest of the crowd.

The food was good; the dancing, the mingling, the stories as satisfying as Sam had imagined they would be. The decor was chosen to evoke the *biergarten*: fairy lights, a *volkspark*-like bar. Sam was completely busy with keeping it running smoothly and looked around for someone to spell him so he could socialize. He hadn't had much of a chance to talk to anyone.

Finally, Sam dropped into an empty chair at a table.

"Great party, Dance," Alberteen—the former Earl T.—offered from across the table. He had filled out, now that he was nearing thirty, and Sam realized that he'd served with boys and that he had been a boy himself.

"Oh yes," said his wife, a martini in one hand and a cigarette in the other "Thanks."

Alberteen said, "Say, want to join us on our trip to Berlin? The wives want to see it. We're thinking about organizing a group."

Sam was startled. "Are you sure it's the best place to go right now?" Stalin was presently trying to starve the Allied-controlled sector of Berlin, isolated from the rest of West Germany by a fifty-mile swath of Soviet-controlled territory. Truman had ordered that food be flown in; the Berlin Air Drop was in full swing. They were still struggling to rebuild the city. Not much had been left at the end of the war. He remembered it as the landscape of Armageddon. He couldn't imagine what these women would do in such a place.

Alberteen fished the olive out of his martini and popped it into his mouth. "No better time. Dollar's way up."

"I don't doubt that." The battle between Stalin and the West had begun over currency devaluation.

"Everybody's talking about it," said Jake's wife. "I just read a piece in the *New Yorker*. Nightclubs, shopping. What did they say? A showplace of postwar prosperity."

"What?" asked Sam, straining to hear over the Bird recording the DJ had just put on the record player. The sharp array of notes hijacked his thoughts, his being, and the world seemed to jump with the octave jumps, move between two different keys, with such ease that it seemed like the most natural thing in the world, when in fact it defined a radically different way of looking at music, of playing it, of experiencing it.

Two different scales. *Two coinciding events, which come from their own pasts, share a few beats of unison, and then diverge into their own futures.*

"My company just got a big order from a plant in Berlin," said Alberteen. "That's what got us thinking. I could make it a business trip."

Sam could not speak for the enormity of what he was hearing.

It had worked.

But not for him.

Then Wink walked in the door.

Sam was dumbfounded.

Wink's face lit in a huge smile when he spotted Sam, and he hollered "Dance!" over the myriad conversations, the jumping drums and hi-hat accents of bebop. He grabbed a drink on his way to Sam's table, gulped it down, and picked up another, all in an instant of smooth, utterly Winklike grace.

Feeling ill, Sam made his way toward him.

"Damn, it's good to see you, Dance." Then, "What's wrong?"

His face was unlined, still boyish; his eyes were that old party-merry that Sam remembered, and his nasal New York voice still ruled the room.

"What's wrong is that Mutt and Jeff over there are taking their wives to Berlin. It's the hot spot. The place to be."

"That's pretty much true. What's wrong with that?"

"No Soviet blockade?"

Wink suddenly looked completely sober. He lowered his voice. "No."

"Well then, what is Stalin—"

"Stalin's dead. Assassinated right after the war by a bunch of Poles. Don't know how they did it. Molotov went into hiding. They got a new top guy. I can never remember his name, but he's one of the old Bolshies who'd survived in exile—a White Russian."

Sam shook his head. "No. Uh-uh. This is different."

"Different than what? How many fingers am I holding up?"

"Something happened."

Wink looked at him steadily.

"That's not the way it is. In . . ." He was at a loss for words.

Wink stared at him. "Christ on a stick."

"Truman president." Sam ticked off the main points as they sat in a dark corner, their voices masked by the music. Two draft beers stood reassuringly on the white tablecloth.

"Yes."

"Attlee is prime minister."

Wink shook his head. "Churchill."

"No, no," said Sam. "Attlee, Churchill's nemesis, called an election in 1945. Right in the middle of negotiations at Potsdam with Stalin and Truman about postwar

Europe. Churchill had to leave Potsdam for a few days. The negotiations were fumbled, especially after Churchill lost the election and then came back to the table. Except they weren't fumbled by Stalin. He got what he wanted, pretty much."

"Impossible!" Wink's single word was vehement. "After Stalin was killed, Churchill held negotiations together. Got us—the Americans—to agree to a less punitive peace for Germany than what Marshall and Morgenthau wanted. After the Allies took Berlin—"

"No. Eisenhower let Stalin take Berlin. Was Stalin killed before that?"

Wink looked somewhere over Sam's shoulder. "No. But the Russians *didn't* get to Berlin first. There *was* an agreement to let them take Berlin first. Eisenhower was fit to be tied and sent Patton east. We took it."

"That is quite different. Maybe that's when it happened."

"Maybe. Or maybe it was about the time we were on that strange tour in the Pacific."

"Or right after. What if Sunny hadn't gotten us on the boat? We would have been sent to Berlin for the occupation."

"In *your* world," said Wink.

"This *is* my world," said Sam, getting irritated. "I'm here. Kocab's here."

"Yes, but you have other memories. And I'll bet you any money that when this reunion is over you won't be able to find me again. Or Kocab. And I won't be able to find you. I mean, where the hell were you on Easter Eve? Go ahead. Tell me. I'll bet you were at Minton's. And I was too."

"Who was playing?" asked Sam.

"Bird. You would have loved it."

"No. I did see him, and I did love it. But he was playing at the Three Deuces, with a kid named Miles Davis on trumpet. I watched him there, then blew most of my money on a cab to Minton's because I was late. Monk was there. But Bird didn't show."

"This is my theory," said Wink. "See what you think. The device was activated in the Pacific. It was spewing out—whatever—some kind of subatomic particle that has an effect on that whole delicate mechanism that Hadntz described in her paper. You know, the genes, consciousness, the sense of time . . ."

"And it affected the whole group," said Sam. "At Camp Lucky Strike, and then on the boat."

"There must be others," said Wink. "There were a lot of people on the boat."

"So why didn't it affect me?"

"It did. Obviously. But for some reason were each in a slightly different time—"

"Slightly!"

"We still have the war in common. I think."

They began to thrash through their war experiences, telling their war stories.

They were pretty well synched. Finally they gave up. "It's impossible," said Wink. "It could be any little thing. Maybe it was right after we got off that observation plane."

"No," said Sam. "It was just a series of hops till we got to France. Tinian to the Philippines. The Philippines to India. India to Palestine. Palestine to Libya."

"Palestine to Morocco," said Wink. "The plane went to Morocco."

"That's it, then," said Sam. He gulped down his drink, set the glass down on the table, hard. "I went to Libya."

"We must have looped apart then, because—"

"We met up again. Yeah. Flew to Paris, and took ground transport to Camp Lucky Strike."

"Back together—at least for the camp?"

"What did we play? At the last."

" 'Salt Peanuts'."

"And who won the most money at cards on the boat?"

"That's no mystery. Wild Card Zee. I guess nobody figured out how he cheats."

"I did. He deals himself six cards, doesn't fan them out, at some point discards two. Risky, but he's slick. Let's try something a little more difficult."

They finally agreed that they had both crossed the Atlantic on the *Robin Sherwood*.

Sam said, "Then who's that Wink that died in . . . in my world?"

"Look, didn't Hadntz postulate that time is constantly splitting? Instant by instant. But our consciousness doesn't register that. Seems to stay steady. So there are probably uncountable selves, uncountable worlds, uncountable realities."

"All with their own share of misery, obviously."

"I don't know," Wink said. "She seemed to sincerely believe that, in some time-line, war would end. Through the use of her device. People would somehow become less aggressive. There was some gene that caused people to . . . like one another. To get along."

"Now that I think about it, it sounds like Sunday school."

"With a twist, though. Where would you rather live? This might really work. I mean, what did I tell you? We're *not* at odds with the Russians. We're not spending money maintaining troops in Europe. We're not amassing a nuclear arsenal, which I presume you are. We're on a big kick to make the schools better. Train more engineers and scientists. A bill just passed in Congress mandating equal rights by federal law to Negroes. A whole lot of them kicked up a fuss after the war about the way they were being treated after having served their country."

"Can I switch?" Sam was being sarcastic. Wink knew it, but deliberately took him seriously.

"It might be too late. I mean, we won't have this critical mass for long. These guys will be gone tomorrow. Kocab seems to be the link."

"He probably has different memories too. We didn't really talk about it much. What are you doing now?"

"I finished my degree at MIT and I'm working at a big research facility."

"What are you researching?"

"Peaceful uses for atomic energy."

"I'm saving people from fires."

"Good man."

They were deep in conversation at four A.M., as were a few other guys, sitting at various tables, all of them extremely drunk.

Then Wink excused himself to use the bathroom. Zee, disheveled and grinning, teetered across the room and said, "G'night, Dance. Great goddamned party. We gotta do it again."

The rest of the men left with Zee. And Wink did not return.

"Damn!" said Sam, when he realized what had happened. "*Damn!*" he shouted.

But that did not bring Wink's world back.

Sam went outside, his head spinning. The stars sprawled across the night sky. He lit a cigarette and smoked it furiously, wondering what he ought to do now.

The first thing he did was go to his parent's house. He got the device and brought it back to Cleveland.

In his apartment kitchen, he took it from its lead box and examined it carefully.

It was no longer clear, but smoke-gray.

The following day, he went through three newspapers, listened to the news, talked to his officemates with such enthusiasm about history and current events. He kept this up for two weeks, until he could see they thought he'd gone around the bend.

The HD2—the second incarnation of the Hadntz Device—still did not respond to his touch. Things remained constant.

As far as he could tell.

He considered his next move carefully. If the OSS was on their same clockwork schedule, they would arrive in a week and give their pitch. They could, conceivably, ransack his apartment.

He put the HD2 back in the lead box and returned it to the radio at his parent's house, satisfied that, for the moment, it was quiescent.

After that, he tried to look up Kocab. Found, through his mother-in-law, that Kocab and his wife had moved to California. "It was so sudden," she said wistfully. "I miss the baby. Sure, I'll send you their new address, as soon as they're settled."

At least he wasn't dead, Sam told himself.

He never did get that address, and the next time he tried, he could not reach any of Kocab's contacts.

Maybe Kocab had segued into that other time as smoothly as Bird segued from key to key.

Yes, it worked. But how? Did it need another nuclear blast to work again?

He considered creating another device, or taking the HD2 to the nuclear tests he was sure were taking place, somewhere in the world. Perhaps that would activate it. He didn't have access to that information, though.

It seemed best to leave things on an even keel. That, in itself, was not doing nothing. It was doing something.

It was leaving well enough alone.

His own world was strange enough.

I helped set up the Cincinnati office of the insurance company I worked for as engineer in charge.

Wright Aeronautical had built a huge war plant at Evendale, a suburb of Cincinnati, which became surplus at the end of the war. It consisted of five very major buildings ranging in size from about five to forty acres.

A new secret project occupied one of the smaller buildings, which I inspected, to develop a nuclear engine for an airplane that would never land (or not very often—details were sketchy), which I inspected. In one of my early trips through the atomic engine plant, I ran into a classmate from college.

Ed was affable enough, but I would have to rely on subsequent articles in *Pravda* for details on what progress was being made. I wasn't cleared to know anything else about it.

Sam did some of his own research, and discovered that the atomic airplane was supposed to be a perpetual warship which never had to land, since it would never need refueling. The design proposed an airship large enough for a thousand men, a village of warriors patrolling the globe from the air as submarines did beneath the oceans, with breaks only every few months, armed with nuclear bombs.

Atomic bomb games, atomic razor blades, and atomic golf balls, among many other "atomic" items, filled the stores. He reviewed atomic blast emergency plans from the point of view of fire protection.

The bomb had definitely changed this world.

⊰ 28 ⊱

Bette

ONE NIGHT IN JULY, Sam was awakened by a ringing phone.

The glowing dial on his bedside clock, blurry without his glasses, seemed roughly aligned to a three A.M. position. Instantly, he thought of his parents. In his hurry to get the phone, he stumbled over a stool in his dark kitchen and caught himself on the sink.

"Hello?"

The line hissed. Definitely long distance.

"Sam?" Her voice was small.

"Bette?"

Silence.

"Are you okay? Where are you? When can I see you?"

The phone went dead.

He could not sleep, so he made some coffee. After frittering around his apartment for an hour or so, he was relieved to hear the paper thump onto the front stoop. Putting on his robe, he retrieved it. Though he combed it from front to back, including the personals, he found nothing out of the ordinary. Finally he got dressed and took the streetcar to his office.

The next night, he didn't even plan to sleep. It was Friday, and Ellington was out at the pier, but Sam stuck by the phone, deciding he would do so as long as it took. It was summer, and his apartment windows were open. Humid air off the lake put a sweat on his Yuengling, and he brought the phone on its long cord into the living room and got out a bag of peanuts. Later, he might hear gunfire. As his mother repeatedly pointed out, Cleveland was not the best place in the world to live. He opened a Mickey Spillane novel he was reading to the marked page.

The phone did not ring.

It did not ring on Saturday night, Sunday night, Monday night, or Tuesday night.

It did ring on Wednesday night. Again, it was around three in the morning.

Bette's voice was stronger this time. "Sam?"

"Bette! How are you? It's been a long time."

"I know. Listen. I'm going to be in Washington this weekend and I'd love to see you."

"Where will you be?"

"The Mayflower."

"I'll be there."

"And Sam?"

"Yes?"

Her voice broke a little. "It's just lovely to hear you."

"You too."

He hung up, his deep glow of happiness edged with worry.

Union Station was a madhouse. Passengers ran to catch trains, the clicking signs rotated constantly with new trains, times, and destinations. He pushed back his feeling of nagging dread and stepped into the hazy late-afternoon sunshine of the nation's capital.

To his left, the Capitol blazed white. Columbus Circle, in front of the station, echoed all the lovely gardens and squares of the city, and was presently graced with purple lilies and pink, white, and red begonias.

Normally, he would have walked down 14th Street and checked the club scene. Instead, he grabbed an *Evening Star* from a newsboy and caught a Mall-bound streetcar.

The Mayflower had shed its shabby wartime business suit. The lobby was posh, elegant. Elegante, he thought, and smiled. It would take a goddamned month's salary for him to stay here. The Y, if it was still on 17th and K, was only a few blocks away. He turned to leave, and Bette was there.

His heart was beating hard. "Hello!"

"Hi!" She stepped forward into his open arms. She offered her cheek and stepped back, and stared at him, eyes brimming. "Um—let's get a drink and catch up. Have you heard from Wink?"

He considered, then said, "No."

She seemed to relax.

They went out into the hot, hazy evening. She steered him right. "Think we're going to have a thunderstorm soon. I love the storms here."

"How long have you been here?"

She glanced around. Though the sidewalks held plenty of pedestrians, none of them were particularly close. "I just got back from Moscow. I've been there for two years. Frankly, I'm frightened."

"You! I don't believe it."

"The war never ended. It may go nuclear. Did you know we're working on a hydrogen bomb?"

"No. I've been pretty much out of things." Except for seeing Wink. And that had taken him somewhere passing strange.

"Would you like to join the CIA?" she asked.

"You want to recruit me?" His heart sank. Not again. The OSS was now the CIA—same mission, same deadly dull black suits. They knew he'd seen Wink and they knew what was going on and they'd lured him here with Bette.

"And to ask you if you want to get married."

He stopped and turned to her, took both hands.

"When?"

"Let's talk about it."

"You're going to be offered a job," she told him over oysters at Hogates. She squeezed lemon on her sixth and sucked it down with gusto. Apparently she was no longer in worry mode.

"I've *been* offered a job. Several times. How much are they offering now?"

"Ah, practical you. Enough to raise a family on."

"Who the hell is following you?"

"SMERSH, probably. Russian intelligence. And you too."

"Why?"

"You'll be briefed."

"Maybe I should be briefed first."

"First before what?" Bette raised smiling eyes to his.

"Before we get married. I don't want to marry you for any other reason than the fact that I love you. What's your reason?"

"The absolute same. I'm thinking about quitting this line of work. As much as I possibly can. I'm telling you now, straight up, that there will always be ties. I want to have children."

"How many?"

"Two girls and a boy."

"What if the ratio is off?"

She grinned. "I can take anything you dish out, Dance."

"That goes both ways."

She sobered, and said in a fervent tone, "I hope so." She reached across the table and grasped his hand tightly.

"Absolutely not." Sam sat in Roscoe Hillenkoetter's office and turned down his generous offer. Hillenkoetter was presently the director of the recently created CIA.

Bette kept her poker face. He supposed that she was pretty good at that.

"If it's pay—"

"No."

"Well then, what?"

I don't want to hand over Wink's universe to these folks who fucked up the peace on a platter, thank you. "I can't accept your offer because you want me to give the—"

"Hadntz Device," Hillenkoetter prompted.

"To the government. Or whatever you are. I don't have it."

"I don't believe it."

Sam did not look at Bette. He was starting to get angry.

"You can't make that a condition of his employment, Roscoe." Bette was out of her seat, strolling matter-of-factly back and forth in the large office, hands in the pockets of her slacks. "That wasn't part of the deal."

Sam was relieved to hear that, but on the other hand, it could just be a game she and Hillenkoetter were playing.

"And as for you, Miss Elegante, I don't want to lose one of my best agents. This is all completely unreasonable."

"I agree." Sam got up and moved toward the door.

Hillenkoetter got up, followed him, and grabbed his arm. "Fine. Then I have another proposal. You'll be part of my new black ops department."

Bette was standing behind Hillenkoetter as he said this. Her eyes widened for an instant.

"Better pay, fewer duties."

"Which are?"

He laughed. "Never in writing. You'll have to move to D.C. Basically, you'll be on the payroll until we have a need for you. Till then—nothing. Maybe never."

"Well," said Bette. "He has a perfectly fine job with an insurance company, and that's okay with me. I don't think this will work out. But thanks, Roscoe. I appreciate it. You'll have my resignation by next Monday."

"I'll think about it," said Sam. They both looked surprised.

His main thought was, maybe I can get in touch with Wink, using whatever information *they* have, and figure out something between us. He had no intention of telling them he had the HD2, but he could find out what they knew.

Then he realized he was thinking like Them.

Well, maybe it was time to get with the program.

Hillenkoetter shook his hand with a firm, dry grip. "Welcome aboard, Dance."

They got married, he took a job with the U.S. Navy, found an apartment, and moved to Washington within a week.

∦ 29 ∦

Crossing Puzzle Creek

THE MORGANTOWN BRIDGE seemed like the gateway to a new world, a new wilderness of time. Bette's folks lived up north, in Michigan, and were summering at their place in East Tawas, on the shore of Lake Huron. After visiting them, they would loop down through Middleburg, and Bette would meet his folks.

And he would pick up the device. He hadn't told Bette this part. He still wasn't sure where she stood.

"It's so strange," Bette said, as they stopped at A&W for hot dogs and root beer floats. A girl roller-skated their order to the window tray.

"Root beer?"

"I just never thought I'd ever feel so . . . normal again."

"I don't suppose we've ever seen each other in normal circumstances."

"There's just that tie. Of thinking about you without end."

"I'm glad it got to you. " He leaned over and gave her a brief kiss.

"But there is a lot we ought to talk about."

"Like what you've been doing the past few years?"

"That's classified."

"So tell me."

"I can tell you in a general sort of way." She finished her hot dog and wiped her hands on a paper napkin. The summer wind rushed through the car and blew the napkin out the window. It skittered across the parking lot. She leaped out of the car, retrieved it, and stuffed it into a trash can. She got back in the car, but just stared out the window at the menu.

Finally, she spoke.

"It's Moscow. It's February. I have a fur coat, fur gloves, I look like an exotic animal. I'm in a café and my contact comes—"

"Your contact?"

"He's in the Kremlin. Risking his life, like all of us. And my aunt, she's—"

"What?"

"She's dead. Shot." Bette's voice was flat. "Purged along with thousands of others." She threw her float out the car window. It arced across the parking lot and smashed, foamy white, on the black pavement. The man in the next car looked at Sam with pity.

Bette covered her face with both hands and he held her close as she shook. "It's horrible. It's so horrible. Worse than the war. And I just . . . can't . . . stand it any more."

"You don't have to."

She flung herself against the door. Her pale face was red and blotched. Grabbing a napkin, she mopped at her face and blew her nose and laughed. "No, Dance, that's where you're wrong. I always have to. Always. There is no escape from this knowledge."

"Knowledge . . . of what?" he asked gently.

"Of the never-endingness of war. *We are still at war, Dance.*" Her tone of voice was fierce, angry. "And I want it to stop."

Sam took her hand. "At some point you just need to give it a rest. They were after it, you know. The OSS. They visited me several times."

"It?" Her tear-washed eyes were very blue.

"Hadntz's . . . device."

She stared at him. "Have you seen her again?" Her voice was level and restored, almost as if she had not been crying a moment before.

"Who do you have to tell if I tell you?"

She looked out at the roller-skating waitress. "You're right. Say nothing, then."

"So you're not out."

"No. I can never be out. I told you."

"I didn't know exactly what you meant."

"I'm telling you now. I am to be what is called a sleeper. They could wake me up at any time. I feel . . . the importance of it. Maybe I could cry and tell them that I'm a woman, I don't want all this, but it's the responsibility of . . . my soul." She looked at him gravely for a moment, then grinned wryly. "Want to annul this deal, Dance?" Her eyes were wide and full of absolute permission, but her expression reminded him of Keenan's before he dove off the high rock at Puzzle Creek Falls into swirling waters terrifyingly far below, something neither Sam nor any of their other buddies would ever attempt. For Keenan, it was part of his bargain with life: give and take no quarter. Test it, do it all, to the limit, head-on, with naked honesty, knowing all the risks. No matter how dangerous. For no one's satisfaction but your own, because otherwise you were not alive.

"Not on your life, Mrs. Dance."

So when he went up into the attic at home, he went alone, while his dad took Bette out to the orchard to show her the early-ripening Transparent apples. Unscrewing the back of the radio, he reached inside.

It wasn't there.

Deeply chilled, he went downstairs to look for a flashlight. "Going to visit Sarah later?" his mother asked. His sister had been asking him to see her new house.

"I think so, Ma. She wants to have us over for dinner. I want to meet my nephews."

He forced himself back up the stairs, thinking that perhaps the world had changed, that the device had never been there in the first place, even hoping for that: a burden lifted. Responsibility vanished. So easy.

This attic room had been the property of himself and Keenan. They had put down the floor, hammered up lath, and plastered the walls. The girls had taken over the sleeping porch for their territory. Neither area had been heated, so it took a certain amount of fortitude for the kids to avail themselves of privacy in the crowded house during the winter months.

Often when Sam had come up here, he had found Keenan reading in an old overstuffed chair in the corner. His taste as a boy ran to adventure books about the frozen north written by James Oliver Curwood, tales of isolation, courage, and moral triumph.

Sam unscrewed the back of the radio and removed the board that covered the insides. Shining the light into the radio, he was almost disappointed to see the lead box. He reached inside, pulled out the box, and opened it.

The device had changed.

It might be a radio, except that it was impossibly small, with no room for tubes. It was round, about the size of the cavity magnetron, but was a lightweight device of white plastic with one dial that was an on/off switch. Another controlled—volume? And another, frequency? What could this mean? This hadn't been built. This . . . *thing* . . . had rearranged itself in the past few years.

He leaned against the wall and shook with quiet laughter.

Maybe he should dial up Wink? Perhaps he could make him loud or quiet—how convenient. Or maybe he could move the antenna a bit; get a slightly different Wink. Change the frequency, and he might be in Wink's world and Bette gone. Dial in possible realities, and then fine-tune them. The possibilities got more hilarious by the second.

No, really. The physical appearance and characteristics had changed radically. It felt soft and warm, unshatterable. He ran his finger around one edge and a spectrum of soft lights appeared.

Fascinating.

If there was an antenna, it was inside, and there was no apparent source of power.

It was endlessly seductive. Combinations of colors beckoned, different sequences of access. But to what, he did not know. A square inch of something like a radar screen appeared, giving him several visible vectors of information. But of what?

It was a marvelous, intriguing puzzle. Funny to think that it had sprung from those equations he'd looked at back in his Washington room a lifetime ago.

"What's that?"

He turned to see his mother leaning over him.

"Oh. I didn't hear you coming up."

She reached over his shoulder and lifted it from his hand before he had a chance to object. "Some kind of machine . . ." The thing emitted a soft glow in the dim light.

She gasped, and dropped the thing. He followed her glance.

"It's . . . it's Keenan. Sam. It's Keenan." She was breathing hard, and put one hand to her chest.

Keenan indeed sat in his chair in the corner.

Sam did not move. Quietly he asked, over the pounding of his heart so loud that surely his mother and Keenan and the men in black suits and even Stalin, ten thousand miles away, must hear. "What is he doing?"

She forced out a whisper. "Reading."

"What?"

"*Popular.*" She cleared her throat and her voice became a bit stronger. "That's all I can see. A magazine."

Sam indeed recognized a recent issue of *Popular Mechanics*.

"How old is he?"

"Grown. Like he would be today if . . . he were alive."

"What is he wearing?"

"Green plaid shirt. He has a beard. He never grew a beard."

Keenan looked up from his reading and broke into a wide grin. "Oh, hi. I didn't see you."

His mother whispered *No,* and ran down the stairs. Keenan got up from his chair and walked toward Sam.

He vanished as he walked.

Sam grabbed the device and spent an hour patiently moving the two dials, methodically trying different combinations and sequences and writing them down so as not to repeat himself. He finally realized that he needed the computing power of the SCR-584 or better, and high speed, to run through all the possibilities. And then, if there was nothing to focus on, it would find nothing, infinitely.

Hadntz had proposed, in her paper, the creation of a quantum computer. Was this it? Perhaps it *was* working, even now. The heart's desire of both himself and his mother had appeared. Another world glimpsed?

Hearing footsteps, he turned. It was Bette.

"Sam, it's time for—" Then her eyes dropped to the device. "Mom seems kind of upset. She went for a walk. I've been getting dinner ready." She knelt beside him. "Something happened."

He sighed deeply. "Yes. We both saw Keenan."

Bette stared at him. "It . . . works."

He shrugged. "Something happened. Now it's stopped happening." He looked her full in the face, searching her eyes. "What do you have to do about this?"

"Nothing," she said decisively, putting her hand on his shoulder. "I didn't see anything."

"Treason. You'll be shot."

She stood and walked over to the window, her hands in the pockets of the ruffled apron she wore over plain slacks and a white shirt. She looked out the window for a long time. "What's all that stuff shining on the barn across the road?"

"Bottles. Johanstien strings them up by their necks and they clank together in the wind. Makes an unholy racket. He's been doing that as long as I remember. Dad says, Of all the places in the world why do I have to live across the road from a god-damn bottle farm?"

Bette laughed quietly. Then she turned, her face serious. "I meant it, Sam. I've had enough of war. I'm not even curious any more. Maybe something's wrong with me. I can't believe there will ever be a cure. It's like a dog chasing its tail. And the cure might be worse than the disease." She started downstairs. "Dinner's in ten minutes."

After a moment, Sam put the thing back in the radio and replaced the cover. He was sitting crosslegged on the floor when his mother came back up and sat on the top step. With the attic door open he could hear that the table was being set, and that his dad was listening to the evening news.

"Sam? What happened? What's going on?"

"I had to know. If we were seeing the same thing. Have you ever . . . wondered exactly what's going on?"

"As in, why are they charging so much for electricity?"

"Cosmically. Philosophically. Scientifically."

"Oh, sure. I ransack the library. I read philosophy. I read the Bible. What do you think religion's all about? Sometimes at night I might get into a funk looking at a dining room chair or a pot on the stove and wondering what it is, really, and why I am here. I guess you come by it honestly. But after Keenan—I just kind of stopped. For a while I didn't care what was going on. My curiosity failed completely. Just went away." She looked over in the corner. "Did you really see him?"

"I did."

"The mind can do funny things. After your grandmother died, I thought that I saw her once. It was downtown, on Fifth Street. I'd just come out of the baker's and she was on the next block, walking toward me, just like she had so many times when we went shopping together. It was a sunny day. Cool, in the springtime. Hedringer had daffodils growing in the barrel out front of his hardware store. For a moment it was like she had never died. It was the most uncanny feeling. She looked at me while she was crossing the street and my heart just raced. And then as she got closer, I saw that she was a complete stranger. She saw me staring at her and smiled at me as she passed.

She went on in a low, steady voice. "Sam, Keenan is dead. I went for a walk to try and think, to . . . to *recover.*" She took a deep breath.

"That was not Keenan we saw. It wasn't anyone. I don't like not caring a fig. I don't like just going through the motions. Neither do I like crying morning, noon, and night. But I simply cannot believe that Keenan is somewhere, alive. It's not in me. I don't have the energy for that anymore. I don't want to pin any hopes on a hallucination. Even if we both had it."

"You sound a lot like Bette."

"What do you think happened?"

"I don't know."

"It had something to do with that radio thing you had."

"Yes, it did. I'm pretty sure about that. But I couldn't . . . find him again. I've been trying ever since."

"I'm not saying that anything is impossible. I guess, given enough time, anything might be possible. You're dad's all worried now that the Russians might have the atomic bomb and that pretty soon they'll drop it on Middleburg and we'll all die like the poor Japanese in Hiroshima."

"I'm sure that they're working on it."

"I've lost one son to war, Sam. That's my limit. Whatever you're doing, please be careful."

Sam went down to Puzzle Creek alone the next morning.

He walked down a country road for a half-mile. The June corn was practically singing on both sides of the road and the sky was a clear blue bowl overhead. Heat was rising from the road already. One car approached him and he recognized April Mysen, a distant cousin, and waved as she passed.

When he got to the bridge he scrambled down the steep embankment and passed beneath it. A narrow trail accompanied the creek downstream on its way past old sycamores and gravel screes where it was at one time easy to find Indian arrowheads. Sam recalled days of smashing the thin ice over air pockets with a stick, or of swinging out on a rope over the deep swimming hole around the bend, letting go, and sailing down into the cool green depths.

After another half-mile the Puzzle deserved the appellation of small river as it gathered itself for the plunge into a larger waterway. He could hear the dull roar of the rapids now as the gorge narrowed. Sam rounded a bend, sweating, and sat on a boulder just at the point where he could see the whole railroad bridge.

The trestle was fifty feet high and a hundred feet long. It looked as if it was built for the express purpose of daring boys to walk across.

In fact, he saw movement in the woods and then three boys arrived at the end of the trestle. Obviously arguing.

He stood up and hiked up the hill toward them; his noise caught their attention and they watched his approach sullenly. One of them started an overhand volley of rocks, trying to hit the trestle.

"Morning."

"Hi," said one of them. Straw-colored hair stuck out below a Reds cap.

"Sam Dance."

They looked at each other. "Oh yeah," said Reds cap. "You live down Route 3, right?"

"My parents do."

"You're a vet."

"Right."

"My dad knows you," said the tallest. "Rob McElroy. He's a vet too."

"So you're Rob's boy."

"Bobby."

"Did he ever tell you about the day my brother got caught on the bridge with a train coming?"

They looked at him with new respect, then quickly looked away, trying to seem bored.

"Were you here too?" Rob's boy looked a lot like him at that age, thin and gangly as a colt, with a diffident slouch and a quiet, determined face.

"Oh, yeah," said Sam. He knew it was a minor local legend, one that these boys might try to match. "Can you imagine being out there on the track, the train whistles, you see it cross Route 3 there?"

"I'd just do what he did," said Bobby. "Grab hold of the tie, swing down . . ."

"What if your hands slipped?" asked Sam.

"My hands don't slip."

Sam persisted, that day's long-ago terror resurfacing. "What if the train was real, real long and your arms got tired?" That train had seemed endless as his brother hung there.

"My arms never get tired."

"Well, what if a bug started biting you?" asked one of the other boys, taking up the game.

Bobby McElroy stuck his chin out. "What if no train came? What if I just walked across? I mean," he said with a shrug. "It's not like we don't know the schedule, right?"

"You could always just *plan* on being on the track when the train comes, McElroy," said Reds cap. "Isn't that your plan?"

"Where's your brother now, Mr. Dance?" asked Bobby McElroy. "I'll tell my dad."

Sam looked out at the trestle. "I don't really know."

It was then he realized that he'd been hoping to see him, down here, in the land of their shared childhood.

He turned and walked toward Route 3 on the crunching gravel of the C&O's right-of-way.

When he got back to the house, he went to Keenan's bedroom and sat on the bed. A model zeppelin hung from the ceiling; the radio he'd sent away for with cereal coupons and built sat on his desk, but his mother had set up her sewing machine in front of the window. She could look out at the orchard, see clumps of big-leaved rhubarb and a row of pink peonies as she made shirts, pants, dresses, and curtains. Sam imagined that, with grandchildren, she was once again busy with patterns, fabrics, and pins.

He thought about how the new radar system had been installed at Pearl Harbor, and about the fact that it had actually worked.

The man on the receiving end hadn't reported it. That enemy planes might be approaching was a simple impossibility, beyond the scope of his imagination. A reality that simply didn't exist, except when it came into sight a few minutes later, setting the harbor and airfields aflame, sending the ships to the bottom of the harbor, and it was too late.

What, precisely, was *he* trying so hard to ignore?

Keenan rose up around him, not visible, but a presence streaming upward, dense with time, event, thought, action. Though the bed, the desk, the dresser, and the sewing machine were still there, objects embedded in whatever "here" was, it was as if they were also streaming upward, downward, into infinity in all directions, to places and frequencies to which he was not tuned and to which he never could be tuned. They both existed and did not exist. Sam just sat there, somewhat bemused, simply experiencing it: the presence of Keenan, and his goneness, concurrently.

"It's a pleasant room." His mother touched his shoulder.

"What if you could change things," he asked. "What if they could be . . . immeasurably better? Would you do it?"

"How could you ever know if they were really better, Sam?"

She could always get to the heart of things. "I'm not sure, Ma. I'm just not sure."

"It would surely be better," she said, sitting beside him and putting her arm around him, "if your brother were still here. Just about all we can do, though, is remember him."

"At least we can do that."

⫴ 30 ⫴

Metamorphosis

IN WASHINGTON, D.C., throughout the 1950s, Bette and Sam kept their pact about not talking about the device—sometimes uneasily, sometimes wholeheartedly. United against disclosing anything to the CIA, they tried to start their family and made frequent trips to New York to assuage Sam's hunger for live jazz. They got an apartment in Georgetown, and enjoyed Washington to the fullest.

They assumed Hadntz was dead.

Jill was born in 1950; Brian in 1952. Sam worked at the Navy Yard, where many government projects involving fire protection kept his interest.

Bette maintained a keen interest in world events. She still had relatives in the Soviet Union. "There's not much difference between the Soviets and Nazis," she said once, after receiving a particularly distressing letter, most of which was censored. "They have camps. They've killed millions. Many more millions than the Nazis, actually. I know things, Sam. I know things. And they're horrible." She was restless for weeks after that, in a perpetual black mood, saying that she should never have quit, that the war continued, that it would never end.

But they put all of their attention into raising their family. Megan was born in 1955. They were busy.

And then it changed.

One Sunday afternoon, Bette took the kids to the zoo, and Sam checked on the device.

He kept it in their town house's basement, in a space he'd created by chiseling several bricks from the old wall and then hollowing out a hole behind. He visited the cobweb-draped corner about every six months, and between times resealed it in with mortar. Bette, of course, knew where it was—not that he'd told her, but after all, she was a spy. However, Sam felt that the bricks and mortar kept both of them from becoming obsessive. He had spent solid weeks, when he'd had vacations, trying to decipher the thing that had revealed the dimension in which Keenan lived, whether it was the past or the future. He wondered whether it had called forth the reunion, and Wink too. He put it through rigorous, methodical tests set up to isolate any property, any function he might have missed. He got out Hadntz's papers, which had never been published, and pored over them, thinking of the whole thing as an intellectual exercise, a puzzle, trying to put his emotions aside and approach it rationally. But it appeared to be inert, as if its possibilities had been exhausted when it had shown him a glimpse of Keenan.

He could have created another lab, made another device, but it apparently required a nuclear reaction in order to function. The public was told of the tests at Bikini atoll, but if he'd wanted to get anywhere near it he'd have had to get permission from the government, and then he'd have to hand it over to the CIA. They might then be able to do . . . something. Something that might rock the foundations of the world, as had the atomic bomb, but even more drastically.

Was the risk he might have to take in order to create an unknown result—possibly good, but also possibly negative, in new, unanticipated ways—worth the price the rest of the world might have to pay?

And so he limited his compulsion to strictly delineated events, such as this Sunday afternoon check, when he was alone.

Setting his cold beer on a ramshackle table, he moved stacked-up boxes of books, got the ladder and his chisel, and to the background of a Sunday afternoon radio show, liberated the lead box. In his mind, never written down, were the series of tests he planned to perform this time.

He dropped into the ragged easy chair next to the table and opened the box that held the device.

It had changed.

Bewildered, Sam stared at the ivory-colored substance in the box.

Where was the tuning apparatus?

He pushed on the substance. It indented, then resumed its previous shape.

He set it on the table, got up, lighted a cigarette, and paced the small basement.

What did this mean?

This evidence of its continued vitality, its continued evolution, shook him to his core. Memories of Wink and Keenan and all his old war buddies, all the old war stories, flooded back. England. The death camps of Germany, about which he still had nightmares. Their laboratories, smelling of chemicals and solder and heavy machine oil. Radio swing music; the Perham Downs. Bebop, Rafferty, bombs, fires, hunger, and disease.

The long, aching tale of war, still unfinished, which would not be finished, as long as humans remained unchanged.

He heard a sound and turned, startled.

"So," said Bette. "Something's happened."

Something had happened.

The old fire planted by Hadntz had awakened.

"We can't just throw it in the ocean, Dance, much as I'd like to," she said, gazing down at it. She hugged herself, rubbing her hands up and down on her arms. "How do you think this happened? You're the engineer."

He laughed. "Believe me, I know nothing about this process. A lot of what Hadntz posited *is* real, and we know it now. DNA, developments in biochemistry. They're discovering all kinds of subatomic particles. So maybe this change is just part of the process."

"I think . . . we should go with it, Dance," she said. "I mean, you should." She abruptly started back up the stairs. "I think I hear Megan crying. She'll wake them all up."

She stopped on the third step, turned, and said, "I never saw this, and I don't want to hear anything more about it."

"Still."

"Still. We are still at war, I am still a part of the war, and I don't want them to even *think* that this thing really and truly exists. You have no idea what little signs people make that they are thinking about something, or know something. Even this is too much. But—I know things, and they are not good." She had started to cry, which surprised Sam. She rarely cried. He climbed the stairs and embraced her tightly. She laid her head on his shoulder.

Megan cried again, this time angrily. Bette wiped her tears and said, "Please."

Then she hurried up the stairs.

The Blue Pacific

1957–1960

SOVIET FIRES EARTH SATELLITE INTO SPACE

—*New York Times* headline
October 4, 1957

I think I had it in the back of my mind that I
wanted to sound like a dry martini.

—Paul Desmond
alto saxophonist for Dave Brubeck
and composer of "Take Five"

Atomic Toasters and
Little Green Army Men

A ROUND DAWN, the Big Island hove into sight, a massive green, white, and brown mountain swathed in cloud and set in an impossibly gemlike sea. From the air, few shallows appeared; the ocean dropped immediately to intense blue fathoms.

"Wake up," Sam told his children. "Look out the window!" And then other islands appeared in the window, blazing green in the dawn, curving in a long line across the sea.

It was 1957. In the wake of the Sputnik launch, the Navy got the space program contract. Sam had landed the job of inspecting the installations of the satellite tracking stations being built throughout the Pacific, across the scattered islands that were now U.S. territory—Guam, Kwajalein, Midway; the Marshalls, the Marianas. The tracking stations would also do double duty as early warning systems for incoming enemy intercontinental missiles, part of the DEW line, the Distant Early Warning system. The Soviets had done as good a job appropriating German scientists and technology as had the Americans. The world was full of the descendents of the V-2, aimed at one another, this time with nuclear warheads.

He and Bette had both agreed that he should take the Hawaii job. It was not spoken, but Sam knew that Bette, as well as he, saw these developments in the Pacific in the light of the change in the device.

Room for them on the DC-3 had suddenly become available the night before. They boarded a bus where they had been billeted in San Francisco, then boarded the plane, Jill with her round white patent-leather case full of comics, Brian clutching little green Army men, their feet stuck to a green plastic puddle, Megan asleep on Bette's shoulder.

The plane made a sharp turn, and Oahu was below. Waikiki, Honolulu, Hickam Air Force Base.

And Pearl Harbor, where Keenan lay, trapped within the *Arizona* forever. Sam covered his face for a moment as grief swept through him. Brian tugged at his sleeve. "What's wrong?"

He took a deep breath. "I'm fine," he said, and put his arm around Brian. "See? That's where we're going to live."

"Really?" Brian sounded doubtful.

Bette went over the kids' faces with a wet hankie and combed their hair. She told Jill crossly that no, she couldn't wear her Davy Crockett hat this morning. "We have to look nice."

"That's why I want to wear it," Jill said.

Half an hour after their first glimpse of the Hawaiian Islands, they stood on Hickam tarmac. A breeze whipped the kids' hair, undoing Bette's work.

A dark-haired man wearing a white short-sleeved shirt and dark slacks approached them. "Bill Eggston," he said, holding out his hand. "Sam Dance?"

Eggston herded them through a huge open-ended concrete hangar with hundreds of seats.

"Where are we going to stay?" Bette was clearly exhausted. Megan woke, looked around, and wailed. "These kids need a place to sleep. Now."

"Don't worry, Mrs. Dance." They were through the terminal now, and out front. Palm trees, and flowers Sam did not recognize, were everywhere. Bill helped Bette and the kids into a blue Chevy. The driver said, "Aloha. Chet. And you are?"

"You don't look Hawaiian," Jill said accusingly, hauling her bag of comics onto her lap.

Chet laughed. "I'm not. I'm from Vermont."

"Wait!" said Brian. "I lost Ralph."

"I don't see how you can tell those soldiers apart," Jill told him scornfully.

Chet said, "How would you like to go to the beach?" As the car pulled away from the curb, Sam felt the brunt of Bette's most exasperated look. He had to admit that the Navy didn't seem all that able to understand the needs of a traveling family—particularly one that was not an enlisted family. And then they were gone.

"Any idea where he's taking them?" asked Sam.

"Ala Moana, I think. And breakfast. Let's take care of the paperwork." Bill's office was a pale and depressing shade of green, but a tantalizing flowery scent came in through the open window. A phalanx of battleship-gray file cabinets lined one wall. A picture of his wife, who looked Japanese, was on the desk. After they sat down with coffee, Bill unlocked a bottom drawer and took out a large envelope marked FYI. He slid it across the desk to Sam with no comment.

Sam pulled out several heavy, embossed documents, a small black bound book, a stapled contract that said U.S. NAVY on the top, and a sealed, bulging letter-sized envelope. Bill half rose from his seat and reached over the desk. "There should be— yes." Sam shook out a cardboard ID card. Bill frowned. Then another slid out and he nodded.

"You have two. That fancy one—yeah, that's it—is top clearance." He smiled wryly. "Mine is not. You're a civilian, so . . ."

"So I don't have to salute."

"Well, that, among other things. Keep this card in your wallet at all times."

Sam picked up the other card. "That's the one you'll use most of the time," said Bill.

Sam compared the two and looked up. "So most people aren't supposed to know I have this clearance level."

"Correct." He opened another drawer and pulled out a file. It contained a small pile of crisp, white papers. He lifted the first one, scanned it, and slid it to Sam. "That's your address. You're with the enlisted men. Navy housing."

"My wife is going to love this. We weren't supposed to be on the base."

"She really won't like the fact that you're smack at the end of the runway. You'll get a good close look at the underside of every plane that takes off. Screws up television reception."

"Thanks, but this wasn't the agreement."

"It's just until you get settled and your furniture arrives. It should be here in about two months."

"Two months!" Sam was beginning to remember why he had run when his discharge papers were issued.

"It'll give you time to decide where to live. She'll have neighbors. Most of the men there are on subs, so they're gone for weeks at a time. The women are pretty close. They'll help her get oriented."

"Good of you to think of that."

"They're town houses, so they're all real close."

"I want officer's housing, at least. A duplex or a single."

"I'll put in for it, but don't hold your breath. You can move out any time you find another place to live."

Sam sat back in his chair. Obviously they wanted to keep an eye on everything. Maybe it was the long trip, but somehow all of these details didn't seem that important once he registered them. This job was his entree to the places he needed to be. It was kind of like MAD—Mutual Assured Destruction, the latest acronym for the atomic buildup. He knew something, or *was* something, that the government needed.

He carried the HD4 with him, in his pants pocket. Its resemblance to clay had inspired him to divide it up and roll it into cigarette-like cylinders and put them in a silver cigarette case. As he had rolled them, he almost wished that just touching it might once more affect him like lightning, change him into one of Hadntz's new, infinitely better humans; split time—

Except for Bette and his children.

He would not have continued to work on it if he thought that would happen, but it seemed quiescent, and was. The forces that had changed it had left it in this form, and it was his responsibility to decide what to do with it.

They only suspected he had it. On the other hand, they had all the access, all the power, all the inner workings of the mystery he needed to solve, the one that seemed newly urgent.

Nevertheless, he took his time reading the contract before signing.

After Bill locked up his desk they shook hands, Bill grinned. "Think it's too early for a beer? You need to know where the Officer's Club is."

They soon found that the television schedule existed only because someone had thought there ought to be one, but the actual shows bore only a loose relation to their scheduled times. Sharp-beaked orange birds-of-paradise bloomed next to their front porch. Hibiscus, double-ruffled and peach-hued, edges blazing brilliant red, bobbed in their neighbor's hedge. Ephemeral showers washed over several times a day. When the banana trees rustled in the wind it sounded like it was raining, and Bette always dashed out to take the clothes off the line, only to find that she had missed the actual rain.

Keenan had probably walked the same routes at the Navy base as Sam now did, prowled the same hallways as he trained as a radio ensign. Sam never lost that awareness.

Out in Pearl Harbor, a flag, flown at half-mast, and a plaque marked the site of the sunken USS *Arizona*.

At dawn one morning he took a boat and cast a lei over the site. It floated on the crystalline water while the sun rose, swiftly as it did here near the equator, and Sam wished then that he truly did have the power and the courage to change history and give Keenan back his life. What might Keenan have done? He was always quicker, more intelligent, more sure of everything.

Sam became involved in designing the fire protection for a proposed *Arizona* Memorial.

It was Saturday. Sam was brewing tea and Jill was at the kitchen table paging through a Superman comic book, her chest tan. She never wore a shirt because it was always so warm and sunny. She seemed to have taken to the place well. She fashioned a covered wagon out of her Radio Flyer and a bamboo mat and pulled her brother and sister, using her Huffy bike as a stand-in for horses. She could walk to the library, and read fairy tales incessantly in fat collections with different-colored covers. She got to buy a new Hardy Boys book at the PX every week. As far as Sam could tell, she was in hog heaven.

"Daddy, when are we going to get an atomic toaster?"

"What?" He measured out tea leaves.

"An atomic toaster. I just saw a show about it. *Our Friend the Atom.*"

Sam shook his head in semi-disgust but said nothing. He did not like Disneyfication, which seemed to be reaching into all corners of the known universe, but his kids were steady fans of the *Wonderful World of Color*, which they watched every Sunday night, although in black-and-white. The horror of Hiroshima was being whitewashed; atomic energy was a marvelous boon, granted them by a magnanimous genie.

But he and Bette were doing the same thing with the HD4, weren't they? Ignoring it.

Jill continued enthusiastically. "The whole world is made of Ping-Pong balls but they're so little we can't see them. They just found out about them. A genie let them out of the bottle. And now we're going to have atomic toasters and atomic everything."

"What's so good about an atomic toaster?"

"It's cleaner."

"Cleaner than what?"

"I guess you don't have to clean out the crumbs all the time. I don't think it burns the toast, either."

"We'll think about it. Let me know when you see one in the PX."

Sam sighed as she turned another page. Jill was crazy about her comic books. She stacked them on the back of the toilet next to his crossword magazines. She sprawled on the couch with them propped on her stomach. She rode her bike to the drugstore every Tuesday afternoon to be there when the shipment arrived.

Superman was hard at work saving the world and protecting his secret identity. Lois Lane loved Superman, but not his secret identity, Clark Kent. Letters to the editor marveled over discoveries of all the double-L'ed characters—Lana Lane, Lex Luthor, as if Superman had fallen onto an alphabet planet where such things were of prime importance. He weakened in the presence of green, glowing kryptonite. Bizarro was his pathetic, mineral-white counterpart.

The easy division between good and evil in the world of Superman bothered Sam. Because there was no such thing. Nevertheless it was there in everything the culture fed her. Black and white. Easy-to-identify sides. Bad guys simply bad; good guys simply good.

He imagined his own comic book character, Air Girl. Air Girl had her own plane and solved mysteries and caught crooks. Air Girl captured spies. Air Girl was Bette and Her Pals, during the war, smart women with good-paying jobs. They were much more possible than Superman. Their limit was that they were real.

He wanted Jill to be Air Girl. Why wasn't there a comic book for her? Supergirl's powers seemed limited, subordinate to Superman's.

"Get ready," he said. "We're going to the beach." Holding his glass of iced tea, he stepped into the backyard.

Brian was next door, as usual, with his best friend Danny, and his warren of blasted battle territory. "Put that platoon over there—no! Behind that hill." Danny was the imperious commander. Brian, a few years younger, appeared to be the private who had not yet learned the value of lying low and keeping out of the sight of officers.

"Good." Danny bent and chose carefully from a neat pile of rocks. "I think this is a job for the eighty-millimeter."

"Can I fire it this time?" asked Brian hopefully.

"Get out of the way." Danny threw a fast underhand and all of the little green soldiers Brian had painstakingly assembled went flying. "Ha!" he crowed. "Direct hit on the Germans." Because of their environment, which included not just Japanese, but Koreans, Chinese, and many other Asian nationalities, Danny was forbidden to fight any battles that involved the Japanese.

"Hi, Mr. Dance," he said, dusting hands together in satisfaction. "Did you see that? Okay, Brian. Now they're sending in the tank reinforcements. They have to cross the river—fill up the river, okay? Looks like it dried up."

Brian obediently trotted over to the hose. When he wasn't playing with Danny, Bette had to shoo him away from the television set. With Danny, he was working his way through every movie about WWII that happened across the screen.

"We're going to the beach," Sam told him. "Get your stuff."

"Take the amphibian!" Danny shouted as Brian dashed into the house. The screen door slammed.

Waves chased one another across an immense fetch to finally burst against lava rock outposts in a wild clash of foam at Kaena Point, Oahu's remote northwest tip. The water sluiced through tiny crystalline pools where otherworldly creatures of impossible pastel delicacy flourished. The briny smell of these pools, the sharpness of the rocks upon which his children often cut themselves so that brilliant red blood ran down their thin brown legs without them noticing, the green dense fleshy fringe of naupaka all transported them in a group, a tableau, to another time in which they existed perfect, in relationship to themselves and to the world, the lines between them taut and straight as the schematics in a pool shark's brain, stretching and changing constantly, singing lines carrying a current of love.

He watched Brian bend to examine something in a tide pool, the boy a stubby curve of brown bisected by a dash of bright red shorts. Jill's long hair flowed this way and that in the wind; Bette hovered over Megan, only two. Bing Crosby crooned as if a celestial voice from their transistor radio that every cloud had a silver lining.

Sam, right here, right now, saw only the silver. Having his family here where Keenan had been was strangely like having him here as well.

The rocks were a graceful scallop along the shoreline beneath the perpendicular, brownish-green cliffs of Kaena Point. The steep plunge of land into the blue Pacific was interrupted only by the narrow dirt road along which they had bumped to reach this place. The wind held the fresh scent of infinity, sweet and salty and fully ionized. A dark cloud boiled up a few miles east along the coast but would spend itself in swift showers soon. A military plane from Dillingham a few miles away took off and veered Maui-ward.

Sam pondered a great deal over how much of his country was top-secret, hidden from civilians. Two thousand feet above him and half a mile back from the Point was a golf ball–shaped installation, part of the DEW line. Fly across the country and if you knew what you were looking at from forty thousand feet the land was a quilt of off-limits military property.

Bette was right. They were still at war in what was now called peacetime, and bright plastic Hasbro toys, Krazy Ikes and Mr. Potato Heads, the residue of wartime research, shone like beacons to children from black-and-white television screens, leaving the kids to imagine the colors. Jill got up at six every Saturday morning and watched the test pattern until hours of cartoons played out, then watched *Rin-Tin-Tin*, *Sky King*, *Fury*, and *Lassie* until *American Bandstand* came on with "those boring teenagers," at which time she finally went outside to play. All against this backdrop of quiet preparation for the next war, which, from his point of view, permeated the entire world.

Swooping up Megan, Bette stood straddle-legged in a tide pool and raised her against the sky, jouncing her up and down. Sam could hear Megan's squeal of delight mingle with the wind.

The Pacific, the present, was primary colors, brilliant light. The war was somber browns and greens and blacks; black trees sketched against white fields, their fractal filigree stark against gray winter sky, and camps of the brutalized dead. This light washed that from him.

It was a little after ten at night. The banana trees flapped in darkness, sounding like leathery cloth being rubbed and scraped by diligent eternal launderers. Sam, at the kitchen table, finished his newspaper and climbed the narrow stairs, stuck his head in their bedroom door. Bette was snoring.

He looked in on the kids. Jill had the upper bunk, Brian the lower, and Megan slept on a cot.

The bookshelf that formed Jill's headboard was crammed with comic books. Sam's new Philco transistor was hidden beneath her pillow, tuned to top-ten hits like "Itsy Bitsy Teenie Weenie Yellow Polka Dot Bikini." Every night after she fell asleep he got it out, turned it off, and put it in the bathroom so he could listen to it in the morning while he shaved.

Reaching beneath her pillow, he was startled when she turned, wide awake, her face wet with tears. "Why are they doing it?" she asked.

"What?" He sat down on the side of the bed.

"Killing each other. People are killing each other all the time, and hurting each other."

"You've been listening to the news," he said quietly. "You told me you turned it off."

"I do when it's on KPOI. It only lasts three and a half minutes."

"So what station is this on?"

"The BBC. There's always news. Wars and murders. People are dead all the time."

"That's from England. The British Broadcasting Corporation."

Fresh tears welled in her eyes. "How can people be so mean to each other?"

"Nobody really knows."

"I'm going to find out and fix it."

"I hope so, Jill. That would be just wonderful." He brushed back the hair from her head.

"Can I keep the radio longer until I fall asleep?"

"Are you going to listen to the BBC?"

She shook her head. "No. I want to hear music."

She wanted to fix it.

Maybe he needed to turn his mind back to fixing it, as well.

The postwar lull, here in the States, was just that: only a lull. People were more prosperous, on the whole; many more could afford a home than ever before. Organized labor had provided a good living wage for factory workers, and for years, they'd produced all the food for Europe.

Economic improvement had not done away with human violence, though, and it had not done away with war.

In two minutes of radio news, Jill was getting only the slightest, distanced glimpse of what he had actually seen, what he had experienced, during the war. If, as Hadntz so fervently postulated, her device was going to change the ways in which people regarded one another, wasn't it time to start doing something with it?

He decided, then: Whatever it was, he would distribute it across the Pacific.

Sam flew to Kwajalein and to Guam, inspecting Navy satellite tracking stations.

That a space program was under way was not known to many in 1957; it was a government secret, one among a legion of secrets.

Sam lived in a separate world on these trips. And a separate world within that one: He took with him his cigarettes of HD4 and planted one at each locale.

Now, he was on his way to South Point, on the Big Island. The highway passed through jungle, high above the sea, and the land rolled below clothed in swaths of glittering palm heads, shining green coffee plantations, and ranches. The towns were casual collections of wooden buildings with a general store and a barbershop, but usually little else. Pickup trucks full of mangoes and sugar cane passed him now and then, impatient with his slow, savoring pace, leaving him in the dust, for the road had turned to dirt not too far out of town.

South Point was dry and stunning. Rolling hills held few houses. The dish reared up before him, outlined against the sky, a new, unnatural object in this wilderness. Waves smashed against the headland, shimmering across the lava rocks after a tall rush of foam that might leap thirty feet before subsiding into the next blue wave. Three fishing craft lay half a mile off the point, cabled to iron rings set in the volcanic rock. The current here was fierce.

Sam parked the jeep and followed a path through tall grass flattened in random circles by gusts of wind. He fished in his pocket and found the key that unlocked the metal door of the graffitied control bunker.

Inside, after he closed the door behind him, it was quiet. A bare bulb hung from the ceiling. DON'T FORGET TO TURN OFF THE LIGHT! read a sign next to the switch.

He pulled a flashlight from his bag. He spent two hours inspecting the wiring, making sure it had been done right. He performed tests on the computer, printed out test results on a chattering machine. The place was air-conditioned, completely sealed, but still there were signs of corrosion and he made a list of parts that needed replacement. He tested the tracking mechanism, the radio, the radar. Finally he climbed up the ladder, opened the hatch, and crawled out onto the top of the tower. Buffeted by wind, he ascended the ladder that brought him into the dish.

Once there, he took from his rucksack a package he'd stowed in the bottom. He carefully unwrapped it, took out a cylinder of HD4, and pressed it onto the dish. It was warm and malleable. *What am I doing?* he asked himself as usual. *Spreading peace? Or complete devastation?*

And if it *was* an active, evolving material that actually did something, was he doing the right thing to distribute it as he did, scattering its beams throughout the Pacific in tandem with their war beams disingenuously named "peacekeepers," and the beams aimed into space? Would he be doing the right thing if he did not? Did it do a damned thing? He often hoped it didn't, that the past was just a trick of his imagination.

But something had happened, and he was left with this responsibility, with only Wink's vision to guide him. In Wink's place there was no cold war. In Wink's world technologies were used for good. In Wink's world, the Soviet Union and the United States were working together to put a man on the moon.

He went over his checklist and descended to the top of the bunker. There he sat and watched the ocean until the fisherman pulled his boat back to the cliff, unhooked his rope, and headed home.

:| 32 |:

The Zendo

BETTE STARTED GOING to the Zen Buddhist temple with Patrice, their Japanese neighbor. Patrice was breezy, friendly, helpful. She taught Bette how to cook rice and talked her into going to the temple over on Kamehameha Highway at an ungodly hour of the morning. They'd leave at four and be back at five thirty, and Bette still had half an hour to fix breakfast before she got the kids up. This was perfect for Bette, who was an insomniac. "It's a lot more interesting than lying in bed awake," she said.

Bette explained to Sam that Zen wasn't a religion. "It's a practice. It's something that you do, not something that you think about, or profess to believe."

"So what do you do at the temple? How can the kids *eat* this stuff?" He tossed the handful of Cocoa Puffs he'd grabbed from the box into the garbage.

"We sit."

"Sit? That's all?"

"Yeah. Look." In the living room she pulled a thick, round, black pillow from behind the couch. "Behold, the zabuton. We sit on it. Like this." She settled her butt on it and easily twisted her legs into the lotus position.

"So, now you're sitting. Do you close your eyes?"

"No. You kind of lower your eyelids."

"Do you think of anything?"

"Of course I do. A huge gushing engorged stream of stuff. It's amazing. The point is to ignore that."

"How do you ignore what you're thinking?"

"I don't know how yet. It takes practice."

"And then what happens?"

"Who knows?"

"Well, sounds like fun."

"It's not really fun," she said, pausing to think. "It's . . . refreshing."

Their home was becoming more Asian. Shoes were to be removed at the door. The kids wore tabis—Japanese socks with a slit between the big toe and the rest of the toes like a hand mitten, which fastened at the ankle with a metal hook. Bette placed breathtakingly simple Japanese bowls she found at yard sales along an upper window ledge. She began to talk about building a koi pond.

She was different here. The tropical ease of the place drew her out. She laughed more, throwing her head back. She was brown and strong.

One Saturday afternoon the kids rushed into the house giggling and snorting and rolling their eyes at one another. Sam was sitting at the kitchen table and put down the comics page of the *Honolulu Advertiser*. "What?"

Then Bette walked in, with a mischievous smile, carrying a bag of groceries. Her hair was purple. The kids let loose screams of laughter.

"There was a lady at the International Market Place—"

"Heloise!"

"And she was spraying all the ladies' hair weird colors—"

"At first nobody wanted to do it but then Mom said she would!"

"I wanted green," said Brian.

"I wanted red," said Jill.

"But I have always *longed* for purple hair," said Bette, sliding the bag of groceries from the GEM store onto the table. "It is *so* satisfying to fulfill one's dreams."

"I never knew, honey. Gee, you look great! It'll go good with that purple muu-muu."

"And a red plumeria behind her ear," insisted Jill.

Brian grumbled, "I wanted stripes, but she wouldn't let me. She said you'd be mad."

"Nah," said Sam. "I wouldn't have been mad. We could all just get a job at the circus."

"Well then can I have a crew cut?"

He looked at Bette. She'd been keeping his hair long and curly. Her quirky smile combined resignation and a message: It's time.

"Sure, kid." Sam pushed back his chair. "I need one too. Let's head on down to the barbershop and let Mrs. Chang do her thing."

Bette itched to move out of Navy housing. Sam initially found it amusing that the MP's could not ticket him for storing his packed barrels on the porch, but the fun had worn off quickly as it moved toward the harassment end of the scale.

She found a houseboat on the Ala Wai Canal for sale. It belonged to a Navy guy who was now stationed in Norfolk.

They were enchanted. It was surprisingly spacious. Megan ran across the deck, flinging out her arms and *aaack-aaack*ing like a seabird. Jill took the wheel. Brian climbed ladders with alarming alacrity. Sam and Bette talked it over while the agent indulged in a panic attack about the kids and followed them around so they would not fall in the water and drown.

"The price is right," said Sam.

"We could walk to the beach."

"Wouldn't want to take it out in the ocean."

"We could ride over to Honolulu Harbor, anyway. Nice sunset cruise past Ala Moana with martinis. Just off Waikiki the water's pretty tame."

"I'm mainly worried about the school," said Bette. "The kids have friends there. It doesn't seem quite fair—they just left their other friends in Washington . . . if they stay at Nimitz, there's no bus. It's a long drive." Bette folded her arms, thinking. "But it seems so perfect."

"You have to go past her school to take me to work anyway."

"Yeah, but she gets out of school a lot earlier than you get out of work."

Bette drifted away to examine the kitchen. Sam tried out a deck chair and sat looking at the canal.

It was a calm day, so boats and palms were reflected with exquisite clarity in the perfect mirror of the canal. Then a little catamaran passed by, setting up a pattern of ripples.

The visual surface of the water was fractured into a series of teardrop-shaped reflections. The palm trees were still complete, with trunk and coconuts and bushy fronds, but were now divided by intervals of turbulence into perfect, but separate, segments. Between smooth shards of sky and cloud, a school of wrasses flashed red.

Sam stared, startled by a thought: *What if all we see is just a reflection?* What if, somehow, that reflection was shattered by an eddy from some unknown source, so that we might live through days of mirrors and then suddenly see beyond, like blue sky vanishing at night, revealing stars. What if just inside, just beyond, just on the other side of *this* reality was another, or an infinite number of them. As close as the Ala Wai Canal on which this houseboat floated. Was that how it worked?

Maybe, he thought, the HD *had* affected him.

The vision was shattered by a huge splash as Brian cannonballed off the port side, narrowly missing the boat docked next to them. As the real estate agent shrieked, he sank down for the full effect of appearing to drown. Sam didn't even get out of his chair. Bette started to laugh.

"He's so little!" shrieked the agent. "He can't swim!"

"Time he learned," said Bette, then he popped up, dog-paddling, and grinned. "Man, it would be *great* to live here."

Sam searched his mind and came up with: "You know better than to go swimming in your clothes, young man."

"I'm not sure the canal is all that clean," said Bette. "Get out. The ladder's at the back."

"No!" he said, and his little rear came out of the water as he kicked back under.

"I think I just changed my mind," said Bette.

"We can make rules."

"Really, it's the school," she said. "And I'm not sure I want Jill to be riding her bike in city traffic."

"It might get a little cramped," said Sam.

"The salt air smells *so* nice."

Sam pulled Brian up with one arm as he reached up from the ladder, and set him on the polished teak deck.

He turned to face the panorama of the Koolaus, intensely green mountains that were Honolulu's backdrop, shaded by dynamic clouds, white, black, gray. As he watched, some were drawn swiftly into the steep creases of valleys, where rainbows arced through misted distance. To their left was Punchbowl's volcanic crater, with its neat long rows of crosses, all for servicemen who died in the Pacific. To their right was Diamond Head, whose cauldron held a Navy tracking installation he'd just inspected.

What might be inside or beyond this bright, shimmering façade? More war? A different family? Elsinore and Keenan, restored? A billion combinations of uncounted times and possibilities, each fully lived, with their own glimpse of Other; perhaps, of *this?*

What was it, then?

Teeming life, expanding to fill the vacuum, pulled into the medium of time and present rainbows. Death, destruction, misery; stupidity and grace.

Bette put her arm around him. Megan tugged on his hand. "Daddy, are you okay?"

"What say we head over to Ala Moana and think about it."

"Did I ever tell you about the morning we got here and that guy brought us over here?"

"What about it?"

They sat next to each other on bamboo mats. Bette was lazily smoking a cigarette and watching the kids playing in the shallows. The beach was wide and full of families. Behind them were naupaka-bordered showers, cool stone dressing rooms, green lawns shaded by broad boa trees with many scattered picnic tables beneath, all of them full midday on Saturday.

"We were the only ones here. It was so peaceful. The wind wasn't stirring at all. It was so . . . delicate. These tropical trees, the air, that white edge of waves out on the reef. I let the kids take off their shoes and socks and go wading. They seemed like . . . flamingoes, the way they lifted their feet so deliberately, all the way out of the water, and set them back down without disturbing anything. They were amazed. They *stared* down into the water. They were reflected in every detail, even the looks on their faces. I don't know. It was just . . . so utterly *perfect.*"

She smiled at him. He looped her hair, with its still-purple streaks, behind her ear and kissed her.

Bette's new zendo was in a hill-perched rambler in Manoa, the University District. Bette parked the car down the block. Sam followed her, barely awake, as they climbed the stairs to the main level of the house, which had been remodeled into one large room.

In darkness and in silence, those who "sat" assembled in the zendo and, well, sat. The room was full of people silently sitting. In fact, it was about the most profoundly silent place he'd ever been in.

As quietly as possible, he settled next to Bette on one of the zabutons they'd grabbed from the cubbies in the hallway. She used the lotus position and he the half-lotus, just situating one foot on the opposite thigh. "It's the straight back that matters," she'd told him. "You can do this in a chair as long as you keep your back straight."

He didn't close his eyes, either, but just lowered his eyelids as she'd prescribed. And paid attention to his breathing, giving each breath a number.

Immediately he found that the mental space between each number seemed to last an infinity. Thoughts grew thick as a forest, each with many branches, and he followed that thought until he realized that he'd forgotten to count and started again . . . *one* . . .

The absolute, attention-filled silence was strangely energizing. A car drove past the zendo; solitary bird calls gathered others until they formed cascades of sound. He felt his attention drifting upward, until he seemed to hover above his body . . . *Whoops—yet another thought . . . one* . . .

He might never make it past one . . . *Damn, that was another thought! . . . One* . . .

A deep gong reverberated and around him the sitters stirred, stretching, picking up their zabutons.

"Like it?" asked Bette.

"Definitely interesting."

And then—

Was that Hadntz across the room?

He felt that rush of thinking a stranger might be someone he knew, and the scrambling to match old mental pictures. It had been ten years, and she was a master of disguises. This woman's hair was white. What made him think it might be Hadntz? Her large, dark eyes? Simply the way she moved as she bent to pick up her zabuton?

Dawn, which came quickly here, flooded the room and she met his eyes, *yes*.

He tried to control his spin of disorientation. The war, Keenan's loss, the wave of darkness returned—all the things he'd worked so hard to mitigate. "Did you know she'd be here?" he asked Bette.

"No," she whispered, a sad, resigned look in her eyes.

Hadntz walked over to meet them. "The two of you together. Perfect."

"I haven't seen you in a long time," said Sam. Apart from his surprise, he was very apprehensive.

"No," she said.

Her long hair, though silvery white, was still vibrant and curled wildly. Her face was tan and weathered, with deep lines. She wore loose, black cotton pants and a plain white T-shirt. Sam could not read the look in her eyes, but then, he never had been able to.

There was a moment of quiet, when none of them said anything.

Then Hadntz said, "This is not a coincidence. I planned to meet you here. Come, let's go for coffee."

Numb, Sam stashed his zabuton in a cubbyhole; the two women did the same. Bette appeared to be as shocked as Sam.

Out on the street, with its mixture of little shops, cheap restaurants that catered to students, and older, shabby houses brightened by potted plants and friendly chairs on porches, Sam began to feel more normal. He could breathe again.

He realized that he did not welcome this impingement of Hadntz, and all that her presence implied, into his life.

They followed her into a Vietnamese pastry shop. Sitting at a Formica table on aluminum tubular chairs while students lined up for coffee and pastries at a window outside, they all ordered Bette's favorite, sweet, strong, iced Vietnamese coffee.

The three of them had never been together before.

Or had they, in some configuration of time he no longer recalled?

Hadntz seemed more hesitant than she had ever seemed before, as if doubt had eroded her previous certitude. "I was hoping I would see you here. I mean . . ." She searched for words and shrugged. "We need a new vocabulary for concepts of time and space."

"It's like bebop." Where scales intermingled, with explosive results. *Two coinciding events, which come from their own pasts, share a few beats of unison, and then diverge into their own futures.*

"As I said before, jazz gives you a supple mind. I am a professor of physics at the University of Hawaii. Somewhen, anyway." An ironic smile crossed her face, then faded. "Here-now? Nowhere? Anyway, we have work to do."

"What kind of work?"

"All right. I actually live in . . . otherwhen." Another quick smile. "You would think that with speaking as many languages as I do I could think of a good term for this." She picked up her strong iced coffee and took a long swallow. "I am only here for a short interval. So here is my news: In otherwhen, I have finally developed a device for averaging the future potentials any particular instant holds."

Sam glanced at Bette. She was regarding Hadntz with utter seriousness.

Hadntz continued. "The probabilities of consciousness are manifold, infinite. Each instant of time, as we know it, is composed of uncountable units of consciousness. You might call them quanta of consciousness; they are measurable and discrete and composed of infinite layers which we are only beginning, in otherwhen, to be able to sense, to measure, to *use*, as here you are using nuclear energy to generate electricity. Just as we were able to delve into the atom when our sensing tools were refined, we are beginning to be able to understand the roots of human consciousness in all of its plasticity. So many variables feed any instant of sensory awareness! The outer and inner world meet in what I can only describe as an exquisite dance."

Sam relaxed into her poetry, realizing that she was trying to describe the indescribable. He imagined, in her otherwhen, a College of Consciousness Studies of which she was the head.

"Intent, desire, and will emerge from our cellular roots. We now know, in the timestream in which I live, how to describe these systems hormonally, electrically, biochemically. We can actually *see* which parts of our brains are used in various and very specific tasks and thoughts. It's all quite astonishing. For instance, people can actually laugh themselves to death if the wrong part of the brain is stimulated.

"We have sciences which strive to understand social patterns, social will, happiness, fear, love, hate. We are finally learning what the physics of *life* are. Our individual minds filter *this* moment"—she raised her hands in a graceful gesture that took in the entire room, the mountains, the universe—"down to a specific set of describable phenomena through unconscious, precise biological processes which do not present the information gathered to the conscious mind. Consciousness is a tool that preserves the organism. In the same way, histories at some point become either concrete or discarded. For instance, I might think about getting up to fetch another cup of coffee, and then discard that thought for reasons I might not understand at all, reasons that are fed by underlying phenomena deep beneath my conscious mind. We are able to pinpoint these instants using various technologies, and thereby study the processes. In the same way, we are able to treat the world as one organism, and to pinpoint tipping points in history. They are often small, seemingly inconsequential. Our computers can map these possibilities."

"The computers must be huge," said Sam.

"No. They are actually very, very small. But they are widely distributed."

Sam thought immediately of the HD4. From the startled look on Bette's face, he knew she was too. Was the HD4 simply so fine, so small, that what he had now was an unimaginably huge number of them?

"They are in constant communication, like a single organism. I know, for instance, that there will be very few times when I will be able to meet you in this way."

"So you know everything that is going to happen?"

"No, of course not. But we do understand what makes a time well and what makes a time sick, if you want to use the analogy of a body. We are subject to fewer illnesses; we understand what makes the human psyche go to war. It was a pretty unanimous decision for us to decide that war is not good for humans, that it only leads to more and more war. Death, tragedy, unhappiness, revenge. Is there another trajectory, one that leads to more and more health? A social environment in which people, no matter what their differences, have the ability to respect one another? More and more happiness, satisfaction, the creation of an environment in which all of our creativity and possibilities can bloom? You might think that this sounds like a rather bland sort of place, but, as Jesus said, consider the flowers of the field."

"The lilies," interjected Bette. "They're the lilies of the field."

"Yes. Consider biological reality in all of its complexity and beauty. We are the only species that systematically kills others of its kind. This propensity has become a serious design flaw. There is a way in which we are able to make another human being invisible, to deny that their suffering is real. We convince ourselves that their suffering is necessary for the survival of ourselves and our children."

Her voice was low, persuasive. Her Eastern European accent did not seem out of place in this many-accented environment. Sam was dimly aware that numerous philosophical conversations were taking place around them, and that the college students, if they happened to overhear, would not think that anything unusual was taking place.

Bette's face had lost the hard-won happiness she had lately effused. She lit a cigarette with a nervous movement. He knew that movement, that look. She was making decisions, becoming Bette of Wartime, in a war that hadn't ended, not really. He also knew what she was thinking—that she in particular had made herself hard, paradoxically, to the suffering of others in the process of becoming happy.

"Bette," he interrupted, "happiness is not necessarily selfish."

"Mine is."

Hadntz said, "She is right, Sam. And I am actually here to give you information so terrible that it is almost impossible to understand."

Sam looked away from both of them. The students at the other tables were all young, filled with life. A young Korean man spoke earnestly to an audience that included a Thai woman, an African woman, and a Hawaiian man. The clatter of the coffee shop, the shouted orders, the smell of exotic pastries and potent espresso defined this present, along with his foreboding.

He looked back at her. "What is it, Eliani?"

She paled, and seemed to find it difficult to speak, which surprised him. Then she surged into it, her words coming rapidly.

"In this when, which is the when to which I seem to be most deeply attached emotionally, there is not much future. Relatively speaking. In all probability, this when will reach nuclear winter within the next hundred years or less. The technology of nuclear weapons will proliferate until someone—it doesn't much matter who or why—releases them. Like a deadly bloom. This event could well lead to the cessation of *all* whens. We have determined," she said quietly, "that *here* is where the problem lies, in your timestream. Like the root of a cancer, when the cell mutates. *This* is the point. This, and the next several years, and an event we have yet to define, but which could rocket through many whens, changing them profoundly. Just as life appeared, it can also disappear."

"What can we do?" asked Bette quickly.

"I'm not entirely sure," she said, surprising Sam immensely. "But I keep thinking of time and consciousness in terms of flowers, seeds, and potential."

"So we have to cross-pollinate?" asked Bette.

"Sort of. Yes. But we need to gather and disseminate more information. I see it as a process, with no particular end. I only feel the need to intervene, as one must when a child is suffering and you have the means to relieve them."

"What if this does—work?" asked Sam. "*Does* something, anything—how could I . . . deliberately initiate changes? How could anyone possibly make such choices?"

"It would not be just your choice. It would be the choice of many. Sensed deeply, biologically, in an evolutionary sense. We are still evolving, all the time, adapting to what is happening. This is a new adaptation to a new circumstance—that of the possibility of complete annihilation.

"Or—this might be a more useful analogy for you. Think of these seminal events as V-I rockets. And think of us—yourselves, me, Wink—as the M-9 Director. We each have different functions in the workings of this antidisaster mechanism. As it becomes more refined, we hope that we can accurately pinpoint the key events and simply vaporize them, nullify them, shoot them out of the air, out of the realm of possibilities. I left you, in London, with the plans for the M-15, and it has evolved, here, into the M-17. I think you call it HD4. The next generation, the M-25, is presently collecting information at a speed which is getting closer, all the time, to the speed of light."

Sam was not completely happy with this news.

"Wink will be your contact in the future. We are living in something that might be described as a woven piece of music. There are resonances, harmonics, intersections of rhythm and melody, overtones that spread like ripples in a pond. It has unimaginable complexity. We are feeling out the new dynamics through time, improvising when necessary. Evolving into a new biological paradigm."

"Like bebop," said Sam.

"Whatever you need to think. Something previously unknown in history, but that can change what we think of as "the past," modify it with a corrective current. Something like the telescope, the microscope, the printing press, technologies that open up the mysteries of this medium in which we live."

"And move, and have our being," said Bette. She smiled. "I'm an Episcopalian, and they live and move and have their being in God. That was one of the things I loved saying when I was a kid. It made everything so . . . immediate. Intense. So whatever God is, this is it. This is God. This is satori."

"Atomic satori," Hadntz mused.

"In the land of American sushi," responded Bette.

Sam didn't know what to say. He just imagined, as he sat in the Vietnamese coffee shop up the mountain from Waikiki, that he was back with Wink and Charlie Parker, rearranging time with the tool of tone, leaving swing and living, quite briefly, in a future no one knew was happening until it was long past.

"My daughter," Hadntz added, standing up, "is only in this time. It is the only time possible for her and for her children."

"Can we—" Bette stood at the same time Hadntz did, reaching for her, but she was out of the shop by then, walking downhill with a fast, long stride, melting into a crowd of students changing classes.

"Jasmine," said Bette, staring down the street.

"What?"

"She was wearing jasmine perfume."

⊰ 33 ⊱

Midway

A FEW DAYS LATER, Sam's intercom crackled. His secretary, Lelani, said, "Will you take a call from a Mr. Winklemeyer? . . . Sir, there is no need to use profanity—"

Sam picked up the receiver and pressed the flashing button with foreboding. Wink would reconnect him to a past and a future which was, he realized, the silver-lined cloud of which Bing Crosby sang.

His voice, when he picked up the phone was unsteady. "Wink?"

The trans-Pacific cable hissed. "Dance! How're things in alohaland?"

Midway Island is a part of the Midway Atoll, which lies about 1,100 miles northwest of Honolulu. I believe it was so named as the midpoint of an enterprise, either the seaplane airline or the cable crossing.

The interval between Kauai and Midway is dotted with a series of atolls—Necker, French Frigate Shoals, Lisianski—all with Polynesian names as well. Beyond Midway, there are others—all continuations of the Hawaiian chain, created as a tectonic plate moved over a volcanic hot spot, ending at Kure.

Picture an island about a mile and a half long and about a half-mile wide at its widest point, triangular and twenty-three feet in elevation at the highest point, which you need to know to respond to a tidal wave alarm. The long runway overruns the island at each end, as does the short runway, at a right angle to the long runway. The atoll itself is roughly circular, ten miles in diameter, making the lagoon a ten-mile circular shallow lake. There is a Coast Guard station on the far side of the lagoon. (Where do the Coast Guard personnel go for leave? Beautiful downtown Midway, of course!)

On the eastern side of Midway is an island called, aptly, Eastern Island. Eastern is a desert island, very little vegetation, several small buildings erected for various forgotten projects.

On the other hand, thousands of people have lived on Midway; about four thousand when I visited. At that time Midway was a vital cog in the DEW line. A long-range, highly instrumented plane would take off every hour and fly about a twelve-hour mission to watch for hostile rocket launches. As far as Midway was concerned, though, the handwriting was on the wall. At the time of my visit in 1961 the rumor went around like lightning that the Alaska DEW line radar station called the Midway flight control tower to ask the type of plane that was clearing the runway so they could adjust their radar software! The Alaska facility was taking over.

On his trip to Midway, Sam carried, in the grip containing his clothes and toiletries, a small amount of HD4, and thought about how he and Wink had flown over this same territory in August 1945.

But he also wondered, as he idly watched the empty sea below, whether he was actually recalling a past that had really existed, or someone else's past, the past of another Sam Dance, injected like a brilliant transparent slide into a carousel to infuse the reflections in his brain like a justifying skein, an interpretation of atoms which he arranged into cause and effect when there was none, when it was just a trick of his brain, the way that it arranged an imagined, dwelt-in, drenching dimension called time.

What was the cloud in Wink's silver-lined world? *This* reality, perhaps, this place where the dark side of man held sway. Perhaps *here* gave weight to *there*. Perhaps

Niels Bohr was right, with his theory of nonlocality, and both places instantly knew each other, were invented by each other, were informed by each other, so that whatever lay in between—time/distance—was as nothing. Perhaps if they were steered toward each other both would vanish in the collision and create a new sun. They would both return to the elements, and the stars would dream new worlds, the cosmos would reinvent consciousness. Perhaps this happened constantly, and he was always being newly created; perhaps unimaginable eons informed each instant, though his brain did not register it as such.

However, in the timestream in which he found himself, Sam was allowed two weeks to complete his inspections and reports.

Then the trip was at an end; he saw the three islands of Midway below. The runway, cleared of gooney birds, was short. When they were on the ground, the stewardess retrieved a plastic bag full of leis from an ice chest. "There aren't any flowers on Midway," she told him as they waited for the door to be opened. "Or any water, for that matter. It's all shipped in by boat."

A man in front of the small terminal waved wildly when he ducked out of the hatch of the plane. Sam hurried toward him.

Wink was heavier. His thin face had filled out. His bushy eyebrows were pale and his flat-topped hair was fading from red to gray. He wore shorts and an aloha shirt, unbuttoned and flapping in the wind.

His wide smile was the same, though. And so was the mischievous light in his eyes.

As he approached Sam shouted, "What the *hell* are you doing here?"

"It's just the cosmos, man." He slapped Sam on the back. "You know. Midway. Right now midway in the cosmos it's time for a cold beer. He grabbed Sam's grip and tossed it into the waiting jeep. "I see you brought your sax. Great. I borrowed a horn from the Navy band."

They drove through a small military town, with its barracks, single houses, bowling alley, PX, and thousands of battered bikes. The Sand Bar was a faded wooden shack with a rusted metal roof, open to the lagoon shimmering in the late-afternoon sunlight. Nearby, a wooden pier stretched out into the lagoon, and children played on the beach.

The bartender liked jazz—Wink had checked this out earlier—and kept a steady stream of LP's on the record player—the Modern Jazz Quartet, Miles Davis, Monk, Trane. "You want a goddamn hillbilly juke box, go to the Monkey Bar," Sam heard him tell one irritated patron.

Sam could think of no finer or more perfect place for their reunion.

"It's kind of like a space station, this habitable place in the middle of the ocean," mused Wink, as the bartender set their first cold, foaming beers on the table. "The only survivable place in a vacuum desert. Midway. In the ocean, and in time."

"Why can you call me? I can't call you."

"Things are different in . . . my timestream. I think I told you that we're moving along at a fairly quick pace, in terms of research and development. With the right technology, I can convert the timestream information into a graph of sorts, and see the places where they intersect. But not very far into the future. So I—or my computer—averages out the possibility of contact within, say, the next twenty-four hours, and at that point, I make a try. The program is running constantly, and alerts me to these possibilities. I've tried to make contact many more times than it's worked. There's . . . static."

Sam said, "But it seems as though there's no gap. I flew from Honolulu into this kind of space. Is it the same for you?"

Wink nodded. "A completely smooth transition. It's like making a travel reservation to St. Louis and then going there. Or walking across the room and arriving at the other side. I keep coming back to this: each human being is in his own world anyway. We intersect with our family, with whom we probably have the most contiguity and the most overlap of worlds, at least at first. But our meeting now really isn't much different than the meetings of most people. We each see history and objects differently, from different perspectives, filtered through our own consciousness. It always appears to be seamless, doesn't it?"

"Yeah, but—"

"Look, a hundred years ago if you left home the only way you could communicate with those left behind was through letter delivery. Then the signal got more abstract, jumped to a new level: the telegraph. Finally we got voice transmission. Distances shrink. Now this other kind of 'distance' has shrunk."

"Can you contact other timestreams?"

Wink shook his head. "I have an emotional connection to this one. Emotions are the key to consciousness. Emotions might be so baseline that we don't even recognize them, like air, but they're always there. I have no emotional connection to other timelines—or . . . think of them as patterns, endlessly emerging. You are embedded in a particular, ever-changing pattern, as am I. Occasionally, our patterns, being intimately related, merge."

"Here's another slant. Let's say that our consciousness is not just in our brains, but in every cell of our bodies, and are, obviously, in constant communication with one another. Consciousness is a whole-organism phenomenon. All the cells in both of us went through a transition that put us into the same quantum state, but nonlocally. We're both one photon, or one cell. We were made one particle, then went in different directions. But somehow, we're still one particle, a single quantum state, separated by the medium we call spacetime. Shrodinger, in his *What is Life?* lectures—the ones that Hadntz quoted in her paper—said that cells are aperiodic crystals. Physically, *crystals*. But constantly fluctuating, unlike inorganic crystals.

We're a constantly changing orchestra of frequencies. And," he smiled, "we seem to be a jazz frequency."

"Thank God for that," said Sam. "What's your hard theory of why we can meet here?"

Wink grinned. "That's easier. Zee and Kocab are here right now. Well, actually, they're on that island across the lagoon. Kocab is stationed here, and Zee came in on a boat a few days ago. He's in the Coast Guard. You saw how small this place is. I figured it was worth a try."

The sun set. Artie Shaw's classic "Begin the Beguine" wound sinuous enchantment through Wink's reason-laden voice with nonrational, purposeless beauty. The world was this bamboo bar, mechanics and pilots and secretaries taking their ease in the tropical night as dark palm trees tossed with their peculiarly soothing frond-hiss in the salt wind that moved them.

Wink leaned forward and extracted his wallet from his back pocket, flipped it past an ID which looked mildly foreign, not quite right to Sam's 1959 U.S. eyes, different fonts or something, and took what seemed to be a plain sheet of paper from one of the slits. "Ever heard of lysergic acid?"

"Didn't Hadntz's paper mention it?"

"Synthesized in 1938 by Sandoz Labs. Neglected, in . . . what shall we call it . . . our old shared world?"

"I guess we can just call it ours, before we got to yours and mine. Obviously where we are now is also ours. Why don't you just give me a phone number that works this time?"

"It's like I was saying. It's like we're both on journeys in which sometimes there are mountains or oceans that prevent us from communicating. The Pony Express guy has been shot off his horse. The telegraph signal is obscured by static and we just don't know how to tune it in. Yet."

"Maybe the static is information too."

"It's not easy for me, Sam. I've got at least two histories to keep straight." He signaled for another beer. "Wait till I get old. That will really be fun."

"So, do you ever see Hadntz?"

"Occasionally. But ever since she won the Nobel Prize, she's been more difficult to—"

"For what?"

"Biochemistry."

Suddenly Sam was the stranded one.

"To get back to your question," Sam said, "I do know that they're using lysergic acid in the CIA. Mainly, it's used to disorient people, as an interrogation tool, to drive them crazy. It's a new weapon for them to play with."

Wink always could express irony with his fast quirk of a smile. "Of course it's considered a weapon here. Everything they lay their hands on is a potential weapon. It definitely is quite powerful. A lot of people take officially sanctioned lysergic acid sabbaticals. They last two weeks, and in government you're entitled to one—or some other kind of therapy-oriented colloquium—every three years. Generally, it functions as an empathy enhancement. That's one of the blind spots in humans. Empathy is useful in various circumstances."

"But contraindicated when you have limited resources and want to keep the other guy from getting them."

"Right. It used to be more efficacious to beat the other guy's brains out to keep your own family fed than to learn to communicate, to anticipate the other guy's concerns. But now—" Wink shrugged. "It seems as if we need to come up with more creative solutions to supply and demand."

"Like communism?"

"Communism is very crude. As it's practiced here, all the control seems to come from the outside, the top, and not for altruistic reasons, or even to redistribute the wealth. It's just a way to control people, not much different than National Socialism. No, this would be a free market affair, but everyone would have a level playing field. Universal volition—a realization that this alternative really does work better than others—would be a key factor, and that depends on universal literacy and universal access to information. You'd channel resources to parts of the world that live in ways we find hard to imagine, and die of diseases they don't have to get. Remember where Hadntz described augmenting a genetic propensity toward altruism?"

Sam picked up the rough, soft paper, about the size of a business card. "Of course. That's what it was all about, in the end."

"This is one approach. Lysergic acid has an effect on the VMAT2 gene."

"The what?"

"It's a gene that regulates the dopamine level in the brain. It's complex, but that's the simple explanation. This stuff temporarily enhances the biochemistry of spiritualism—not religion, just a sense of being connected with the rest of life. In that sense, it's crude—it gives experimental results that point to an avenue that is promising, in terms of Hadntz's goals, but that needs refinement and study. You can't take this all the time—you become nonfunctional. But the memory of the experience lingers, and people who take it have more empathy, overall, than those who don't."

"Empathy is measurable? Maybe the only people who decide to take it are the ones who are already more empathic," suggested Sam. "Those who aren't often treasure their lack of empathy. For instance, has Zee taken it?"

"Wouldn't know. Might smooth his rough edges, though."

"I always got the distinct impression he liked them. You've taken it?"

"Sure. Gives you a new emotional perspective. Hard to come by in any other way.

People don't usually take it very often because the experience is hard to assimilate. Mostly, those who indiscriminately take it are kids, but—"

"By kids, you mean?"

"Teenagers. Sixteen or so through maybe twenty-five."

"The age most of us were when we were fighting the war."

"Brains still growing. Anyway, Hadntz specifically got the Nobel for tracing the hormonal processes that keep the brain growing, as it were, and figured out how to replicate those states in us old, stupid adults. Keeps the brain in learning mode. If you want to learn a foreign language, a branch of mathematics—"

"Which a lot of people do, of course." He tried to imagine Wild Card Zee having such aspirations, and failed.

"More than you might imagine."

"I don't suppose people have to work in your timestream."

"Of course they do. And most people actually want to. Their work is emotionally satisfying because most of the deadly dull boring work is taken care of by machines."

"Wow!" said Sam. "The technological dream of the early twentieth century has come true!"

"Be as sarcastic as you want. It's true. The technologies of our two timestreams are diverging rapidly. I've been reading the newspapers. Here, you're scrambling to catch up with Sputnik. There, ISES—the International Society for the Exploration of Space—is planning to put a team on the moon next year."

"What? This must be jealousy I feel. At last."

"It's expensive to live on the moon. We can afford it. All your wealth, and the wealth of the Soviet Union and the countries they're sucking dry—is still tied up in war. A cold war, no explosions, but a war nonetheless."

" 'Your wealth,' " Sam mused. "Let's just call your place Wink's World. It's a whole lot different than Sam's World. Very shiny." He sluiced condensation from his beer glass with one finger in the shape of a circle.

"Humans are definitely becoming different than what they've always been. We're evolving—*consciously*. We can see a future in which criminality is greatly minimized. Where enhanced communication and science improve public health to the extent of diminishing the aging process. The war ravaged everyone. Now that there's an alternative to war—"

"I'm just not sure what that alternative is, yet."

"It's not just one thing. It's a lot of things."

"Gee, is there anything bad in your world, bud?" Sam signaled for another beer.

"Sure. Unfortunately. Not everyone loves the way things are going and there is, of course, no ethical way to persuade them that things like curing diseases and exploring space and educating children and adults are good things. They can cause a lot of trouble in the good old-fashioned way—bombs, assassinations, and so forth. Sometimes it seems as if there's going to be a real divide, a real breakdown in society based on whether people choose to grow with technology or impede its progress. The living world is unimaginably complex, and it's true that we might make some sudden changes that turn out to be nonsustainable. We can't know all the consequences of our actions. It's a slow process. I'd be called a lunatic radical in a lot of quarters."

"That's kind of a relief. Tell me, who's president?"

"Kennedy. Same here, I see." Wink tapped a beer-rippled newspaper left on their table.

"Right. So. No worms in your political apple. No wars. No—"

"I didn't say no wars. China is changing fast, and that kind of turmoil causes problems. A lot of postcolonial wars in Africa. Heartache aplenty, I'm afraid."

"But for you the good news outweighs the bad."

"Maybe that's just from where I'm sitting. One step forward, two steps back. Sometimes I think that time has a shape, that it's like a braid or something that weaves and overlaps and intersects at certain points, as it is for us right now."

Sam nodded. "I think about the shape of time a lot. Maybe it's like a piece of music. Diz and Bird. You remember that, don't you? Two scales coming from different directions, sharing the same notes for a few beats, then diverging."

"Seems like that's what started it all, for me. A major jolt for my brain."

"A form of ecstasy."

"And a collaboration that depends on deep individuality. I think that Bird lived in several spacetimes at once."

That night, Sam took the lysergic acid. Several hours later, they reopened the bar—just a matter of walking beneath the roof and turning on the power—and rifled through the bartender's record stash. Some were old '78's.

Sam held up a find. " 'Ornithology'! I'm going to recommend this bartender for a military commendation."

They listened to it well over a dozen times, absorbing the astounding harmonic mind of Parker. Then Sam slowed it down to 33⅓, and proceeded to lay his own saxophone over the notes. He'd heard it so many times—not just tonight—that it was already well lodged in his brain. But actually playing it, the kinetic experience, was learning on a much deeper level.

They turned off the record player then, and began to play, to move away from Parker's vision into something completely new.

It began separately, each of them stating a slightly different theme. Then they wound the themes together.

It would have been difficult to say how they did so. It was a collaboration informed by the musical thoughts of each man. At times, one followed the other, and then the roles would reverse. Finally, they'd hammered out a completely new tune that had nothing to do with "Ornithology."

"What shall we call that?" asked Wink.

" 'Timeocracy.' "

He and Wink talked through the night and wound up at dawn walking the beach past forbidding concrete bunkers from the war, looking for Japanese fishing floats. Everything that Sam saw set off a million instant associations, but mostly he felt a marvelous and transparent sense of well-being and happiness.

By midmorning he had slept, was back to normal, exhausted, and missing his kids tremendously. Because of them, and because of Bette, Sam was not at all envious of Wink's world, his future, his enhanced horizons. If he were there, he would not have his children; he would not share his life with Bette. But then again he would not have wept for hours, as he had the night before, for the refugees of the world, those without homes and food, those caught in the political machinations of others. In Wink's world, these problems were being slowly addressed and eradicated.

"Well, that was interesting," Sam said, later in the day. "But I don't consider it world-changing."

"I didn't say it was," said Wink. "It's just another tool your CIA is using to try to harm people, while we're using it to help people. Context is everything."

They'd come to no conclusions, made no concrete plans. Somehow just to see each other was enough; it solidified their sense of having a larger, shared purpose. And Wink could not stay longer than a day.

"Or you'll turn into a pumpkin?" asked Sam.

"Oh. I almost forgot." He took a small, flat case from his shirt pocket. "The HD10. You only have the HD4 here, right?"

Excited and disturbed at the same time, Sam opened the box. Inside was a thin card. He picked it up. It was smooth and slippery. "Plastic?"

"No. It's a new, completely different material. All of the components of the original device are in there, but there have been a lot of augmentations. A lot of new information about the mind and how it functions."

"It's pretty small."

"Molecular engineering. Everything is getting small."

"I'm not sure I want this."

Wink sighed. "Dance. We are affecting—influencing each other."

"No kidding," said Sam.

"Remember nonlocality? You're the one who first told me about it."

"I do."

"This will retrofit the HD4."

Sam shook his head. "I can't go around and revisit all the ones I've put on these islands. The Navy won't pay for it."

"You don't have to. This is already doing it for you. You don't have to do anything."

"How?"

"Using the principles of nonlocality."

Sam regarded the small, thin device. "Maybe you should take it back where it came from. Maybe we're doing just fine here. Look, I don't want to be the one responsible for . . . whatever happens. I have kids, Wink. It's going to be their world now. They're going to have to live in the world that I—that all of us here—make for them."

"Right," said Wink. "All those H-bombs are good, right? The Berlin Wall? Russian gulags? Keep it."

"And what can I, as the grateful colonial recipient of your world's largesse, do for you?"

"It's not like that. We're in this together. Joined at the hip, so to speak. One can't exist without the other. At some point, the balance will inevitably change. The smallest thing could change it. There's something I want to tell you," said Wink, almost as an afterthought, as the plane that would take him from Midway taxied toward them.

"What?"

"There's a fellow doing some interesting work in physics. I've read his work, and I met him at a conference last year."

"What's his name?"

"Keenan Dance."

Sam felt like giving Wink a bear hug and punching him at the same time. "Why didn't you tell me!"

"I'm sorry. It's . . . complicated. This Keenan has three sisters, and a brother who died in Europe during the war."

"Huh." Sam rubbed his jaw. "I see."

Wink shrugged. "Just thought I ought to tell you."

"Yeah. Well"—he tried to grin—"keep in touch."

Their conversation stopped when the engines of the plane started up. The propellers doused them with hot wind. The door of the plane stood open.

Wink picked up his bag with one hand and with the other accepted the green fishing float he'd found on the beach the morning of their strange journey. They stood there a moment, knowing that they might never meet again, and then Wink turned and walked toward the plane.

During the next two weeks, as Sam did his inspections and prepared his reports, he went over to Sand Island to see if his Army buddies were there.

Zee's ship had left the same morning that Wink had, and Kocab was on leave in the Philippines.

But his main job was to inspect the facilities there.

The Distant Early Warning mechanism looked like a giant golf ball on legs—that was the radome. It was linked to mammoth dishes, and a beacon tower reached into the sky.

Sam chatted with the radar ops guy in his room of sweep-arm screens and stacked-to-the-ceiling electronic components, then went through his fire safety check.

When he emerged from the radar hut, he walked to the foot of the huge antenna and opened his cigarette case.

When he saw the HD4, he felt a chill.

For the first time in years, it had changed. It was again clear, as it had been when they had first created it so long ago in Germany.

He took one of the sticks out of the case. It was still the same neutral temperature. He pressed it to one leg of the aluminum tower. As usual, it adhered firmly, forming a strong bond with pressure. He watched it for a few moments. It remained clear and flat for a moment, and then began developing the colored threads he'd seen in earlier versions.

He now knew exactly how Bette had felt when she felt Bette-of-Wartime returning.

When he was younger, he had welcomed change. Now, because of his children, he was not all that keen for it.

He tried to think of Keenan, Bette, his children as parts of a pattern, and failed.

The Nixon-Kennedy debates were on the television set. Sam cradled his quart-sized glass of iced tea in both hands and sat on a kitchen chair pulled up close to the set so as not to miss a word, while Brian and Megan romped behind him in the living room. Jill stood next to him.

"Do you want to be president?" she asked.

"No."

She looked surprised.

Nixon was sweating. Kennedy was cool and in charge. Brilliant, with energy and verve and vision. A soldier, whereas Nixon was not.

He longed to tell her that there really were no heroes. Despite his own history, he never felt heroic or singled out. He was just another node of being, doing his best. How could any person, he wondered, have the audacity to take any action that might result in the deaths of others?

The Bay of Pigs fiasco was in the news. Bette was incensed at the way the CIA was used to attack the revolutionaries. "They're *napalming* the sugarcane fields, Sam. Trying to destroy the crops of those poor people."

"How do you know?"

"Unfortunately, I know." She sighed. "They are creating a threat where there wasn't really one. Castro kicked out the rich people. So what? It's a socialist revolution, sure. But it's really none of our business, in my opinion."

"Didn't he conduct a lot of purges? Kind of along the lines of Stalin?"

"Yes, but—"

"Your politics don't seem to fit in with the professed intentions of your organization, honey."

"You think I don't know it? Kennedy's an idiot for stirring this up. And it was bungled. That's what happens when you use a pack of lies to justify an action."

"Is that why Dulles has been fired?"

"He's one of the scapegoats."

Sam was surprised at Bette's unusual candor in talking about these top-secret matters. "You must be really angry."

"I am. I just don't know what to do about it."

Kennedy was setting up NATO schools all across Europe. As a result, Sam received a very good job offer in Oberammergau, Germany.

Bette refused to consider it at first. "No. It's too close."

"Too close to what?"

"To *me*, damn it!"

"To the war."

"To Russia."

"It's a great job, Bette."

"I can see that, Sam. It's just that it's in Europe. Germany."

"West Germany."

"Why do we always have to be at war?"

"This is NATO. NATO is maintaining the peace."

"Right."

"I'll be teaching at the NATO school."

"On a military base. In Oberammergau. Which is, as we have ascertained, in Germany. Relatively close to East Germany, Berlin, and Russia. You'd be teaching in the service of war."

"The kids will love it. We can take them all over Europe."

"I've been all over Europe. I didn't like it. It was full of dead people."

"They can learn German."

"They're learning Japanese here."

But in the end, she agreed, reluctantly, to go.

Germany

1961–1963

Can we carry through in an age where we will witness not only new breakthroughs in weapons of
destruction—but also a race for mastery of the sky
and the rain, the oceans and the tides, the far side
of space and the inside of men's minds?

—JOHN F. KENNEDY
July 15, 1960

Germany

BETTE LOVED OBERAMMERGAU. Instead of shopping at the PX, she went to the German shops in the small village, and made friends among the Germans, many of whom were professors or former professors.

Sam, in a switch from fire protection to his long experience in ordnance, was teaching the latest advances in antiballistic missiles to officers. He and Bette attended classes in political theory. Bette soon stopped going. "I know more than they do," she said. "And it's all depressing."

In October, soon after they arrived, the entire base was suffused by almost unbearable tension. The Soviets were installing missiles in Cuba, missiles that could easily carry nuclear warheads to Washington, D.C., in minutes, too quickly for any fire director, such as the M-9 or its present incarnation, to intercept it.

Amid the fall glory, the family hiked up the Lauber, one of the peaks that surrounded Oberammergau. Nearby, the Lauber Bahn, the cable car that ascended to the top, languidly pulled cars toward a *biergarten* with a panoramic view. The kids ran on ahead, and Bette vented her anger.

"It's Kennedy's fault. He gave the Soviets an opening. Castro obviously *needed* those missiles to keep the United States from taking over Cuba after the U.S. tried to take over the country with the Bay of Pigs invasion." She moved quickly up the mountain, stabbing her walking stick into the trail as she climbed. Sam could barely keep up with her.

"Well, what do you think is going to happen?" The aura of fear was great, and he could imagine that it was paralyzing in the eastern United States. In the Washington, D.C., area, schools had closed early the day of the announcement that Soviet missiles were in Cuba. The children were hustled home as air raid signals mourned in the voices of prehistoric beasts, but not on their appointed weekly schedule, when schools did their duck-and-cover routine. This was *the real thing*.

And it *was* the real thing. No doubt. All that Churchill had warned of. Soviet aggression extending to their own backyard, ninety miles from Key West.

"Maybe World War Three is going to start," said Bette. "Scuttlebutt is that Kennedy is going to sacrifice some of our missile bases for theirs, though. He is negotiating, unfortunately, from a position of weakness. He can't attack Cuba again. If he does, the Soviets will use it as justification to take the rest of Berlin. All we can do is wait and see. Just wait and see. Fuck it. We can just all go hide in the Messerschmitt caves until the fallout blows over, right? Oh, except that the Soviets have missiles aimed *here*, too. There's no place to hide. It's insanity. Absolute insanity."

"Would it be better," Sam asked, puffing alongside her, "if Nixon were president?"

She glared at an innocent hemlock tree, and then at him. "Hell no, Dance. This is *Nixon's* idea. Nixon's and Eisenhower's. To invade Cuba and get them all stirred up. Kennedy merely took it over, like a dunce. All that anticommunist rot that they've been using to try and control everybody infected his brain too. Well, I'm not a Red, and I'm not red, white, and blue, or the color of any flag. Maybe I'm . . . green, the color of life. Just plain blue, the color of the sky and the sea."

"Green and blue. The Hawaiian Islands and the blue Pacific."

"I told you I didn't want to come."

The crisis subsided, just as Bette predicted, except that the public didn't know that Kennedy had given up one of their missile bases in exchange for the dismantling of Soviet missiles in Cuba.

Brian ran wild on the mountain along with the other boys on the base. One day he brought back an SS knife—the exact same kind that Company C had given as prizes in the athletic games they'd put together the summer of '45 in Muchengladbach, bought for ten cents from the factory in Essen.

After some intense questioning, Sam found out that Brian and his friends had discovered access to the bombed entrance of the Messerschmitt factory and were going in with torches of rags wrapped in kerosene. Bette hit the roof.

"What, Bette? Do you want them to grow up in ignorance of what happened here?"

"They're too young. I found Jill with a library book about concentration camps last week. I don't know why they let her check it out. It was an adult book. She was crying her eyes out. Now she can't sleep. I can't sleep. I'm up half the night."

"You always are." Usually, she read. Sometimes, she cleaned.

"That's beside the point and you know it."

"Look, Dad. There's the entrance."

Sam and Brian were high above the lush Bavarian valley. It was a beautiful place to live, with plenty of things for them to do. The family had biked to Neuschwanstein the week before and visited one of the legendary castles of King Ludwig, all of which had bankrupted his country.

The valley was almost completely walled in by mountains. Crosses adorned the surrounding peaks. A passion play was performed here every decade to fulfill the bargain the villagers made with God in the seventeenth century. It had worked; the plague bypassed the valley.

The village itself, far below, might have been a miniature train model of a Bavarian town. Sam picked out the violin shop, the woodcarver's shop, and the *biergarten*. The white steeple of the Catholic church gleamed in the sunlight, and the huge city pool, filled directly with water that had quite recently been icemelt running down the mountain, glittered.

They had been climbing over boulders for almost an hour, having followed a barely visible footpath Brian pointed out that passed through a cow field. Finally, they rested on a boulder and watched a hawk circle overhead against the clear blue sky. Sam was sweating and wished he had a cold beer. He took a drink of water from the canteen slung over his shoulder and got bratwurst and rye bread from his pack. "Want some?"

Brian wrinkled his nose. "I brought Oreos."

"With a perfectly good bakery in town?"

"Are you finished yet?" Brian was eager to show him the cave, after sulking so hard about being banned from it that Sam had arranged this outing.

It was the danger, Sam told himself as they climbed over more boulders. There were no doubt unexploded charges inside the facility—a huge network of tunnels stretching to Munich. The Army had set charges to close this entrance, many years ago, but a landslide must have opened it.

They paused in the cold wind that emerged from a space between the rocks. "You've got to put on your sweater," Brian told him, getting his own out of his pack.

Sam carried a heavy battery-operated floodlight and had provided Brian with the strongest light he could comfortably manage. "Stay behind me."

"Oh, Dad."

"No whining or we'll go back. This is dangerous."

"I've been in here a million—"

"Brian?"

"Okay."

As they stepped inside Sam switched on his light. The area was so vast, and the darkness so complete, that his light did not reach any limits, but illuminated only a tiny portion of the network of tunnels he knew were there.

"We used rags wrapped around sticks and soaked them in kerosene. They worked a lot better."

"But that's not very safe."

"Jack said that one time he got all the way to the concrete road. I think he got scared and came back. What did they do in here?"

"They were building rocket planes."

"Why did they have to build them here?"

"Because the Allies were bombing Germany. They would bomb any installation, supply depot—in the end, just about everything above ground."

He could almost see the brightly lit network of German efficiency as it must have been only fifteen short years ago. Twenty-two miles of air-conditioned tunnels, on three levels. He'd seen it in a report. It was honeycombed with offices, supply depots, and housed an entire airplane plant, a facility so modern that it still would be considered cutting edge. It had been rumored that a Nazi superweapon, one of those that captured SS soldiers bragged about, was being constructed here—another superweapon that would win the war for Germany at the very last minute.

And indeed, it had been a very near thing. A change in only a few variables could have had them under Nazi rule this very day.

The superweapon. They had it now, all right, super as all get-out. The atomic bomb.

This outer citadel was ruined, with a musty, ancient smell, and strewn with blast-twisted machinery. "Look," Sam said, training his light on a scattering of grenades. He could almost feel Brian quivering with excitement, like a dog on point.

"Wow! Wait till I tell Jack!"

Sam could not believe that he was sweating in this cold. The darkness was all-devouring, a vacuum, sucking him outward into the cold, vast reaches where he had seen pure evil.

"Let's go back."

"Da-ad."

"Come over here. Be careful. Here's the track."

"A train track?"

"Yes. There were three levels here. If the war had gone on longer, they might have been able to use this facility to help win."

"Why didn't they win?"

"Because a lot of men died so that they wouldn't. Because we had better radar. Because they drove away their best scientists. Because they picked too many fights. Because Hitler was an idiot. Because the Germans did what they were told. Because they ran out of money."

"Oh. Well, when you were in the war, you had fun, didn't you?"

"I did some satisfying work. But I didn't have to fight in any battles."

"Because you were so smart. That's what Mom says."

"A lot of very good and very smart men and women weren't so lucky, Brian. War isn't fun. It's one of the most terrible things that can happen. It's something that humans do to themselves. If you don't die, you can still be terribly injured, lose your loved ones, lose your home and everything that you have worked for and that you own. Your mother and I would do everything we could to prevent another war from ever happening."

"Well, let's go," said Brian. "We never came in this far. I never saw any hand grenades. You take all the fun out of everything."

"This place takes all the fun out of me, that's for sure."

They hiked over to the ski lift and took it up to the top of the mountain. Brian had a hot dog and a root beer float. Sam had a beer.

In three days, a heavy chain link fence covered the opening to the cave.

Before he had it closed, Sam went back in, all the way to the concrete road, where the shrine to the construction of secret weaponry began. Germany had built their vengeance weapons, the V-1 and V-2, underground, and had planned many more along that line.

There he knelt and planted a small cube of HD10, Hadntz's answer, perhaps now to grow an M-17 or better, something that might navigate the deeps of time, take aim at heartache, disease, suffering, and war, and vaporize it, as the M-9 had ultimately deflected most of the V-1's Hitler had fired toward England. It would be a missile piloted by the concerns that made up the best of humanity's desires. Right now, those desires seemed focussed in John F. Kennedy, who was leading the world away from war with strength and insight and technological progress and education, despite Bette's present irritation with him.

But now, Sam was in a dark cave. Suffused with wrenching memories, he turned and found his way out, heading toward the brilliant entrance, the weight of futility lightened by just the smallest shred of hope.

Early one November morning, Brian burst into their bedroom. "Mom! Dad! President Kennedy is dead!"

Bette sat bolt upright. "What?"

"It's on the radio. Hurry!"

They crowded into Brian's little bedroom under the eaves. Brian had a radio he'd built from parts a German electrician, one of their friends, had given him. Every morning it was tuned to the BBC and he woke up to it. Brian burrowed back under the covers and Sam and Bette sat on the bed. Jill came in the door. "What's up?"

"Listen."

The President of the United States has been assassinated by a gunman in Dallas, Texas.

Bette shook her head slowly, staring out the window. Absently, she took Sam's hand. "It's over."

"What's over, Mom?" asked Brian.

She was silent for a moment and bit her lip while the announcer gave more details. She nodded to herself.

"What?" asked Brian again.

Jill turned and left the room, her face pale.

"Things will change," Bette said, and followed Jill.

Sam had a sensation of a steep, fast fall. Outside Brian's small window, it was snowing.

"Dad, what can we do?" asked Brian.

He sighed. Had he done all he could? Was Kennedy still alive in Wink's shiny world? "We'll just have to see."

Talk was rampant on the base. At home, Bette was uncharacteristically silent. She took long walks alone in bad weather. Sometimes in the middle of the night, Sam woke to the staccato sound of her typewriter. One day she said that she was going shopping in Munich for Christmas presents and would spend the night there. Sam left work early to take care of the kids.

She returned the next evening, her face haggard, after Sam had put the kids to bed. Blowing snow followed her in the door and she shut it gently behind her, setting two large bags of gift-wrapped boxes in the foyer.

"You're back." Sam put his book down and helped her with her scarf and coat. She sat on the wooden bench next to the door; he knelt and pulled off her rubber boots. "Nasty weather."

"Very nasty. Very bad stuff out there, Sam. Like they say, it's cold. On the large scale of things, we're headed for the next ice age. Better than the hot stuff, I guess. I told you I didn't want to come here." She threw herself into their largest, softest chair and drew up her legs, making herself compact, tiny. Sam went into the kitchen, heated some cocoa he'd prepared for her earlier, and carried two hot cups into the living room.

Bette took hers. "Thanks."

She looked fragile, her face white, her eyes wide and blue, the fringes of her blond hair wet with melting snow. Sam poked the fire and waited for her to talk.

"It just makes it so easy for them. To use me."

"I guess I shouldn't have taken the job."

"No, I don't think it makes any difference, honey. It made it easier for them, but that's all."

"So you would have had to go Christmas shopping in Munich even if we lived in Honolulu."

"That's about the size of it."

"I suppose the money is untaxable."

She laughed and cocoa sloshed from her cup. She brushed it off her ski pants in an impatient motion. "That's one good thing, isn't it. Same old Swiss account. I hope the kids don't waste it all on unwise choices of mates or something. I guess I was naïve to think that it could ever be over." She looked at him keenly. "But that was the promise, wasn't it?"

Hadntz's promise.

He got up and put on Coltrane's "My Favorite Things." He liked Trane's sinuous subtlety, the marvelous tone of his sax, and his musical concepts, which sometimes could be even more abstract than Bird's. He went into the kitchen to get a beer.

"Bring me one too," Bette called, when she heard the refrigerator open. She lit a Camel, assumed the lotus position, and situated an ashtray in front of her on the cushion. He opened two bottles of a particularly fine local beer.

"Where is it, Sam?" she asked, when he stood once more in front of the fire.

"Who wants to know?"

"I can't say. But I will tell you one thing. Remember the work on radar, the work on the bomb? The same kind of work is going on now in Russia, regarding the device. They seem to have a copy of the plans."

Sam laughed. The beer and the music merged; avenues of thought opened. Which version? What if, what if? "What if it worked?"

"Maybe it does." She crushed out her cigarette and lit another. "Have you heard from Wink?"

"I thought we agreed not to talk about it."

She nodded. He could tell she was starting to get wired from the cigarettes. "We might have to."

"Why?"

"Gulags. Ghosts. My ghosts, in particular. The promise of more to come. Satellites with warheads. Awful, awful weapons, Sam. New kinds of chemical warfare. The Nazis didn't use their sarin."

"It dissipates too quickly."

"Well, the Russians have huge stockpiles. They have an H-bomb. They have anthrax. We have all the same stuff. It looks as if Hadntz was right. Neither of us is going to quit until we're all dead, using whatever methods we can find. Switching sides and ideologies until it's all over. It's not the ideologies that matter. It's something deeper. Something that she was on to. That's my opinion. There will be no world for our children. If the Soviets were gone, it would be someone else. That's why it's vital—"

He seated himself on the back of her chair and massaged her neck. She arched back and pressed against his hand.

He said, "I'll think about it."

"That's all I'm asking." She lifted her face to his. He bent down and kissed her, set the ashtray aside, and gently uncrossed her legs. He lifted her up with a grunt, at which they both laughed, and staggered over to the stairs.

"This isn't going to work, Dance. We won't fit." She pulled several layered shirts off over her head as he followed her up the stairs, and let him complete the job once she locked the door behind them.

❧

The following day, after much thought, he took Bette for a walk downtown for coffee. On the way, as they passed between the huge piles of snow on either side of the sidewalks, he told her that he had the HD10, and how he had gotten it from Wink on Midway.

She nodded as he talked. "We knew someone had this. And I was pretty sure it was you. Now here's what we're going to do." She squinted her eyes against the bright winter sun.

"What's that?"

"Nothing. Absolutely nothing. Now that I know where it is, I can relax. The only thing missing is Perler's version."

"Perler!"

"Remember him? Your phone guy in Muchengladbach."

"I remember him well. He took back his device and vanished. And you're the one who gave it to him in the first place, right? In the interest of full disclosure."

"Yes, Dance. I gave it to him. He was part of a bona fide assassination plot, and it was my job to help him however I could. Hadntz gave me that device—the one I gave Perler—when we made the deal about dropping you in France. I've always kept my knowledge of the device from my superiors. I suspected that Hadntz was on to something from the beginning; I was assigned to shadow her, and I became fascinated by what she was trying to do. I never told anyone about it; in fact, for a long time, I was the only one in the organization aware of it at all. I was operating outside their parameters."

"So you're a traitor."

Bette nodded. "I suppose you could look at it that way, but it's really only a very tiny part of what I've done as an agent. They've always suspected both of us; that's the main reason they've kept you on the payroll." She pulled out her pack of cigarettes. "I guess I shouldn't have been surprised that Perler went over to the Russians. It must have been shortly before they entered Berlin. No one hated Hitler more than the Russians. They'd hated Germans for centuries, and vice versa. But—" She lighted her cigarette and snapped the lighter shut. "Get this: *Perler is the only reason our wonderful intelligence organization has any idea that the legendary device exists at all.* They found out about it from *Moscow.*" Her laughter rang out in the sharp, cold air.

"So the Russians have one too."

"Yes. But the thing is, they have no plans. I think I bought their only copy of the plans from that guy in Berlin. He didn't know what it was; didn't care. Hell, at that time, if I'd known the right people, I could probably have gotten the heavy water too."

"Maybe the Russians have their own version of Wink, filling them in."

"You really think so?" asked Bette.

"No. Actually, I don't. And Hadntz hated them too."

"They killed a lot of her relatives. I don't think she's to blame. It couldn't have been her. It's completely my fault."

"What do we do now?"

"You just keep it. I don't even want to know where it is."

"So you can't talk under torture."

"You think that's funny."

"No, I don't."

"You know I'm supposed to carry a cyanide pill?"

"Bette! You don't, do you? What if the kids get hold of it?"

"No, of course I don't, for that reason," she said. "And it wasn't issued to me to kill myself in case my own guys get nasty, which is a scenario that is much more possible than my capture by SMERSH, which seems to have lost interest in me. But that's what I'd probably use it for, particularly if my own guys thought that I was a double agent. They wouldn't hesitate to use torture. They've got a lot of tools at their disposal."

"Lysergic acid?"

"That's one of them, but most are infinitely less pleasant."

"*Are* you a double agent?"

She grinned. "Would I tell you? You're not very tough. You'd spill the beans right away. But no. I guess I am in this sense, though. I don't want my organization to know about this, and I'm not going to tell them."

After his assassination, most of Kennedy's international outreach programs were canceled. The NATO school was closed. Within months, the Dances had said good-bye to their German friends and packed. As the plane taking them to Washington took off, Bette said, "Things could have been so much different. It's a watershed. Things will change. For the worse, I'm afraid."

Washington, D.C.

THE SIXTIES

Things fall apart; the centre cannot hold.

—**WILLIAM BUTLER YEATS**
"The Second Coming"

:|| 35 ||:

1964

A FTER THEY RETURNED from Germany, Sam went back to work for the Navy as a fire protection engineer. He and Bette bought a run-down mansion in D.C. On one side of the house was a long tree-covered slope that ran down to a creek, across from which was parkland. The creek flowed into an enticing viaduct beneath the street, which Sam declared absolutely off-limits to the kids, though he was sure they ventured into it nonetheless. What kid wouldn't?

Their next-door neighbors, the Hansons, were black, and delighted to see someone move into the long-empty place. Jackie Hanson was a schoolteacher and her husband, Terence, was a pharmacist. They had a boy, Doug, who was Brian's age. Doug and Brian became best friends. Most of their other neighbors were black, as well, with a few whites and one Chinese family. Sam's family was a welcome participant in neighborhood activities—the Fourth of July block party, Christmas caroling, and kids playing at one another's houses.

Sam and Bette were happy to have found the place, similar in some ways to the multicultural environment they'd grown used to in Hawaii. Sam was also pleased because he loved Washington and because he could ride the bus to work. They could make do with one car. As the children grew, they rode the busses to the far reaches of the routes, an education in itself, and mastered the schedules.

Built in 1902, Halcyon House, as they called it, was turreted and solid, with plenty of hiding places for the kids. The entire family worked on the house, room by room, as 1964 unfolded, re-lathing old walls and plastering them; carrying boards and nails from room to room, and learning to use tools. Bette decided to become a Montessori teacher, which was, she said, the best way to change the world. After she completed her training, she opened a school in the back of their house, which helped pay the mortgage. Sam had long since ceased to be startled by her sudden changes of direction. He supposed this was just her new cover. But she seemed to enjoy it.

In summer, the favored place for game-playing was the huge screened-in side porch, which overlooked a gully that roared during heavy rains with the swollen creek. Most evenings, after the dishes were done, the family gathered there. Sam tried to read, but was usually drawn into a game of Clue or Mouse Trap. To help them become well-rounded, he taught them how to shoot craps and play poker.

With huge-winged moths batting the screen and cars passing now and then in the summer night, they tossed the dice, spun the arrow, and formulated private strategies for winning at canasta or spades beneath the light of an old, yellow-shaded floor lamp. Another table always held a jigsaw puzzle. The present one was pure white.

Sam also taught them gin rummy. "I lived on card winnings when I was first in the Army," he told them, as they played gin one Friday night. Rows of cards snaked across the table. "I only had three dollars in my pocket when I went in, and they didn't pay me for six weeks. I lived on my winnings, and I've never been broke since."

"I have no such heroic tales," Bette said, and laid down her winning hand. "Gin."

One of the things Sam liked best about their house was that it had a real attic, accessed by a real, though narrow, staircase. It came complete with some old unwanted trunks and dressers the former owners had left behind, and was now filled with the mysterious, evocative remnants of several generations of his and Bette's families.

It was there that Sam hid the clear, soft, plastic-like substance that the HD4 had become when Wink introduced the HD10 to this world. Into the bottom of the lead box went the thin, smoky piece of plastic, anonymous and unfathomable, and then he locked the box. He pried up a floorboard in a corner where the roof came down to the attic floor, stowed the box, and screwed down the board tightly. He shoved a trunk over it, and loaded it down with old, dusty mathematics books. Then he set up a barricade of broken chairs, empty picture frames, an ironing board, and other assorted junk abandoned by, he suspected, a long line of previous owners. When he was finished, his hiding place looked just like the rest of the huge attic—another pile of unappetizing debris.

The rest of the house, old-fashioned and welcoming, pretty much suited his idea of what a house should be. A friendly tricolor collie they found at the dog pound, dubbed Winston, and a tabby cat, Eloise, followed the kids around. Sam built a treehouse for the kids, which Jill used for reading and Brian and Doug as a command center for their bike-riding explorations of Washington. Bette's crossword puzzle magazine was always on the kitchen table, open at the difficult ones at the end, something to do while she waited for food to fry, boil, or bake.

Sam cultivated the antique roses and peony bushes already in the yard. He planted hundreds of bulbs, with the grudging help of Bette. Starting his flats indoors in March, he tended the seedlings with care. Seeing them grow, bloom, flower, and fruit was a source of satisfaction, and he actually enjoyed weeding. Forced forsythia blooms brightened the living room in February, and during the summer, bouquets of zinnias and delphiniums. He foresaw each month's tapestry of color in intricate detail, red tulips flanked by yellow daffodils; pink roses rimmed by spikes of purple iris, as he labored in the plain dark earth. The garden prospered, a respite from experiments, tests, reports, and frequent trips to the Naval Research Lab in Maryland.

Lyndon Johnson was president. On November 23, 1963, less than twenty-four hours after Kennedy's assassination, he signed a reversal of Kennedy's draw-down plan in Vietnam. Instead of winding down the war, as had been Kennedy's proclaimed intent, he ramped it up dramatically.

Megan joined the Brownies, Brian was a Boy Scout, and Jill quit the Girl Scouts when she discovered that the troop's focus seemed to be on feminization rather than learning how to tie knots, build a bivouac, and survive in the wilderness.

To the distress of his children, he continued to play the saxophone, practicing his scales frequently and working on new compositions. He kept the radio tuned to a station that played music of the forties. One day he overheard Jill saying to Brian, "That music's *fifteen years old!* When is he going to get *over* it?"

He began to amass a fine, current record collection: Monk, Trane, Miles Davis. Their new cool jazz seemed in accord with the cold war after the heat and speed of war and postwar bop, and was the background to their game-playing evenings and to the long nights afterward when he often sat up reading or playing solitaire, which gave his hands something to do while he was thinking. Gardening was also useful in that way.

He made a few trips to New York, but The Street—the 52nd street jazz clubs—was gone—now mostly strip joints and adult bookstores. There was jazz to be found, and the shaggy men he'd seen in Minton's years ago on his Easter trip to meet Wink had evolved into a distinct breed, beatniks, who sat around in the clubs getting gone. He heard a lot of the jazz lingo he'd grown up with—*cats, man, bread, square, dig, daddy-o*—spoken there. Hardcore jazz was still there, of course—cooled down, smoothed out. But the decline in The Street was depressing.

Bette's interest in flying did not wane. She often took the kids to a small airfield at Bailey's Crossroads in rural Virginia to admire the small planes, and watch them take off and land. On her birthday Sam rented a plane for her and she took them all on a flight over Washington, up the Potomac, over the Blue Ridge, and back over the Piedmont. The kids were thrilled. They ate weekly at a small, downstairs restaurant in the District's Chinatown, where the proprietors chatted with them about Honolulu.

Bette began taking afternoon and evening classes in developmental biochemistry at Georgetown University. Every six months or so, she let her assistant teach the kids in her school while she was gone, somewhere, for a week. She told the kids she was giving teaching seminars.

Sam did not ask where she really went.

It was August. Sam was on the Baltimore-Washington Parkway, driving home from a colloquium stirred by the lecture on a new, and, once again, secret technological avenue: a quantum computer. He thought it would probably be years before the world heard anything about its mere existence. Development would pose challenges that looked almost insurmountable. Of course, research and development were occurring in the context of weaponry.

In Wink's world, they had reached this stage a lot sooner. But one of the main concerns with this technology was one that Wink had not mentioned—the possibility that it might lead to an uncontrolled chain reaction that might have the power to change literally everything. All matter.

How did this synch with Hadntz's ideas, in which she posited a chain reaction of caring, a biological change in human biochemistry that would lead to the cessation of war?

He merged onto the Beltway, jockeying his way automatically through the fast-moving traffic, and his thoughts wandered.

Every individual was the focus of a unique, but also shared, history. Every second, infinite stories combined, separated, trajected, and formed another history. What kind of matter reflected consciousness? What kind of signals did the brain emit; how could they be tracked?

His HD10 was a potential weapon. He recalled the then-top-secret Rad Lab, the Radiation Lab, set up by Alfred Loomis and Vannevar Bush at MIT in 1940 to quickly develop short-wave radar into a potent tool of war. Had he been recruited, so long ago, as an engineer in an unseen Rad Lab of time? And could Hadntz really vaccinate humanity against the disease of war?

The Beltway was hypnotic. Green, fast summer rushed in through the open windows of his car. Leaves had reached their apex.

Time expanded, became wider.

Summer was Bette, her body familiar to him as his own; lying nude on white sheets sweating, even her closed eyelids sheened. Fall was Jill in a miniskirt and go-go boots, heading to Georgetown and returning from that same trip wearing combat boots and green, flat-pocketed army pants, a surplus pea jacket rounding out her military fashion ensemble. Winter was Brian spinning the car on parking-lot ice as Sam gripped the dash, trying to teach his boy to drive safely on ice. And spring was delicate, dancing Megan, presently a committed ballerina.

And all of it was controlled by Hadntz, her ideas like bullets, ripping into his life. All of them, everything, children, the war, his wife, his work, his thoughts, rushed through the car, couched in wind that smelled of city, of greenness, of an approaching storm.

He saw his exit approach, and pass by, not as if he were passing it intentionally, but more as if he were sitting still and everything moved except himself, in puzzled surrender of all volition.

⁊

When he finally got home, he said hi to Megan, who was playing jacks on the front porch, grabbed the mail from the box, and let the screen door slam behind him. Loosening his tie, he set each piece on the foyer table as he looked at it. The electric bill, Bette's crossword puzzle magazine, a letter from his sister. And then—

A letter to him, in an envelope of crisp office stationery, the address typed, from Allen Winklemeyer.

The monotonous thump of Megan's jacks ball and the sparkling metallic scattering as she went through foursies and fivesies receded. He took the letter, went into the living room, and sat in his easy chair. When he opened it, a formal announcement, printed on embossed card stock, fell out: WINKLEMEYER NAMED DIRECTOR OF QUANTUM COMPUTER DEVELOPMENT AT NAVY YARD.

Sam let the notice drop to his lap. Of one thing he was sure: this letter was not from his own Navy Yard. How had it gotten here? What was the cryptic announcement supposed to do? Was a nexus about to occur? Were their ever-fluctuating presents moving closer together? Would their two differing scales meet, and produce the new music of which Dr. Hadntz had dreamed?

He reached out, feeling the air against his fingers. Within this medium, Wink. Within it, Keenan, Elsinore, Dr. Eliani Hadntz.

But also within it himself, Bette, their life.

In the attic, hidden in a box in a locked trunk, the latest incarnation of the Hadntz Device. Exuding, perhaps, viruses, DNA, radio waves, infinite spacetimes. A repository of the multiverse; a cipher.

"Ever hear of a 'quantum computer'?" he asked Bette, as she entered the room carrying two glasses of iced tea garnished with mint from under the back porch. The two words evoked a highly advanced, functioning spectrum of molecular engineering applications.

She stopped for a second and lowered her head, as if listening to something far away.

"Yes," she finally said, when she had sorted through something, Sam knew not what. "Actually, I have."

But, of course, she could say no more.

Sam continued to keep his diary, but it had long since ceased to be for Keenan.

Maybe his children would be interested in it someday.

One of the first things I discovered upon assuming my post as District Fire Protection Engineer of the Potomac River Command was that my predecessor was a firm believer in keeping his feet on the desk whenever it was possible. Everything avoidable was avoided.

The first battle was with the Chief of the Design Division who thought the fire protection guy should sign only the cover sheet of a project, and withheld whole sections of the project. I had to go to the commanding officer and convince him that I was the only one who could determine the relevance of a given drawing to fire protection, and then, only after I had seen it. The Captain shrugged, and later that day a new directive was issued.

My first customer the next day slammed a single drawing on my desk and said, "There, sign the goddamn thing."

The function of a building had been security classified, requiring a fence. That was the change in the drawing; one fence. Just inside the fence was a fire department hydrant.

"How does the fire department get to the hydrant?" I asked.

"Sonovabitch," he murmured, grabbed his drawing, and scooted.

This was Sam's work. It was a constant war against ineptitude, against people—officials—who didn't care about things that mattered, who got by the easy way, signing off on reports they never read, leaving all the work to those who actually did care, like Sam and those other invisible bureaucrats who took their charge seriously.

Sometimes, it was enough.

⊹| 36 |⊹

1966

ON AN OVERCAST AFTERNOON in January, Sam and Bette were in the kitchen with Ed Mach, drinking coffee. Ed—thin, tall, with an overshot jaw and reddish hair—wore an immaculately pressed black suit. He'd been a dinner guest at their home when they'd first moved there and were getting acquainted with the people Bette called the "home boys," but this time he'd knocked on their door uninvited.

"How about another piece of coffee cake?" asked Bette.

"No, thanks. I'm sorry to bother you at home, but—" He wandered around the kitchen, then leaned against the wall next to the phone.

"You skunk!" yelled Jill from the living room.

"Sam, go see what they're doing and tell them to be quiet," said Bette.

Sam did not want to leave, but pushed back his chair. Essentially, Ed was Bette's guest—if you could call him a guest—but he had been sent to spy on Sam as well. Jill's *Mad* magazine, featuring the cartoon "Spy vs. Spy," was closer to the mark than she might imagine.

The kids were sprawled on the living room floor around a metal tray embossed with brilliant colors—some sort of game board, though Sam had no idea what the game might be. It looked as if it might support all kinds of different games, so intricate and varied was the surface. It seemed to move, to shift, beneath his eyes. He blinked. Jill, eyes closed, sat cross-legged, shaking dice in her cupped hands.

"Cranabule!" shouted Brian at the moment she released the dice, and giggled as she looked at the results in horror.

"Stop it!" She grabbed Brian's shoulders.

"Look!" said Megan, and put her hand over her mouth. The three of them leaned over the game board, blocking Sam's view of it.

"Why don't you kids take that upstairs," Sam told them. "Your mother and I are trying to talk to someone."

They all looked up at him in the same instant, their faces filled with wonder, as if he'd grown another head.

"You do have your own rooms."

"Right!" said Jill, after a second's silence. "C'mon, let's go up in the attic." In an instant the paraphernalia was tossed into an old burlap bag, and they were pounding up the stairs.

"Look, I'm just saying that we need to know where it is," Ed was saying as Sam resumed his seat.

"And I'm saying we just don't know." Bette lit a cigarette and leaned back in her chair.

"There's no use in lying. We have tracking data that shows it is here, in this house, and active."

Bette snorted. "Ed, I know what you're talking about. That misconceived junk you're calling a tracker couldn't find an elephant in a medium-sized ballroom."

Ed started in on Sam.

"We don't have it," Sam said. "We gave you the prototype years ago." At that time, Bette had sacrificed the "cow pie" she'd confiscated from Wink and him in France.

Ed said, "As I was telling Bette, it doesn't do anything."

"What is it supposed to do?" Sam asked. "Have you figured that out?"

"It's completely inert. There is apparently no way to power it, to turn it on, to test it. It's like"—he picked up his coffee mug—"this object, here. Doesn't go beyond itself."

"No one ever said it would," Bette said.

"No," Ed said doubtfully. "I guess not. But we think that something is missing. Some catalyst. We at least need a new set of plans."

"Plans?" asked Sam. "What plans?"

"You must have a copy of the plans."

"No."

Ed lit his own cigarette with a sharp snap of his lighter, and inhaled as he returned the lighter to his pocket. He looked Sam in the eye. "I don't believe you."

"I can't give you something I don't have."

Ed said, "Is it money? Because if it is—"

Bette stood up. "That's it. Get out. Now."

Ed stubbed out his cigarette. "If that's the way you want it."

"We're not doing this for money. We—both of us—have devoted the past twenty years of our lives to our country."

Ed said, "Maybe you're getting money from someone else."

He was beginning to get to Sam. "Listen, you moron—"

"Sam!" said Bette. "Ed, here's your hat."

Ed looked back and forth between them, then walked down the hallway to the door, stooped and silent. Sam followed, opened the door, and let him out.

In the kitchen, Bette was sitting on the floor, running her hands over the bottom of the table. Sam upended Ed's chair. Together they combed the hall, the front door. They found one bug next to the wall phone in the kitchen and set it on the table between them.

"I can't believe he said that," said Bette, speaking to the bug.

"I wish we had some plans," said Sam. "I really wish we did."

"Megan, don't climb up next to the phone with that Coke. You're going to spill it. Get down off that stool right—" Bette dropped the device into a glass of water. It exuded a stream of miniscule bubbles as it sank.

Bette said, "That was really tiny. They're getting better." They went out onto the back porch and closed the door. She lit another cigarette. "They're also getting a lot more pushy. You're absolutely sure that Ed is wrong?"

"I checked it just last week. Nothing's happening."

A few days later, Sam and Bette were sitting in the living room watching *Hawaiian Eye* when the kids filed downstairs.

"What's wrong?" asked Bette. She stood and turned down the television. "You look like zombies."

"Nothing," said Brian. They headed for the kitchen. Sam heard the refrigerator door open.

"What have you been doing up there?" Bette said. She and Sam followed their kids into the kitchen.

"Just playing a game," said Jill.

"I feel like a pizza," said Bette.

"You *look* like a—" began Megan, but shrugged and flopped into a chair at the table.

"I'll call Bazzano's," said Sam. He ordered a pepperoni pizza to be delivered and hung up the phone.

"What difference does it make?" said Brian. Jill glared at him.

"I mean, why bother to eat? We're all going to die."

"Oh, eventually," said Bette lightly, but Sam could tell she wanted a cigarette.

Megan burst into tears. "No, it will be soon. Because of nuclear war."

Bette leaned over from behind Megan and hugged her. "What's brought this on?"

Jill looked aggravated, but then said in her cool-and-collected voice, "We, uh, saw a movie about it. In a school assembly." She glanced at Brian.

"Yeah," said Brian, picking it up. "And we had one at our school too."

"Nuclear war is not very likely," said Bette, gathering Megan on to her lap. Megan's long legs hung down to the floor.

"Yes, it is," said Megan. "No matter what we try."

"But the Soviet Union—" Sam started to say.

"It's not them," said Brian. "China is going to start it."

"Oh?" said Bette. "That's what they're telling you in school?"

"Sounds kind of strange, doesn't it?" asked Sam.

"Well, they *are* all communists," said Jill, as if that decided it. The doorbell rang. "The pizza's here. Where's the money?" She rushed off to the front door.

The kids calmed down as they ate. Bette insisted on a round of spades, and soon they were all laughing and joking.

After they went to bed, Bette and Sam went outside and sat in a little grotto Sam had made near the creek. It was spring, and they both wore sweaters. Koi swam in the pond next to him, and Bette's meditation nook, defined by bamboo, was the place for her morning retreat unless it was raining or snowing. The roaring water made it a good place to talk without being overheard. The dog, Winston, lay between them.

"I think the kids have found the HD10," said Bette. "No thanks to you."

Sam didn't say anything for a while. The sounds and smells of the night filled him with Bette's Chinese poetry.

> Whirr of cicadas rises and falls.
> A night-bird sings, a clear flute piercing darkness.
> Wei Creek runs full and loud.

The clouds shift; moonlight drenches all.

Self vanishes: only this remains.

It reminded him of the first time he had touched the device, back in Tidworth, when it first coalesced . . .

"Sam!"

He snapped back to their dilemma. "If you're right, what can we do?"

"Oh, I guess we can sneak around and spy on them."

Sam said, "We could confront them and ask them about it."

"Right. Good idea. Kids, your dad hid some strange thing in the attic and we think you've found it. Then if they really *haven't* found it, they soon will."

"Last time I looked, it was still there."

"What do you mean, it was still there? It *mutates*, Sam. Part of it walked off and climbed into their ears one night." Her hand trembled as she lit a cigarette. She was furious.

The next morning, the kids came down for breakfast as if nothing had happened. They seemed cheerful, happy.

"Feeling better?" asked Sam.

"Oh, yes," said Brian. "We're all feeling *much* better."

"Why is that?" asked Bette. "Is there anything you want to tell us?"

"No," said Jill.

"We just think that it's not going to happen," said Megan, and smiled brilliantly.

"Well, that's a relief," said Bette. She hugged them all tightly before they left for school.

"Damn it," she said, when they were gone. "When Megan smiles like that, she's always hiding something. They've gone to ground. I want you to show me where it is. Now."

"You're sure?"

"Absolutely."

They went up to the attic. Bette helped him move the broken kitchen chairs and shove aside the heavy trunk. Kneeling where the trunk had been, Sam got a screwdriver out of his pocket and unscrewed the plank. Lifting it up, he removed the lead box, unlocked the padlock, and opened it.

"Well, there it is," he said, relieved.

"Yeah," said Bette. "That's where *some* of it is."

"All of it. The box is full."

"It *expands*, Sam."

"Well, it doesn't look to me as if they got into it. All of my threads were exactly as I left them. Every last detail."

"The kids aren't stupid and neither is this stuff," said Bette. "You put it all over the Pacific, and in Germany, and probably all over D.C. and every other place you've been in the past five years. Sam, I think it's changed again. That's why Ed was here. They have all kinds of incredibly sensitive equipment."

"What can we do? Toss it in the ocean?"

"It's too late for that."

⊣ 37 ⊢

Quick Triplet

ON JANUARY 27, 1967, Sam got a call. A flash fire had killed astronauts Gus Grissom, Ed White, and Roger Chaffee in their Apollo capsule. The capsule sat atop an unfueled Saturn rocket and was fully sealed; they were going through a training exercise.

By the time the news became public, he was on a military flight to Cape Kennedy.

When he returned, he told Bette in the kitchen as they fixed supper, "It's a tragedy. Not just for the men and their families, but for the whole space program." He later testified about his investigation as an expert witness before Congress.

In Wink's world, they had a functioning moon colony. They were probably getting ready to explore Mars, by now. Here, they couldn't even get off the ground.

Their own space dreams, begun by Kennedy, seemed further and further away.

Oxygen supports combustion. Fuels combust, explode, in the presence of pure oxygen. The richer the oxygen, the more likely it is that the fuel will cause combustible materials to burn, or explode. The space program used 100 percent oxygen. They were aviators, not scientists. They were used to taking oxygen through a facemask, the more the better. In a capsule, pressurized with oxygen, any tiny amounts of combustibles could explode.

The space capsule was littered with trash.

After this episode, the space program was forced to hire and listen to fire protection engineers. One of my protégés was hired to oversee the program.

The temptation to do something with the HD10, to release it to the world, to facilitate the changes it might bring about, was never as strong as at times like these.

Jill became ever more involved with the antiwar movement. She organized and attended rallies, marched, chanted, and came home wrung dry. Bette and Sam refused to let her travel out of town for events. "There's plenty happening here," Sam told her.

Now, the latest protest, a huge march on the Pentagon that required national coordination, was on the evening news. Megan dragged them into the living room to watch.

"Look!" said Megan. "That's Abbie Hoffman! They're all going to levitate the Pentagon!"

"After that, I have a few other jobs they can take care of," said Sam.

"Who's that putting a flower in the Army guy's gun?" asked Bette nervously, getting up close to the screen.

"Not Jill," said Megan.

It turned ugly later that night. Sam bailed Jill out of jail at four in the morning amid undaunted chanting that poured out into the street.

"You know," said Sam, as he drove them home through dark streets, "I think you might be doing some good."

On April 4, 1968, Martin Luther King, Jr. was assassinated.

The family was all in the kitchen, just about finished eating dinner, when the phone rang. Bette picked it up.

"What? No, I hadn't heard. Oh my God. That's terrible." A pause. "I don't think so. Where would we go? No, no one is going to burn down our house." She turned around and said to them, "Martin Luther King has just been assassinated."

"He can't be dead!" Jill turned pale. She had been volunteering at Resurrection City, where participants in the nationwide Poor People's Campaign had gathered. Dr. King had helped develop the campaign.

"I think it's true, honey," said Bette, gently.

Jill pushed back her chair and ran upstairs.

Bette said, "Your sister thinks that we need to leave. She says that all the whites in D.C. are going to be killed."

"Rather unlikely," said Sam. "This is just awful, though. I couldn't blame people for getting mad." Sam wasn't sure what would happen, but he didn't think he or his family were in imminent danger. Their own neighborhood was tightly knit. Their latest neighborhood project was ongoing—fighting the proposed highway that would cut through the District, isolating blocks and people from one another. They had a good organization with good communication—a phone tree to inform everyone of a new development or to call a meeting quickly.

Terence Hanson, their neighbor, came over to the house a few minutes later.

"Come on in," said Sam. He got both of them beers from the kitchen, and they settled down to talk in the living room.

Terence was a quiet, soft-spoken, graying man. Being a pharmacist, he regularly chatted with Bette about her biochemistry studies. "I think we should keep an eye on the boys."

"Do you think we're in any kind of danger?"

"Not if we all stay home. There's probably going to be trouble, but I'd say that businesses and offices will be targeted. I don't think anything will happen here. But the boys are . . . boys. Is Doug here?"

"I think so." Sam yelled up the stairs. "Brian? Doug?"

They pounded downstairs, a matched pair in bell-bottoms, T-shirts, and plaid overshirts, each with a Coke in one hand. And tall, Sam observed for what seemed the first time. They were what—sixteen?

"I don't want you going out for the next few days," Terence said to Doug.

"But Dad—"

"No buts. Just stay on the block and you should be fine."

"That goes for you too," Sam told Brian. Brian scowled.

Terence said, "This is serious. People are very angry right now. There will be a lot of dangerous situations. All it would take is a few professional agitators to stir people up. I don't want you involved in any of it. I imagine that soldiers will be sent in. I wouldn't even be surprised if some people get shot."

The boys looked wary, but excited.

The riot started down on 14th Street that evening. Sam decreed that everyone stay home. "I mean it," he said, making a special trip to Jill's room to tell her.

During the next few days, smoke billowed from fires just a few blocks away as business were looted and set afire. Brian and Doug were not to be found for half a day, then rolled up on their bikes and said they'd just gone over to a friend's house on the next block, what was the big deal? Finally they admitted that they'd ridden down to the Washington Monument. Both were grounded. Troops marched through the streets, including their own, where not one of the predicted rampagers had set foot.

They all stood on the front porch and watched them pass.

"Pigs," Jill muttered.

"I don't ever want to hear you say anything like that again!" said Bette.

"Jill hates policemen and servicemen and the National Guard and the war and anyone who's doing a good job for their country," said Brian. "Didn't you know?"

"Everything is going wrong," Jill raged. "First it was Kennedy! Now it's King! Who's next? Only the bad survive. Thousands of boys are dying in Vietnam. Johnson will never pull out. We all have H-bombs aimed at each other! All they have to do is get in a bad mood and push the button! And this whole city, the nation's capital, is full of the poorest people in the country and they're all—surprise!—black. What are we waiting for? We need to *do* something! Now!"

After it was again safe to go out, she immediately found her way to the Robert Kennedy campaign and volunteered.

A sense of sadness and resignation pervaded the neighborhood. The Darts, a white family, quickly sold their house and moved to Arlington. The entire social fabric of the city was changed. Alliances between blacks and whites were severely tested, and many were broken. Many neighborhoods would probably never recover. Optimism about progress in race relations evaporated.

Just two months later, Robert Kennedy was assassinated. After this event, the third major political assassination Jill had experienced in her short life, she grew silent and intense. She withdrew to her room for days on end, and refused to attend school, though she did go the library from time to time.

"I'm worried about her," said Bette.

"What can we do?"

"I don't know. Get her involved in something positive."

So they were happy when she became even more involved with antiwar demonstrations.

The political situation was deteriorating fast. The country was up in arms, particularly students, who were becoming more and more militant, along with Black Power advocates. Nixon was nominated to run again for the presidency. He was taking a hard line against anyone who criticized his policies. The National Guard and the police were more and more a presence on college campuses. The long, hot summer was filled with tension. Jill went to the Democratic Convention in Chicago, giving her parents a very nervous week as they watched the mayhem on television. She returned excited, invigorated, with a large bandage on her forehead from a police clubbing, filled with more fire than ever for antiwar and other social causes.

"It's as if she's taken vitamins," remarked Bette one day, after Jill had given them a long lecture on imperialism.

Bette herself had to leave, this time for two weeks. When she returned, she was alternately exhilarated and depressed. Sam was worried.

"What's wrong, Bette?" he asked one evening as they sat in the kitchen. "Anything I should know about?"

"Actually, there is," she said. "But I'm not going to tell you."

"Let me guess. It's for my own safety, right?"

"And mine. And our children's."

"Where were you? Can you tell me that?"

"Germany."

"Where in Germany?"

"This is a fun game. Oberammergau."

"Oberammergau. Hmmm. That sounds really strange to me. What for?"

"I had to pick up an airplane and bring it back to the States."

"So why is that upsetting you?"

She lit a cigarette. "This is upsetting me, now. That's all I'm going to say."

For years I had read various articles about the tender loving care lavished upon the original Declaration of Independence, mounted in a hermetically sealed heavy metal box, filled with inert argon gas, protected from infrared and ultraviolet rays with specially formulated industrial-strength glass. After viewing hours (or in case of a vandal's attack), a built-in vault elevator lowers the viewing box into the reinforced concrete storage vault under the public floor for safe keeping. A perfect solution for the hazards of public viewing!

We were preparing to install sprinklers throughout the National Archives building and collections, and I was sent to observe some of the details.

I met with the Archivist of the United States, discussed some of the fire protection problems, and began my escorted inspection. When we got to the Declaration of Independence display, I expressed my interest in inspecting the vault where the Declaration spent its "down time."

The vault was smallish, maybe ten by twelve feet, but pretty well occupied. There were four standard metal workmen's lockers with their street clothes hanging inside. A large stack of what appeared to be creosoted railroad ties, which we found were used as dunnage to support the vault elevator when the elevator was disassembled for inspection or repairs. To round out the ambience were an open fifty-five-gallon drum of grease for lubricating the elevator machinery, a couple of folding chairs for hanging out, and a butt can for smokers.

The Archivist of the United States immediately pledged to have the place cleaned up *that day,* and the cupboard was bare the next day when I returned. That vault was on the Archives' wish list for no sprinklers, but they really didn't fight it when we insisted.

Sam finished his entry, and closed his composition book.

It was two o'clock in the morning—not an unusual hour for him on a weekend. He was sitting on the screened-in porch. Two guys on the radio were talking about Red Rodney and his contribution to jazz. A tall glass of iced tea sat in a pool of condensation on a saucer next to him.

He smelled cigarette smoke.

Pushing his chair back, he went out the door and down the wooden stairs to the bamboo grotto near the creek. Sam had recently laid flagstone and erected three walls of lattice, then added a tin roof so they could use it in the rain. Vines now hid the lattice, and kept it cool on hot days.

The creek rushed past; it was a lovely, starry night. Winston, who lay on the ground, thumped his tail when he saw Sam but did not get up. As he had expected, Bette was there, her chin resting on her knees, one arm holding her legs close to her body as she sat in a wicker chair, smoking.

"I didn't know you were out here," Sam said. "Worried about something?" He sat down himself and put his feet on a hassock.

Bette didn't answer, just smoked absently while Sam enjoyed the immense, pulsing whirr of the cicadas. He reached over and rubbed Bette's neck. She turned her head so that her cheek rested on her knees and looked at him.

"Yes."

"What is it?"

She finished her cigarette and wrapped both arms around her knees. "I am in possession of something that could be . . . very dangerous."

"What's new about that?"

"This isn't a joking matter."

"I'm not joking."

"For the first time, I'm afraid for us. Really afraid."

"Can you give me any details?"

She shook her head. "Absolutely not. They grilled me from here to kingdom come last week. It's . . . wearying. All the more so because we're supposed to be on the same side. And I guess I'm not on their side anymore. The only trouble is, there's really no particular side that looks good. No other side I'd rather be on." She smiled then, and took Sam's hand. "Except yours, Dance."

And then, the matter was closed.

⊣ 38 ⊢

The Gypsy and the Game Board

IT WAS A RAINY Sunday afternoon in late January 1970. Sam knocked on Jill's door. He heard blaring rock and roll music. Jimi Hendrix, he guessed. She was nineteen now, and had a show on a local underground radio station. It was just a few hours a week, but she got a lot of free records out of it, and free tickets to concerts. She was attending American University and had a heavy course load as well.

He knocked again, harder, and was rewarded with a cross "What?"

"Can I come in?"

"I guess."

Sam cautiously opened the door.

Jill's tower room was filled with houseplants. They twined on windowsills, crowded together on an old table, hulked elephantine in huge pots set on the floor, and fogged the windows with humidity. He tried to imagine how she'd gotten all this dirt up to the third floor. Next to an antique bed and dresser, her closet overflowed onto the floor, and an old oriental rug was almost invisible beneath stalagmites of books. She'd taken over his collection of science fiction, and those books covered one of the narrow back walls. He glanced at some of her other titles. *The Pill versus the Springhill Mining Disaster. Trout Fishing in America. Tropic of Cancer. One Flew Over the Cuckoo's Nest. The Electric Kool-Aid Acid Test.* Several thin volumes by some-one named Denise Levertov next to her Chinese poets, Li Po and Wang Wei. Under-ground comix—*Zap* and the *East Village Other*—were strewn across the floor. He thought he smelled a faint whiff of marijuana in the room and hoped that the neighbors never did.

Jill, on a tall stool, hunched over her drafting table. She wore jeans with holes in them, Mexican haurachis, and a T-shirt that ordered UP AGAINST THE WALL. On her left upper arm was the black armband she always wore since joining the SDS.

"Can I look?" he asked, shouting over the music.

She shrugged. She didn't stop drawing, but swayed to the right on her stool so he could look over her left shoulder.

"What is this?" he shouted.

She reached over and switched off her stereo. "My comic book. *Gypsy Myra.*"

"Your comic book?"

"That's right. Elmore and I are going to publish it." Elmore was Jill's latest boyfriend, a thin, intelligent guy who was also in the SDS. Sam had spent many eve-nings chatting with him about politics. "This is the second issue. We already pub-lished the first with the SDS mimeograph."

"No color."

"Too expensive."

"This looks pretty interesting. Can I see issue number one?"

She looked at him in disbelief, left her nibbed pen in the jar of black ink, and tugged a copy out from beneath a pile of books. The thin, wrinkled tome was sta-pled on the left side. A little box in the corner read 15¢.

"You're getting paid for this?"

"What's so strange about that? I'm donating the money to the cause."

"The cause?"

"The antiwar movement."

"Sounds like a good cause." He opened it up to the first page.

He felt as if he had been punched in the chest. He looked around and collapsed onto what he thought was a chair, obscured beneath piles of clothing.

"Dad, are you all right?"

"I just—yeah."

He caught his breath. The woman wore an unlikely costume: swirling Gypsy skirt, white blouse. But her face was uncannily, undeniably, the face of Hadntz.

And, come to think of it, this was what she had worn when he saw her, briefly, at the halfway house in Muchengladbach, where he, Wink, and the Gypsy refugee had created a marvelous fusion of jazz and gypsy violin music.

"She's, like, a superhero," said Jill.

"Oh?"

"Yeah. She has superpowers that can stop the war."

"How does that work?"

"Well, it's a secret."

"Do *you* know how it works?"

"No. She's from another planet—"

"Like Superman."

"Not exactly. She's from another planet just like this. Only better."

"How did you . . . how did you happen to think her up?"

Jill smiled. "Oh, I just did."

"Look, Jill, have you kids . . ." He paused. Have you kids what? *Have you kids found anything strange in the attic?*

"What?"

"Nothing. Who are these people here?" He pointed to an old sepia photograph that obviously came from the attic, stuck on her bulletin board. Maybe he could lead into it that way.

"Oh. That's the family who used to live here. And that's Evvie."

"Evvie?"

She walked over to a bulletin board and tapped another picture, of a girl in a white dress. "Evvie. She's from the attic. Here's her mother, Fern"—she tapped another picture of a woman wearing an ankle-length dress—"and her father, an exiled Russian count."

"Really?"

"No, not really," she said impatiently. "We just made those stories up about the family who used to live here. When we found the pictures. They did all kinds of things. They had balls in the living room."

"Small ones."

"But grand. The cream of Washington came to them. Evvie was sickly, and had to spend a lot of time in bed. Her grandfather, who was also Russian, gave her a special game to play. A thinking game—a board with beautiful colors. It changes."

"Can I see this thinking game?"

"Uh, I don't know where it is right now."

"Well, can you tell me more about this Gypsy Myra?"

"Oh." She shrugged. "There are just a lot of stories. Lots and lots of stories in . . ."

"In what?"

"Oh, just everywhere. Look, Dad, I have to get back to work, okay?"

❧

A few hours later, while Sam was laying a fire in the fireplace, the phone rang.

He ran down the hall to the kitchen, picked it up, and watched Bette through the kitchen window. She was pulling back the tarp over the woodpile and going through the logs, picking one up, tossing another down.

"Hello?"

"Dance!"

The unexpected connection, carrying Wink's voice, was clear and pure.

"Well," said Wink. "Cat got your tongue? What are you up to?"

"Contemplating a career in philosophy. You know, ivory tower, all that."

"Coward."

"Easy for you to say."

A pause.

"Where are you?" asked Sam.

"You have to mean, when am I."

"I'll bite." Bette had selected a few logs as satisfactory, handed some to Brian, and then took an armload herself. They slogged up the hill through the rain.

"Beijing, 2010, the Book Mart."

"Of course. Doing what?"

"Hawking my biocube. Life story. You know, 'Technology From Another Dimension,' all that."

"This isn't a collect call, is it?"

Huge Wink-style laugh.

"Will I get an advance copy?"

For an instant, he seemed elsewhere: *Wink's eyes, gleaming, as he laid out his understanding of time interwoven with undanceable bebop at Monroe's, Parker and Dizzy dazzling their brains, rearranging electrons instant by instant by instant, sliding infinite landscapes into their ears.*

Wink's worried voice on the phone brought him back to his own kitchen. "Some of that stuff you put everywhere is going to be activated."

Sam opened the door for Brian and Bette. They wiped their feet and trudged down the hall to the living room.

"I think that some of it already is."

Wink didn't say anything for a moment. "This is going to be everywhere. If it all works out." He laughed. "It's going to go to all the kids. Free favors and things like that."

"Is that a good idea?"

"It's the only one," said Wink, his voice bleak. "Out of all the possibilities. It's the only one that will work. Our worlds are like . . . DNA. It's organic, a genetic link.

The two helixes have to be able to read each other. They have to match up. Otherwise . . ."

"I don't know what you're talking about."

"I don't either. Not really. Not deeply. But I do believe it's true. And in the process, things will be lost."

"Things?"

"People. It's a war."

"Which people?"

"No way to know for sure."

Sam was quiet. A war. Watching Brian as he took off his coat down the hall, Sam realized how tall he'd become. He'd be eighteen in a month, and subject to the draft.

"We have to have a reunion," Wink said.

"When?"

"You mean where."

"Spacetime coordinates, please," said Sam.

"Your town. End of April. The Sheraton. I'll handle the invitations."

"Great idea. Say, sport, what gives you the impression that we're heading for this dire situation?"

"It's a nexus. It just shows up as a nexus."

"Fine. A nexus. That's informative."

"All of these emerging patterns are shown as topology. And at some point, this particular nexus, they all become too dense, too interconnected, to decipher. That's all we know at this point."

"What if you're wrong? That would be wonderful, wouldn't it?" He had more than half a mind to ignore all of this, pretend it wasn't happening. He did not like Wink's portents of death and loss.

"I'm right." His voice tightened, darkened. "You might have to—"

The line went dead. *"Damn it!"* Sam yelled, and slammed the phone down.

Bette came into the kitchen, pulling off her gloves. "What's wrong? Who was that?"

"Wink," he said. "Of course, the conversation was over before I had a chance to ask any questions."

Brian came into the kitchen. "Who wants hot chocolate?"

Many hours later, the kids had wandered up to their rooms. Sam shut the French doors to the living room and told Bette about Jill's comic book, and Wink's call.

"What do you think, Bette?"

They were drinking the last of some very good brandy that they'd been saving. Winston lay in front of the fire, and Bette's hair gleamed in the firelight. It might be a perfect evening except for the fact that his daughter seemed to have met Dr.

Hadntz, who lived in otherwhen, and his old war buddy Wink had told him that not just *this* world, but *all* worlds, might end soon.

Sam said, "Somehow, Jill knows something about Hadntz. But I don't know how, I don't know how much, and she wouldn't talk about it."

"It's very disturbing. And it makes me mad. Hadntz is trying to put pressure on us."

"To do what?"

"To use it, Sam. It's been a few years since we saw her, and at that time she told us that nuclear winter is inevitable. To tell you the truth, I'm coming across more and more people in the government—high up, generals—and officials in the CIA who would jump at the chance to use nuclear weapons. They're hoping the Vietnam war will escalate. They want to use them there. They've even got very specific plans."

Sam said, "The only problem is that we don't have any idea *how* to use the HD. I *have* continued to distribute it. Other than that, I don't know what to do. I kind of wish it would turn back into the device that I used to see Keenan. At least that would give me something to work with. I was under the impression that the HD10 Wink gave me at Midway would make some kind of a difference."

"Maybe it has. Maybe that's what he was trying to tell you."

"If that's so, it's a damned disheartening difference."

Bette smoked in silence for a few moments, then said, "I don't know about this organic time idea. But things are pointing more and more, from what I've been learning at Georgetown, toward an organic model for our future. The DNA of bacteria carrying information, melded into every part of our body. I can imagine the kind of brain enhancement Hadntz described. It wouldn't be done with just one component. But the latest brain studies show that serotonin, a brain chemical, is tremendously important for one's mental health. Tip it one way, you're united with the universe. You *care*—about everything, everyone. It's the empathy thing we talked about so long ago. I mean, think about how you care about your plants. You look at one of them, think about it needing more sun, more shade, more fertilizer, and you fix it. You experiment. In the classroom, I think about the whole class as one organism. I concentrate on all of the children at once, while thinking about exactly what little piece is needed for this particular child to understand—deeply, kinesthetically—what addition is, or how they could actually use reading and writing to communicate with others. Once they're opened up in that way, there's no stopping them. Just think of a future, a world—Wink's world, maybe—where this kind of understanding of the whole is embedded everywhere, optimizing opportunities, eliminating waste."

She took a drag from her cigarette. "And if you tip the serotonin level the other way, you care less and less, until you reach the Hitler end of the scale. You care only about yourself, and your plans. You become suspicious and paranoid."

"So it's all chemistry."

"Well, it's genetics too. The way serotonin is regulated seems to have a correlation with a particular gene, VMAT2."

"Hmmm. That's what Wink said."

"They're doing research on it at the National Institutes of Mental Health. But it's slow! The nuclear winter that the kids saw was not all that far away. And things are getting worse here."

"I don't know," he said. "We'll see."

"We're not children," she said. "We can't just *see*. We have to *do*."

But Sam felt terribly sluggish. Or terribly, *locally* happy. He examined his happiness, the happiness of his family, their very lives, and measured it against the seemingly boundless happiness of that world where Keenan Dance still lived. His own happiness seemed much more important than continued happiness for Wink and that distant otherwhen, which intruded only to bring news of catastrophe.

Finally, he understood how the Germans had felt during the war. Do nothing. Don't interfere. All the bad things are happening to somebody else.

But it hadn't been true then, and it wasn't true now. His family was deeply involved in what Hadntz had started.

"Let's get going on the reunion, then," he said.

"We can do that. But what can we do right now?"

"Jill said something about—what? A thinking game? What could that be?"

The next morning, after the kids left, they went through the house. They took out all the games stored under the bench in the screened-in porch. They found some very strange games, but nothing unexplainable. They made a search of the attic, again checking on the HD10, which once again appeared to be intact. That took several hours.

Finally, they got to Jill's room.

Bette stepped across the cluttered floor gingerly. "I don't think I lived in this kind of mess. She's nineteen—wouldn't you think she'd want to be a little neater?"

"She's taking a heavy load in school, isn't she?"

"This is a jungle. Some of these plants are monstrous," said Bette.

"I think they're pretty nice. Look, this angel-wing begonia is in bloom."

"Get to work, Dance. I'll start with the closet." She knelt and started pulling out clothing. "I need to throw this away—she doesn't need to be wearing this raggedy plaid shirt. It would be nice to get rid of this skirt too—it's the size of a handkerchief."

"Bette, we're doing something a little more important here."

"A thinking game . . . a thinking game. What could it be? Every game is a thinking game, isn't it? Maybe it's just a deck of cards."

Suddenly Sam remembered the board they'd been using when Ed Mach had visited them, and his fleeting impression that the board had changed as he looked at it. He hadn't thought much of it at the time—he had just supposed his eyes were tired.

"I think we're looking for a metal board, like a tray, with raised edges. It has legs that fold under. Like you could use it while sitting in bed."

"That's a lot of welcome specificity. What gives you that idea?"

"Remember when Ed was here, and they were making noise in the living room?"

"That was a while ago. Hmmm. Yeah, I guess so." Bette's voice was muffled. The pile of clothes, boots, and shoes behind her was getting very large.

"When I went in to see what they were up to, they were playing a board game. The surface of it . . . seemed very intense. It moved. Kind of like a pattern in a tile floor seems to move if you stare at it long enough."

"Maybe that's just what it was. A pattern."

"Underlying, and continuously evolving, changing." Sam was lying down and pulling things out from under the bed. It was old-fashioned and sat high off the floor. "So that's where the broom went. I guess she wanted to make sure that the whole house looked like her room." He sneezed when he pulled out some dusty cardboard boxes, and then a stuffed rabbit. "Bunny rabbit? Didn't she have this when she was three?"

"Yeah," said Bette. "Brian tore the ear off. The anguish! Come on, we have the whole house to go through."

"Wait! I think this might be it!"

He pulled out what he recognized as the game board. "Bingo."

She turned from the closet, pushed herself across the floor, and sat next to him, her back propped against the bed. "You think this is it?"

It was blank, just plain gray metal, except for a small black dot in the center.

"I think this says 'touch me.'" Sam powered it on.

The surface flowed with wavering lines that seemed three-dimensional. "It's a holographic flow analysis," said Sam. "Amazing. We use these sometimes to observe and measure heat distribution."

The curved, concave lines seemed to flow endlessly from two different directions, two different dimensions, then intersected, setting up new lines in a three-dimensional display that appeared to hover above the board's surface. The lines themselves were dark green and the shimmering spaces between them were a much paler green.

"Okay," he said. "The interference is being set up by something that the raised edges of the trays radiate. Imaged wave interference can be caused by different agents—radar, lasers."

"Timestreams."

"HD10's." Sam's heart beat harder. "Kind of like early radar, really—except this must be extremely short-wave, with an extremely short antenna. Maybe just molecular-sized. This is . . . amazing. But how did it—how was it—manifested?"

"There's something I should tell you, Sam," said Bette.

"What?" asked Sam, his hands moving over the board, touching the varying patterns to see what would happen. "This just keeps changing and changing . . ."

"When I went to Germany last time, I brought back a plane."

"You told me."

"This is a very special plane. It's kind of the same as this."

Sam stopped what he was doing. "What do you mean?"

"Okay. Now you tell me. Did you put any of the HD10 in the Messerschmitt cave?"

"Are you sure you want me to tell you?"

"Sam!"

"Yes. I did. Before I had the entrance sealed off again, after Brian found that knife there."

"Well, it mutated."

"Into . . . what? A game board?"

"No, Sam. A plane. A very special plane. The CIA doesn't know about it. But all this—Hadntz's paper, the physics of life, all the things I've been learning about biochemistry, your research into fire dynamics, physics—it all seems to come together in that plane."

"How so?"

Jill's Army boots were in front of them. Sam looked up. She had her hands on her hips. She was very angry.

"*What* are you two doing in my room?"

"Isn't it obvious?" asked Sam. "We were looking for this board."

"It's mine."

Megan and Brian were in the doorway. Megan looped her long black hair behind her ears nervously; her face became pale. "It's the Infinite Game Board. Jill, I thought you said it was lost."

"Yeah," said Brian. "You haven't let us use it in years, you pig."

"I think I should just move out," said Jill. "Then I'd have some privacy."

"With what money?" asked Sam.

"I could get a job. I could move in with Elmore."

Bette said, "Young lady, if I ever hear—"

"Look," said Sam. "Let's get back to the matter at hand." With some effort, he got off the floor, gave Bette his hand, and hoisted her up.

It had to be said. "Did you kids ever get into some . . . stuff . . . in the attic?"

They all laughed until they were almost hysterical.

"What's so funny?" asked Sam.

Megan said, "What *else* is there in the attic?"

Brian said, "You know what they're talking about. That plastic stuff."

Bette sank down on the bed. "Yes. That plastic stuff."

Megan said, "The stuff in the metal box under the floorboard under the trunk full of books?"

"Exactly," said Sam.

"Well, yes," said Jill. "We needed that trunk for the side of a house we were making, and we tried to move it. It was too heavy, so we took out all those books. When we moved the trunk, Megan noticed that there were new screws in the floorboards. She was reading spy books then. She thought she was going to be a spy."

"It seemed pretty obvious that something had been very carefully hidden," Megan said. "So I was careful about observing every little thing, like the threads that were there, and putting them back the same way."

Bette gave Sam an exasperated look.

"We opened it up and just saw that clear stuff. It was like Jell-O, only stiffer. You could pinch off a little piece and the rest of it just relaxed, sort of, to fill up the space."

"It was actually kind of dull," said Megan. "Disappointing. I put it all back together the same way I'd found it."

"I thought the box would be full of gold," said Brian.

"I thought it would be full of old letters," said Jill.

"So then what?" asked Sam.

"Then—nothing," said Megan. "We never looked at it again. It seemed like a lot of trouble."

"Did you take any of it?" asked Bette.

"No," said Megan. "I pinched that little piece off, but then I lost it somewhere. Why? Did I ruin something?"

"No, honey," said Sam.

"What's that got to do with the game board?" asked Jill.

"We were wondering where you found it," said Bette.

"We found it in the attic too," said Brian. "I don't remember when. After that, I guess. We found lots of toys in the attic. Old dolls, some kind of racetrack game, a really nice chess set, a baseball glove—you know, stuff like that. We made up the family that might have lived here. The ones who built the house. Made up stories about them." He smiled as if to himself. "I'd almost forgotten. It seems like a long time ago."

"It does," said Jill.

"But the game board was a lot of fun," said Megan. "Until it got scary."

"What happened?" asked Bette.

Megan leaned against the dresser. "I don't like to talk about it. I tried not to remember it."

"Fires and death," said Brian. "There were a lot of stories about war in there. I can't remember any of them, either, exactly. They all seemed to happen so fast. Like they were happening inside your brain. And you had to make choices about what to do, and sometimes you died. But mostly, a lot of other people died. Kids, parents, old people. Everybody. Sometimes you were there when they died. Sometimes you killed them. It was kind of like playing with my green plastic soldiers when I was a kid. But a lot more . . . real."

"I'm sorry," said Sam. "I'm so sorry that you kids had to see that."

"I'm not," said Jill. "For one thing, it got me thinking about how to do some good. For another thing, it had the Gypsy Myra stories in it, and they're pretty interesting. They make good comics. They help me think about how to make the world a better place."

Sam picked up the board, which was once again blank. "We need to keep this now."

"That's okay," said Megan.

"*We* won't miss it," said Brian, glaring at Jill.

Jill said, "No. I need it. For my Gypsy Myra comics. Look, they're a big hit. We're actually making money after we pay all the costs."

"I'm sorry," said Sam, holding the board against his chest. "Really. I'm sorry for everything."

He went down the stairs with slow, heavy steps.

He had not felt this terrible since Pearl Harbor.

Bette put the board in "a better place."

"Our closet?" asked Sam. "That's a better place?"

"For now." She finished piling up hatboxes and gave Sam a long, tight hug. "Sam. It is not your fault."

"Are you kidding? Of course it is."

"It's Hadntz's fault," she said.

"It's my fault," he said. "Absolutely, completely my fault."

"It's my fault too. I could have insisted that we get it out of the house. But I thought that here it would be more secure."

"All the things I wanted to protect them from—they've seen it all. The events that have given me nightmares my whole life. They're scarred. It was so bad that Megan doesn't even want to remember it."

"Those events made you want to do something," said Bette.

"Yes, and what have I done? Just left that device for my kids to play with. And I've put it everywhere I possibly could. The Pacific. Europe."

"Speaking of Europe," said Bette, "I told you about the plane, didn't I?"

"Yes," said Sam. "Something about the Messerschmitt caves."

"Maybe you can help me figure out what it does."

"Some other day, Bette. I'm not feeling very good right now."

The next morning he put the HD10 in a safety deposit box.

⊣ 39 ⊢

The Gathering Storm

EARLY IN FEBRUARY, Sam parked his car next to a mound of depressing gray slush. He and Bette had spent the past few weeks in intense, nonstop preparation for the reunion, and this evening they would do more of the same. As he climbed the front stairs, he scanned the front flower bed for early irises, as usual. No luck.

He heard shouting, and hurried across the porch. He opened the door to find Bette yelling at Brian.

"I can't believe—oh, Sam! Thank God you're home. Tell him, Brian."

"Dad, I've enlisted."

Sam tried to be calm. "With who?"

"The Navy."

Sam looked back and forth from Bette to Brian. Bette's face was splotched red with anger and wet with tears. Brian had a stubborn, yet patient look on his face. Sam knew at once he couldn't be moved, that he did not regret his action. And he knew why. Terence had just come over last week, agitated because his son Doug had joined the Army. Doug's cousin had died in Vietnam a month earlier, just after Christmas. They all knew the boy, and attended the funeral. Sam kicked himself for not understanding that Brian would want to do the right thing, as he saw it.

"Shall we go sit in the living room?" Once they were seated, he said, "Why the Navy?"

"I want to be on ships. Or maybe fly planes."

"How long have you been thinking about this?" asked Bette.

"About six months, I guess."

"Why didn't you talk to us about it?" asked Sam.

Brian looked at Bette, rolled his eyes, and said, "Isn't it obvious? Look, it's what I wanted to do since I was a kid. Now's the best time—there's a war."

"Now is the worst time," said Bette.

"It's what Dad did."

"I was older."

"Yeah, but you would have done it when you were younger if the war had started, wouldn't you?"

"I guess, but—"

"But what?"

"It was a different kind of war, Brian," said Bette.

"You enlisted too, Mom."

"I did. I—" She looked at Sam for help.

"I enlisted because Germany was a growing threat," said Sam. "My older brother—"

"Keenan. I know. He died at Pearl Harbor."

Sam regretted allowing Brian to wear Keenan's perfectly kept pea jacket and bell-bottoms for the past year. "*This* war just doesn't make any sense."

Jill came in from work and closed the front door as Brian was saying, "Communism is a big threat. Once China gets hold of Vietnam, all of Southeast Asia will become communist. We held them back in Korea. That's what we have to do now."

"That's bullshit and you know it," Jill said, hanging up her coat and scarf.

"You need to speak more respectfully to your brother," said Bette.

"We've been over it a thousand times."

Brian said, "You're just a radical hippie, Jill. And you're a girl. You don't have to make a choice."

"I'll ignore that first part, seeing as how I'm working on a degree in political science. And I'm sure you'll make the right choice."

"Right. You want me to sneak away to Canada like your friends did. Well, I won't. I've enlisted."

Jill stared at Brian. Tears trembled on her eyelids. "I'm sorry." She went over to him and hugged him tight.

Brian sighed. "I'm sorry, sis," he said, when she withdrew. "I guess I didn't think it would be such a shock to everybody."

Jill perched on the edge of a chair. "But we've been talking about it for months. You've been accepted at MIT. You'll get a deferment."

"Brian, you can do a lot more good once you know something," said Sam. "I'd had three years of college."

"The Navy will train me. And pay for my college too."

"You've always known that's not a problem," said Bette.

"I'd rather do it this way. I'm going to be a SEAL."

Bette lit a cigarette and shook out her match. Finally she said, "They're not going to follow through. That's just what they told you, Brian." She got up and looked out the window. "Why do you think those recruiters have been sharking around at your school? That's what they're doing, isn't it?"

"I went to their office," Brian said.

"Sometimes I hate this country," said Bette.

"You don't mean that." Brian's eyes were wide with shock.

"Right now, I absolutely do. I hate all countries, all nations, every entity that forces children to go to war. Do you know what the original definition of a nation was to the first United Nations? A nation was a group that had the capacity to wage war. Period. Not, a nation is a unique cultural entity. Not, a nation is your homeland, the place you love because your family lives there. No. A nation is simply that which makes war, and I don't like it, and I've never liked it, and that's why I enlisted. I don't think that nations are a good development at all. And this particular military involvement is based on greed, Brian. Pure greed."

"I don't believe that!" he said heatedly.

"I can prove it. Unfortunately." Her cigarette crackled as she drew on it hard. Finally, she said, "I'm going to get you out. I can do that, Brian."

Brian stared at her. "What do you think I am? Some kind of coward? Do you all want to die in a nuclear war? Where do you think they'll aim the first missiles, anyway? Kansas? I grew up hiding under my desk at school once a week. I don't want my kids to have to live that way."

"She just means that we love you," said Sam. "We just want to make sure that you have a chance to—" He stopped.

"To live!" said Jill. "We want you to *live*, you idiot! Not get killed like Doug's cousin!" She burst into tears and hurried from the room. Her sobs became louder as she ran up the stairs.

"That's what I plan on doing," he shouted at her. "But I don't want just *me* to live. Don't you understand? I want *everyone* to live!" He turned back to Sam and Bette and now Megan, who'd come in from the kitchen. "All of you! I'll be fine!" He grabbed his coat and left, slamming the door.

Bette watched him go down the walk and sighed. She shook her head. "I'm completely at sea."

"I wish he'd talked to me first," said Sam. "I don't think I ever . . . glorified things. Did I?"

"He's always been impetuous." Bette sank into a chair, thinking. "I'm not sure what I'll do. They're training SEALs for covert operations. He's too young for that. He's just a kid."

"He's a young man, Bette," said Sam gently.

"SEALS are involved in extreme missions. Dangerous ones, the ones that no one else is remotely qualified to do. The main point, for me, is that it's not necessary. They're just using the patriotic feelings of these boys and their families. It's very cynical."

"He'll hate you the rest of his life if you pull any strings. And honestly, I don't think it would be a very good thing to do. It would remove his dignity."

"Don't you think I know that? I know it with every bone in my body. He's my boy and this is what he's going to do. Damn this country! Damn all these goddamned idiots! How did this happen? Millions of people died so that this wouldn't happen again. But war is like quicksand. It just sucks everybody down again. We'll never get out of war. Never. We've been at war this entire century. And all of the other centuries too."

For a few weeks after Brian left for basic training, Jill was inconsolable. "It's my fault," she insisted, even though everyone told her again and again that it was not.

On April 30, Nixon announced his plans to escalate the war by invading Cambodia.

"Yeah," said Jill at dinner one night. "He got elected because he had a plan to end the war. *This* is the plan! He's been bombing Cambodia for a year already, did you know that?"

Bette and Sam looked at each other.

"No," said Sam.

"Yes," said Bette.

Nixon's decision ignited the firestorm that had been smoldering throughout the country. Students, and many professors, took over campus buildings in protest. Four important staff members of the National Security Counsel resigned. Huge student marches swept the country.

Nixon's way of dealing with this was to crack down, to limit protest.

To send out the National Guard.

⊰ 40 ⊱

Now's the Time

I T WAS SATURDAY, May 2, 1970.

The reunion attendees able to come on short notice grumbled about every little thing—the accommodations, the tours Sam and Bette arranged, the food, and the unseasonable heat that had settled over the District. They complained about plane service into Washington and about how everything seemed strangely old and shabby here. They never mentioned, though, the fact that they were in frightening downtown, Washington, D.C., recently the center of some of the most terrible riots in the country. To tell the truth, Sam wasn't sure what they saw, what they knew, or how discontinuous this reality might seem. They were only here, hopefully, as Wink's vehicle, though Wink had as yet not shown up.

"It doesn't seem to me as if they are living in a better world," Bette commented as they trailed the group up the broad marble stairs of the Natural History Museum.

"Yes, it's so much better that this place is miserable. They just can't exactly figure out why."

"That Jimmy Messner hates his job in China."

"His wife hates it. Did I tell you that he used all the money we made on the *biergarten* to marry her?"

Bette laughed. "What did you guys do?"

"Nothing. I guess he could afford to pay it back now. They're not all grumbling. Grease—Bob Crick—is pretty excited about being a consultant for the international moon base project. I sure would be."

"I'm so sorry." Bette touched his arm. "You're still upset about the astronaut fire, aren't you?"

"I probably always will be. It was a terrible way to die, senseless and unnecessary. I don't know if our space program will ever get back on track."

"Is that why you didn't want to take them to the Air and Space Museum? You just want to show them some stuffed animals instead?"

"I guess that's kind of silly. I mean, the whole sociopolitical construct is different here. But . . . they're here."

"I heard Mrs. Crick say that this was just a backwater." Bette laughed. "You don't have to be from another time to think that. You just have to be a New Yorker."

"Maybe that's how they mentally adjust."

"What do they think when they read the newspapers?" Bette looked around for stragglers, waved to one couple down on the sidewalk.

"Maybe they just see a different newspaper. Different news. That corresponds with their world, where JFK is about to pass the crown on to his brother. Like this city is just a tiny intersection; as if they are somehow able to just ignore small details that don't fit, such as Nixon is president here and we're mired in a war that nobody but the generals want. That's my theory, anyway. Hey, Jake, glad you could make it. Go on inside."

Bette said, "That's actually a viable theory. There's a lot of research showing that people can tune out an awful lot of information if it doesn't correspond with what they think they ought to be seeing."

Sam paused on the broad portico at the top of the stairs, turned around to survey the Mall, thick with tourists. The carousel was running gaily just opposite them, but there was no traffic, for some reason, on the one-way street in front of them, which would have been heading toward the Washington Monument, their next tour stop. "Where the hell is Wink?"

"What the hell is that?" Bette pointed down the Mall.

A crowd advanced down the narrow street. As it came closer, the antiwar slogans grew louder.

"It's Jill!" said Bette, pointing. "See her?"

Sam took off running down the stairs. He caught up with Jill and fell into step with her.

Her long brown hair flowed loosely down her back; her cutoffs were raggedy, she wore no bra beneath her tank top, and her costume was completed by her black armband and black Converse basketball sneakers. Under one arm was a rolled-up *Washington Post.* She did not stop walking, but unscrewed her Army canteen and took a long drink. "Water?"

"No, thanks."

"What's the plan?"

"We're going to sit on Constitution Avenue and stop traffic. Nixon can't get away with invading Cambodia. It's barbaric. All those innocent people. They're going to be driven from their homes, just like the Vietnamese, their children murdered—"

Then Wink was beside them, strolling easily through the noonday haze, mostly bald now with just a halo of pale orange frizz. "Can I go with you?" he asked.

Sam said, "Jill, meet my Army buddy, Wink."

"You're Wink," Jill said. She stopped walking for a second and looked at him closely.

"That's me."

Later in the day, Sam climbed uphill from the bus stop, relieved to see a small figure, which was Bette, at the top of the hill. She wore a tropical-print dress and a pink headband, to absorb sweat generated by the heat and humidity. The afternoon sky was that smoggy no-color that promised a spectacular thunderstorm within hours.

When he reached her, she looked at her watch. "I wish the caterer would show up. I'm getting nervous."

"This really is a lovely spot." He could see the Capitol, the Washington Monument, the Mall, and glimmers of the Potomac smog-muted like an Impressionist painting.

"Did you find out what Wink is doing here?"

"Not really. The only thing I know is that it has something to do with Jill."

"Jill! The hell it does."

"That's what I said to Wink. We followed Jill down to the Mall and sat on Constitution for hours. Lots of chanting. It was too loud to talk."

"And hot."

"Terribly. Jill gave me the Style section to sit on, and gave Wink Metro."

Betty looked at her watch. "Well, I baby-sat this crowd for the last few hours. This shindig starts at six. I think they're all getting drunk at the hotel bar now."

"As I should be."

"As we *both* should be."

The party, at least, was swinging. With food and plenty of liquor, the hardships of days of wearying tourism were forgotten. The boys of the war were re-emerging, not always to the delight of their wives.

Sam stayed for about an hour, until he was satisfied that there'd be no serious problems, or, at least, that they sufficiently inebriated so that if an alligator bit them on the ass they wouldn't notice. He waved to Wink and they ducked from air-conditioned comfort into the hot summer night. Bette had taken a cab home earlier and left him the car.

"Roll down the windows," said Sam as they got into the station wagon. "My a.c. doesn't work." The smell of cooling asphalt wafted through the car as Sam drove home through familiar intersections.

"So what's the nexus?" asked Sam.

"Still not sure," said Wink. "Got a cigarette?"

"Bette might have some in the glove compartment."

Wink got out the pack and punched in the cigarette lighter. He smoked in short, nervous puffs.

"They're starting to say that's bad for you," said Sam.

"It is. But it won't bother me."

"Something's eating you. You sounded frantic on the phone."

"Yeah," he said, and stubbed out his cigarette in the ashtray. "I still am. Even more so. The reason I didn't say much today is that I just didn't know what to say. I've tried my best to get information about what's happening—what might happen—and it's all kind of twisted up. Of course, time is a perpetual event. But this . . . nexus is like a cancer, somewhere, in the body of time, that we have to find and eradicate." He leaned back in the seat and rubbed his forehead. "I'm sorry, Dance. I wish I could tell you more, but I don't *know* any more. Maybe it was a false alarm. Bad information."

"That would be great. It's good to see you, anyway. We need to get together more often. I told you that Brian enlisted, didn't I? The Navy."

"Jill did. She's pretty upset about it."

"Did she tell you about her *Gypsy Myra* comics?"

"No."

"She's been working on this line of comics. It's about this superheroine who looks just like Hadntz. The kids got hold of the HD10. It was in the form of a game board."

"A game board?"

"Full of all kinds of stories. Bette and I have been pretty upset about it. In fact, the last few months have been nothing but upsetting. Nixon is driving the country crazy with this war. Lots of student demonstrations, as you saw today. And some violence—knocked heads, and stuff. But you never know when it might get out of hand. Here we are."

The lights were all on when he pulled up to the front of Halcyon House. When they got out of the car, Megan stuck her head out the screen door, then came out onto the wide porch. "They're here!" she shouted.

His snowball bushes glowed like dim Chinese lanterns in the light thrown from the porch. On the screened-in portion at the side of the house, the lights were on. Winston rushed down the broad front steps, a whirlwind of greeting. Cicadas whirred, their sound burgeoning up from the creek. Bette's ancient poetry seemed fresh as the moment; much of it featured cicadas.

Wink paused on the steps. "Wait a minute. Are we going to have to listen to rock music? Those horrible, pounding, repetitious drumbeats that smash right into my brain?"

Sam laughed, relieved to have light-hearted Wink back. "Our music is not democratically controlled. I'm in charge. I've put together some pretty nice reel-to-reels over the past few years. Monk, Coltrane, Miles Davis—all kinds of cool jazz."

"Miles Davis?"

Sam stopped and looked at Wink as he opened the door. "No Miles? That's a great loss."

"It takes some getting used to, doesn't it?"

They stepped inside. The house was disorientingly neat and clean; Bette had had some of the wives over yesterday and had spent a week getting ready.

"You've done well, Dance," said Wink.

"A color TV, even. The better to see the gore on the evening news. If they had our war on on television, people would have put a stop to it pretty quickly."

"You'd think," sighed Wink. "But people get inured to that stuff pretty quickly."

"Hey!" Bette walked past them bearing a tray piled with snacks—Ding Dongs, Ho-Ho's, Screaming Yellow Zonkers, and several sweating bottles of Tab.

"If we knock the kids off with this stuff we won't have to pay for college," said Sam.

"Oh, it doesn't hurt them," said Bette. "Why don't you show Wink around the house while we get set up." Although her voice was light, her mouth was set in her most serious manner.

"Nice," said Wink, examining Sam's stereo setup. "Of course, *we*—"

"Enough!" said Sam, holding up his hands in mock protest. "I know it's all wonderful."

"But that's what it's all about. Isn't it? Technological advances that cure diseases, enhance communications, create free universal education, boost economies, and allow us to emigrate into space."

"Did I tell you that I've been inspecting the computer Internet the government has set up?"

"That's a start, but because we haven't spent all of our money on nuclear weapons, we have computers that are integrated into our clothing. Most people have a daily free scan that's sent to a place that keeps a baseline and informs them if there's a problem developing. Or you can just go to a screening kiosk and get scanned and immunized or medicated on the spot."

"That doesn't sound very private."

"It's all protected."

"And people believe that? How do you deal with criminals? For instance, sounds like it would be easy for someone or something to custom-design something that would kill you pretty quickly."

"It's a several-pronged approach. First of all, there are various genetic propensities that are corrected with an immunization patch in infants."

Bette came back with some beers. "Come on, let's sit down in the living room. Did I hear correctly? Parents can't say no?"

"Not that simple," said Wink.

"That would be a pretty bad sign for me."

"All kinds of developmental stages have been pinpointed and are enhanced. It's been found that with this kind of emotional satisfaction available, with creativity enhanced, with education available, more people have much more of an opportunity to feel valuable to themselves and to others."

"I'd want all parents to be licensed by me," said Bette. "No kids without Bette Certification. I've been working on a training and testing program for parents for years."

"That doesn't sound very private," said Wink.

"I never claimed that I'm consistent."

"I like this music," said Megan. She was sprawled on the couch, and nodded her head to a fast sax flight of Bird's. "It makes me feel as if I'm traveling at a very high speed."

Sam said, "Megan, we're going to talk about some private things now."

"Nice to meet you, Wink," said Megan, and got up to leave. She ran into Jill, who came into the room, holding the game board.

"Where did you get that?" demanded Bette.

"Oh, please, Mom," said Jill. "We have to play the game."

"Why?" asked Sam.

"Because Wink is in it," she said.

"What kind of game is this?" Wink asked.

"It's not much of a game," said Bette. "Your father and I tried to use it."

"You didn't know how. Sit down," said Jill. "I'm sure it has something to show us. And if not, I'll get some more episodes for *Gypsy Myra*."

"Can I see that?" asked Wink.

He ran his hands across the surface of the board. "Where did you get this?"

"We think it's the HD11," said Sam.

"The what?" asked Megan.

"I think playing is a good idea," said Wink.

Sam sighed. "I don't. But I'll try it. Let's go out on the porch."

The thunderstorm of the night was just over, and the post-storm coolness was delicious. When they were situated around the game table—Sam felt Brian's absence every day, and especially now—Wink said, "How do we start?"

"The board tells us how to start," said Megan. "Every game is different, because it's an Infinite Game Board. Look, I'm not sure that I want to do this again."

"Come on, Megan," said Jill.

"All right. Just one more time. Go ahead and tell it, Jill."

"We're ready to play now, Myra," said Jill.

Sam looked sharply at her.

"How would that do anything?" asked Bette.

"You'll see."

"It's like the computers I was telling you about," said Wink. "Voice-activated. Seems like maybe Jill has set the password. We'd probably all have different ones."

The Infinite Game Board glowed deep blue on the table between them. Sam sipped his beer nervously and tossed some peanuts into his mouth.

The board lit with six green-glowing circles. Wink, Bette, and Sam all looked at one another.

"We each need to put a finger on a dot," said Megan. "I guess there's one for Brian, even though he's not here. It probably remembers him, don't you think?"

Sam touched the board with great trepidation.

"Remember when we had to calibrate the B-17's?" asked Wink. "I think that now we're going to calibrate time."

They were in a plane. The times they flew through, the whens, were as permeable as great sheets of rain, gray and luminous. There were heart-wrenching drops, and Dr. Hadntz appeared during one of them, in a back row, asleep, with a raincoat drawn over her. Her hair was white and splayed across her strong face, now more aged but still just as beautiful, and just as determined, as before.

"Is this how you . . . change whens?" Sam asked Wink. They were sitting in the front row.

Wink shook his head. "I never really do. I just . . . go places and there I am. Turn a corner and I'm in othertime. It's like . . . bebop. Remember when we played with Parker?"

"Yeah, thank God. Wouldn't want to forget that."

"There was nothing linear about what he was doing. And—think about this— the world didn't know it happened."

"You're right. Not until after the musician's strike was over."

"It was a whole history being created that no one knew about. An alternate history that just suddenly appeared full-blown after the war. I think we're involved in something like that."

"Look," said Brian. Surprised that Brian was here, Sam was going to say something, then saw what he was pointing at. Below them was a vast plain, and it was on fire.

Hadntz was standing behind them, unsteady in the turbulent air. A dry sob broke from her and she grabbed the seat in front of her.

"Sit down," said Wink urgently, sitting her down and buckling her seat belt. "We all have to buckle our seat belts. I think we're going to encounter some flak."

Bette's face was grim. "I didn't know this was going to happen. We should have left the kids behind." The door to the cockpit was open, slamming back and forth. Bette made her way to the front of the plane. Then she disappeared into the cockpit.

Sam followed her, and then everyone else was behind him, crowding into the cabin.

Bette, putting on her headphones, looked up at Sam. "It was on automatic pilot."

"I'll copilot," said Brian.

"But where are we going?" asked Megan.

Sam realized, for the first time, that the children were older in this game. Megan was nineteen, as no-nonsense as her older sister Jill had been impetuous at the same age, and Sam knew that she was closing in on a theoretical physics degree. Midnight-black hair fell below her shoulders, framing a pale, freckled face. Brian looked to be about twenty-two, a strong young man whom Sam knew was in the military, studying aeronautic engineering. And Jill was frittering away her life as a comic-book artist and underground DJ, having still not graduated college.

Hadntz was there, behind them.

"We're playing the game?" asked Megan.

"Not exactly," Hadntz said. "We are in a war."

"So now my entire family is in danger?" asked Sam.

"They are here willingly, Sam," said Hadntz.

"That's right," said Brian. "We've been here before. Only you and Mom weren't with us. Wink was, once or twice."

"It's a series in the board about changing history," said Jill. "We've never gotten past this level."

"The device has modified all of us," said Bette. "I'm just guessing."

"Yes," said Hadntz. "Including me."

"So do you know what's happening?" asked Wink.

"Not exactly. Our consciousness is moving us," said Hadntz. "Just as it always has. Our bodies, the world, and all of history is our mind's environment. The main thing is that we are not alone. We carry a huge freight. I don't know what will happen now. Maybe what I've done is terribly wrong."

"I don't think so," said Wink. "We've seen several of the alternatives."

"Centuries of them," said Bette.

Megan said, "I've seen them. In the board."

"We all have, Mom," said Brian. "That's why we're here. We've chosen to be here."

"I think we know more about it than you and Dad," said Jill.

"I don't doubt it," said Sam.

"Well, we don't have time to think about it anymore," said Bette. "We've got to do something. Right now."

Wink said, "We have to find the nexus. Unwind it. Relax it. Transform it. Inoculate it. Let it synch."

"How?" asked Sam.

The plane manifested dials that purported to control dimensional aspects that none of them had ever heard of before, but which Brian attended to with a mixture of delight and wonder. "Okay," he said. "We're going to perform some corrections. Megan, get over here. You're in charge of azimuth. Sit in that chair behind Mom. Jill, you're—I don't know. The radio guy. Keeping us all in touch. There are a lot of . . . factors here."

"I think we're heading for a major quantum event," said Megan, frowning. "Something having to do with Bohr's interpretation."

"Where spooky effects at a distance are actually manifested," said Hadntz.

"Right."

"Isn't every instant a major quantum event?" asked Wink.

They all laughed. With that, the tension vanished.

"No, I mean it," he persisted. "It's just that when we're in this mode, we are more able to know it."

"Like monks regulating their brain waves and heartbeat," mused Bette.

"But even further in," said Hadntz. "Not even at a cellular level. At an atomic level."

"Look, Mom," said Brian. "We've been playing the game for years now. We *know* where you and Dad and Wink and Dr. Hadntz were. We've *been* to those camps."

"Oh, God," she murmured. "I suppose it's a little too late to be irritated with your father for leaving that thing lying around."

"And this is what we have to do," said Jill. "We have to put it in the guns. The anguish that a single death causes. So that when someone, anywhere, picks up a gun, their empathy will get ratcheted up a millionfold."

"That's just one thing. We also have to put it in the kids," said Brian. "Kids have to understand that the pain *they* feel is the same as the pain that *others* feel. You know, like the kids in Dickens's books are brutalized by adults, and when you read the books, you feel for them."

Sam looked at Brian in surprise; he'd complained bitterly at having to wade through Dickens.

"We have to bridge that gap, then," said Bette. "We have to give everybody some kind of touchstone of decency, so that they are able to do what needs to be done to set things right. Some story that they can hold on to."

"You have to spin that dial, there," said Brian.

Spin the dial?

Sam suddenly realized that it was, really, a game. His sense of claustrophobia, of terrible doom, vanished. "This game's over," he said.

He experienced a moment of falling, as if the plane was going to crash.

Then the family was at the table again, the game board in front of them.

Sam looked around. Wink was gone.

Bette was pale and breathing hard. Jill and Megan were the age they'd been when they started playing.

"Who was that woman?" asked Megan. "She seemed to know a lot about physics."

"That was Gypsy Myra," said Jill. "You've seen her before. Don't you remember?"

"Where's Wink?" asked Sam.

"He got up and left a minute ago," said Jill. "He said he couldn't stay."

Sam pushed back his chair and looked out the window. "Which way did he go?"

Sam decided that Wink must have caught a taxi to otherwhen, otherwhere, the other timestream that so weighed on this one, where the war had still not ended, where his son was in it, where his daughter was fighting against it.

This time, he knew exactly where to find that place.

He got in the car, careened through town, parked illegally. As he approached the door, the music got louder.

The party was still in full swing. A shout went up when he walked in the door. "Hey!" said Alberteen, putting his arm around Sam's shoulder. "We've been looking for you. It's time for the Perham Downs to play."

Sam wasn't really in the mood. "Have you seen Wink?"

"He's up on the goddamn stage, waiting for you."

Sam made his way through the happy, drunken crowd and climbed up on the stage to confront Wink, who was running through scales. On the way, someone slapped an Army hat on his head, handed him a jacket that had his bars on it.

All right.

He shrugged into the jacket; straightened the collar. "Why didn't you tell me you were leaving?" he asked Wink.

"Couldn't. It's just packets of information." He handed Sam a tenor sax.

"Packets of information with *emotion*," said Sam. "Right now this packet of information has a strong urge to punch you."

Wild Card Zee stepped up and took his place behind the drums, dusted the hi-hat, made an exploratory *ker-plunk* on the bass drum.

"Reeds, anyone?" asked Kocab, his clarinet under his arm. His hair was white, and he was thin and wiry.

"Thanks. They'll sound real good right out of the box." Sam kicked himself for not even thinking about bringing his own saxophone, and his own carefully prepared reeds. He'd just been so worried. He held the reed up to the light, then pulled out his pocketknife and trimmed it a bit.

"Quit farting around," said Earl T. He played a few bluesy notes on the piano. "Couldn't you have gotten this tuned?"

Grease plucked a few notes on his bass. "Remember Moonlight?" he said. "This is her. Shipped her home from England. Lovely old thing."

"What are we going to play?"asked Earl T.

" 'Jazznocracy'," said Sam, somewhat meanly.

"Can't we warm up first?" asked Earl T.

Sam counted out the time. "One, two, three, four . . ."

Grease laid down a railroad rhythm with Moonlight, plucking fast. The train was speeding through the night, passing small towns, telephone lines, a light-filled flash carrying them all to war.

Wink moved in with the chilling trumpet solo, and the journey was begun.

They moved from place to place. Aberdeen, the Block, Duke Ellington, the top-secret cavity magnetron. The story of Sam and Wink had become the story of Company C; the story of Company C had become the story that would give humans access to the working of their minds.

After ten bars, Sam took off with a Bird-like riff, roller-coastering across the Atlantic, Wink close on his heels, repeating every blisteringly fast note perfectly. Then they merged in unison.

The train again, Alberteen keeping the beat.

They headed to Tidworth. Zee took care of the explosion as if he'd been there, grinning. Then Bletchley Hall, and Hadntz's mysterious house in London. Wink picked up the mute and produced a strange, moody tone on his cornet, and then it was on to France.

Bette's interrogation was a fast-talking dialogue in minor tones, and Earl T. put in the galloping hooves of Hadntz's herd animals.

Germany was dark, dark as the revealed camps, the starved refugees.

For a few beats they just stopped, abruptly. For the death camps, there was only silence.

The Americans beat back the Germans, who descended abruptly until Zee echoed Hitler's death-shot. An uproar of bebop joy.

Another silence for Hiroshima.

A final eruption as the train tracks rolled fast beneath them again. They were on their way home.

When they finished, Company C roared with applause.

It was one of Sam's finest moments. The men lined up, took a quick bow, and headed into a long line of sentimental favorites and the steady dance beat, slow and fast, of the Glenn Miller Orchestra.

Sam and Wink made it back to Halcyon House well after dawn. Wink insisted it was all right, that the Hilbert spaces weren't ready, and something about a torus, and complexity, and fruitfulness. He was drunk.

Wink fell onto the couch downstairs and Sam trudged up the stairs, where Bette welcomed him quite warmly. "Great performance, Dance," she said.

"You were there?"

"Mm-hmm. I took Jill and Megan too. They were dazzled, completely impressed. It was quite fine."

"The torus," said Sam, and passed out.

They woke shortly after noon and were drinking Bloody Marys by the creek when Megan came running out of the house with the news.

"The National Guard just killed four students at Kent State," she said, her voice high-pitched; nearly hysterical. "And Jill is gone!"

Sam jumped out of his chair. "Where?"

"I don't know," said Megan. "She just took the game board and left."

Wink tossed his drink in the creek. He suddenly looked as if he had aged ten years. "Okay. Now I understand. I think I know where she went."

"Where?" asked Sam, as they ran up to the house.

"She's found the nexus. Or maybe it's found her."

Leading Notes

S AM WENT UP TO Jill's room, the rest of them right behind him, and opened the door.

Her room was shockingly neat. On her drawing table was a pile of library books about the Kennedy assassination, and a note. "Please get this to Elmore to print and distribute. It's VERY IMPORTANT." Beneath it was a manila envelope.

Not pausing for moral niceties, Sam ripped open the envelope.

To his surprise, inside were a stack of drawings for several future *Gypsy Myra* issues.

He sat down and read them, quickly, and passed them around.

"Oh my God," said Bette. "I guess she's been planning this."

"Is this what I think it is?" Sam asked, incredulous.

Bette lighted a cigarette. "It is. I think she's going to try and use the device. The game board. To prevent the assassination of JFK. That's here. Issue number seventeen."

"Right,"said Sam, turning pages. "See, here—in Gypsy Myra's world, Kennedy's continued presidency would probably have made our present quite different. More like Wink's. Space travel, education, international outreach, scientific development, communication, monetary changes—all kinds of subtle things would be different. But how the hell could *Jill* do anything?"

"It's the nexus," said Wink. "This is it. It could have been anything, but this is it. A battleground of forces."

"Hadntz," said Wink, tapping a drawing of Gypsy Myra. "Hadntz is going to help her."

"Why Jill?" Sam paced the room, looked in the closet as if he might find her there.

"Why not?" said Bette, throwing down the comic she held. "Goddammit!" With shaking hands she tapped another cigarette from her pack and lit it. "Because we wouldn't. We haven't used the HD10, actively, at all. What do you think the game board is—HD15? Hadntz doesn't need us anymore. It's ticking away on its own; it has its own agenda. And remember, Hadntz told us that her daughter lives only in this timeline—unlike her—and this one looks pretty terrible, at least from Jill's point of view, right now. Jill is a great target. A useful agent. Like you were, Sam, when she used you. Young, impressionistic, brave. Obviously more useful than us. We're old, full of doubts. We have something to lose."

Her hands no longer shook. She picked up another issue. "It looks like Jill has been working on this plan for a while. In fact . . ." Bette turned some pages. "Here it is. I thought I saw this. If Jill doesn't do anything," her voice caught, "Brian will die in a covert action in Cambodia. *This* is her dilemma. Something that she saw in one of the games, I'm sure."

"Is that true?" asked Sam, horrified.

"You know as well as I do that it's an averaging process. That is, not necessarily. She saw this all in the game board. Possibilities, probabilities, all jumping track eventually and leading to one final place. "But . . ." Bette was pale as she set the comic back on the table.

She turned her attention to the huge stack of books on the table. "The Warren Commission report. Seems like most of the volumes are here. These are reference books—she must have snuck them out of the university's library."

She put her hands in her pockets and looked out the open window. The leaves of Jill's jungle plants bobbed in the fresh spring breeze.

Sam could almost see the transformation, could almost see Major Elegante standing strong in her boots, her sidearm strapped on, cunning OSS weapons hidden everywhere, thinking of how to bring her own hopes to fruition using Hadntz's plans.

She was making decisions, cutting through minutiae, moving faster, with purpose. "We have to know what she knows." She stepped to the table, pulled out one of the books, and opened it to one of Jill's bookmarks. "Okay. Here's the map. Indentations—she's traced it. Shows Kennedy's route. She has the Warren Commission's exhaustively reconstructed—and, by the way, fictional—timetable. Her plan is to thwart Oswald.

"The only problem is, he's not the killer. She's heading to the sixth floor of the Texas Book Depository where—she thinks—one man with a rusty, outmoded weapon with a bad scope, three bullets, and a terrible vantage point is going to fire a bullet that will rip through Kennedy, ricochet through his body, and go on to injure Connally. We call it the magic bullet. It just didn't happen. She just doesn't have the correct information."

"Well, Bette, what *did* happen?" asked Sam.

"I'm not at liberty to tell you, wiseass. But I will anyway, as soon as I have time."

"How could she possibly get there?"

"The game board is the HD15. Or who knows. The infinite version, assembling all the information. How does Wink get here? He says he just turns a corner, right?"

Sam was behind her as she ran downstairs. "Where are you going?"

"I have to prepare some things."

"I'm coming too."

"No. You need to get the HD10 from wherever you put it."

"It's in the bank. In a safety deposit box."

"Good. Get it, and come back here. After that, *stay here*. Megan?"

Megan stood on the stairs. "I have to do something. I have to help Jill. What can I do?"

"I want you to stay with your friend Karen until we get back."

"But Mom—"

Bette returned and gave Megan a long hug. "Honey, please. I really need you here. If—well, that's all. I just need you here."

She grabbed her purse. "Wink. Let's go. We'll need the car, Sam."

"I'll get a cab to the bank. Where are you going?"

Bette ran out the door. Wink followed.

"You tell me, Wink!" Sam yelled after them.

"I don't know yet," he shouted as he got in the car and slammed the door.

The car sped off down the street.

On the trip to the bank, Sam became so agitated at the delay caused by construction on New York Avenue that the cab driver threatened to throw him out. When they finally pulled up to the house, after what seemed like hours, Sam tipped him hugely.

The box was intact, the HD10 inside—the malleable plastic substance as well as the thin gray card Wink had given him on Midway.

He paced by the phone; he went to Jill's room to go over the *Gypsy Myra* comics and the Warren Commission report; he made coffee. He became very angry at Bette, then calmed down again. He stepped out on the back porch and was enveloped by spring. He went down toward the garden.

It was not as though Sam had never felt this way before—that something of great import beyond control was about to happen. He'd felt this way plenty of times during the war. But now it all had more pressure, an edge so sharp it cut his being in the place where Jill lived.

He stood at the entrance of his garden, delicately beautiful in its springtime regenesis. The rush of the creek added another dimension, as did the thrush and the mockingbird and the other myriad singers, threading notes into a tapestry of sound which was made whole by scent and vision.

And yet . . . and yet . . .

He could walk into it. He could become a part of it, one of the weavers and at the same time one of the threads.

His entire history lay not *behind* him, but always *around* him and *within* him, waiting to manifest itself, over and over again, in bits of memory that infused his awareness of the present. He was never without that past, those bubbles of time through which he sailed again and again, constantly. Like his own consciousness, his own time, this history was not something he could see from the outside. No map could replace experience. No map could hold that much information.

He got as far as the apple tree, gloriously white with blossoms, and stood there. And, for an instant, just like in one of Bette's Chinese poems, he disappeared, and only the blossom was there.

And yet . . . some future was here as well, influencing this present. Many futures, he supposed, infinite futures. He felt alive. His very body was permeable, and this was a joyous, light feeling, an openness.

Memories once again stacked up and said this is always happening, this Washington, this time. Driving slowly up Rhode Island Avenue on a midsummer Sunday afternoon, shops and houses known and familiar and the home of his mind. Then *this* was happening—the green and pink striped wallpaper in his mother's kitchen, a huge bouquet of yellow dahlias next to the sink, the clear glass vase shimmering with a narrow, precise reflection of the icebox. And the face of Keenan Dance, eighteen years old, sure and not that of a boy, when he said, like Brian, but in that other kitchen, "I've enlisted."

But—what *future*? What future did Sam feel? What future pressed upon his mind; what did he hope for?

It was a future in which Jill was safe again, returned to the normal currents of the world. He yearned for this with a cellular precision that searched and fired with neurological certainty, drawing him onward into the mysterious medium called time, which was biology, emotion.

He heard a deeper music then, and descended on one of the paths he'd built through his stand of brilliant tulips. Rocks he'd wrestled from the creek anchored visages, offered places to stop and sit and breathe as the garden opened and opened, not formal but weaving and drawing him onward. It was impossible, he thought, that this, that *life*, all gardens, of all kinds, gardens of thought and of science and of love and labor, should end because of human folly and human ignorance.

Where was Hadntz's new world? Where was the fix of which she'd spoken to him twenty-five years ago, just a few blocks away, in the rooming house off 14th Street, that fix which spoke of the underpinnings of mind and a new-made core of being— something that, if Bette was right about Hadntz's involvement with Jill, Hadntz herself seemed to lack? For why else would she put Jill at risk?

As he descended on the path, the source of the music finally came into view. There, on the arched bridge, was Wink.

Wink was playing a lively, twining music on his cornet, filled with leaps and gaps and resonances, with overtones that slipped into time and lingered, which one heard and yet could never hear, those phantom vibrations that Bird, with his special mind, did hear, and which he then did play. Maybe he and Wink could finally make real the resonances of time, play those unplayable notes.

Wink was gazing up the creek, into the massive, dark viaduct that carried it beneath ten blocks of city. A fresh smell always issued from this place, one of wet concrete and water unmixed with street runoff, just pure creek. Above, the world of the present rumbled over the viaduct on his residential street.

Sam had always forbidden the kids to enter the viaduct, but of course they did. It was not dangerous except perhaps in flood times, and from snakes or other creatures or from the slipperiness inside. He'd never really worried about them.

But now, he thought, this tunnel leads somewhere mysterious, some place that might be lost when childhood ended. Some place adults could never see, save those gifted with Hadntz's new chemicals of mind. Every path leading outward seemed just as infused with possibilities.

Wink stowed his cornet in a bag hung on his shoulder. "We're to meet Bette," he said.

"Where?"

"At a little airstrip in Virginia. She's got a plane there she brought back from Germany some time ago."

As he stood in the cool wind rushing from the viaduct, Sam had a vision of walking into the tunnel and coming out in the Messerschmitt caves, where the HD4 he'd planted long ago had grown into, not an atomic airplane, a perpetual city of war that would never land, but a sleek machine that slipped through time like pure electrons, shaking hands with otherwhen, shifting what he now thought was the past, realigning information. Somehow, he'd known that was happening, or might happen. Now it had, and his very children were at stake.

But they were not just *his* children. They were Lise, Karl, all the children of war, of poverty, most of them never to blossom. They were an effervescent music, their minds emanating thought, vision, possibility—love and happiness, like the refrain in Jill's rock music. And, as they grew, they would be scarred, and scarred again, when that love was not returned.

Wink said, "Seeing all this makes me think that time is like a garden. Some flowers are picked and some flowers stay to seed. New species evolve. New strains of everything. Making it new is everything. Time reaches backward and forward and in directions of which we cannot really conceive because our brains, large as they are, are really very small."

Yes, this was the old Wink. This was the way he talked.

They were making their way up the creek as Wink spoke, and reached the viaduct. They scrambled up the hill to the road and Wink waved down a cab.

:| 42 |:

War Skies

S AM RODE THROUGH Washington, where he had spent so many years, with a
sense that it was disappearing, all the riot-fired corners still not rebuilt; the
bright white edifices of government, the offices where he'd spent years of his life.

That time was dissipating like a vapor, a particular fragrance composed of stale
coffee, mimeograph ink, the perfume of secretaries, even the smell of paper clips
bunched in the top drawers of massive metal desks. It was also the smell of thought,
of seeing firsthand the technological wonders of his time, the fruit of scientific
thought made real, an incense rising from this world center that could either destroy time or make it whole and new.

They crossed the 14th Street bridge as part of the rush of traffic, passed the Pentagon, and merged into the George Washington Parkway, which twined and flowed
along the banks of the Potomac like string, like a new form of time, one that would
take them to Bailey's Crossroads in suburban Virginia. Not in a day of summer tar-
rying lostness on narrow country roads but on new straight roads, in businesslike
minutes, between impermeable strips of the new shopping centers which had replaced singular, distanced stores and isolated country houses.

Wink spoke as they moved through the circles of time surrounding the city—
Alexandria, Shirlington, Lincolnia—but Sam did not really notice what he said and
then they were nearly in the country. Wink bade the driver turn off Columbia Pike
at the Coca-Cola plant, just past Dawes Avenue, and there was the airstrip, Bette,
and her plane. She ran to the gap in the sagging fence where one walked onto the
field and met them.

"Hurry," she yelled as Wink paid the cabdriver. "We just might make it."

"Where's Jill?" asked Sam. "Is she with you? I was hoping you'd found her."

"No," said Bette, who was miraculously able to run across the airfield in high
heels. "She's not here. Thanks to Dr. Hadntz. Or, as Jill thinks of her, Gypsy Myra.
Some sort of . . . hippie guru magical gypsy woman. A 'madwoman of time,' as issue number four states." Her voice was as hard and as unforgiving as the surface of
water when one fell into it from a hundred feet above.

"What in the world have you got on?" They stopped at the plane, panting.

"Just a nice, low-key Christian Dior suit."

"You hardly look like yourself. Great makeup job. And that hair—how did you do that?"

"Trade secret. It's not easy." She herded them up the ladder, and told Sam to sit next to her. "You're the copilot, Sam. Wink's in back." She closed the hatch.

"Me?" said Sam. "But Wink knows—"

"No," she said. "It's you and me, Dance. We're finishing our mission. Together. Okay. Give me the HD10."

Bette pressed a small cube of HD10 into a portal in the dash of the plane.

There were no dials in the plane. It was smaller, more delicate and light, than the plane in the game. Information flowed through its skin, ran through its body, and manifested in a panel in front of him. There was the azimuth, the elevation, and measurements of several new dimensions of which he'd never heard, apparently being translated much like the M-9 Director had translated polar coordinates into rectangular coordinates, instantly. A small keyboard was mounted to Bette's left; she typed in their present place and date, May 4, 1970, and then Dallas, November 22, 1963.

"How in the world does that work?" he asked.

"You're the engineer. I'm sure that there are a lot of calculations taking place behind those numbers. We're probably all just some unimaginably huge calculation ourselves, embedded in the universe. We are the quantum computer."

They took off from the tiny, rural airstrip with none of the rumbling heaviness Sam was used to in military airplanes. For a moment, he looked out on bright green rural Virginia, the Blue Ridge, and then the windows were filled with color and form, sometimes sharp and discrete, sometimes blossoming like fireworks. Sound accompanied them, almost like a form of free jazz, linked to the colors, but changing too quickly to grasp anything, too fast for Sam's mind to find a pattern or anticipate a change.

Bette, intent on her controls, said, "This is a lovely plane to fly. Radar doesn't pick it up; I found that out on practice flights in Germany. But it's dangerous to land; I don't think it's meant to. I had to fight to get it down every time, like I was fighting wind shear. It's like the rocket plane; simply a focussed weapon, or the atomic plane, not meant to land, but just cruise. Cruise and sample and emanate and transmit and fix. Fix time again and again, inoculate it as each new virus of war is generated."

"Where does the fix come from?"

Wink said, "I think it comes from us, really. It's focussing on a particular outcome and adjusting the variables to create that particular place, that particular *when*. It's a sum."

"This is not World War Two technology."

"You left something in the Messerschmitt cave, Dance. A piece of Hadntz's time machine. Just like the game board, it mutated. It found the necessary shape. It's just an interface, really. Maybe what it really changes is . . . us."

"How did you get it out of the cave? When it was built, the cave had a huge entrance, and a road for taking out the completed planes. But we blasted all that shut."

"Someone in the organization informed me that a local resident claimed to have found a plane in the old Messerschmitt caves. They had a wild tale about it being a Nazi 'superweapon' prototype that never really did anything, but since I was familiar with the area they asked me to deal with it.

"When I saw it, I was flabbergasted. I spent lots of secret government slush fund money to have the road reopened. I took it out, down to the airstrip at the base, and kept everybody the hell away from it—and had the cave closed up again. It took me quite a while to figure out how to fly it as a regular plane. In the process, I realized exactly what it was."

"What is it?" asked Sam. "I mean, it looks like a plane, but—"

"I guess you could call it an M-Infinity Director."

"Instead of the M-9 Director?" asked Wink.

"Exactly. It uses the same principles, but they are infinitely evolved, apparently hooked into whatever supercomputers exist in Hadntz's . . . when, and it tracks a moving target, which is time itself."

"Why doesn't the CIA know what it is?" asked Sam.

"I turned in a lot of fake reports. Flew it here to Bailey's Crossroads and kept it in a private hangar. Ed Mach suspected something, and had me put through the ringer when I brought it back. That's when I was gone for two weeks. Part of that time was for healing up."

Sam grasped her hand tightly. "Why didn't you tell me?"

"So they could get their hands on you too? I'm a tough old bird, Dance. It was worth it. This is a lot more useful than the game board. I think that the board must be giving Jill continuously updated information about what to do, how to get there. But she's in terrible danger. She's blundering into one of the most tightly constructed conspiracies the world has ever known. If she gets in their way . . ."

"I'm not even going to ask how you know about this conspiracy," said Sam.

"You're learning. Actually, I don't think any one person knows everything. It's like any intelligence operation—self-contained cells."

"But why wouldn't Hadntz know this?" asked Sam.

"There's a great deal of darkness and confusion about this nexus," said Wink. "The models show a lot of constantly shifting timelines leading in and out of it."

"Maybe Hadntz does know," said Bette. "Maybe she's been juggling a number of different probabilities. It's been very difficult to have this information and tools— the HD4, the HD10, the game board, this plane—at my disposal and continue to believe that it's best not to use it. But that strategy has to be discarded. At some point a balance tips. At some point you have to use what you've got, show the enemy your hand. Despite all of my—*our* denial—we're part of the tipping."

"What can *we* do?" asked Sam.

"The forces against us are huge. A lot of weight behind them. The problem for Kennedy was that he was actually changing things. He was a terrible threat to those in our own country with the agenda of world domination. A real wild card. When he began his presidency, he didn't have the confidence he needed. But he was a courageous man. Which was his undoing—he was going to try and go forward no matter who threatened him. Think of all of the things he wanted to do."

"Things I don't know about?" said Sam.

"Probably. One, he was actively working with Khrushchev toward nuclear disarmament and peace. Two, he blamed the CIA for the Bay of Pigs, fired Dulles, and said he was going to blow the agency into a thousand pieces. That's huge. The CIA knew he had the power to do it, and that he would. Three, he was going to remove our advisers from Vietnam—in fact, the papers for him to sign that would have started the process were on his desk when he was murdered.

"But, four, if the U.S. *didn't* escalate the conflict that Kennedy was planning to pull out of, LBJ's oil cronies would have lost a shitload of money, and to top it all off he was planning to dump LBJ in 'sixty-four. LBJ faced a possible prison sentence because of his buddy Bobby Baker, who was being investigated by the Senate Rules Committee. Five, Kennedy was going to change the Federal Reserve System. Basically, all these things added up to huge, ambitious, fundamental social change. Shifts in the power structure."

Wink said, "Got any Dramamine? I'm a little queasy."

"I'm feeling sick myself, but I'm not sure Dramamine would help. All kinds of molecular imbalances are occurring right now; our sense of time, much like our sense of balance, is controlled by many biological processes."

"So where *are* we going?" asked Sam. "What are we going to do? When are we going to get to Jill? How do you know this will work?"

"I don't. The only thing I'm sure of is that Jill will be on the sixth floor of the Texas Book Depository around noon. But before and after—I don't know. I have a general plan, but the variables are still being summed by our vehicle. The fuse, whatever those actions might be, will not be lit until we are very, very close to the target. My concern, though, is not history, and, really, not even whether or not Kennedy lives or dies. It's just Jill. We need to get her out. Hadntz couldn't get me there, to the tipping point, so she lured Jill instead, knowing that we would have to follow."

"Do you really think she'd do that?" asked Sam. Bette and Wink looked at him and said "Yes!" in unison.

"Hadntz has a whole different view of everything," said Bette. "I'm not even sure that she's human any more. She may have evolved into a conscious fusion of the organic and the quantum. She could just be some kind of virus, trying to infect all of time, all of memory, all of the organisms that have ever existed or that ever will exist. I've lain awake at night trying to figure out what, exactly, she is, what she might have become. Whatever she is, she's banking on the fact that we're pretty competent."

"Maybe you are," said Sam.

"Dance, you are the most competent person I've ever known." She spoke quietly, with intense confidence. Then she became more brisk.

"Both of you are familiar with the publicized assassination theory."

Wink said, "Didn't happen for me, but I've reviewed the documents, boss."

"Good. Jill will head for the Book Depository and try to thwart Oswald somehow. I haven't a clue what her plan might be. But obviously, he *is* a dangerous man, and there are agents in place protecting his actions to make damned sure he can't wriggle out of his role as patsy once he realizes that he's supposed to take the fall. And then, as you know, before he can tell anyone anything—that he never really defected, never really left the CIA—Jack Ruby will kill him."

"Whose agents are at the Book Depository?" asked Sam.

"Ours, in heavy quote marks. The ones who have maintained their own secret government, their own power, their own priorities and goals no matter who is elected, starting with Wild Bill Donovan and getting more Byzantine with every passing year.

"Okay. The real shooters are in *front* of Kennedy. The back of his head was blown off because a bullet entered from the front. As a backup, a man with an umbrella dart gun that my good friend Prouty—you've never heard of him and probably never will—approved for manufacture will send a dart into Kennedy's neck in case the shooters miss. All of that forensic evidence mysteriously vanished, including Kennedy's brain.

"There will be two men on the sixth floor, not Oswald. I still haven't found out why they're there. Somebody placed a bullet on Kennedy's stretcher in the hospital hall with striation marks matching Oswald's gun. Maybe they just had to make sure that gun was fired. Evidence was suppressed or vanished, witnesses mysteriously died. And so, the mission was accomplished, except for these nagging loose ends that the recalcitrant public seizes on from time to time. But a lot of the papers and evidence are not going to be released for a long, long time. Ample time for loss and obfuscation and for people just not caring anymore."

"I'm getting a headache," said Sam.

"I think we may black out at some point. I've been fighting it. There might be something like the sound barrier—maybe a time barrier—we're pushing these waves, or these particles, closer and closer together and then we'll break through."

Sam looked back. "Wink is already out. Do you hear that?"

"What?"

"The music." The sounds had changed to an actual pattern, beautiful, precise, yet open. Tones traveled across one another, creating resonances that manifested around him like pure being, invading every cell, every atom of his being, and *changed* him . . .

Bette smiled at him. "Certainly not as complex as the music you hear, Dance."

It was indeed magnificently improvised, with thrilling turns and twists. But then, it sounded as if it were actually two pieces of music, so cleverly superimposed that one moved into another, the way a movie might segue into a scene that gave new meaning to what had come before. The rhythm picked up, in both parts, then the new part left the old behind and the music opened up, no longer bounded by the previously implied rules of scale and tone and time, and embraced Sam in a deep, cellular caress. Vision no longer signified anything he found meaningful, until he saw an airfield below.

At first he had to force the words out, then speech came normally. "Are we going to Love Field? Are we cleared to land?"

Bette looked at him. "Good. You're back. No, that's Wallace Field, a dirt strip. I could have landed at Love. I've got this string of numbers that just opens the world to me. Access. Thus it has ever been, at least since 1940. And," she said grimly, "if we are very, very lucky, thus it will ever be. But I don't want to use my clearance—that would surely alert someone. As far as they know, I'm still asleep."

Then the plane dropped precipitously. Her face grim, Bette fought with it, brought it back up, banked and seemed to cut right through those forces, catch them and use them. She laughed, and her laugh was one of sheer exhilaration. "It's a damned fine feeling to cheat death," she said.

She touched down in a quick zip, taxied off the strip, and stopped the plane next to a trailer, the only building in sight. A man under a green-striped awning in a lawn chair waved.

Sam roused Wink and helped him jump down from the hatch. The temperature was pleasant, and the Texas sky was a brilliant blue. They walked toward the trailer as the old man hoisted himself out of his chair.

He was bent and skinny, wearing jeans, cowboy boots, and a stained white T-shirt. He gave Bette a short salute with his left hand; his right held a bottle of beer. His face was shadowed by a cowboy hat; only his grizzled beard was clearly visible. He spat on the ground. "Got your instructions, darlin'. Everything's copasetic."

"Thanks, Leonard. Keep an eye on my plane and *don't touch it*!"

He grinned. " 'Course not. Your car's over there."

"Everything in it?"

"Yup."

A black Rambler station wagon was parked next to a pickup truck. Bette opened the back and pulled out what looked like a large leather handbag with a shoulder strap. She set it on the hood of the car and opened it, and Sam saw that it more closely resembled a briefcase. A breeze ruffled Wink's hair, but Bette's stood firm, fortified by hair spray. "A Walther for each of you. Cartridges. Silencers. Holsters. There's a jacket in the backseat for each of you."

Sam hefted the heavy, unfamiliar gun. "Is this necessary?"

She just looked at him, then set a plastic bag she'd brought from the plane into the open briefcase.

"Are those toys?" asked Wink.

Bette opened the bag. "They look like they're made of plastic, don't they? Let's see . . . here's an astronaut—a *female* astronaut, you'll note. Half are female. All ethnicities—look at the face on this one, the epicanthic fold. All kinds of Africans are represented . . . you're sure to find one that looks like you, no matter who you are. Um, parts of the Mars colony, a space ship . . ." They fell from her hand, a wealth of toys in crackling cellophane, designed for children to covet. "You have to buy a lot of cereal to get the whole set. That should sell the folks in Battle Creek. I'm thinking about the comics in Bazooka bubble gum too. I don't know how I'll get it to kids in other countries yet . . ."

"What are you talking about?" Sam noticed that she had a map of Michigan folded beneath them. Battle Creek, where many cereal manufacturers were located, was in Michigan.

"Vectors. And in case you want to know, I got these toys from the attic." She put them in the briefcase.

Wink said, "Is that a Colt in there? How come you get that one?"

"Bette—" said Sam.

"Check your watches. It's ten-fourteen right now. The murder is scheduled for noon or thereabouts."

She got out a map and closed the bag. She spread out the map on the hood of the car. "Hold those edges down for me, please." She pointed to a spot on the map. "I'm going to try to get as close as I can to the Book Depository. Now, here's the plan."

"Bette, I think we should stick together," Sam said again as they entered the outskirts of Dallas. Now that he was seeing more people, he understood Bette's getup—women really had looked this way in 1963. And it hadn't been that long ago.

"That would be nice." She drove carefully, stopping at every stop sign and yellow light. "Unfortunately, that's just not possible. We have two goals here. Three, really: extract Jill safely, thwart the assassination, and get back safely."

"Get back where?" Sam asked. "Won't everything be different?"

"Not necessarily," said Wink. "Although it's possible. But time is much more elastic and nonlinear than it seems to us. It seems completely counterintuitive, but that's just because of the way our minds work. Our brains adjust. Time . . . adjusts."

"Like your body heals after a tumor is removed," said Bette. "We're removing a tumor. Or—adding a kidney?" She sighed. "It's damned hard to think of models. Okay. I think I turn here . . . lots of people now. I'm going to park on this corner. We're two blocks from the Book Depository."

"What are you going to do?"

"I'm still not sure," she said. She looked uncharacteristically uncertain.

"Okay," said Wink, brisk and assured. "According to you, there are two assassination positions. If you deal with the umbrella man, I can get the guys behind the picket fence up on that hill."

"That makes sense," said Bette. "What do you think, Sam?"

"I think that all of us should get Jill, and the hell with Kennedy."

"I think that having four of us there would really cut down on our chances of getting out, of getting away. We have to run a major disruption operation, distract them from Jill. Wink's plan does that.

"The motorcade approached the Book Depository from the south and should have been in Oswald's sights for an entire block. If he was going to shoot Kennedy, he would have shot then, not after the car had turned, when he'd have a much worse shot. Sure, if one of us could fire a few shots at the motorcade as it approaches the Depository, they'd be alerted and that would probably be enough to thwart the umbrella guy and the shooters. But there are several flaws."

"Such as?"

"Well, like I said, we'd probably never make it out of the building."

"Oswald did."

"That was because he didn't *do* anything. He was just supposed to be seen there, and he was, buying a Coke from a machine right at the moment that Kennedy was shot, on his way out of the building. He was *supposed* to get away. Those were his orders. No, I think that Wink's first plan is the best. Except that, Wink, you take the umbrella man and I'll take the guys behind the fence."

"Why?" asked Wink.

"Because they're going to be hyper-alert, but maybe they won't feel all that threatened if a woman in a suit walks by, looking for a better place to see Kennedy. They'll probably just tell me to get the hell out of there. Wink, you've studied the photographs, right? You know where to find the guy with the umbrella?"

"Yeah," said Wink, looking over the photos again.

"I thought this was all being . . . summed up," said Sam.

"That can only be done up to a certain point. There are too many variables to be any more precise. We'd better get going now. The faster we move, the faster Sam can get Jill out of there."

They came to a barricade in the road. Bette parked on the grass at the side of an already full parking lot. "I'm putting the keys under the seat. You take the car, Sam, with Jill. Don't wait for either of us."

"Where are we going to meet?" asked Sam.

Bette got out of the car and straightened her suit. She bowed her head for an instant, then got out her bag, and slung it over her shoulder. "Just get to the plane."

They made their way through the crowds lining the street and crossed Houston a block north of the Book Depository. Behind the building was a parking lot, with several parked cars and two green Dumpsters.

Bette took a deep breath and squared her shoulders. "Sam, inside that door is the freight elevator. Use that to get to the sixth floor. Just act like you're one of the guys working there."

"Bette, *listen* to me."

She grabbed him, held him close, gave him a passionate kiss, and looked into his eyes. "See you." She turned and hurried away.

Then Wink was off too, walking briskly around the side of the Book Depository.

There was one passenger waiting for the freight elevator. Sam stepped inside next to him. The elevator was padded, the metal scuffed and dull. It labored up to the third floor, where the man got out.

As the door opened on the sixth floor, Sam quickly took stock.

There were no partitions in the room. The east side, where Oswald purportedly stood, according to the Warren Commission report, was crowded with stacked cardboard cartons of books. They were in the process of putting down a new plank floor. Next to stacks of planks he saw a hammer and a sledgehammer. Two half-full Coke bottles had been left on the floor near the window.

He drew his gun.

In the shadows, on the west side of the room, were two men wearing black suits. One had blond hair, the other, brown. Oswald was not there. But the Italian rifle he had purportedly bought through mail order leaned against the window.

Their radios crackled constantly. They were talking, and apparently had not noticed the elevator door opening a hundred feet away. They stood next to a low stack of pried-up boards and a crowbar.

Where was Jill?

He crouched behind some boxes and watched.

The men were intent on looking out the window. "Okay," said the blond man.

The other set his rifle on his shoulder and sighted through the scope.

Sam heard the roar of the crowd outside, getting louder as the president's car approached on Houston, getting ready to turn onto Elm. Through the open window, he could see pedestrian-lined Elm Street, people cheering and waving.

Sam started at a sound. The men whirled.

It was Jill. She pointed a handgun at the man holding the rifle. "Stop! Now! I'll shoot!"

The brown-haired man reached for his gun. Sam fired at him.

He staggered backward and fell against the stacked boards, which fanned out across the floor. The blond man swung his rifle toward Jill.

His partner raised up on one elbow. "No! Out the window! The decoy shot!"

Sam was deafened by a second report. Jill cried out and crumpled to the floor. "Jill!"

The blond man glanced at Sam, wavered, then turned back to the window and pushed his rifle out the window.

Sam shot him.

The man slammed into the wall as the bullet hit him, and staggered to one side. At that moment, Sam heard other shots, from outside, distant pops of gunfire.

❘ 43 ❘

The Long Way Home

HOLSTERING HIS GUN, Sam leaped over the boards and knelt at Jill's side. Her face was covered with blood. He ripped off his shirt and mopped her face, found a gash on her forehead. He wrapped his shirt around her head, trying not to think that she might be dead, though she seemed lifeless. For an instant, the world and everything in it faded away. He felt her neck: there was still a pulse. But for how long?

He eased her onto his shoulders in a fireman's carry, crossed the room, and hurried down the stairs, conscious that someone might stop him at any moment. As the stairwell door closed behind him, Sam heard sirens, distant screams, more shots.

Another man joined them on the second-floor stairwell, shoved past them without a second look, and ran out the door when he reached the ground floor. Sam emerged behind him. He passed the stinking Dumpsters and set Jill down gently behind a parked car. "Jill!"

She opened her eyes. "Dad?"

He hugged her tight, crying with relief, and picked her up once again.

Many thoughts flooded him as he half walked, half ran. He wanted to stay out of sight. He wanted to get to a hospital. He needed to get to the car, so they could get away. He crossed Houston Street, ducked into an alley, turned right, and continued running, breathing hard. Jill had passed out again; her head sagged back. A middle-aged woman, hurrying toward him, shouted, "The president! The president," and then just stared as he pushed past her.

He saw their Rambler ahead.

With strangely steady hands, he opened the back door and gently deposited Jill on the scorching hot seat. She murmured something. He slammed the door, grabbed the keys from under the seat, started the car, and cut the wheels sharply.

Away from the Book Depository. Toward the plane. Toward Bette.

He bumped down the curb into the street, drove too fast for a few blocks, then forced himself to slow down. He kept an eye out for a hospital sign, a doctor's office, anything. But he was in a residential neighborhood.

Jill sat up. "What happened? God, my head." Then she saw herself in the mirror. She pulled the shirt from her head.

"Jill—" Sam tried to turn and get the shirt back around her head.

She rubbed her face with the shirt, then said, "That Esso station. Up ahead."

The bathroom door was blessedly unlocked. He helped Jill inside. It stank. Toilet paper was strewn on the floor, but there was none on the roll. Jill looked in the wavy spotted mirror over the sink and laughed weakly. "I look like something from a horror movie."

He turned on the water and helped Jill bathe her face, rubbing blood off gently, wondering where the wound was. After a few moments it was clear that she had a deep gash on her forehead, which started to bleed again.

Jill stuck her entire head under the faucet. She drenched her hair and face, came up for air, reeled dizzily against the metal stall. "That's better," she gasped. "Okay."

He helped her back out to the car. "Is there a Coke machine?" she asked. He felt in his pocket for coins, found a dime and two nickels, bought two Cokes, and drove off.

Jill upended her Coke and chugged it down.

"You need stitches," Sam said.

"It's just a scratch." She sounded drunk. "I got worse in Chicago. I was out for hours after they clubbed me. But maybe—where are we? What happened?"

"We're in Dallas, Texas."

"Dallas! How did we get here?"

The buildings around them were no longer those of the downtown, but of suburbs. He felt relief as they got farther out of town and into the country. "That's a very good question. Don't you remember?"

"I don't know," she said, looking around. "Everything looks kind of . . . strange."

"Strange in what way?"

"Old. Maybe that's because we're in Texas." She looked up at him suddenly, her eyes meeting his in the mirror. "The assassination."

"Right."

"I'm starting to remember."

"How did you get here, Jill?"

She frowned and closed her eyes. "I . . . yeah." She opened her eyes. "I hitch-hiked. It took three days and nights. The game board had maps on it. They changed whenever I needed a new one. I got good rides, fast. Along the way, things just started to seem . . . I don't know, older. Finally a woman like Gypsy Myra picked me up and I knew I'd be all right." Her voice was dreamy.

They were out on a long straight country road now. Sam pegged the speedometer. "What do you mean, like her?"

"She had long black hair, but she had it pulled back with a red bandanna. She wore western stuff—you know, cowboy boots and jeans. She drove a pickup truck with a saddle in the back. She drank a beer while she drove."

"Great," said Sam. "What did she say?"

"She told me that I was doing the right thing. She said all kinds of weird stuff about biochemistry. She sounded like Mom. She talked about the war. She talked about history. Herd animals. Molecular biology—ever heard of that? It was wild, man. She gave me that gun. She stopped and showed me how to load it and shoot it. I told her I didn't want to use a gun and she said, 'You will.' " Jill looked around the car. "Where's the game board? Do you have it?"

"No."

"We have to go back! I have to have it!"

"No." Sam saw, in the distance, the trailer with a wind sock next to it, practically the only sign of the airstrip. He accelerated, and spun onto the dirt road leading to it. As he got closer, he saw, with dread, that there was no plane.

Leonard was there, though.

Sam pulled up in a cloud of dust and yelled, "Where's Bette?"

Leonard hoisted himself from his crooked lawn chair and hobbled over to the window. Sam smelled beer and tobacco. "She left, son."

"When?"

"Half-hour ago."

Sam felt tremendous relief. At least she was all right. "Was there anyone with her?"

Leonard shook his head and spat tobacco juice sideways, just missing the mirror. "Nope."

Sam felt a moment's emptiness, which reached outward like the flatness of the land, forever, with nothing to break the view. "Did she say anything?"

"She just said to tell you she'd see you."

"What else?"

"That's all, son." He shoved back from the door.

Bette.

Bette was gone.

As was Wink.

Casualties of war.

"There a doctor around here?" Sam asked.

Leonard waved his arm. "Next town. Ten miles down the road. Dr. Innis. On your right. Good man."

Sam found Dr. Innis's office with no problem. There was one patient in the waiting room, but the nurse took them right in.

The doctor didn't seem too curious, except that he did ask what happened to Sam's shirt as he gently pulled the cat gut through Jill's forehead. Sam felt sick; couldn't watch. As he finished up, Innis asked if they'd heard about the assassination attempt.

"An attempt?" Sam asked.

"Bastards didn't get 'im. Sorry, miss."

Then they set off on the long drive home.

⊣ 44 ⊢

In the Slipstream

THE ASSASSINATION ATTEMPT was endlessly dissected on the radio. In a greasy spoon the following morning, he and Jill studied the newspapers. Several men were mysteriously dead. Two had been shot while standing on the bumper of a truck parked behind a picket fence overlooking the motorcade's route. They each had a high-powered rifle, but both had been shot in the head by someone the paper called a "professional."

At about the same time, a man at the train-switching tower a block away had seen a woman in a suit carrying a leather bag cross the railroad tracks; she had met two men on the other side. The switchman watched them pull guns on her, but then they fell. He called the police and then ran to them. Both had been shot. The woman was gone.

Strangely, there was no mention of the two men in the Book Depository, nor of the scoped rifle.

A man on Elm Street with an open umbrella standing ten feet from where the motorcade passed had also been shot. The Secret Service had killed that shooter. He could not be identified. Sam could find no photos of the man, but he was sure it was Wink.

But which Wink? The Wink who had died in Berlin? The Wink of the Chinese book mart? The Wink of Midway?

And which Sam was he?

While they passed through New Orleans, two days later, Jill was fiddling with the radio when Sam said "Stop! Get that back!"

It was Kennedy, giving his speech, delayed by the assassination attempt, at the Trade Mart. He was a stubborn man.

This link between leadership and learning is not only essential at the community level. It is even more indispensable in world affairs. Ignorance and misinformation can handicap the progress of a city or a company, but they can, if allowed to prevail in foreign policy, handicap this country's security. In a world of complex and continuing problems, in a world full of frustrations and irritations, America's leadership must be guided by the lights of learning and reason or else those who confuse rhetoric with reality and the plausible with the possible will gain the popular ascendancy with their seemingly swift and simple solutions to every world problem . . .

This nation's strength and security are not easily or cheaply obtained, nor are they quickly and simply explained. There are many kinds of strength and no one kind will suffice. Overwhelming nuclear strength cannot stop a guerrilla war . . .

We have regained the initiative in the exploration of outer space, making an annual effort greater than the combined total of all space activities undertaken during the fifties, launching more than 130 vehicles into earth orbit, putting into actual operation valuable weather and communications satellites, and making it clear to all that the United States of America has no intention of finishing second in space . . . In short, our national space effort represents a great gain in, and a great resource of, our national strength . . .

Finally, it should be clear by now that a nation can be no stronger abroad than she is at home. Only an America which practices what it preaches about equal rights and social justice will be respected by those whose choice affects our future. Only an America which has fully educated its citizens is fully capable of tackling the complex problems and perceiving the hidden dangers of the world in which we live. And only an America which is growing and prospering economically can sustain the worldwide defenses of freedom, while demonstrating to all concerned the opportunities of our system and society.

We in this country, in this generation, are—by destiny rather than choice—the watchmen on the walls of world freedom. We ask, therefore, that we may be worthy of our power and responsibility, that we may exercise our strength with wisdom and restraint, and that we may achieve in our time and for all time the ancient vision of "peace on earth, good will toward men." That must always be our goal, and the righteousness of our cause must always underlie our strength. For as was written long ago: "Except the Lord keep the city, the watchman waketh but in vain."

∷ 45 ∷

The Lost Note

S AM AND JILL RETURNED to Washington to a season of late fall. While on their way back, the dates had gradually adjusted themselves, just as Sam was so desperately trying to hold on to them.

By the time they got to Virginia, they were in the same year they had been in when they left. But the news was much different. Robert Kennedy was president, and JFK was still alive, a globetrotting philanderer.

Sam had a strange, strong sense of having lived through this past, although he recalled the other past.

"Do you remember, Jill?" he asked.

"I remember everything." She sat quietly in the car, her head bandaged, one arm out the window, staring at the streets they passed as if to drink them in.

Once they got into D.C. there was no sign of the highway construction that had threatened obliteration of whole neighborhoods. There were other subtle differences everywhere, which became more and more apparent. A new office building on the corner of 14th and K. The old YMCA down the block had been replaced too. Their street, when they turned onto it, was much more well-kept than when they'd left. The Kelly's house had been remodeled; the place where the Wentworth's house had been was now a construction site. All of this was new.

"I'm afraid," said Jill, as they drove up to the house.

"Me too, honey."

Brian and Megan had just gotten home from school and were snacking in the kitchen. Brian was in his first year at Catholic University, in an engineering curriculum. Doug was there too; he was going to Howard.

Sam knew these things. He also knew that this was not the way things had been. He was so suffused with dread that he could barely bring himself to say hello.

"Hi, Mr. Dance," Doug said. "So is Jill going to transfer to Texas, or stay at American?"

"I think I'll stay here," Jill said. She stood in the center of the kitchen, looking lost.

"What happened to you?" asked Megan.

"Little car accident," said Jill. "I was driving."

"Is that how you got that clunker?" asked Brian, looking out the window. "A little accident? What happened to the car, Jill? Sounds like you totaled it."

Sam and Jill looked at each other. It was as Bette had said. It had all healed over. But he and Jill were the scars.

He searched the faces of his two younger children to find some clue, but he knew already. Had known since Texas, when Leonard had told him the plane was gone.

Bette was not here.

None of her cookbooks were on the shelf in the kitchen; there was no open crossword puzzle book on the table. Sam knew that if he were to go upstairs to their bedroom, none of her clothes would be in the closet.

And that she had been gone since 1962.

Jill let out a scream and ran up the stairs to her room; Sam heard her sobbing upstairs.

"What's with her?" asked Brian. "The accident?"

"She's pretty tired." Sam pulled on a jacket and went out to the garden.

It was cold, with the nip of winter in the air, and getting dark. The streetlights over the viaduct were on. A few leaves clung to the trees. Their empty branches creaked back and forth in the rising wind.

As he gazed down at Bette's koi—at least they're here, he thought—grazing one another in languid tracings through the water, he wondered: *Where was that life, now? Where had it gone?*

Out of his emptiness rose a hoarse cry, which burst forth and was swallowed by the gusting wind, which blew away the last clinging leaves of fall with a sudden, powerful roar.

⊰ 46 ⊱

After

S AM CONTINUED WORKING, in what he called The After, when everything was
so different, but only to him and to Jill.

Brian and Megan had grown up in a world free of the threat of nuclear war, due
to the Munich Disarmament Treaty negotiated by Khrushchev and Kennedy in
1964. Like millions of other children, they recalled playing with exciting space toys
they got in their boxes of Wheaties and Captain Crunch, which led to an expansion
of interest in science education, which the country had money to fuel.

Toys made of HD10.

After the assassination attempt, Kennedy had more political capital, which he
used to the fullest. The Civil Rights Bill he'd proposed in June of 1963 and which
was being debated in Congress when he went to Dallas. The CIA was, as he had
threatened, "broken into a thousand pieces." He stepped down the Vietnam
conflict, and left the area, which had never been an independent country, to work
out its own fate.

The Dance family remembered Hawaii as an idyllic time, the time before Bette
flew off to Germany, in 1963, on one of her work weeks and did not return.

Her body was never found, which gave Sam a little hope, but not much. They
never had a funeral, leaving the neighbors to speculate that she hadn't died, just run
off with another man. But neighbors came and went with increasing speed as the
years passed.

Sam's garden flourished. He found a jazz club in Georgetown that welcomed
old-timers at a jam session Sunday afternoons, but he never met anyone of Wink's
caliber or fire. He took pleasure in technological advances, but felt stranded,
marooned. His children urged him to date, but he preferred to read, to travel, to
consult.

Jill's bullet scrape left a scar on her forehead. She refused to have it removed. She
remembered what had happened, but didn't want to talk about it; much of it came
out in the alternate worlds of her comic book, *Gypsy Myra*, which became a com-
mercial success. Brian and Megan were left with shadowy memories of the strange
game; disturbing dreams, but not much else.

Jill blamed herself for her mother's disappearance, as much as Sam tried to convince her that it was not her fault.

It was, in fact, his.

He was not interested in trying to recreate the Hadntz Device. It seemed unlikely beyond words that he could use it to find Bette. And if he did find her, what would that shatter? At times, he was angry that she had not tried to return—but maybe she had. Wherever she was, she probably knew more than he did. Maybe she knew that if she returned, something huge would go askew. But if only she could gently return . . . walk in the door one day and say, like Desi Arnaz, "Honey, I'm home."

To Sam, Bette was a casualty of war—missing, but not declared dead. He assumed the emotional stance of Wang Chien, the ninth-century Chinese poet from the book Bette had left him when she had disappeared in Germany so long ago. In his poem titled "On Hearing That His Friend Was Coming Back From the War":

> Yet I never weary of watching for you on the road.
> Each day I go out at the City Gate
> With a flask of wine, lest you should come thirsty.
> Oh, that I could shrink the surface of the World,
> So that suddenly I might find you standing at my side.

To Sam's relief, Jill continued to study political science, got internships and a series of short, contracted jobs in Washington, and was starting on her doctorate. She eventually married Elmore, who was now a lawyer involved with social issues. They still lived in Halcyon House, but were renovating a run-down town house they'd bought for peanuts on M Street at the end of Key Bridge, where they planned to open a bookstore downstairs and live upstairs. It seemed like they'd never be finished working on it, though.

Brian joined the Peace Corps, went to Africa, became an engineer, and married a woman he met there. They now had a little girl. Brian and Doug, also an engineer, formed a small company that was struggling, but had promise.

Megan had a research fellowship in the field of biological physics.

The United Nations actually functioned. Germany had been reunited in 1972, when international communism relinquished its World War II holdings, convinced that a free market would create more wealth than its former system. The Internet, the seed of which Sam had inspected early in the decade, quickly flourished once released from military control.

The ephemeral nature of time was, for Sam, like the flash of sunlight sliding over fields of waving green grass on the plains. Much of the time, he felt as if he lived in the shadow that passed over after the light.

He traveled to relieve this feeling, taking consulting jobs all around the world. He spent a lot of time in the garden, and read more and more Chinese poetry, learning Chinese so that he could translate it, albeit clumsily. It suited him. Time was a great sweep of rain, mountains, and rivers. Poets focused with precision on the small, telling details of the place in which they found themselves, and were filled, always, with longing.

⊣ 47 ⊢

Germany

IN 1980, SAM WENT to Munich on a job. He'd kept away from Germany, but Jill persuaded him to go.

When the job was finished, he convinced himself to take the train to Oberammergau.

He almost did not go. The pain of not having Bette would be too immediate there, too starkly obvious.

But being in Munich was not as difficult as he had anticipated. The main square was the same, as well as the train station where he and Wink had once arrived at three in the morning, but the rest was just a large, modern city. Oberammergau, more of a tourist destination, would have held on to its past and was, thus, more daunting for Sam to contemplate as the train passed through foothills, and then mountains.

He went, though. As if it were something he needed to see through.

The rolling hills of the countryside, fall-brilliant, seemed to undulate as the train passed. It was still pastoral, and the ancient town was again home to a flourishing NATO school.

Hiking up the mountain much less easily than he had when he was forty, although much more easily than he might have, had his arthritis not been cured by recent medical advances, Sam found the cave mouth one late afternoon. It was getting dark; he should not have started so late. The rusted fence sagged, admitting access, seeming to invite him past the barricade he had so long ago erected.

Taking his halogen flashlight from his pocket, he went inside. He made his way carefully through the cathedral-huge space, where the sound of his footsteps was swallowed by distance. He cast his light here and there and walked farther and then his light caught the edge of something he'd hoped to find. He realized, then, that he had put off this trip for so very long because he did not want to find it absent.

It was Bette's plane.

When he sat in the cockpit, the dash lit up. His own heartbeat sounded in his ears.

He pushed various pads that appeared, and when it asked him what and when to search for, he simply typed "Bette."

Ah, Bette.

He felt a plummet, and there was around him just the infinite blackness of the cave. A single, low note vibrated through him, as if someone had plucked a string on a bass.

The memories that rushed through him were almost too much to bear—memories he had tried not to recall for so many years. They simply merged into one entire memory, whole, of a person whose uniqueness was braided through his time, who had made it brilliant and fine and unexpected, a collaboration in the theme of love, with a woman who did not believe in countries, but in people; a woman daring beyond belief. He found himself in a beautiful garden of vision and sound, then he was fighting to stay awake and aware, and lost.

When he regained consciousness, his flashlight was dim. His watch showed that three hours had passed.

He wondered if he'd had a stroke.

At last he climbed down from the plane, found his way out of the cave. Outside it was night, and cold. The little village of Oberammergau lay below, glittering as wind roared in the pines around him. He picked his way down carefully, his light bobbing through blackness, but really did not care much if he were to pitch over a cliff.

He had one more place to visit, though, before heading home. Might as well see it through.

Muchengladbach, Sam found, had officially changed its name to Mönchengladbach in 1950. Now, it was completely built up, a modern city, but he took a cab to Neusser Strasse, just to see it. To his surprise, a chunk of the old neighborhood remained, amid small office buildings and shopping centers.

His footsteps quickened as he walked down the block. Ghosts flocked around him, all the old guys. Earl T., even Wild Card Zee.

And Wink.

He found their town house, still standing in its row, looking well kept. Climbing the stairs, he hesitated a moment. Then he thought, why not.

He knocked on the door.

A middle-aged blonde opened it. Sam cleared his throat. "Do you speak English?" She nodded. "I know this is crazy, but is your name Lise? The aunt of a little girl I knew in the war lived here, and she had no other relatives."

"And you are?"

"Dance. Sam Dance. We were billeted here during the war and—"

"Mister Sam!" She hugged him, tugged him through the door, opened a bottle of wine, brought out a plate of delicious cheeses and thin black bread. Lise's husband came home from work and was introduced. They had two children, both in college.

After dinner and coffee, Sam went online and showed them the wartime photos he'd archived, including one of Lise, standing straight in her cotton dress. Her husband was delighted. "There are very few photographs of that time available. I never thought I'd see a picture of her as a little girl." They insisted that Sam spend the night, and he accepted.

At first he could not sleep, but finally his restlessness subsided. When he woke, it was because moonlight was stabbing his eyes.

Somewhat annoyed at being wakened after his struggle to fall asleep, he pulled on his pants and shirt to make his way down the hall to the bathroom. First, he looked out the window, his old window. He'd been afraid to ask Lise about the summerhouse, but there it was, bathed in moonlight, the marble statue in the same armless condition as thirty-five years earlier.

It was strange to find this past intact, this Lise here.

The garden, illuminated by moonlight, was becoming ragged with fall. The linden tree, now enormous, was still full of leaves, but many were also scattered on the red tile roof of the summerhouse and on the ground.

Go on down. Why not?

Sliding into his shoes, he made his way quietly through the house. Leonid's kitchen was completely modern now, in compact European style. He opened the door, taking care to leave it unlocked, and went down the stairs.

The bar was gone, replaced by some comfortable outdoor chairs. He stood behind one, remembering. The fairy lights, the accordion player, the keg—it had been right here—

"Sam."

He turned.

And there was Bette.

She stepped out of the shadows, many years older, like him, but still slim and beautiful as that night she'd turned up and asked for a drink. Her hair was silver in the moonlight. She wore a red dress, as she had when she'd taken him to Berlin in 1945. He was afraid to speak, afraid she would vanish.

"Took you a goddamned long time to track me down, Dance."

He reached out, and embraced time's released melody.

Coda

J ILL WALKED ACROSS the wide porch of Halcyon House, and descended the steps between washes of pink and violet hydrangeas glimmering with morning dew. She adjusted her small briefpack, and wheeled her bicycle from the shed, noting that the grass needed cutting.

As usual, she would ride to the Georgetown town house and do some work. Elmore would show up later with the truck and they'd ride home together, bike in the back. It was almost ready to move in. They were building bookshelves for the store now. She was taking only one course, Complexity Theory and World Politics, and it would not meet again until tomorrow.

She liked riding her bike very early in the morning. It was quiet; the streets where she had grown up, where so much had happened, were cool and leafy. She made a note in her mind to work in Dad's garden this evening. It was getting overgrown.

The letter she had received from him a year ago still unsettled her, but she accepted that he was gone, like her mother. He had vanished into some vastness that was concrete and yet unfathomable, a place where she had once gone and from which she had never entirely returned.

"Take care of everything, and don't worry," it had said. No mention of ever coming back from wherever he was.

Jill sliced through the cool morning air, shifting gears, taking tree-lined back streets just beginning to stir with people heading for work. She coasted past the recently cleaned snow-white Capitol, and turned at Union Station.

Something made her stop for a moment in front of the park across from the station, Columbus Circle. It had been done up new—overnight, it seemed, the way they changed landscaping in the city—with banks of pink, deep rose, and red begonias. Behind them were stalks of tall purple iris.

The colors blazed out against the green grass, the damp brown tree trunks. It was enough just to look at them. She pulled out her water bottle and took a long drink.

The greenness, the beauty of the city, the white and gray buildings and tall trees all around, through which she rode every day, rose up and embraced her, assuaging the deep pain she'd carried with her for years, ever since . . .

Ever since *then*.

Hadn't her father said that he got off the train here, years ago, when he met their mother and they decided to get married?

They were not here. Yet they were.

It was as if they were streaming upward and outward, infinite in all directions, *there*.

She stood spellbound for a few minutes, breathing the green-infused air, thinking about the war, wondering again what, exactly, they had done. She had seen long-ago glimpses of it in the Infinite Game Board, but they had never talked much about it.

As she inserted her foot into her pedal-guard and readied to push off, she had a thought. She would get those dusty, consecutively numbered composition books of her father's out of the attic and read them.

Their collective title was, simply, *In War Times*.

AFTERWORD

THOMAS E. GOONAN, my father, wrote the sections of *In War Times* that appear as Sam's narratives. Though the novel itself is fiction, these sections are true and factual accounts of his World War II experiences, and of his career as a fire protection engineer. Most are abridged, and only a small percentage of them appear in the book; more appear on my Web page, www.goonan.com, on the *In War Times* page. A discography, photographs of 1945 Germany, and a list of the history, biography, physics, and biology books to which I referred are there as well. Although the war years herein closely follow his Army career, Sam is not Tom Goonan. Although my mother flew for the Civil Air Patrol and owned a small plane, Bette is not my mother—except, perhaps, in spirit. Likewise, none of the men of Company C, as portrayed herein, are meant to portray actual persons.

The 610th, which set up shop in Germany four months before the surrender, was in British territory; therefore the draconian antifraternization rules of the U.S. Army, which forbade any contact between Germans and American soldiers as well as giving the Germans any kind of food (leading to much excess food being thrown away in plain sight of the starving population, and more than one American soldier court-martialed) were not strictly enforced. The soldiers of the 610th, therefore, got a slightly different view of being a conquering army than did much of the American military. This particular slice of the war, as well as the work of those who handled the buildup for Operation Overlord, are not well documented. Sir Max Hastings's *Armageddon*, Dallas's *1945: The War That Never Ended*, the eyewitness reports of journalists, and German accounts of the final days of the Third Reich proved invaluable.

Thomas Goonan's M-9 training at Aberdeen, Maryland, undertaken at a time when the M-9 Director and radar were top-secret, and his subsequent troubleshooting of the circuit boards of the M-9 Director, are true. The M-9 system as finally constituted at the time the Nazis gave up on the V-1 buzz bombs consisted of:

M-9 Director

SCR 584 (radar)

Proximity Fuze

Replacement wire wound cards, which embodied 90mm sun firing tables (instead of 3-inch gun tables originally provided by the Army as "good enough for anti-aircraft work."

During his entire professional life, he has worked on the vanguard of information technologies. As a fire protection engineer working for the Navy, the Veteran's Administration, and GSA, he was involved in projects such as the fire protection for the *Arizona* memorial, inspecting the tracking stations for the space and ICBM programs throughout the Pacific, and the development of voice-directed evacuation procedures and the entire fire protection systems for high-rise buildings. One of my goals in writing this book was to show how those who spend their careers putting their technological expertise in the service of all of us, by working for the government, contribute to our welfare. After retiring from the government, he worked on historic preservation projects, including the South Street Seaport, the Inner Harbor at Baltimore, the Furness Library at the University of Pennsylvania, and the Old Post Office Building in Washington, D.C.

I have likened the evolution of modern jazz, later dubbed bebop, to the creative ferment in science that has led to our ever-growing understanding of the world, nature, and ourselves. Like the development of the atomic bomb, modern jazz remained a well-kept secret until after the war. Unlike the development of the bomb, which can now be known, we can never revisit the original luminous thoughts of Charlie Parker as he and Dizzy Gillespie birthed a new art form. In reality, the physicists, chemists, and biologists of the nineteenth and twentieth centuries birthed modernity and its reflection and interpretation in literature, art, and music. Our art and our science are inextricably linked.